meathaus eight

GW00835937

HEADGAMES

MEATHAUS

volume number eight in a series of
comic book anthologies featuring
several cartoonists who like to rock

Meathaus Enterprises
New York City, Los Angeles, Tulsa

Alternative Comics
Gainesville, Fl

2006

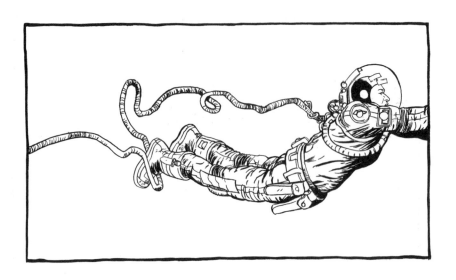

meathaus 8: head games ISBN: 1-891867-92-X
printed in canada   2006.
entire contents are copyright © by the individual authors, meathaus press,
and alternative comics. all rights reserved.
except for review purposes, no portion of this book may be
reproduced without written consent of the author.
published by alternative comics 503 NW 37th avenue,
gainesville, fl 32609-2204. phone: (352) 373-6336.
e-mail: jmason@indyworld.com www.indyworld.com/altcomics.
meathaus e-mail: meathaus@meathaus.com
www.meathaus.com

headgames

Head games

table of contents

meathaus eight

cover and book design
Farel Dalrymple

inside front cover
Mu Dafaka

inside back cover
Thomas Herpich

editors
Farel Dalrymple, Chris McD, Jason Sacher

Publisher
Jeff Mason

meathaus website designer
Chris McD

HEADG

meathaus
number
eight

AMES

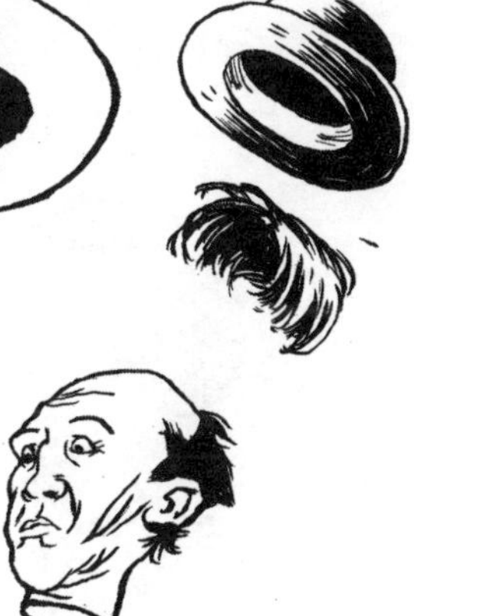

After 8 years of living in that conurbation known as New York City, scene became less important to me than scenery. To preserve my sanity and my consistently depleting funds I decided it was time to say goodbye to all my friends and the metropolis that had such resounding and eternal consequences on my work, art, beliefs, attitude, and personality. Moving to the Midwest saved my life but it is time for me to move on again, head back to the West coast. The overall look of our comic book anthology I have heard described as "New York art school". Fair enough, but the group we had built up from a few New York art school chums has expanded to a considerable web of artists from around the world, tendrils extending out from Brooklyn to the Midwest, the South, the West Coast, Canada, London, South America. This book is dedicated to all of those Meathaus creators, and of course all awesome dudes who like to rock. Thanks for being a part of this. Sorry this one took so long.

-farel

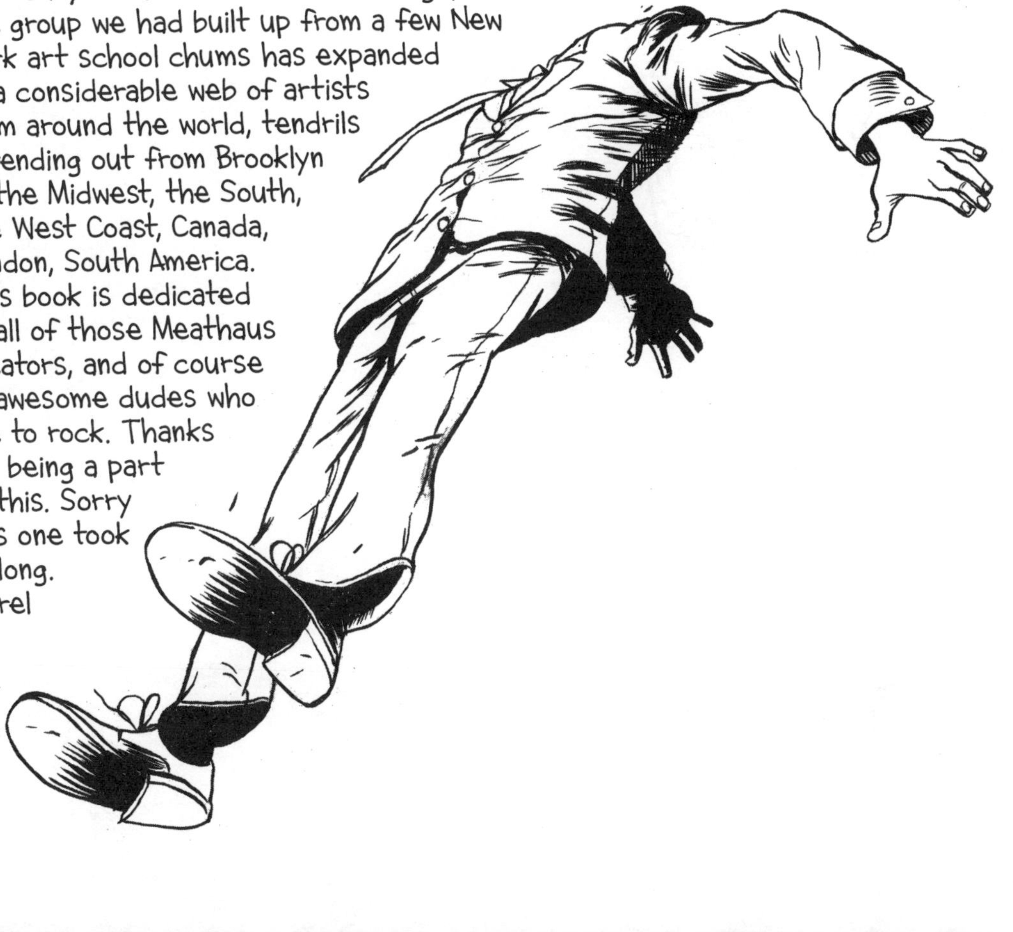

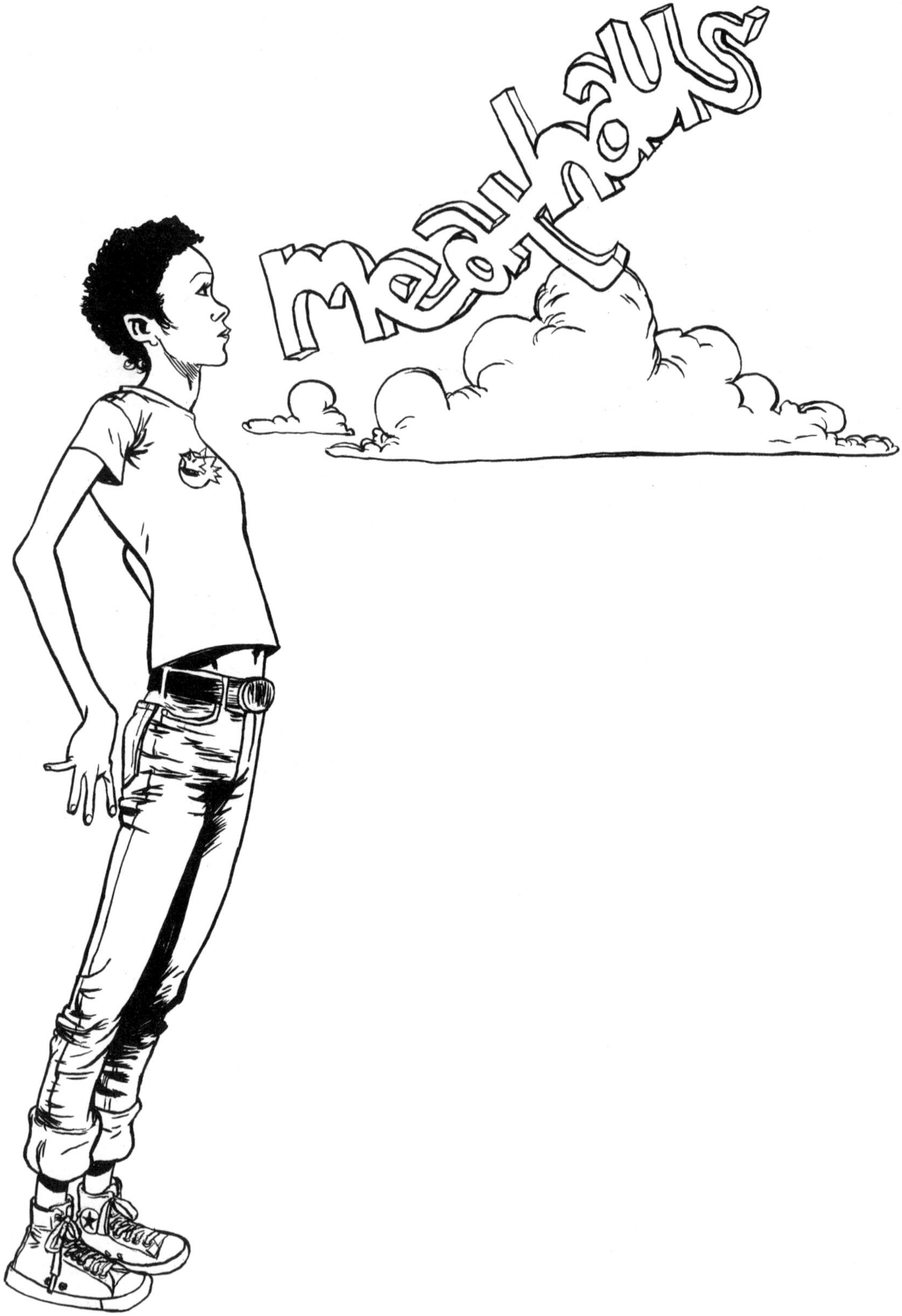
meathaus

Headgames:
Some Thoughts and Predictions from MH correspondent, Jay Sacher
We've got some patterns for you:
Statistically speaking, most mammalian species survive about two million years before stagnation, environmental pressures and competition from new species wipe them off the globe. To paraphrase Princeton's Kenneth Deffeyes, the human species is therefore living on borrowed time. We have already outlived our scheduled extinction. So, like the dancing bear, just about everything we achieve is remarkable. It's not how well we do it, but that we do it at all. This realization takes the pressure off, or at least it should.

There should be no raging against the dying of the light; instead we should raise our margaritas in the air and chink our glasses in mass congratulations. Against all odds, we continue to exist. Work is therefore meaningless. Paper money, politics and automobiles are simply the final disordered gasps of a species well past its prime.

To wit, on Friday April 13th, 2029, Asteroid 2004 MN4 should, if projections are correct, pass somewhere within 22,000 miles of the center of planet Earth. It is the first object to be labeled a 2 (out of 10) on the Torrino Scale. It is about a quarter of a mile in size and will be traveling at somewhere around 5 miles per second. 22,000 miles from the planet may seem like a safe enough distance, but to put it in perspective, consider what the odometer on your family station wagon reads, or remember that on that particular Friday, Asteroid 2004 MN4 will be 216,900 miles nearer to us than the moon, and in fact will be even nearer than the orbiting geosynchronous satellites that provide us with cell phone receptions and cable TV. What was that old sitcom with Ted Knight and Jim J. Bullock called? Exactly.

The probability that 2029 will be the last year of the human race is actually pretty slim. Something like .033%. But really, considering what we've just related regarding the probability of mammalian extinction rates, we should accept that statistics are bunk. This realization can be both comforting and disturbing, considering your perspective.

But we at Meathaus choose neither perspective. We're a playful species, maybe not as playful as golden retrievers or sea otters, but there's no denying the playful gene in our makeup. We all play games, even the big guns. Economists, scientists, Supreme Court Justices, novelists, cartoonists, baby seal-clubbers and fast food purveyors, we're all gamblers. Einstein famously said God does not play dice with the universe. That may be true, and it's probably just as well, since we make up in spades for his reticence with the dice cup. Every moment of our life is a gamble, whether for ill or good, we can't always determine. Like true gamblers, we realize there's no such thing as a moment of life that occurs off of the gameboard. Every single second, every instinct and mistake, they're all part of the game, whether they're in our checkbooks, on the sidewalks, in our bedrooms or in our heads.

Becky Cloonan

Becky Cloonan is so busy drawing comics.
She keeps making them!
SHE CAN'T STOP!!!

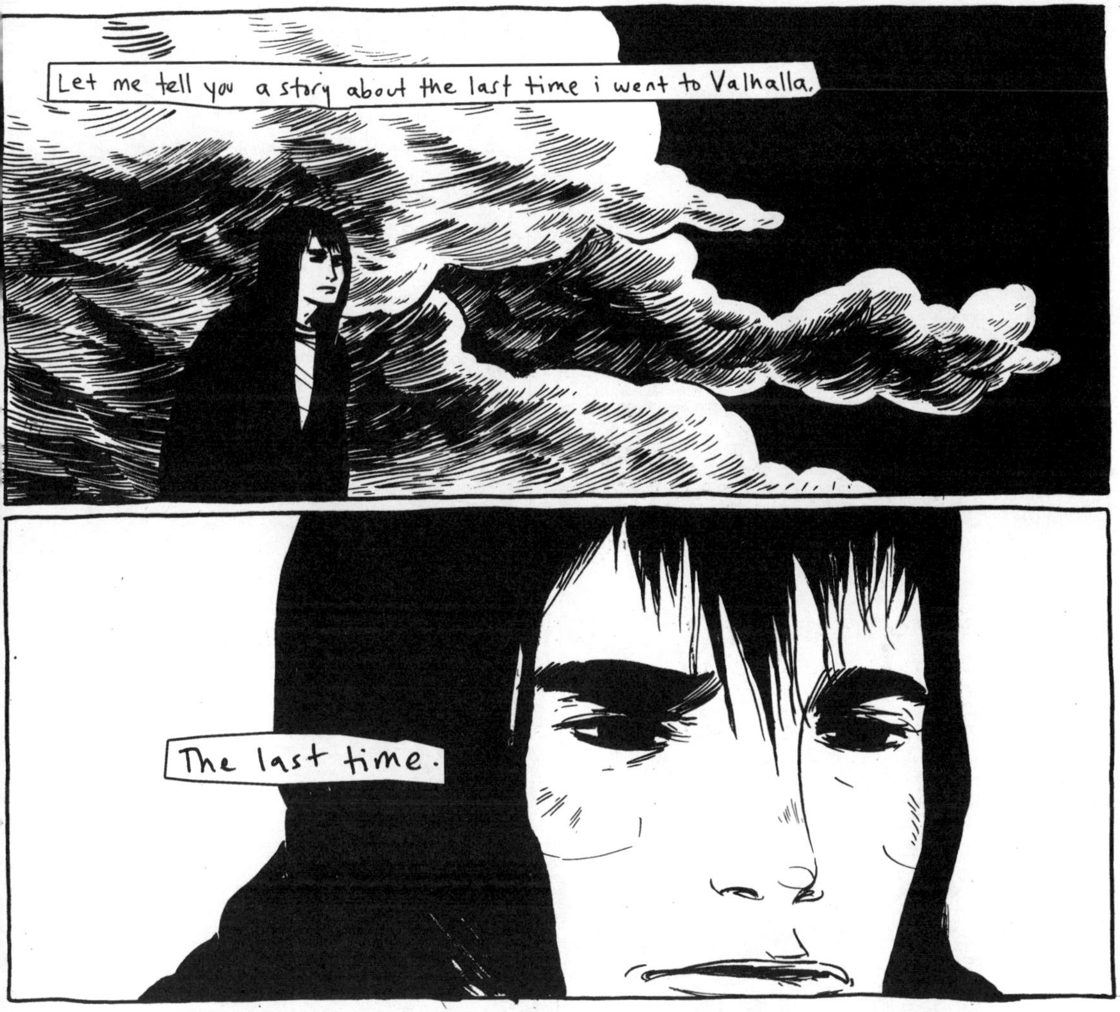
Let me tell you a story about the last time i went to Valhalla.
The last time.

FLOORPUNCH

by becky cloonan

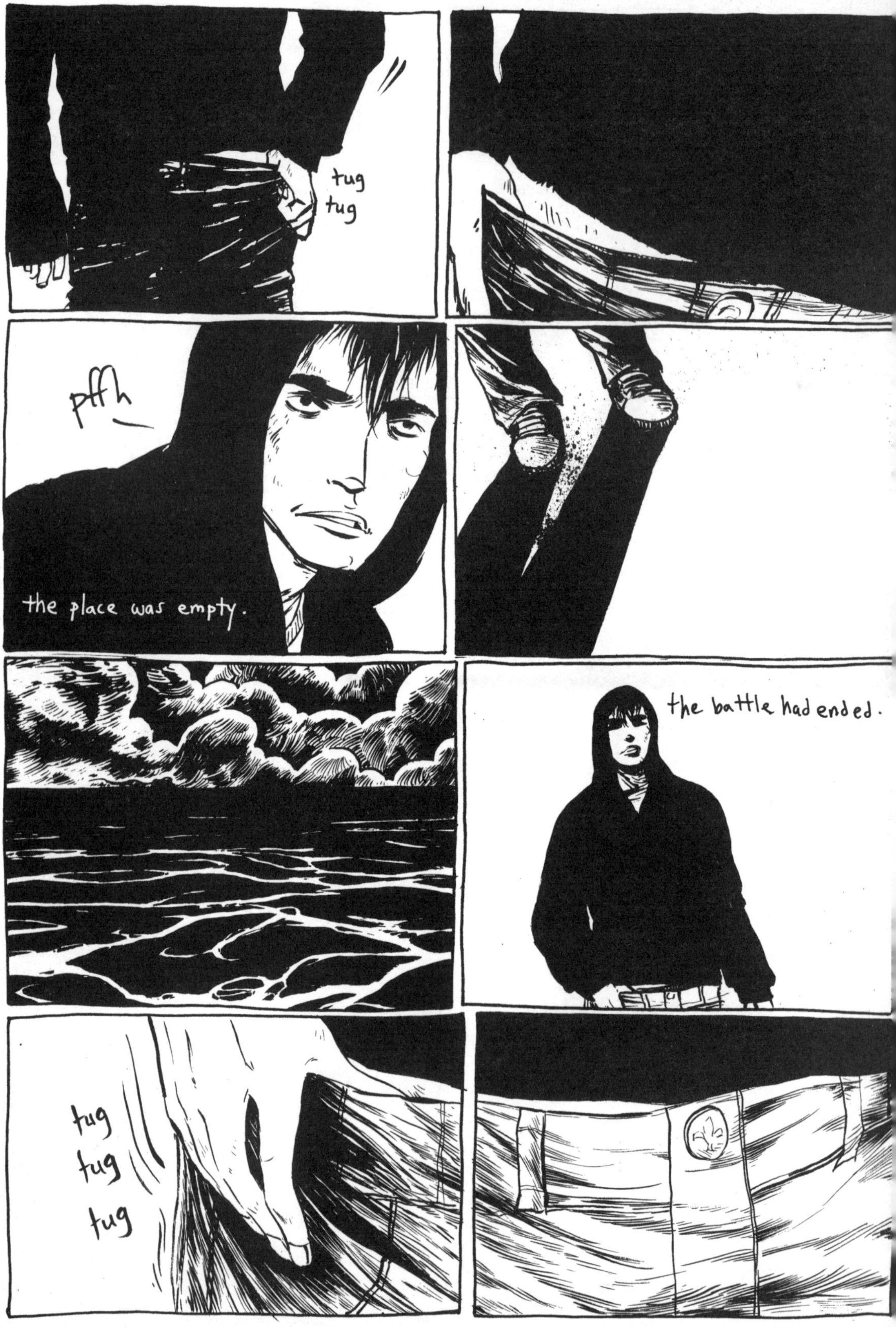
tug
tug
pffh
the place was empty.
the battle had ended.
tug
tug
tug

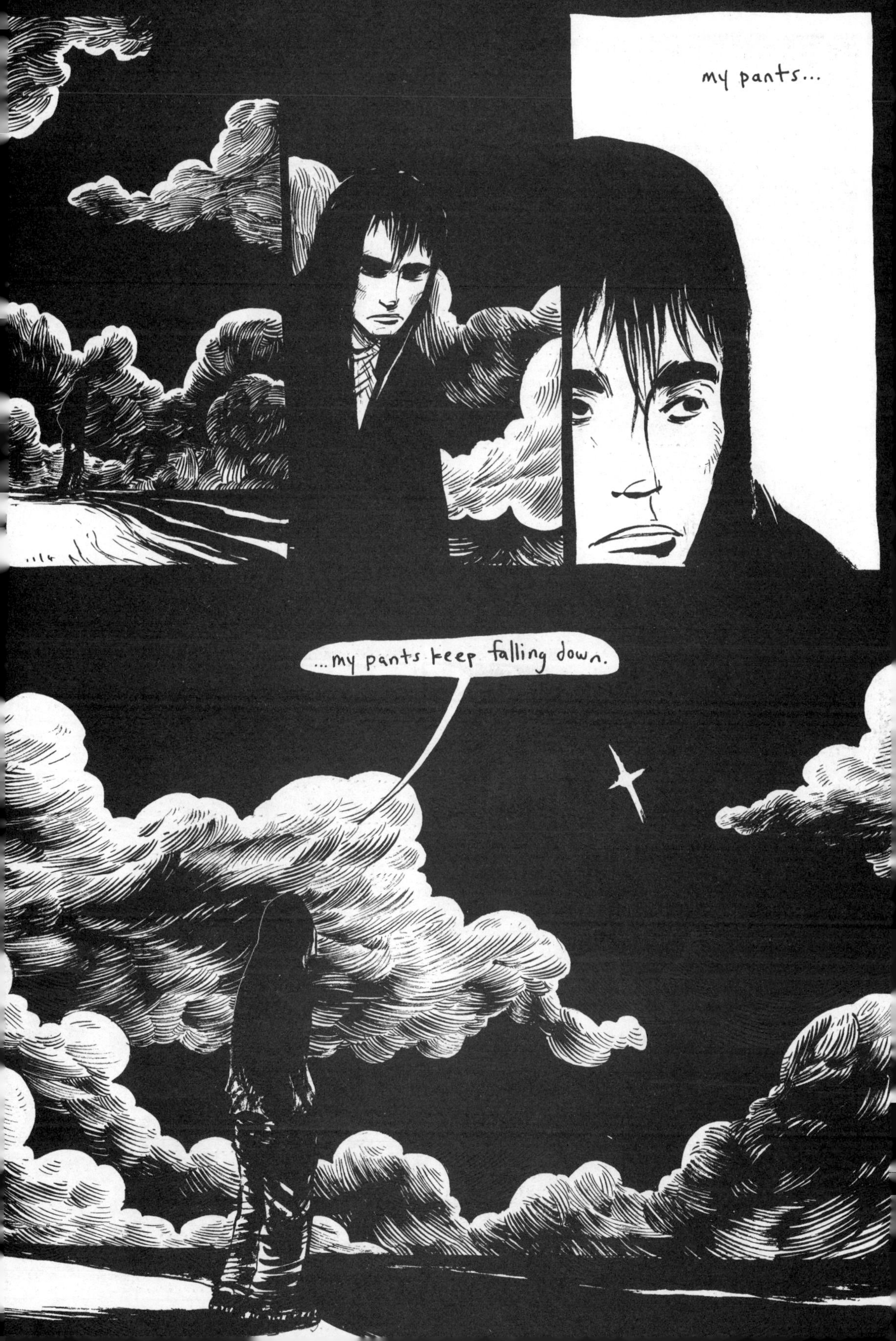
my pants...
...my pants keep falling down.

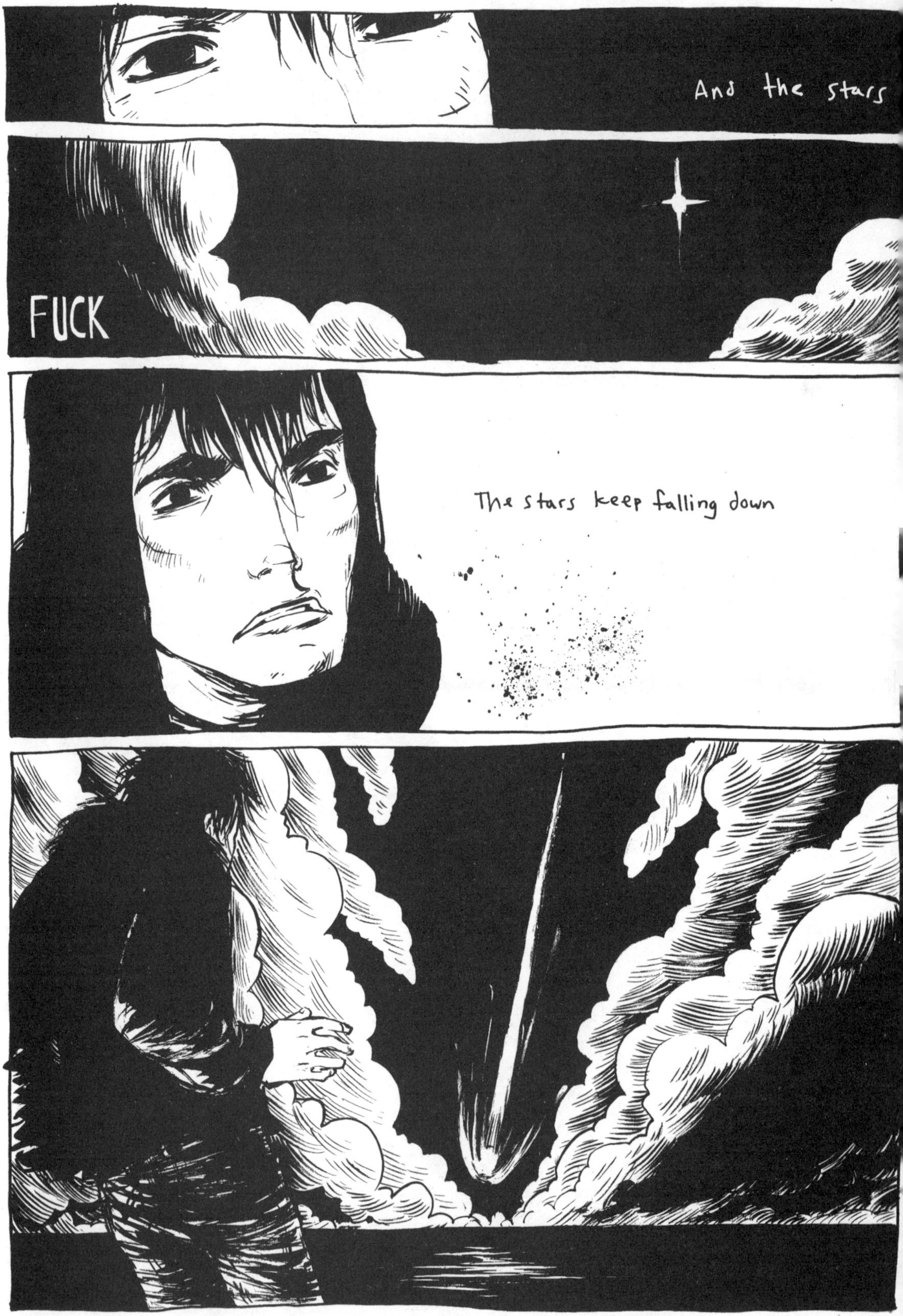
And the stars
FUCK
The stars keep falling down

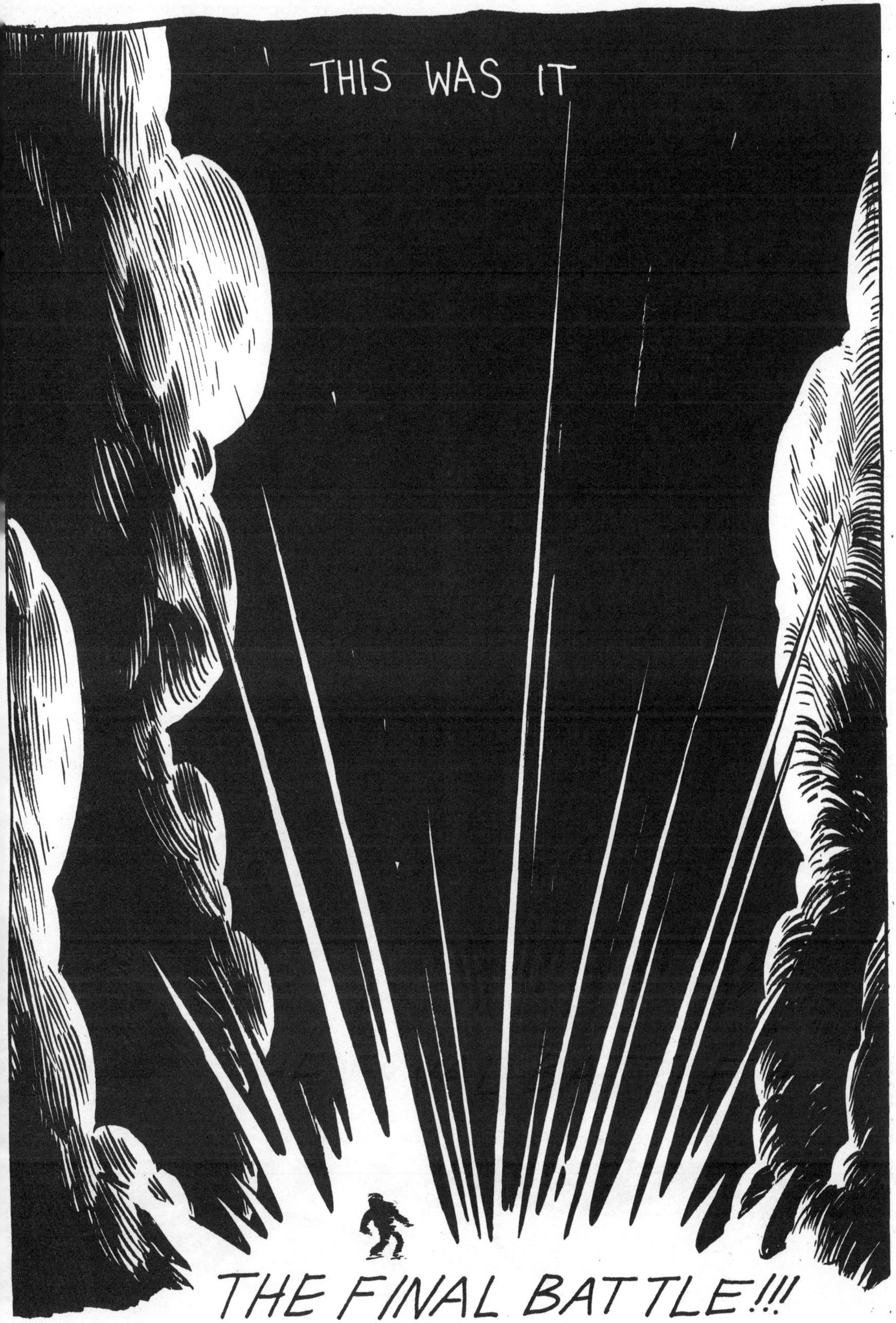
THIS WAS IT
THE FINAL BATTLE!!!

FIGHT

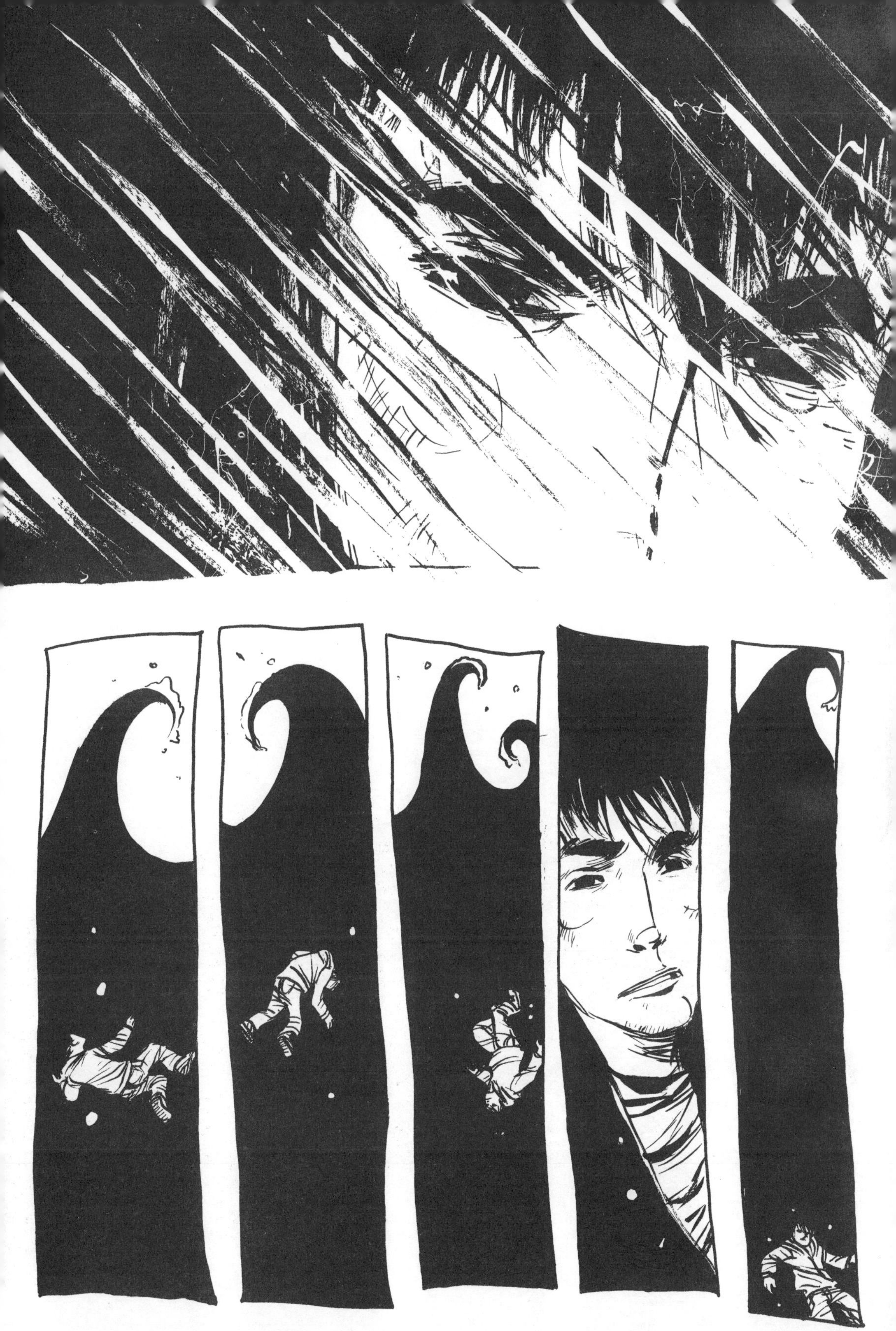

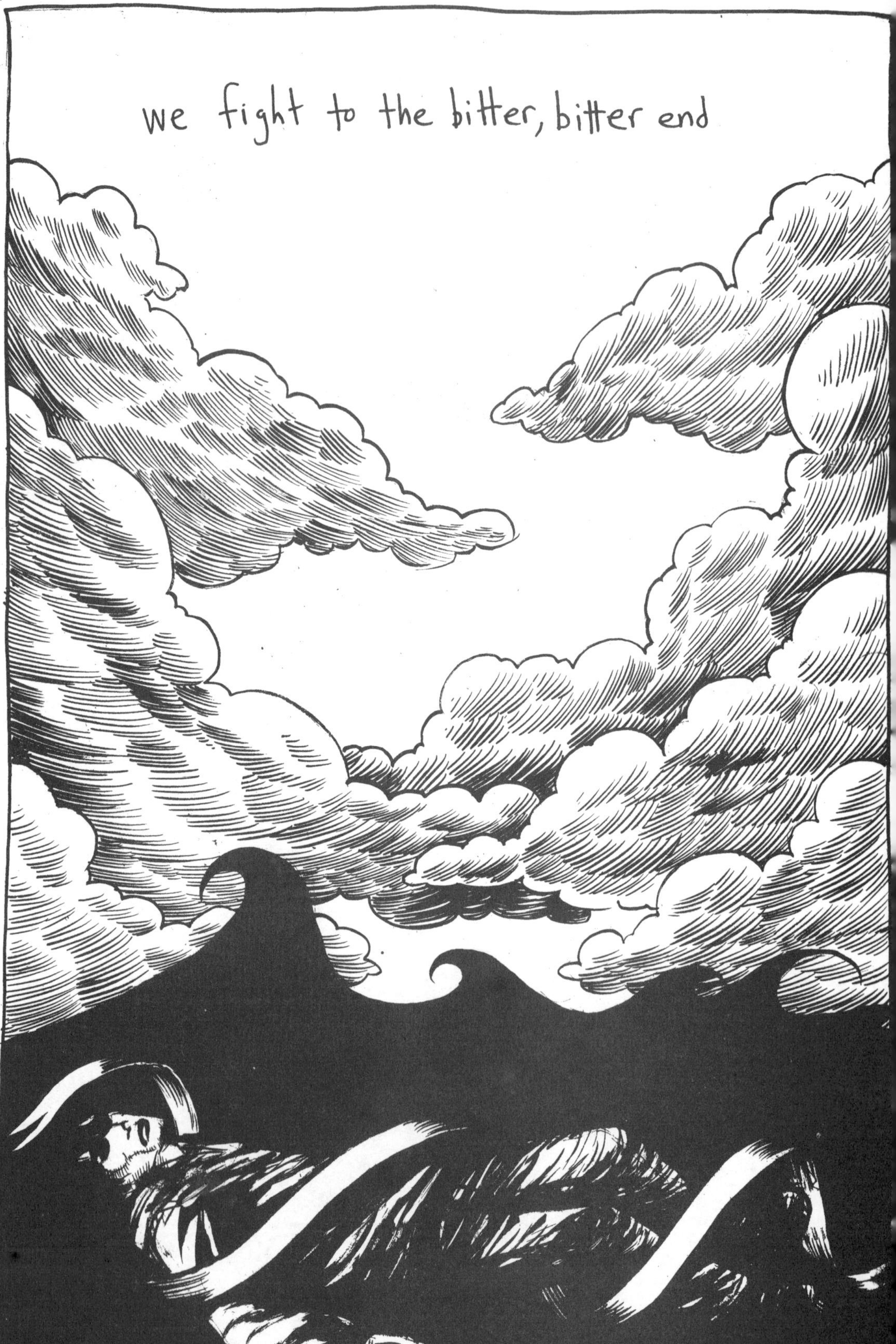
we fight to the bitter, bitter end

Brandon Graham

Brandon draws in parking lots drinking yoo hoo.
He's hard like good comics.
He's got a new books from Tokyo pop, NBM,
and Alternative on the way.
www.brothersgraham.com

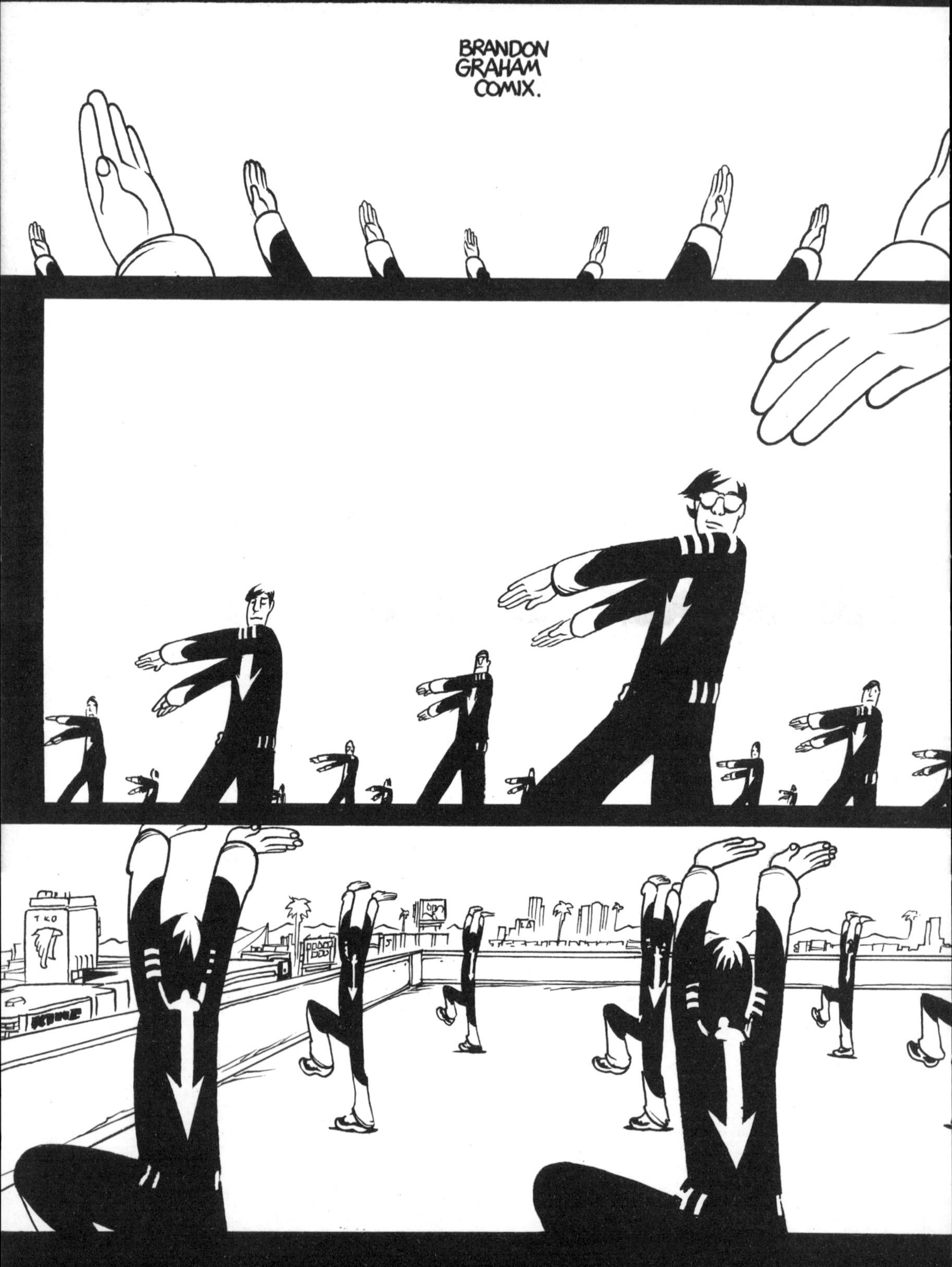
BRANDON GRAHAM COMIX.
TKO

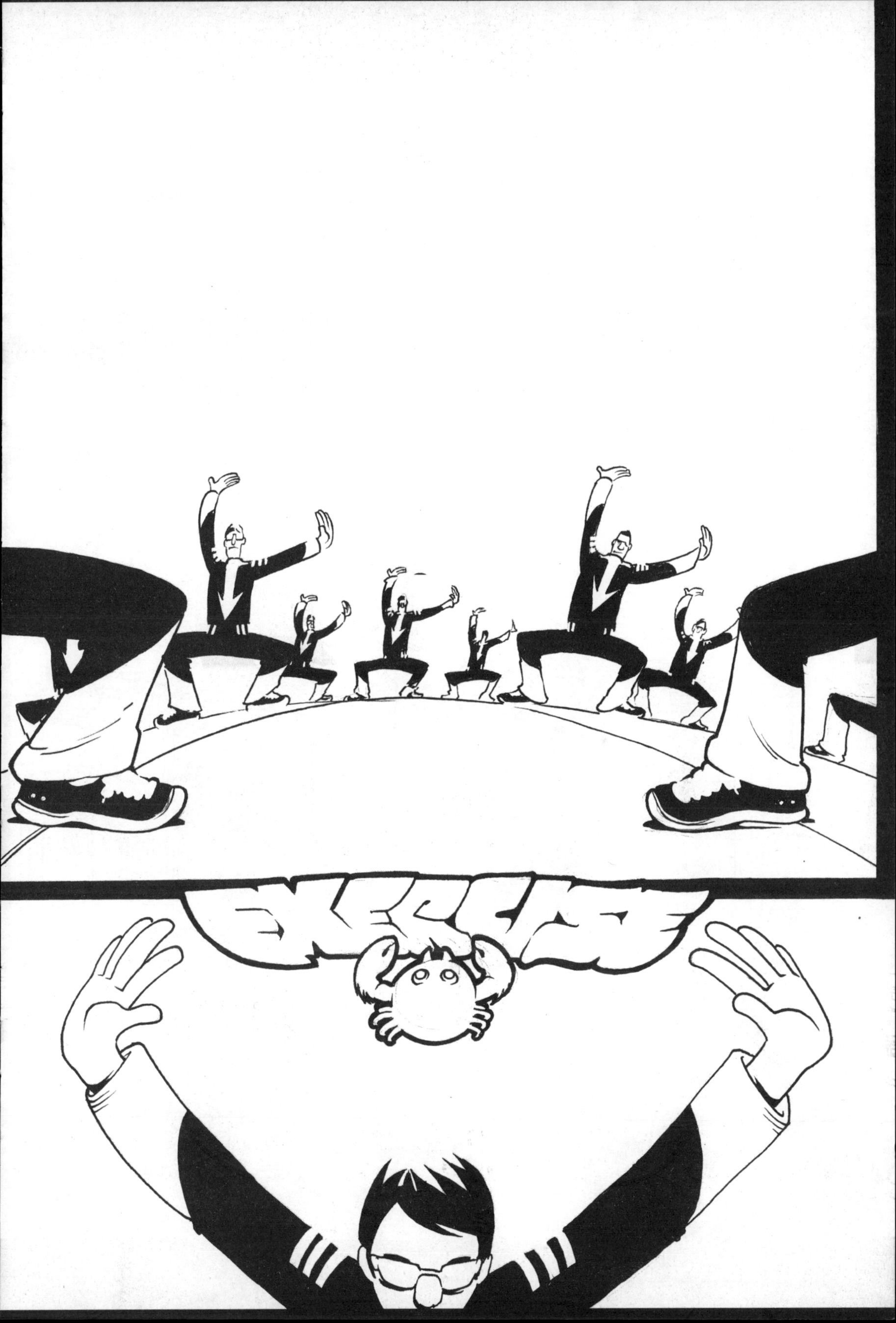

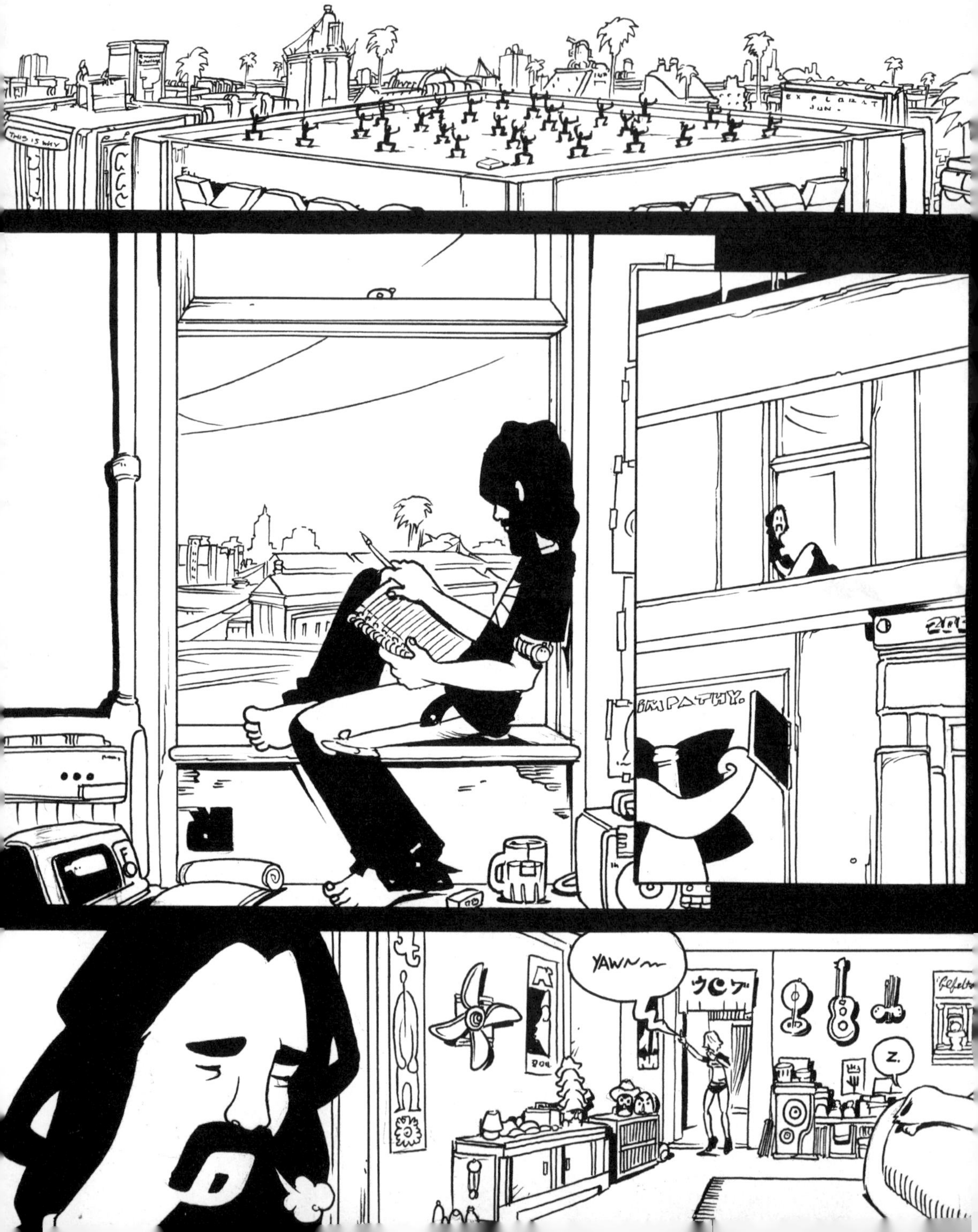
THIS IS WHY
YAWN
Z.

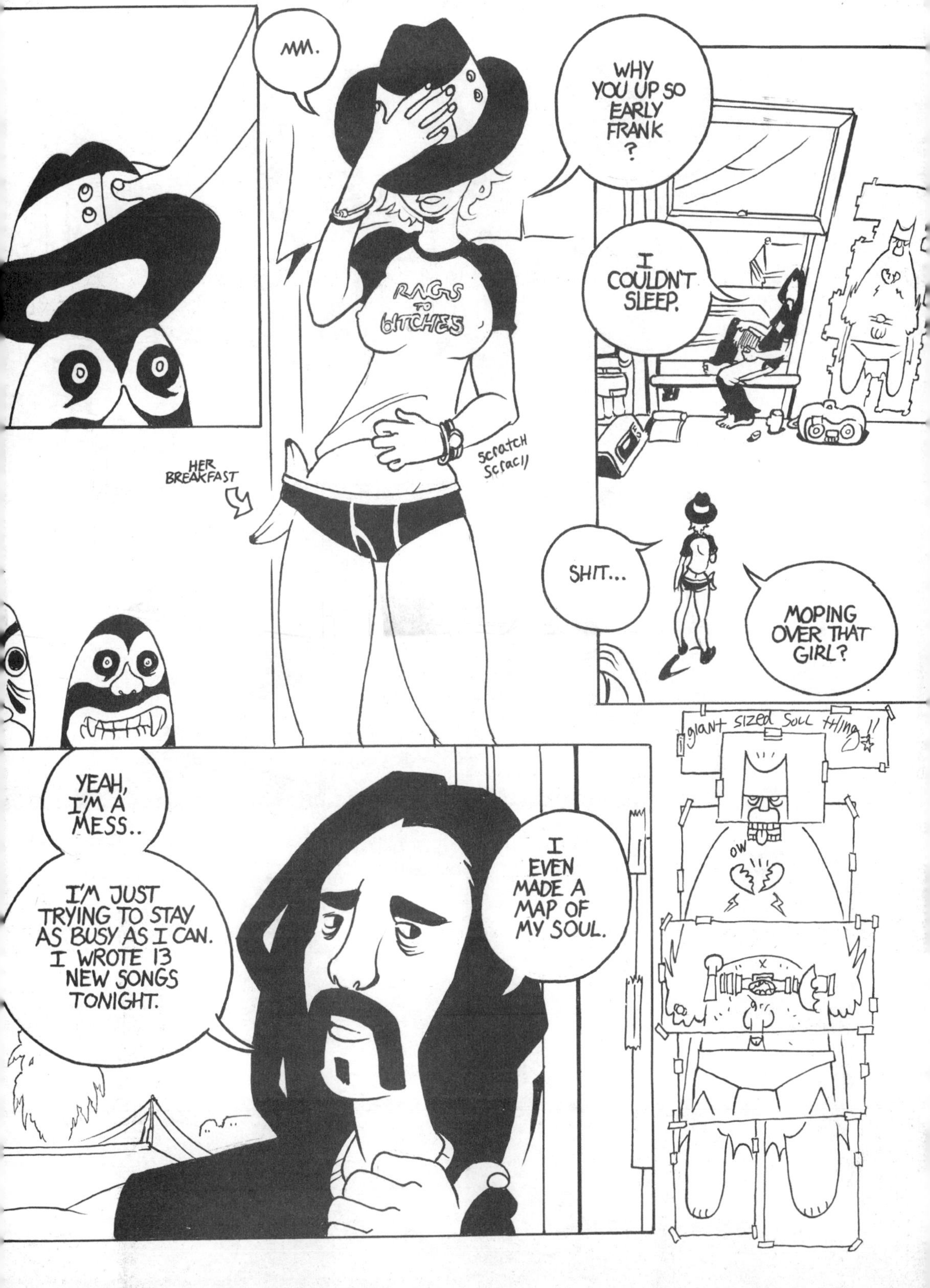
MM.
WHY YOU UP SO EARLY FRANK ?
I COULDN'T SLEEP.
RAGS TO bITCHES
HER BREAKFAST
SCRATCH SCRACH
SHIT...
MOPING OVER THAT GIRL?
YEAH, I'M A MESS..
I'M JUST TRYING TO STAY AS BUSY AS I CAN. I WROTE 13 NEW SONGS TONIGHT.
I EVEN MADE A MAP OF MY SOUL.
giant sized soul thing!!
OW

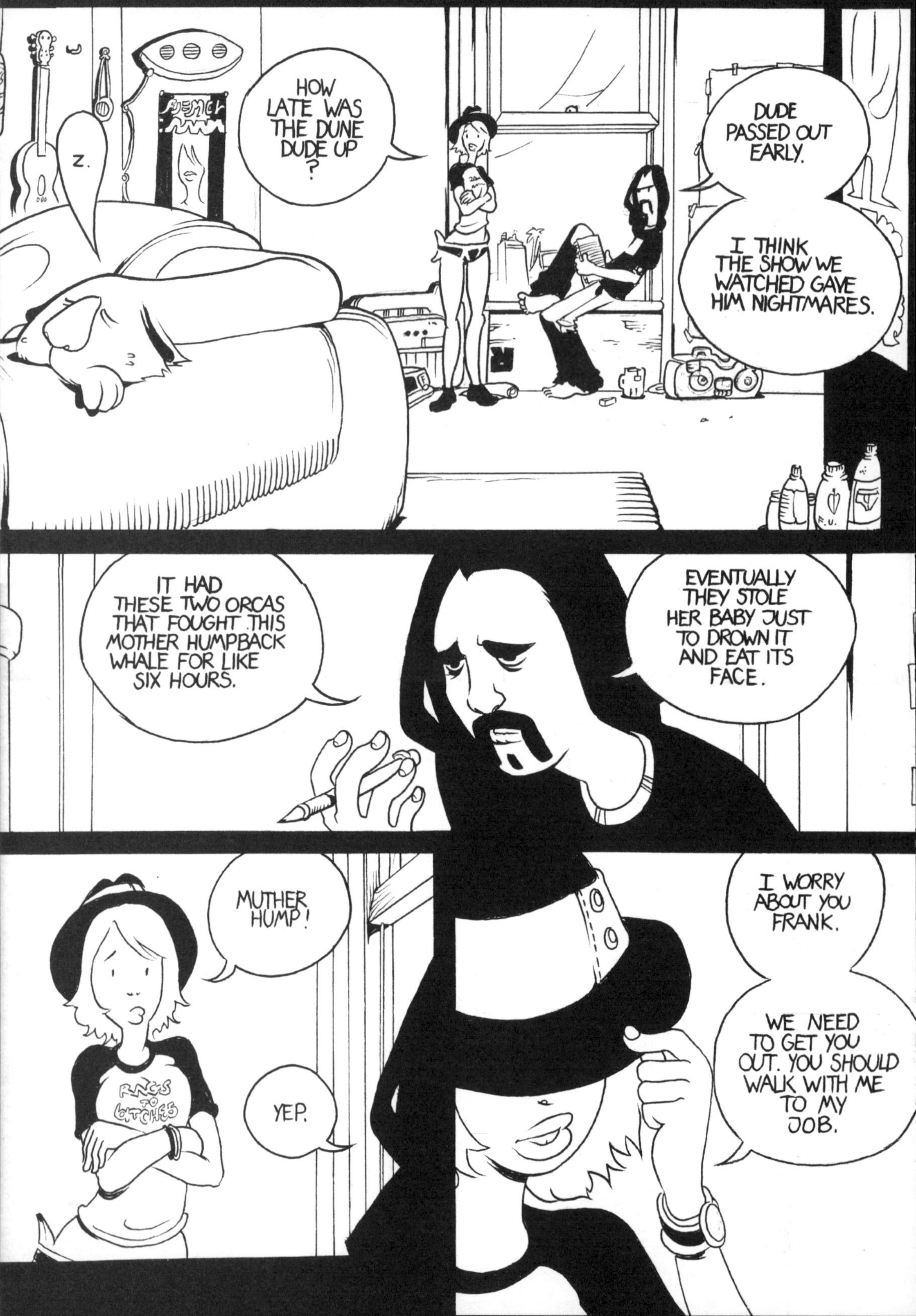
Z.
HOW LATE WAS THE DUNE DUDE UP?
DUDE PASSED OUT EARLY.
I THINK THE SHOW WE WATCHED GAVE HIM NIGHTMARES.
IT HAD THESE TWO ORCAS THAT FOUGHT THIS MOTHER HUMPBACK WHALE FOR LIKE SIX HOURS.
EVENTUALLY THEY STOLE HER BABY JUST TO DROWN IT AND EAT ITS FACE.
MUTHER HUMP!
YEP.
I WORRY ABOUT YOU FRANK.
WE NEED TO GET YOU OUT. YOU SHOULD WALK WITH ME TO MY JOB.

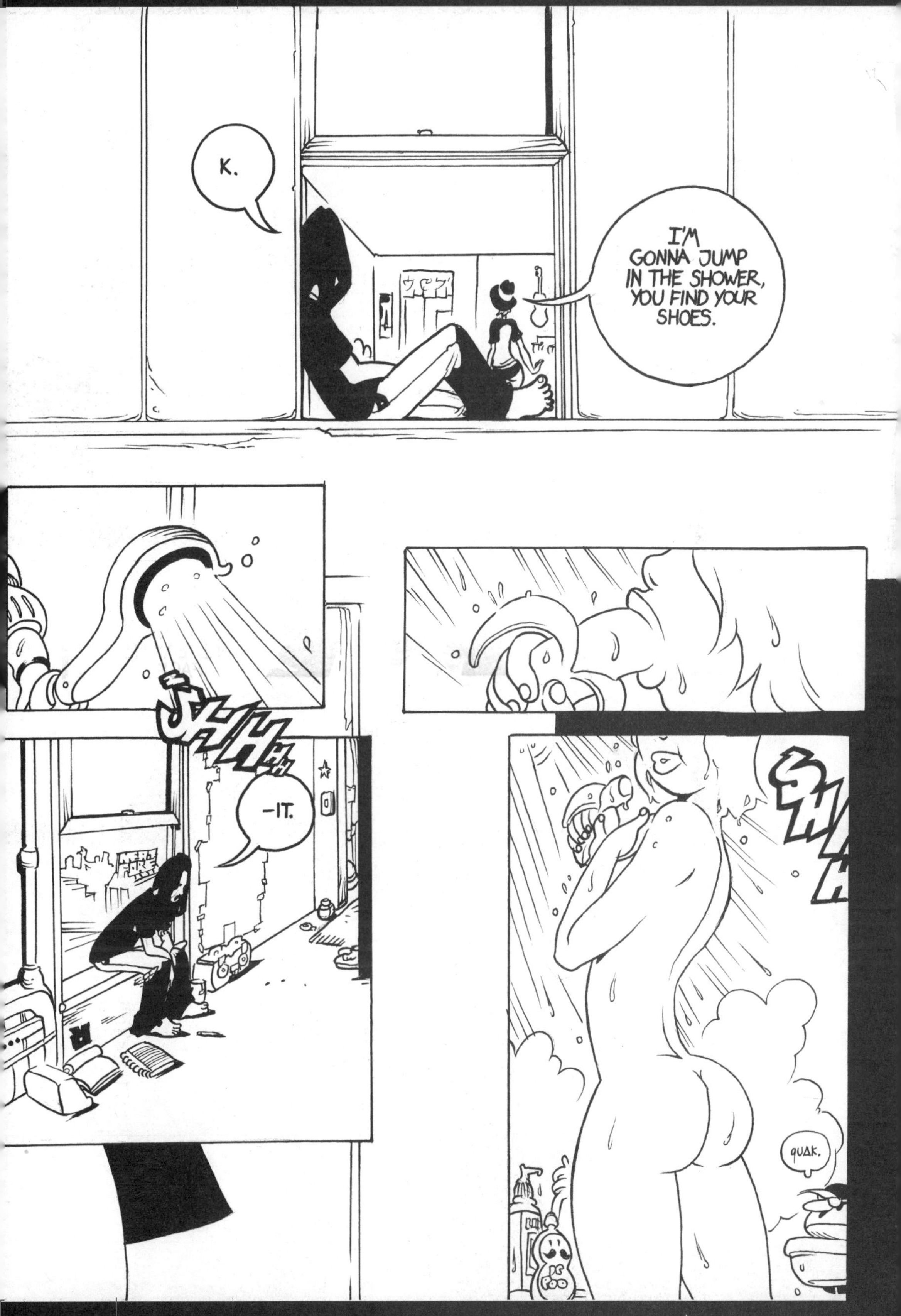
K.
I'M GONNA JUMP IN THE SHOWER, YOU FIND YOUR SHOES.
-IT.
QUAK.

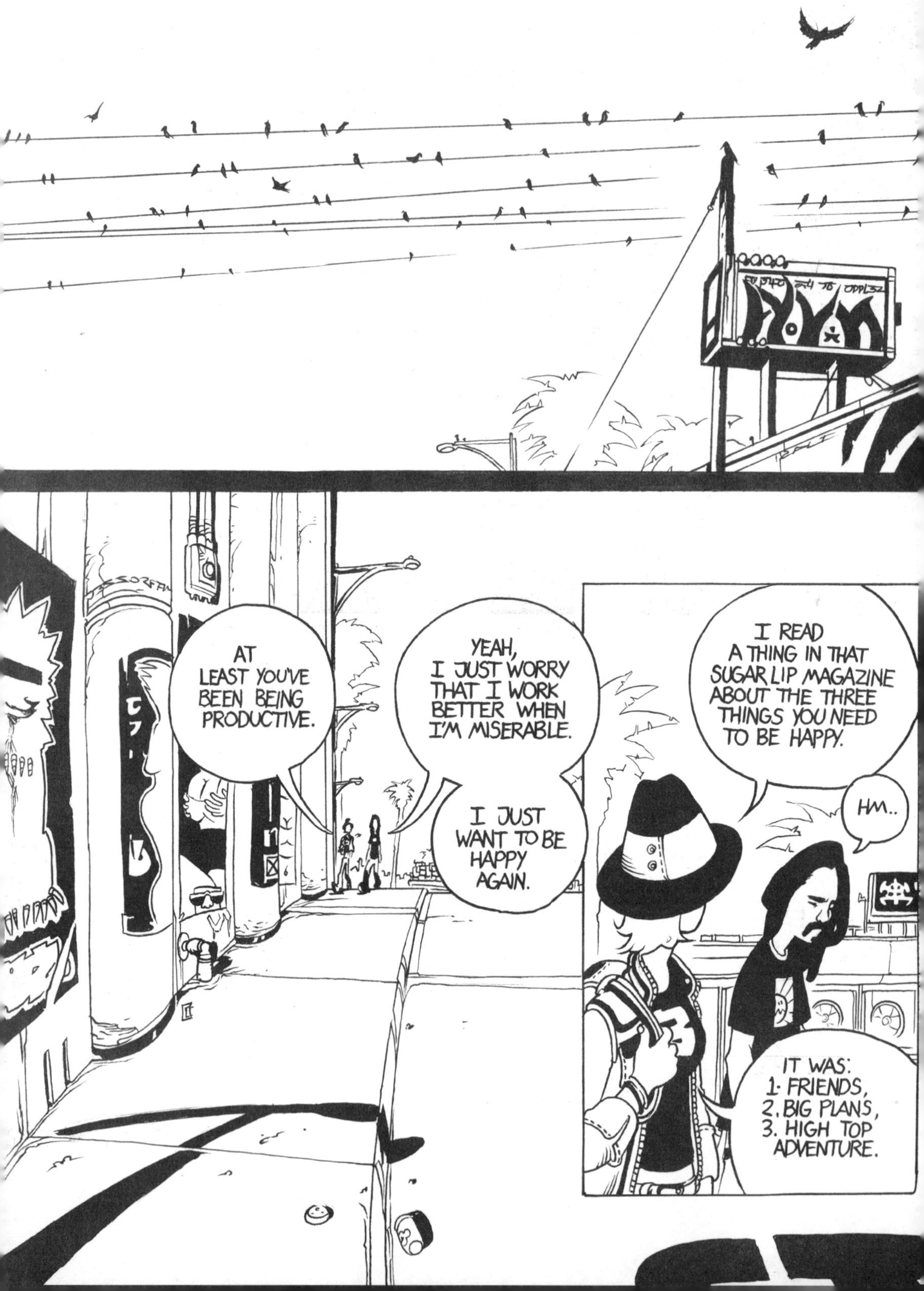
AT LEAST YOU'VE BEEN BEING PRODUCTIVE.
YEAH, I JUST WORRY THAT I WORK BETTER WHEN I'M MISERABLE.
I JUST WANT TO BE HAPPY AGAIN.
I READ A THING IN THAT SUGAR LIP MAGAZINE ABOUT THE THREE THINGS YOU NEED TO BE HAPPY.
HM..
IT WAS: 1. FRIENDS, 2. BIG PLANS, 3. HIGH TOP ADVENTURE.

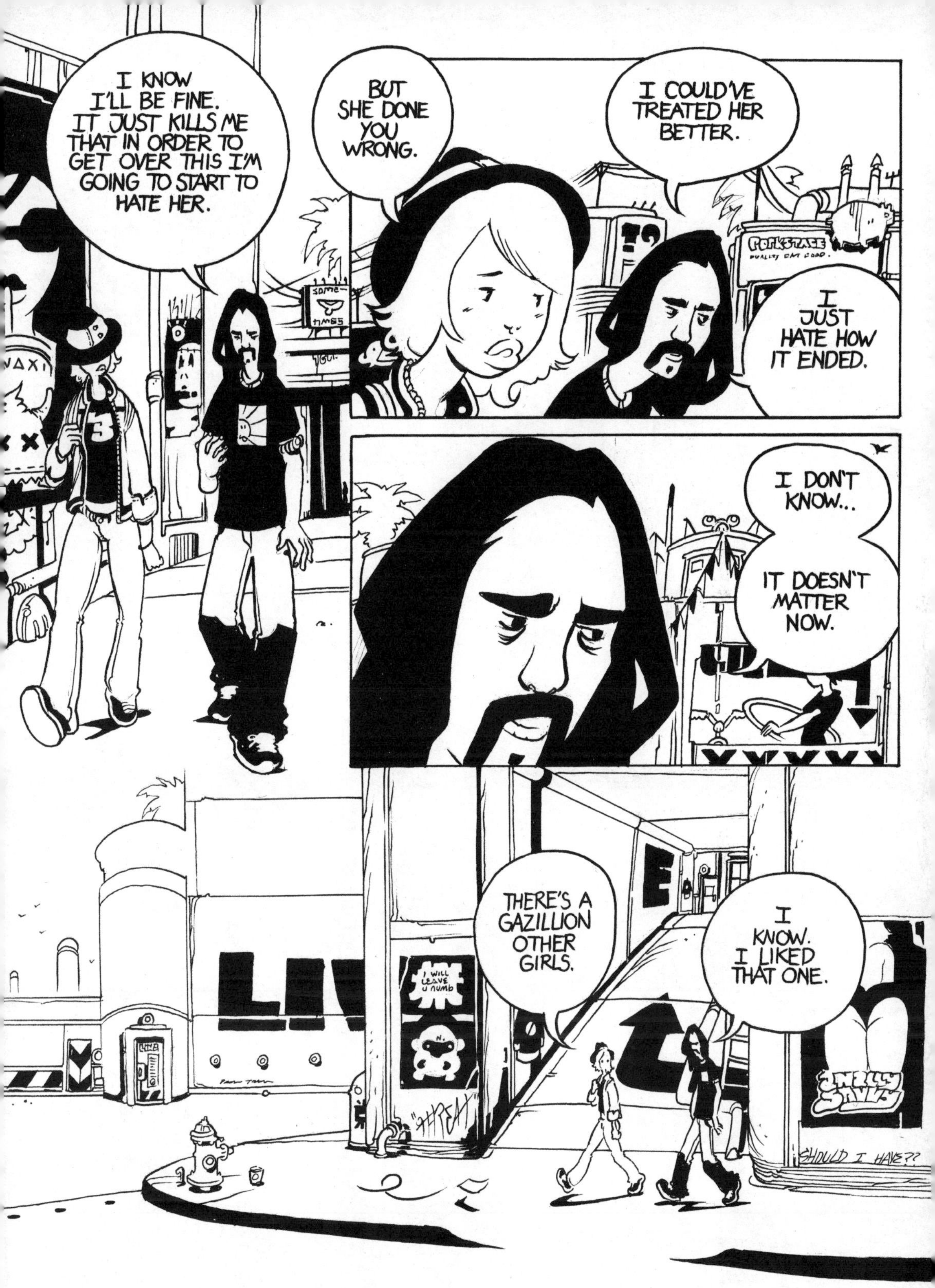
I KNOW I'LL BE FINE. IT JUST KILLS ME THAT IN ORDER TO GET OVER THIS I'M GOING TO START TO HATE HER.
BUT SHE DONE YOU WRONG.
I COULD'VE TREATED HER BETTER.
I JUST HATE HOW IT ENDED.
I DON'T KNOW...
IT DOESN'T MATTER NOW.
THERE'S A GAZILLION OTHER GIRLS.
I KNOW. I LIKED THAT ONE.
I WILL LEAVE U NUMB
SHOULD I HAVE??

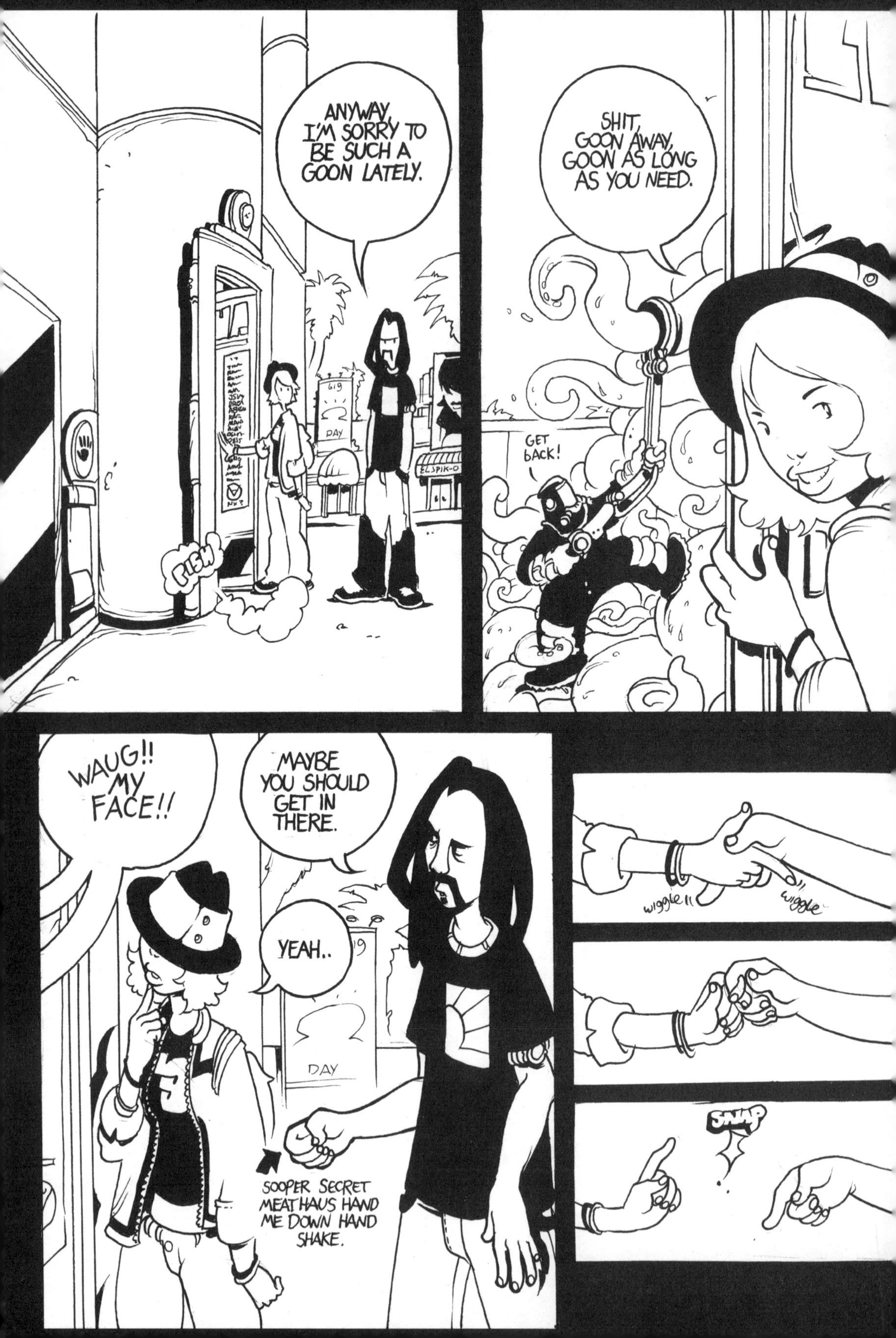
ANYWAY, I'M SORRY TO BE SUCH A GOON LATELY.
PISH
SHIT, GOON AWAY, GOON AS LONG AS YOU NEED.
GET BACK!
WAUG!! MY FACE!!
MAYBE YOU SHOULD GET IN THERE.
YEAH..
SOOPER SECRET MEAT HAUS HAND ME DOWN HAND SHAKE.
wiggle
wiggle
SNAP

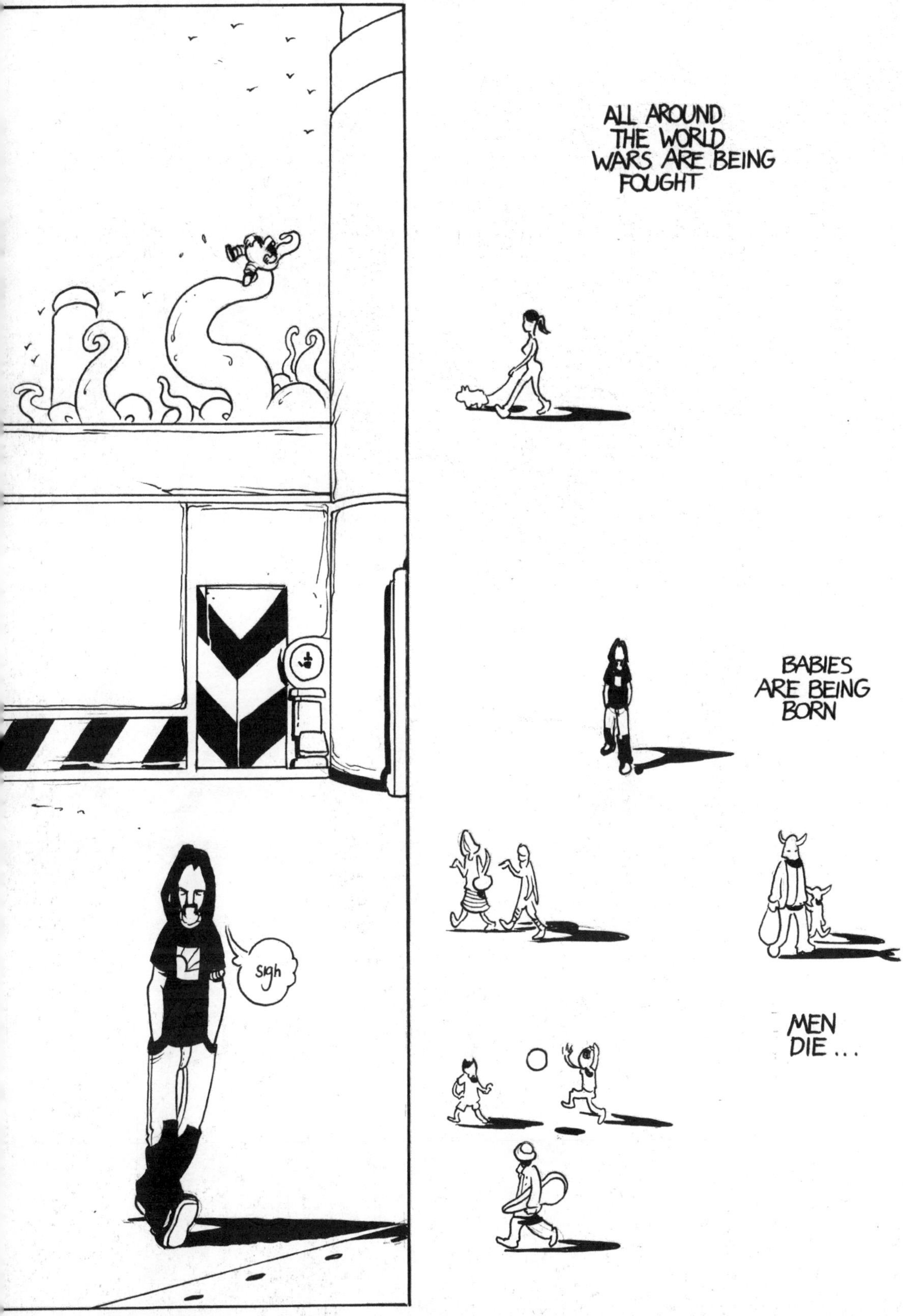
sigh
ALL AROUND THE WORLD WARS ARE BEING FOUGHT
BABIES ARE BEING BORN
MEN DIE...

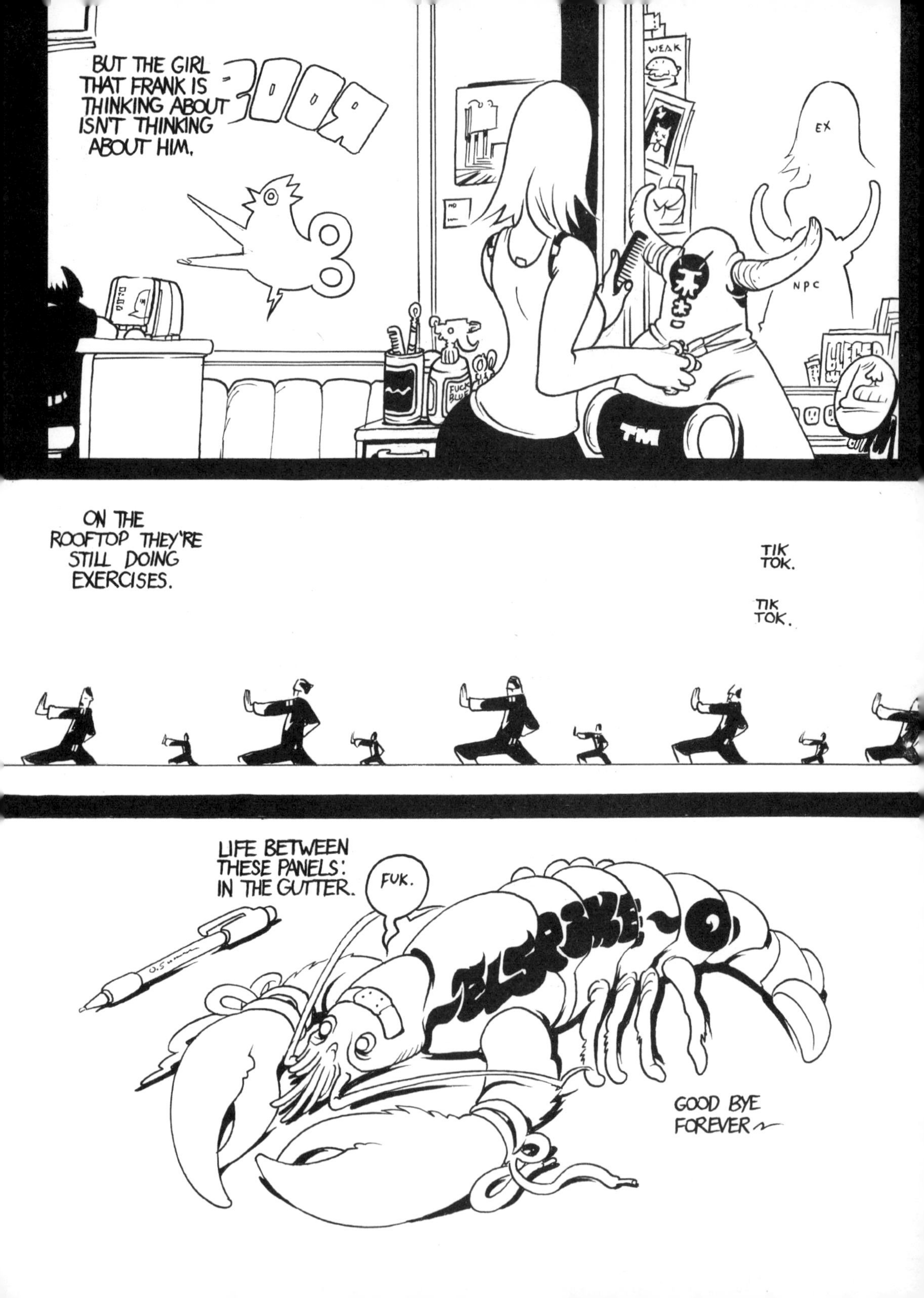
BUT THE GIRL THAT FRANK IS THINKING ABOUT ISN'T THINKING ABOUT HIM.
WEAK
EX
NPC
TM
ON THE ROOFTOP THEY'RE STILL DOING EXERCISES.
TIK TOK.
TIK TOK.
LIFE BETWEEN THESE PANELS: IN THE GUTTER.
FUK.
GOOD BYE FOREVER

Kenichi Hoshine and James Jean

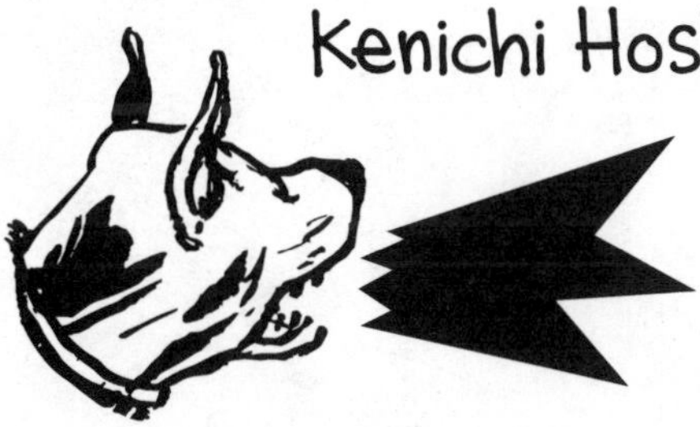

Kenichi Hoshine is an artist from New York City.
He really lives in Astoria, Queens
but likes telling people he lives in New York City
to make himself seem cooler than he really is.
In fact, he is a pretty lame guy.
www.kenichihoshine.com

James Jean is plotting his return into the earth.
Erstwhile, his work has been appeared in many
publications in all over the world.
For pleasure: www.jamesjean.com.

POLITEWINTER

A Conversation

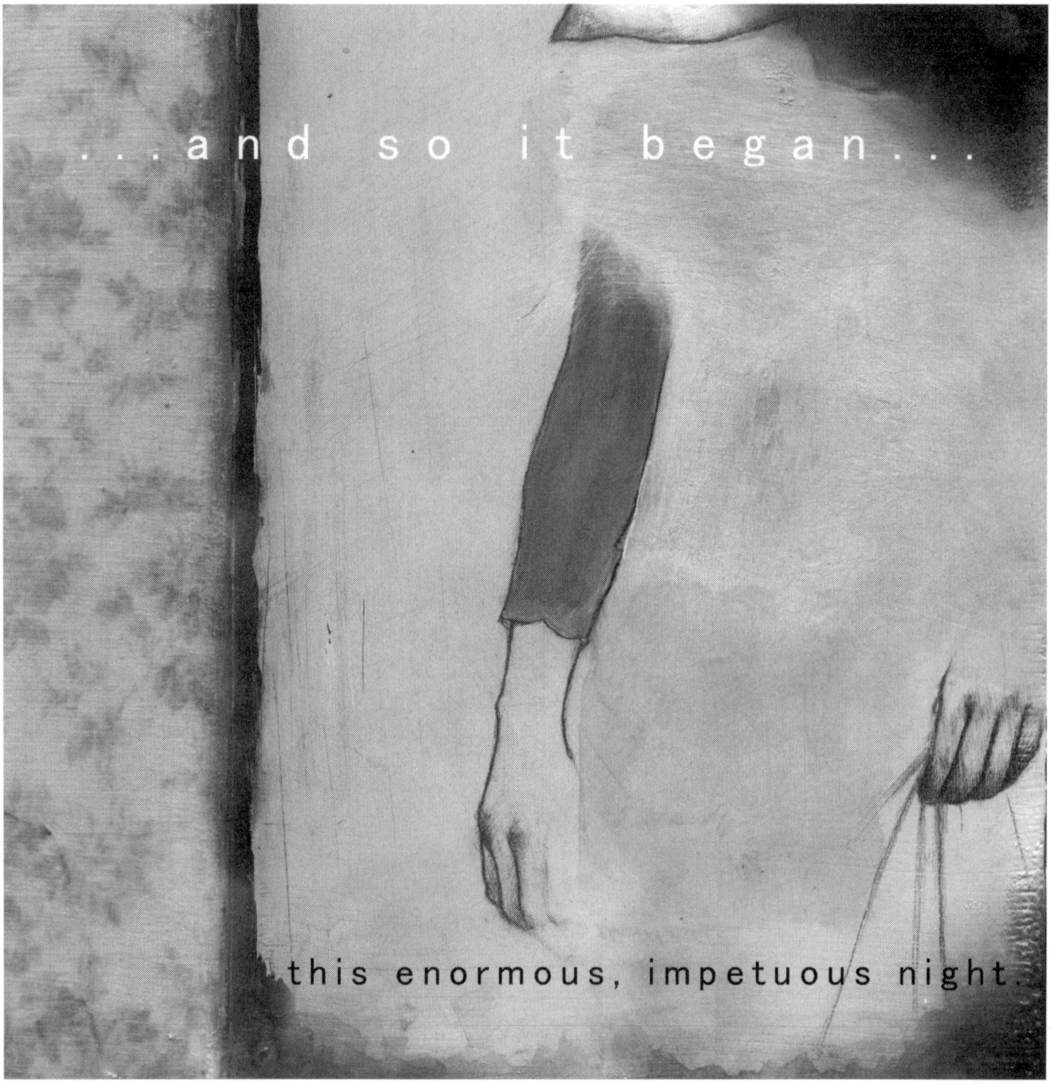

...and so it began...
this enormous, impetuous night.

She remembered the last thousand years with cold

REGRET

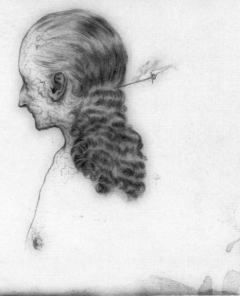

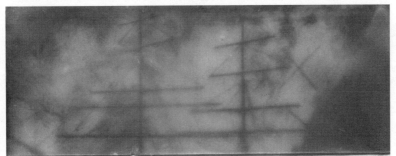

Who are you looking for?

Your tea merchant husband who

perished off the coast of China

200 years ago? Or is it your

august mother who was murdered

a century before that? Her

windpipe violently sliced in two

by your coercive father...

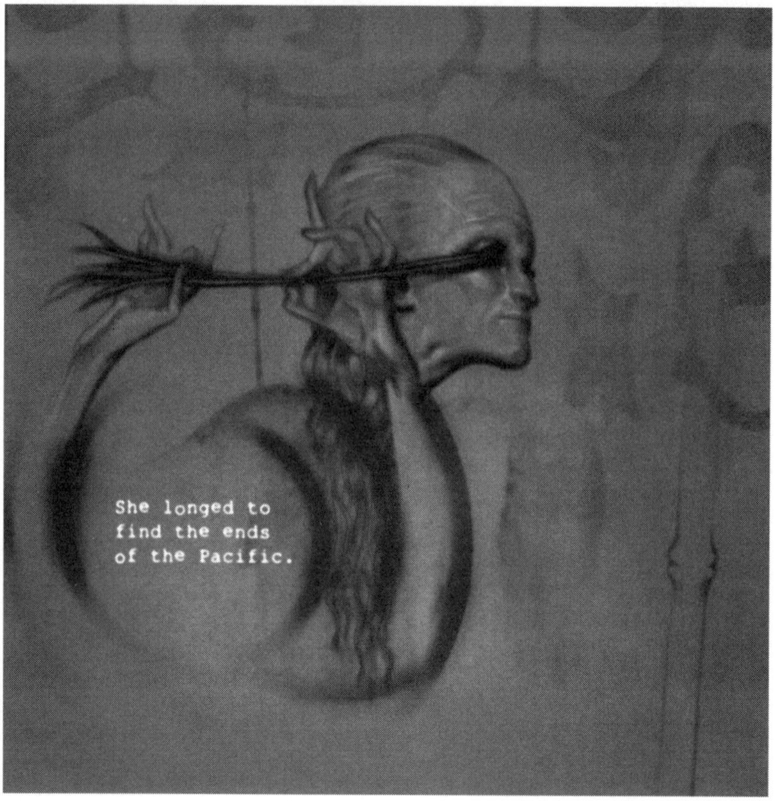
She longed to find the ends of the Pacific.

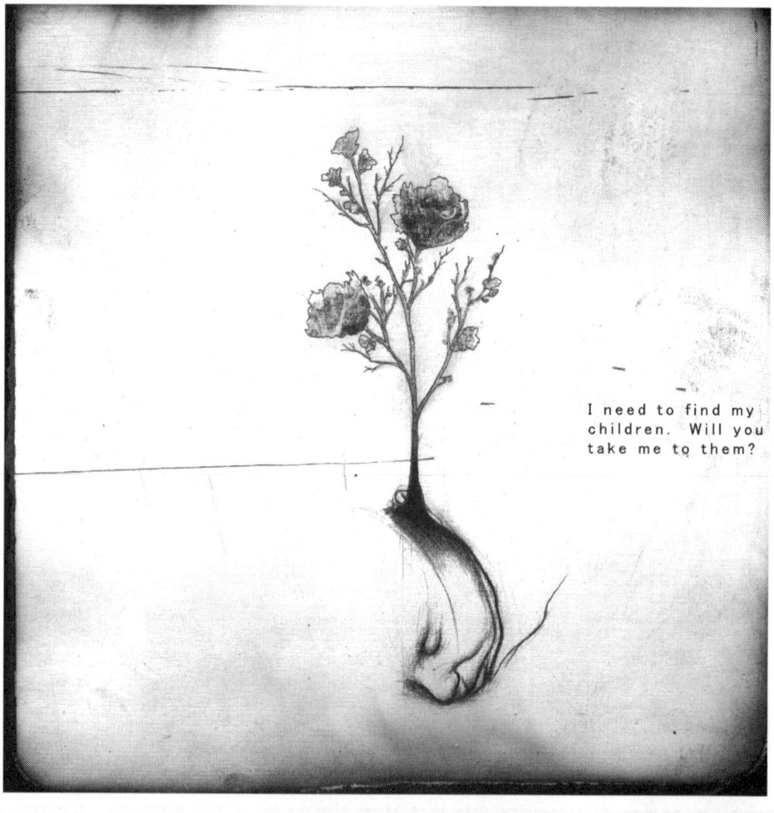
I need to find my children. Will you take me to them?

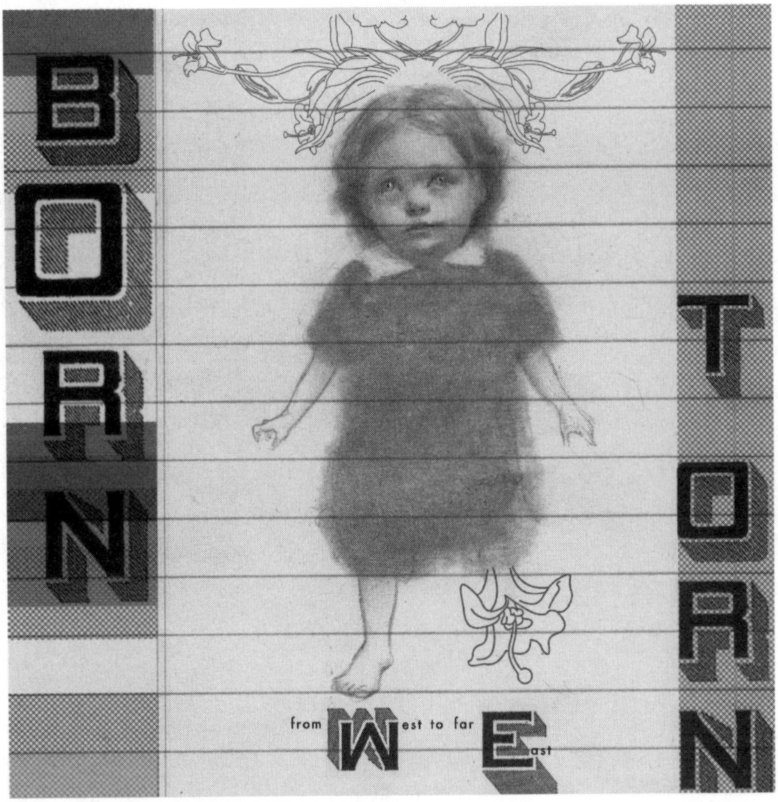
BORN
TORN
from West to far East

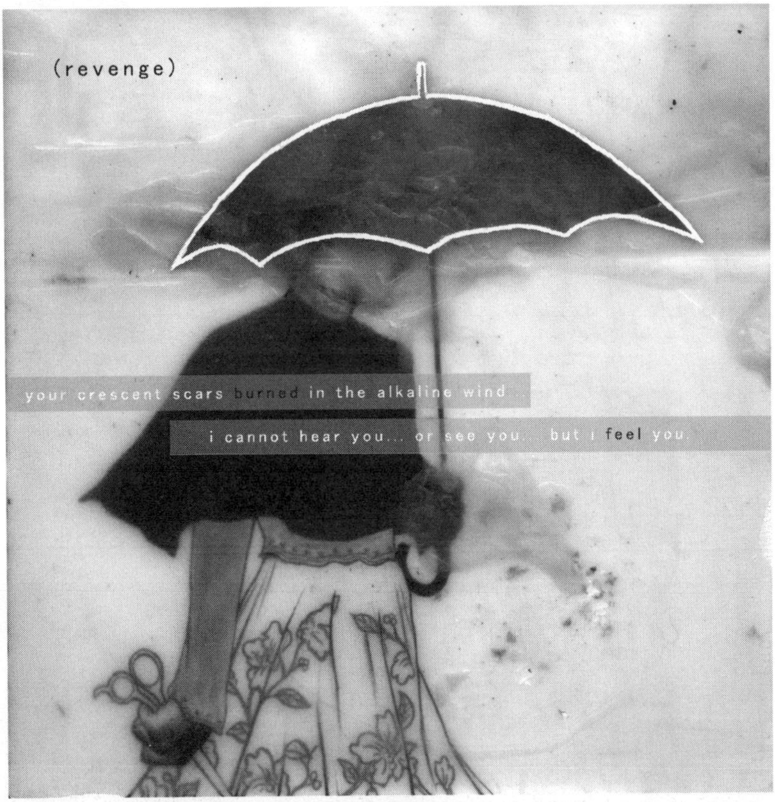
(revenge)
your crescent scars burned in the alkaline wind
i cannot hear you... or see you. but i feel you.

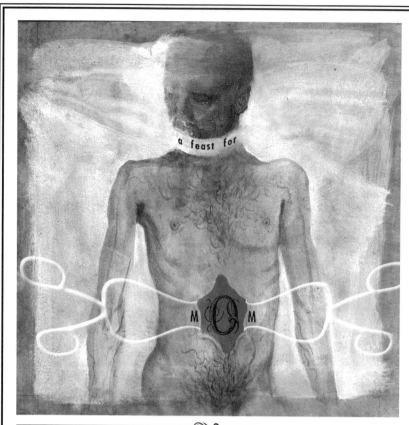

a feast for

M C M

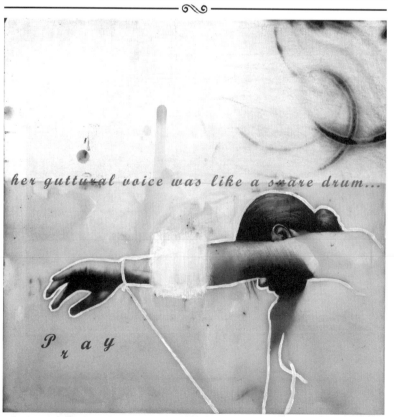

her guttural voice was like a snare drum...

Pray

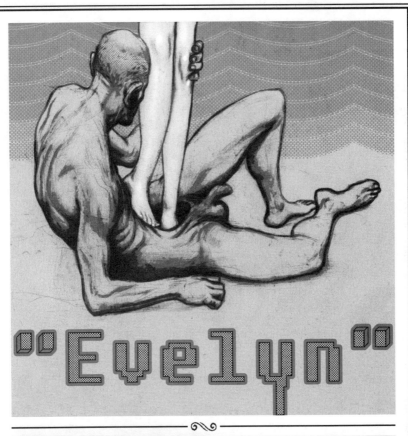

"Evelyn"

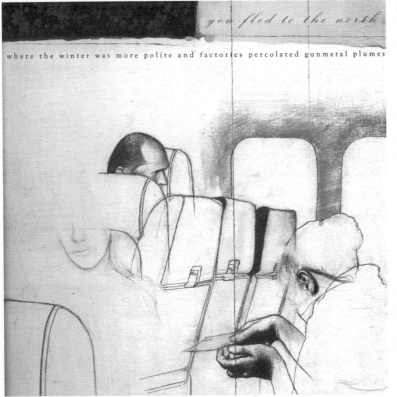

you fled to the north

where the winter was more polite and factories percolated gunmetal plumes

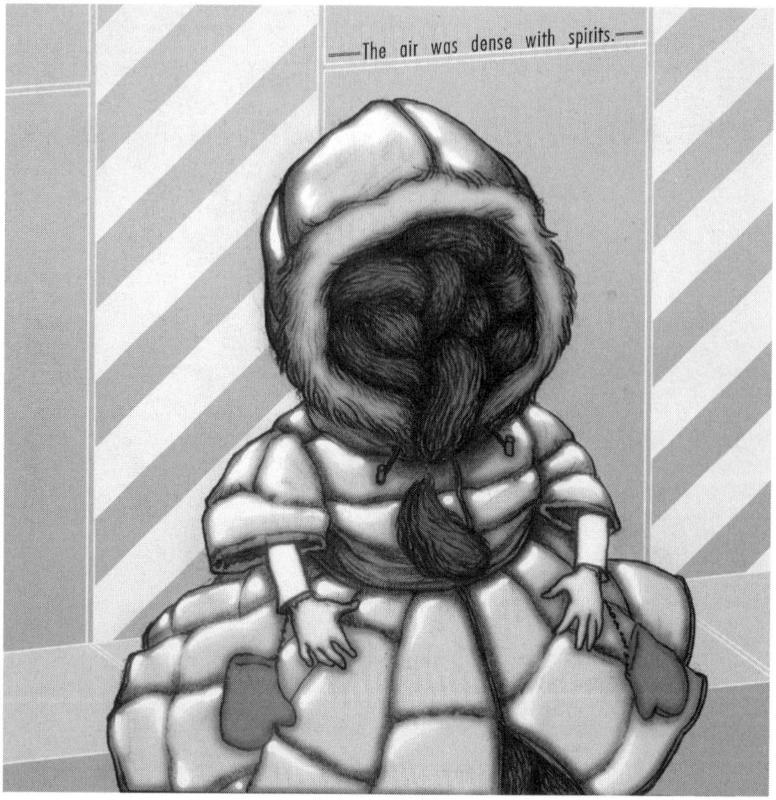
The air was dense with spirits.

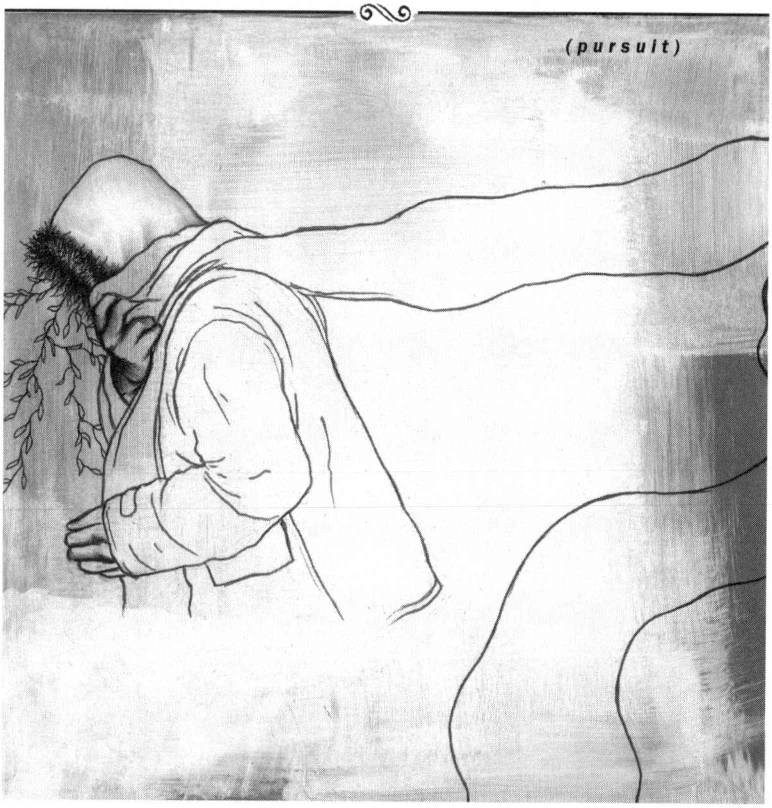
(pursuit)

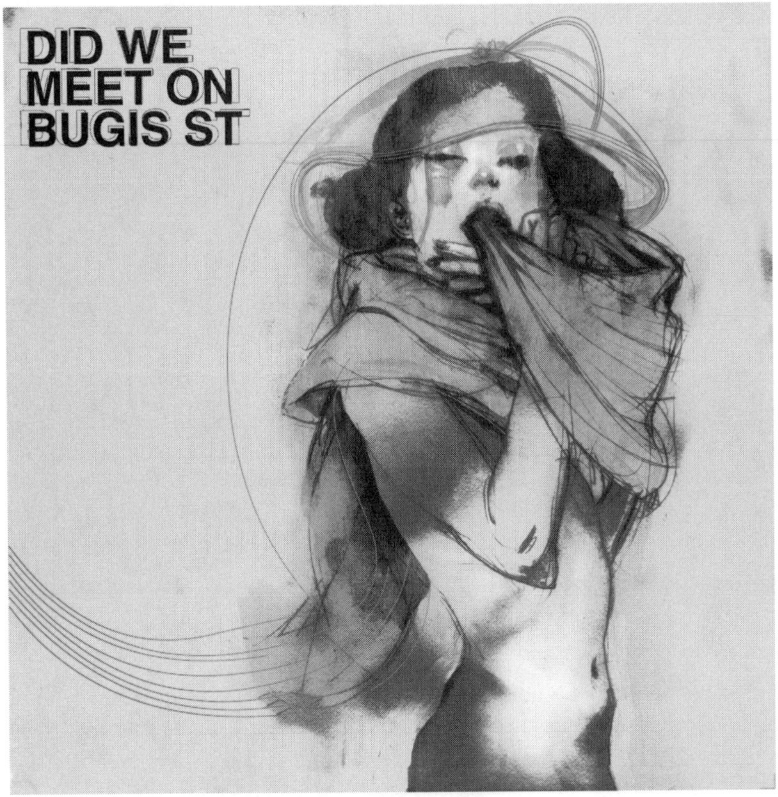
DID WE
MEET ON
BUGIS ST

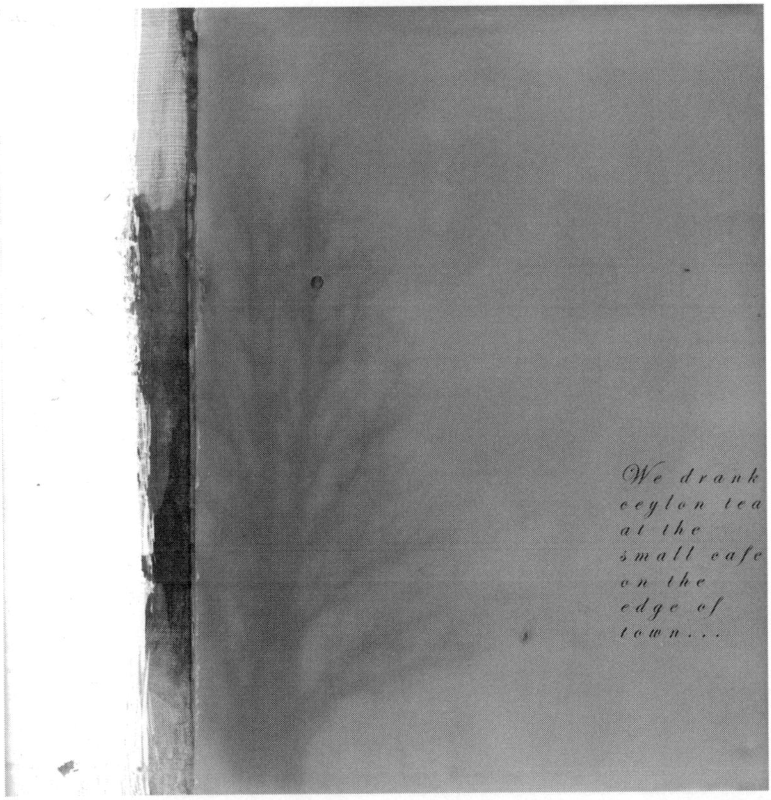
We drank
ceylon tea
at the
small cafe
on the
edge of
town...

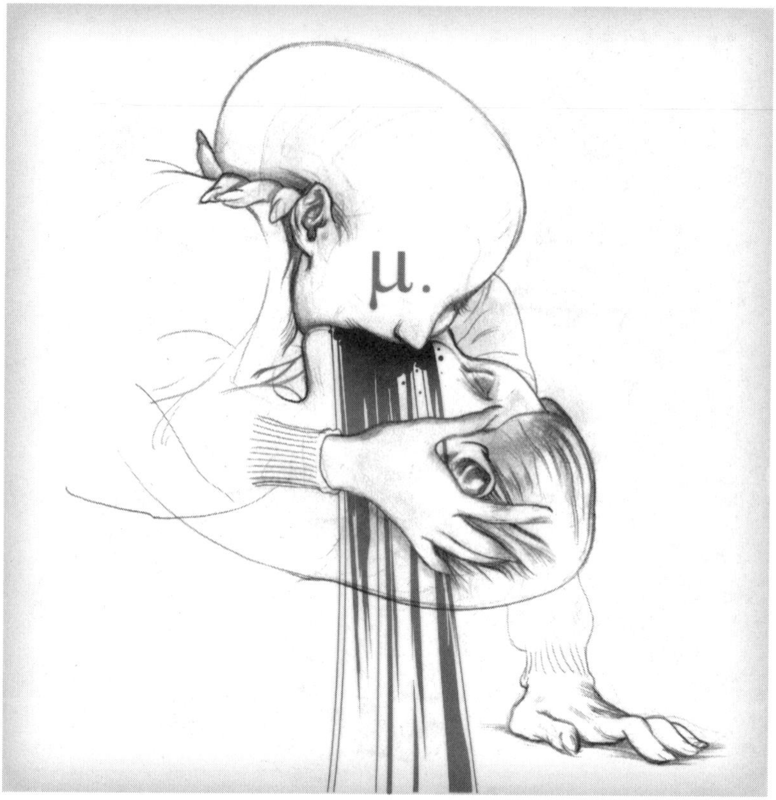
μ.

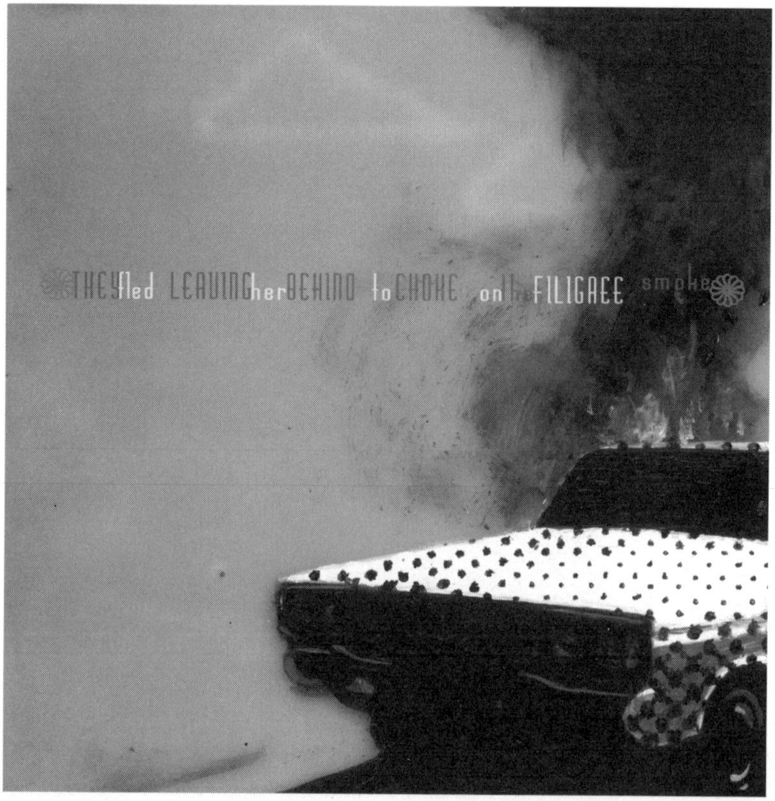
THEY fled LEAVING her BEHIND to CHOKE on the FILIGREE smoke

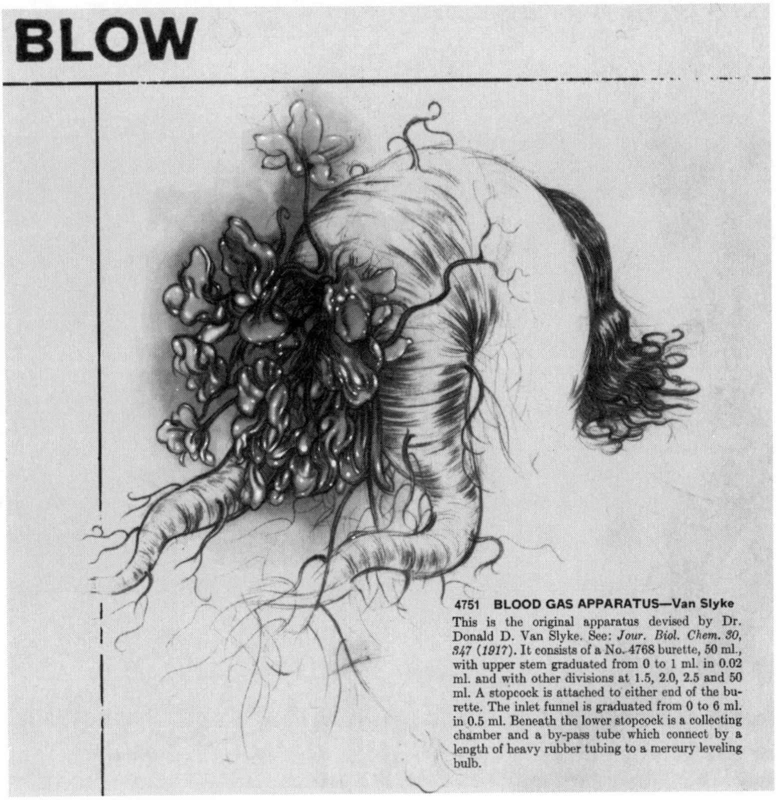
BLOW
4751 BLOOD GAS APPARATUS—Van Slyke
This is the original apparatus devised by Dr. Donald D. Van Slyke. See: *Jour. Biol. Chem. 30, 347 (1917)*. It consists of a No. 4768 burette, 50 ml., with upper stem graduated from 0 to 1 ml. in 0.02 ml. and with other divisions at 1.5, 2.0, 2.5 and 50 ml. A stopcock is attached to either end of the burette. The inlet funnel is graduated from 0 to 6 ml. in 0.5 ml. Beneath the lower stopcock is a collecting chamber and a by-pass tube which connect by a length of heavy rubber tubing to a mercury leveling bulb.

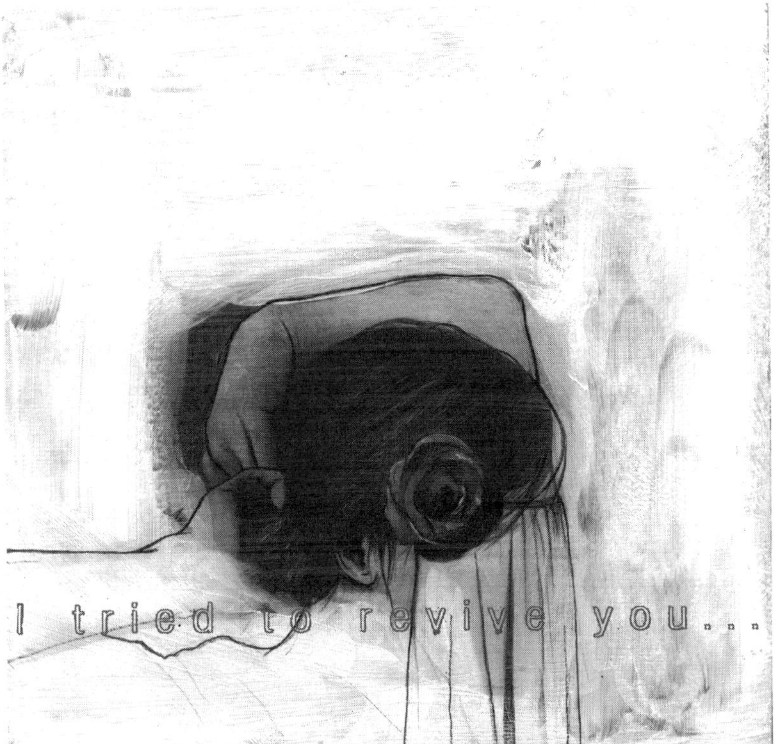
I tried to revive you...

to
be
con-
tinued
∞

www·POLITEWINTER·com

Dash Shaw

Dash is a recent graduate of the School of Visual Arts. now he is homeless.
dash@dashshaw.com
www.dashshaw.com
band website: www.loveeatsbrains.com

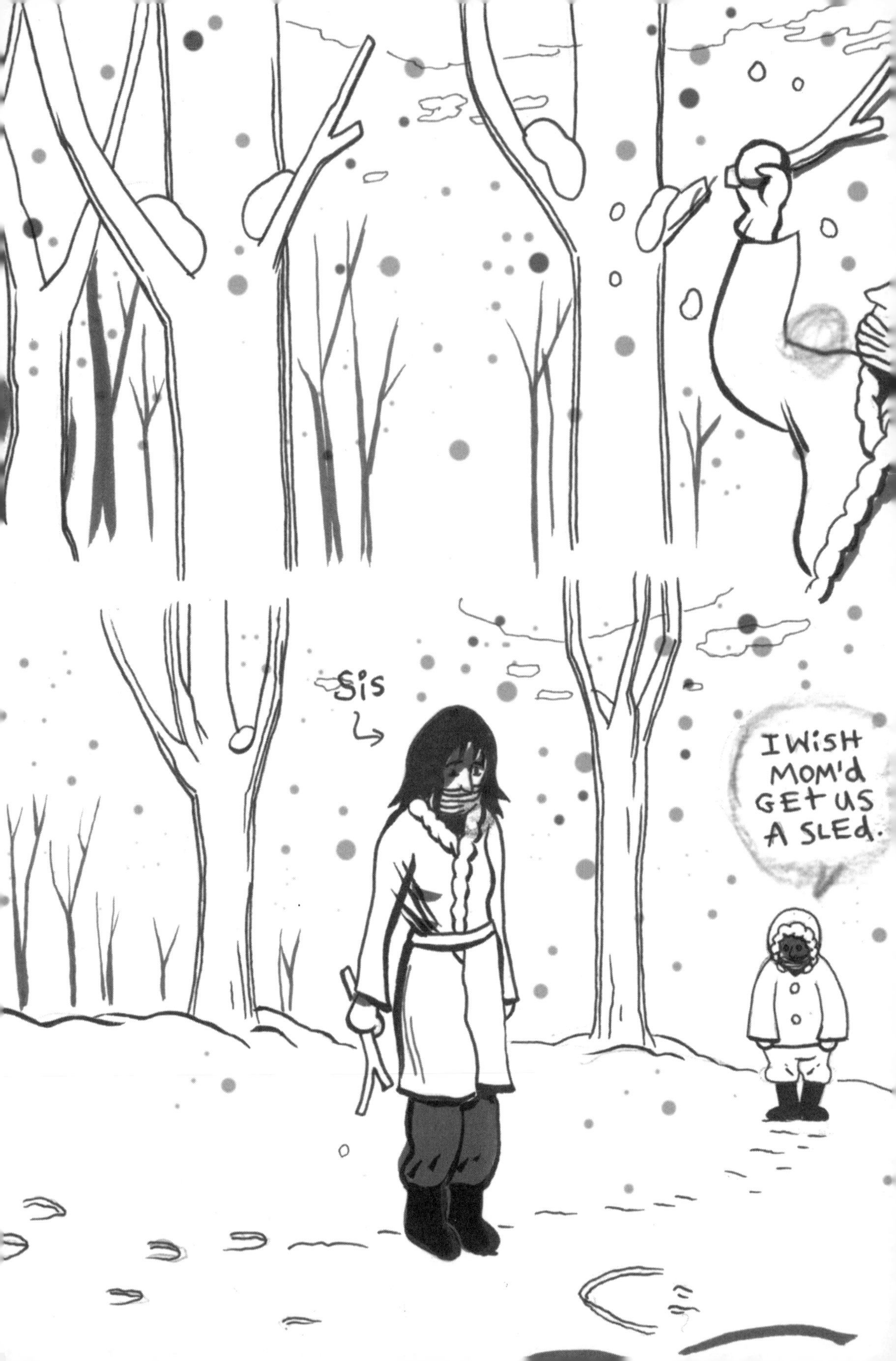
Sis
I WISH MOM'd GET US A SLEd.

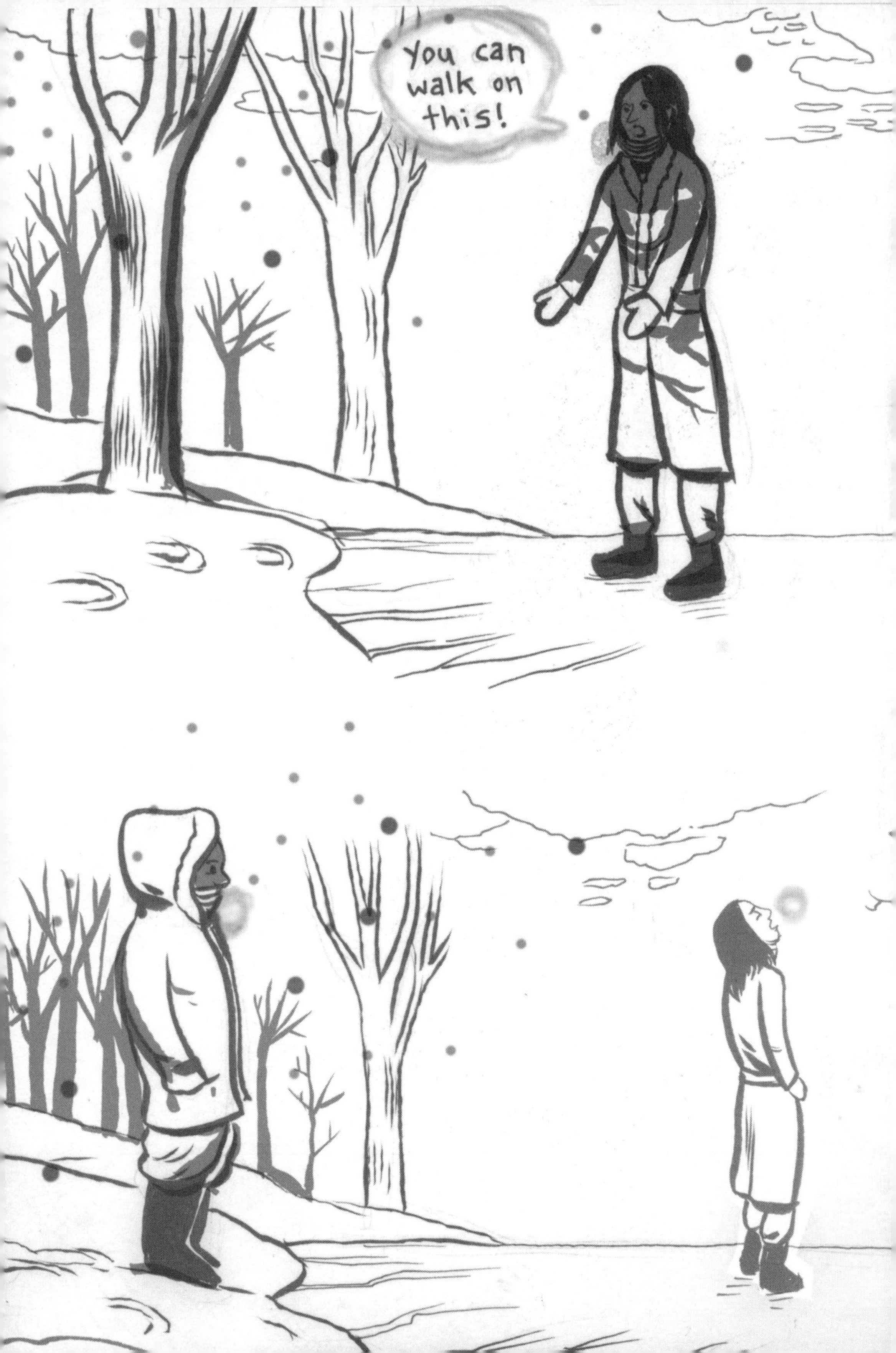
You can walk on this!

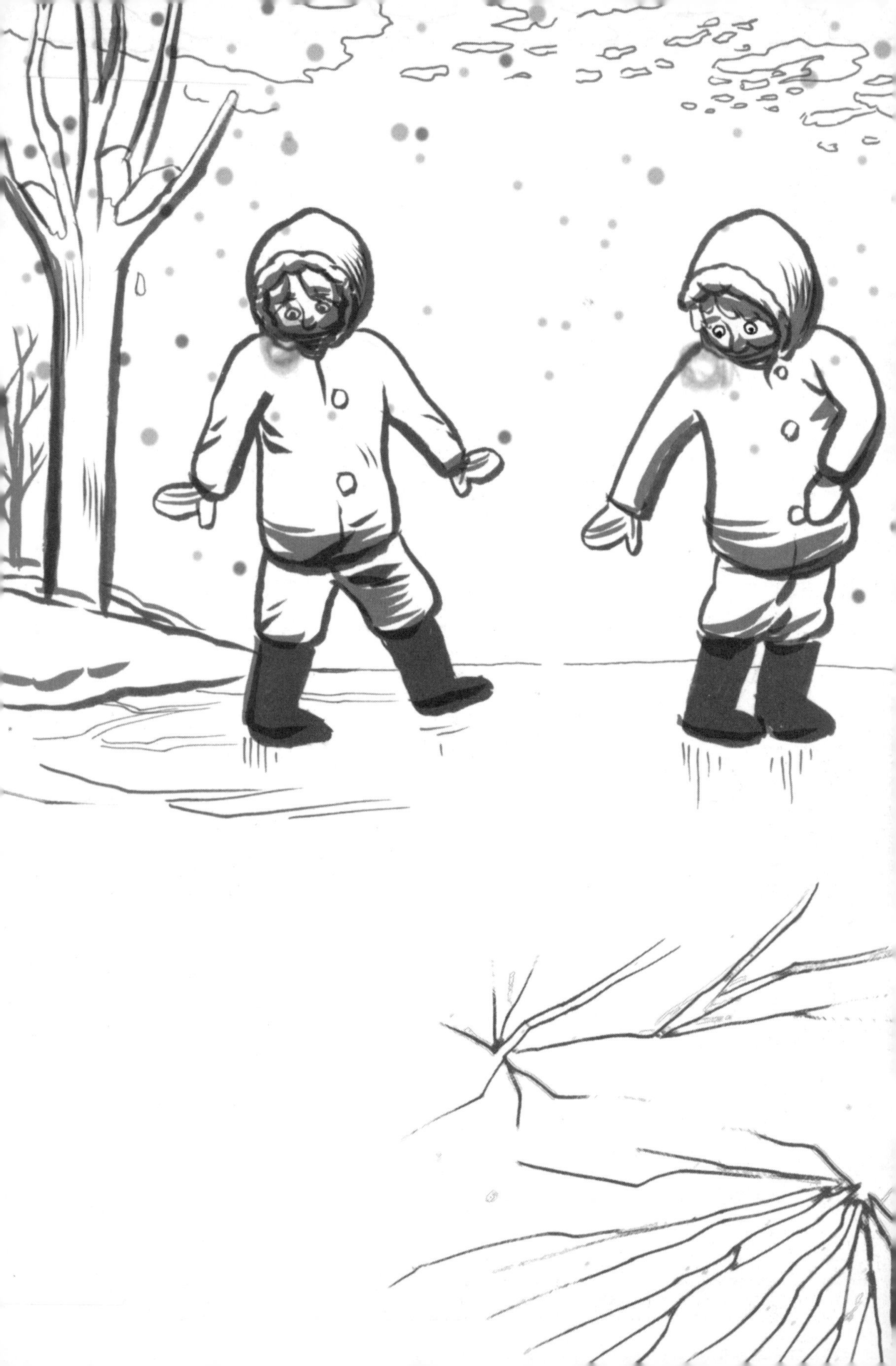

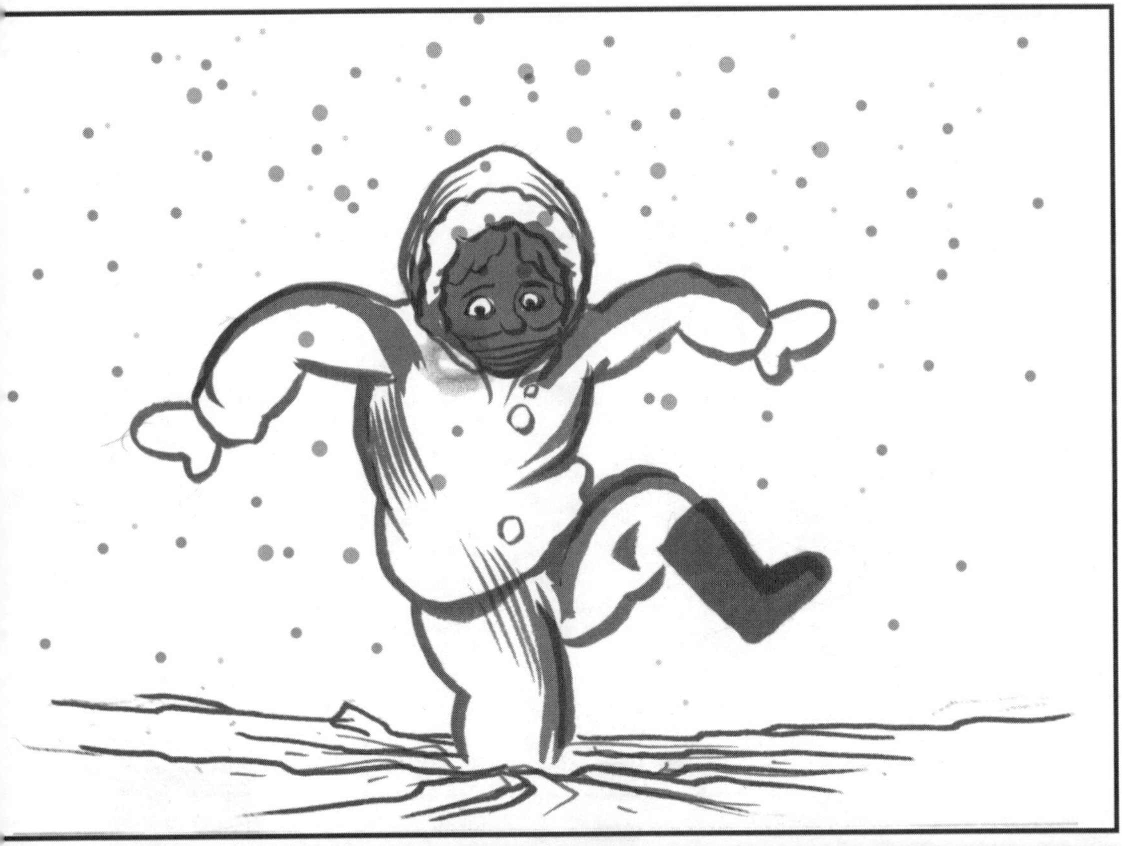

FREEZING C
COLDD WATER

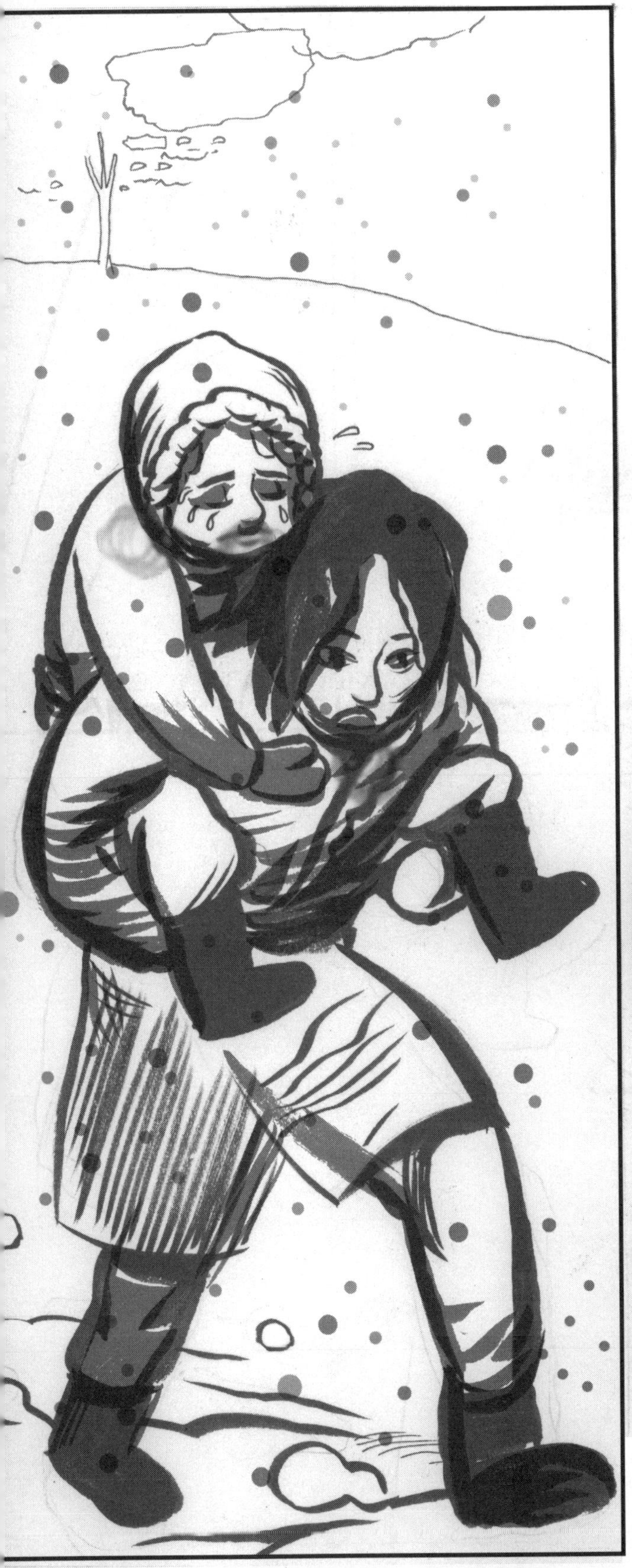

When we got home,
Mom yelled at me
while Nick took
a hot bath.

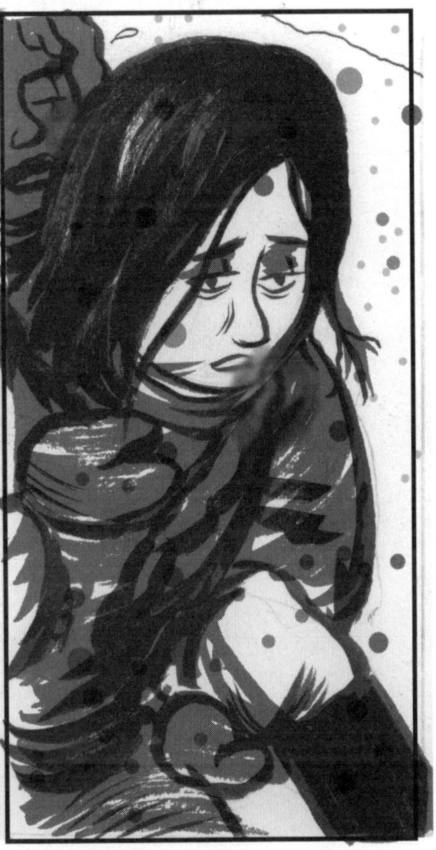

-dash '05

Matthew Woodson

Matthew Woodson lives in Chicago, nobody reads his comics, and quite frankly, there are not that many to read. He is timidly working on a project with Brian Wood for Top Shelf, as well as a book on his own. www.ghostco.org

What youth and beauty these creatures bore

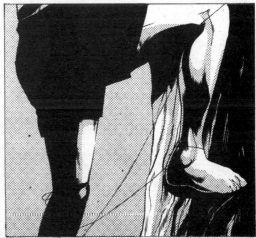

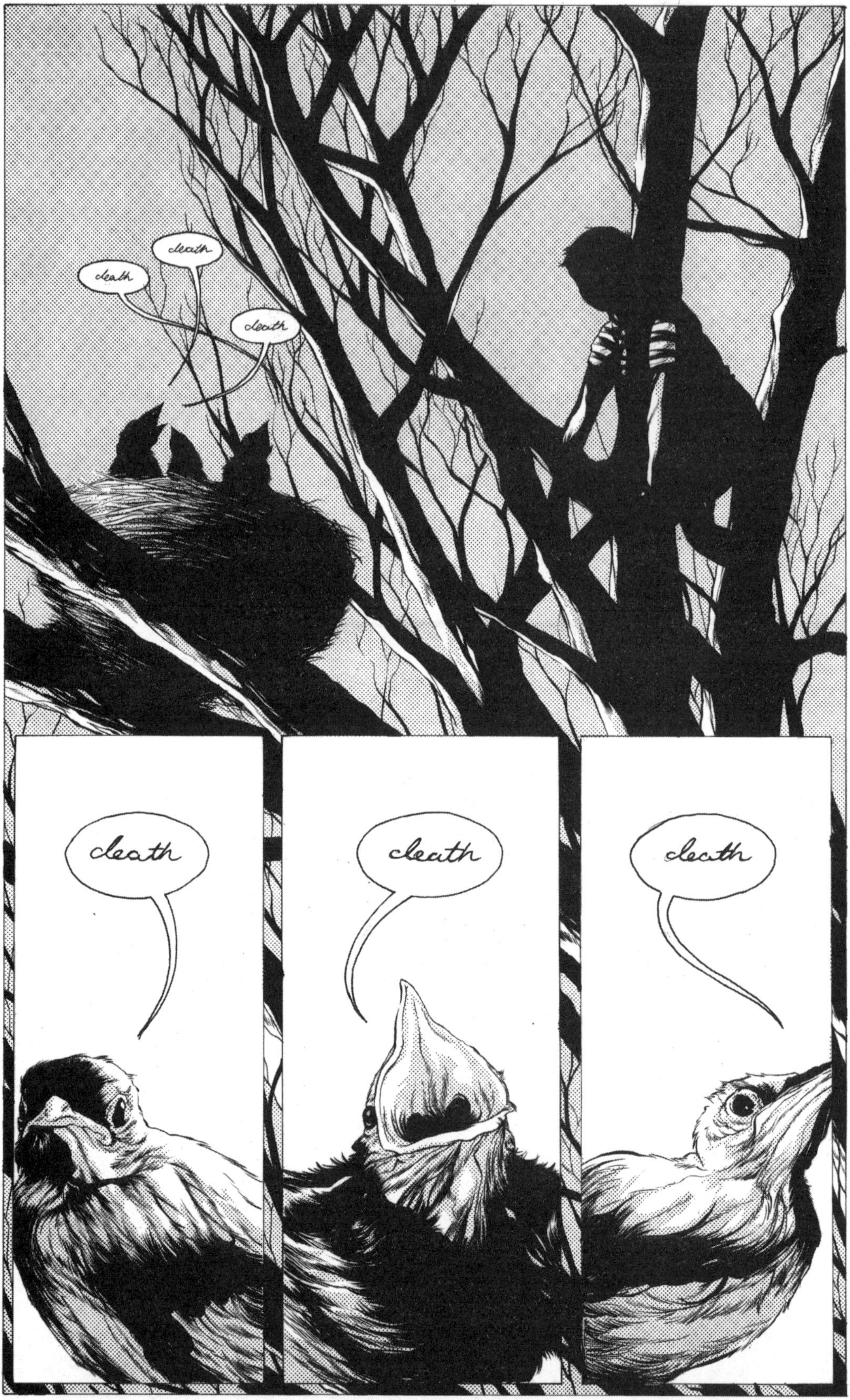
death
death
death
death
death
death

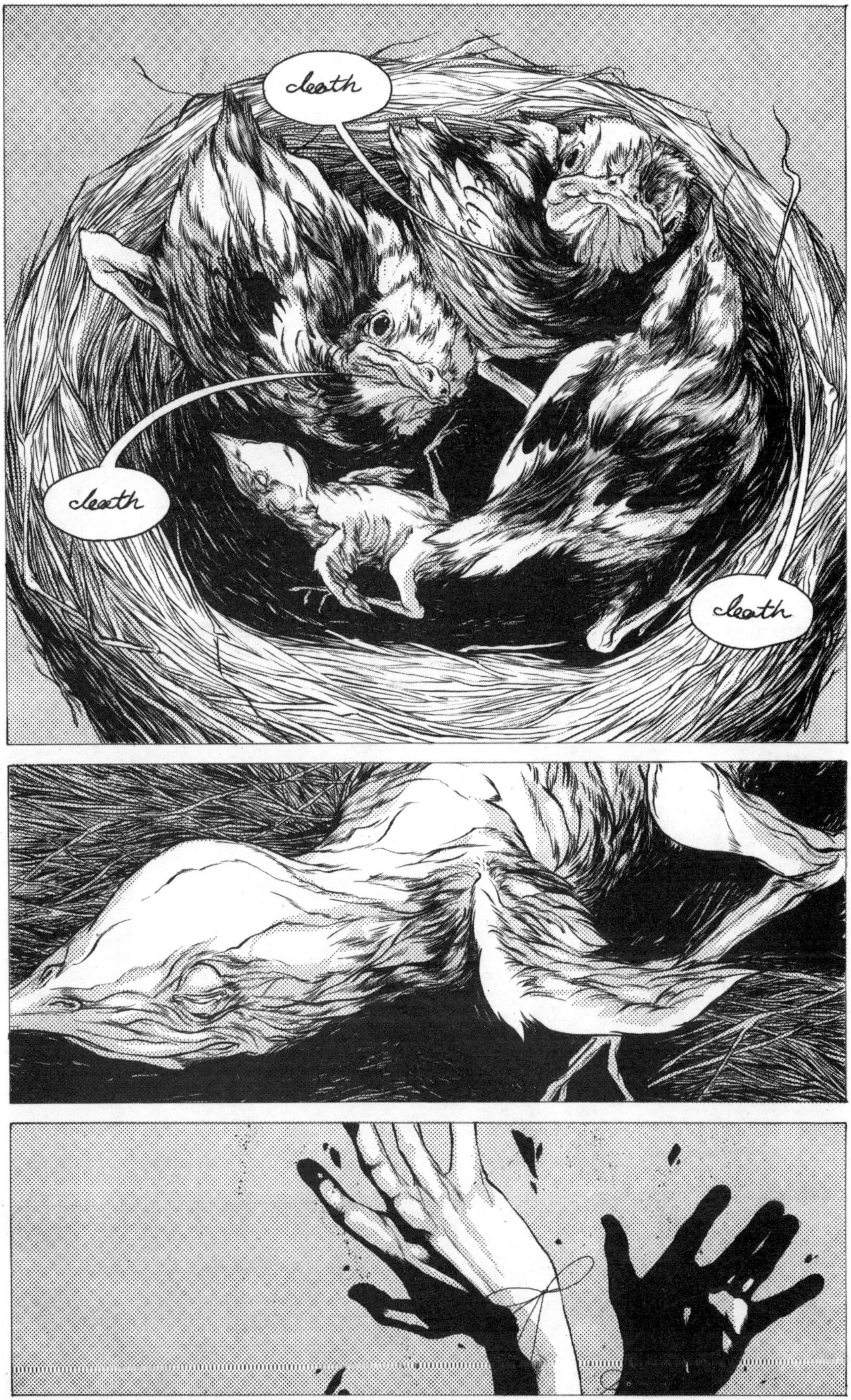
death
death
death

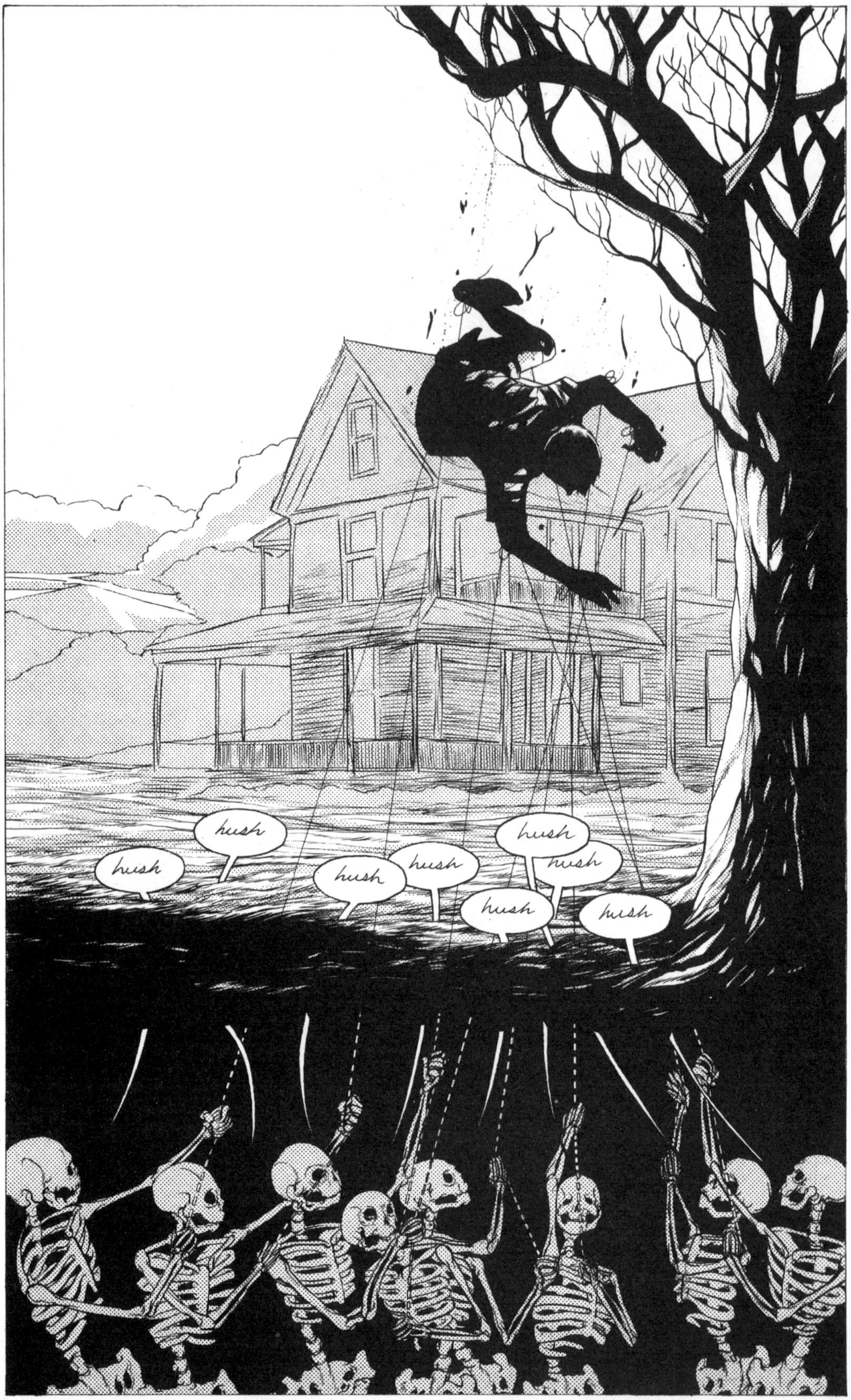
hush
hush
hush
hush
hush
hush
hush
hush

Tom Herpich

Tom Herpich lives in the mountains of North Carolina, where "iced tea" is "sweet tea", and no one has ever heard of Duane Reade drug stores. He has had two of his own books published by Alternative Comics, entitled "Cusp" and "Gongwanadon".
Tom can be contacted at thomasherpich@hotmail.com, or through www.thomasherpich.com.

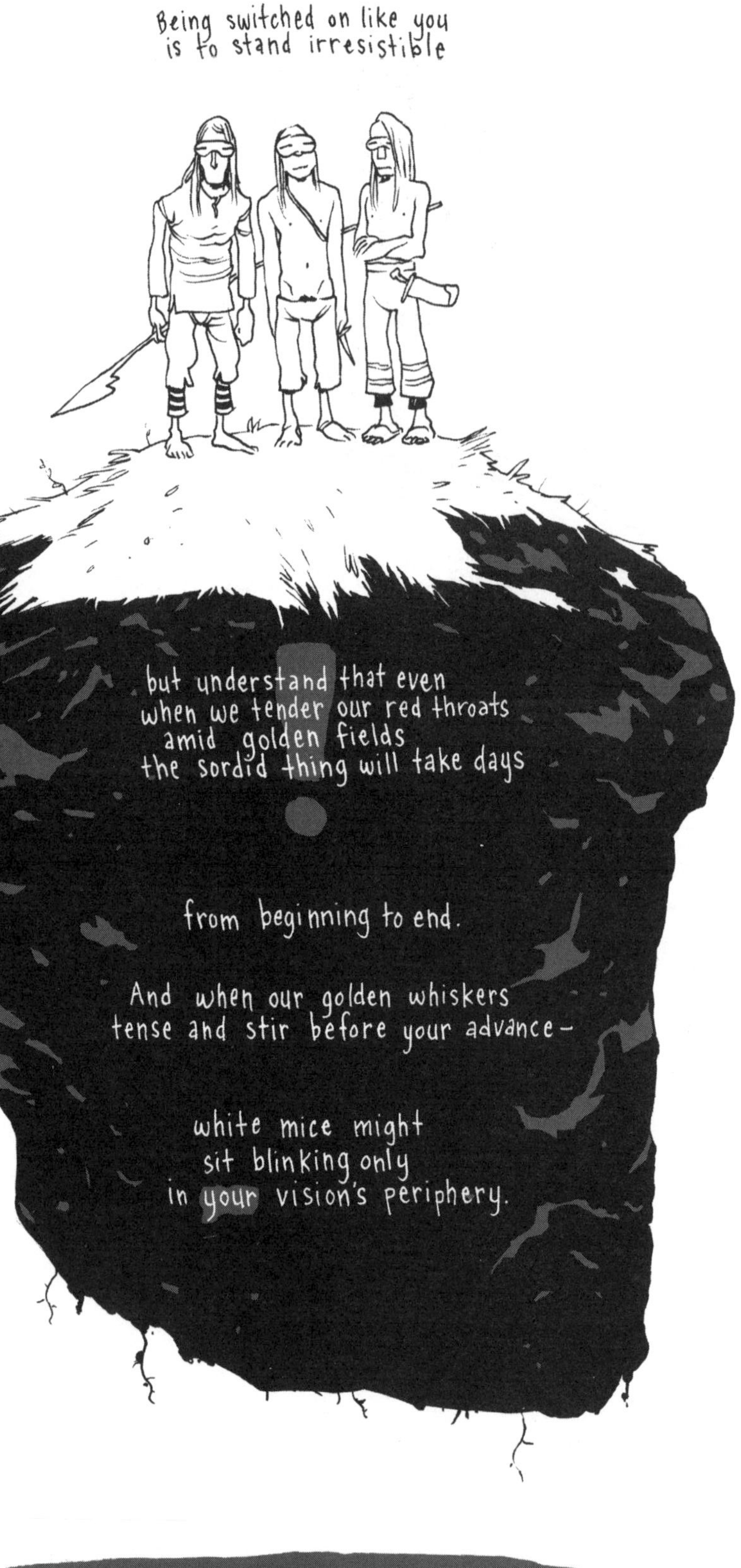
Being switched on like you
is to stand irresistible
but understand that even
when we tender our red throats
amid golden fields
the sordid thing will take days
from beginning to end.
And when our golden whiskers
tense and stir before your advance-
white mice might
sit blinking only
in your vision's periphery.

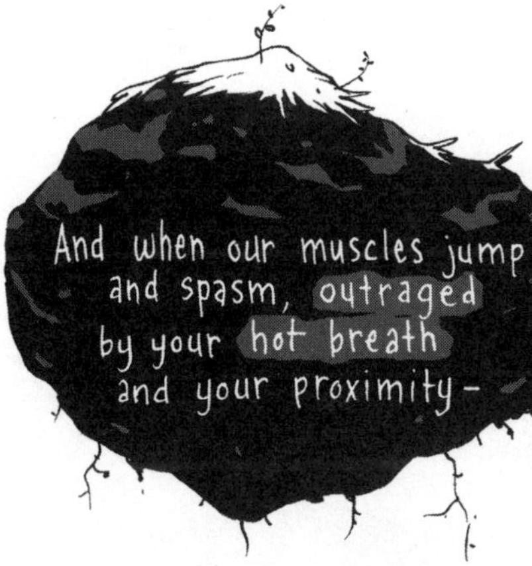
And when our muscles jump
and spasm, outraged
by your hot breath
and your proximity-

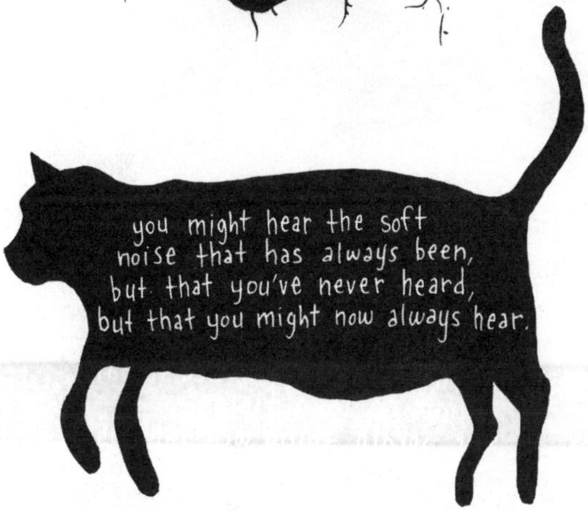
you might hear the soft
noise that has always been,
but that you've never heard,
but that you might now always hear.

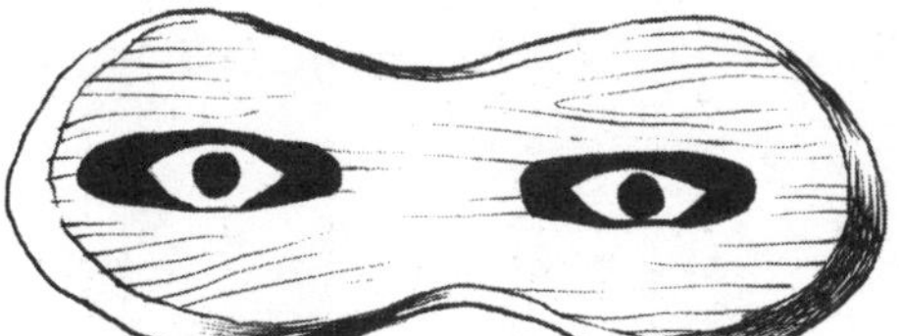

And on the final evening
when I am only a dusty heavy pile in the gravel-

a match struck within your
hermetic stone egg
might reveal a bashful
orange face squinting.

Mu Dafaka

Some times people get confused with me and Mu Pan (Muwen Pan or Mu Wen Pan), but I am not him!! That guy is the most talented artist I've ever known, so sophisticated and profound and funny as well. I am just a lowlife who talks with comics, but I do what Mu Pan doesn't wanna do and dare not to do. Without Mu, I am useless, without me, he is just merely another trained draftsman. http://mupan.com

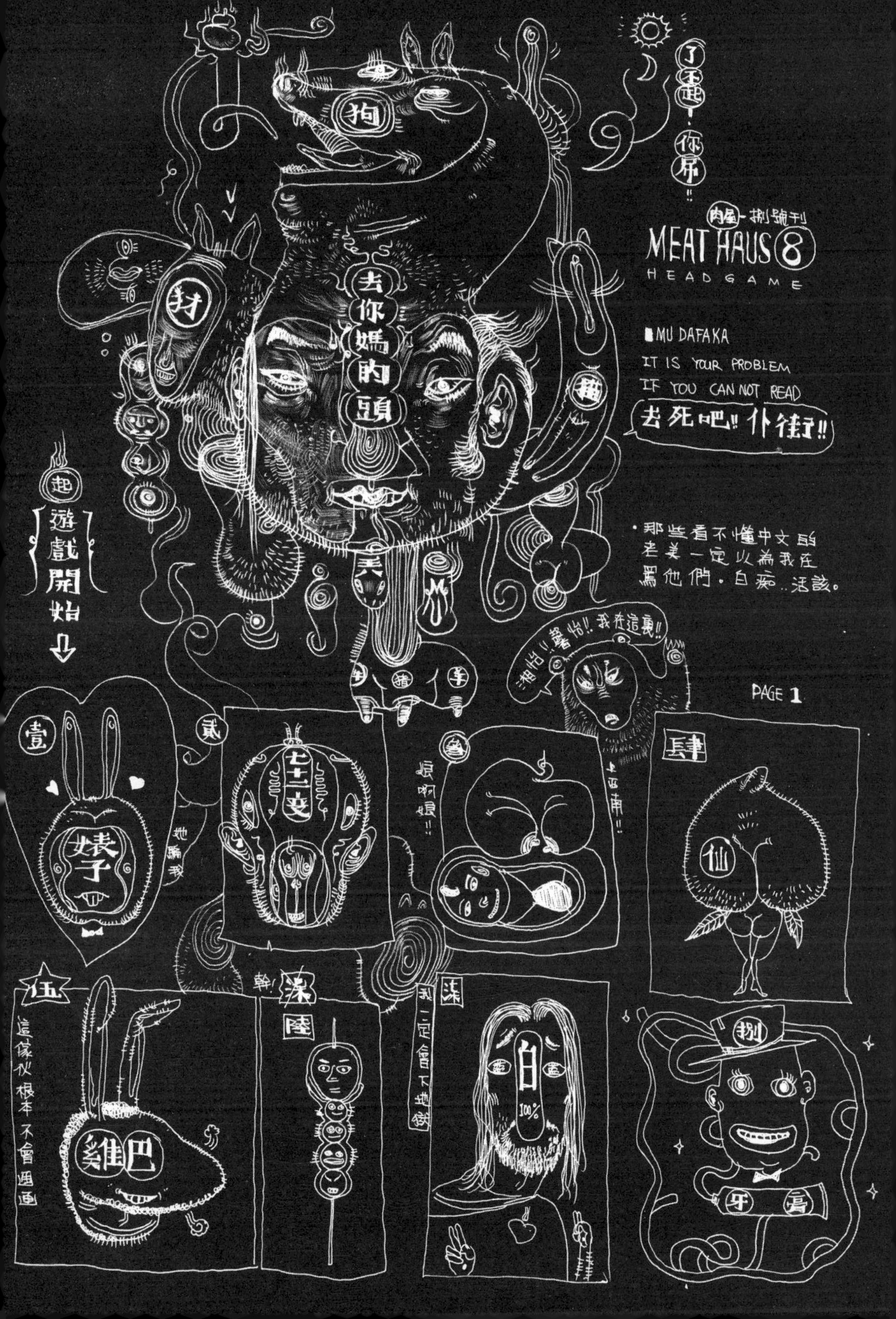

了不起!你屌!!
肉屋-捌號刊
MEAT HAUS 8
HEAD GAME
MU DAFAKA
IT IS YOUR PROBLEM
IF YOU CAN NOT READ
去死吧!! 仆街!!
那些看不懂中文的老美一定以為我在罵他們。白痴..活該。
狗
去你媽的頭
起
遊戲開始
湘怡!! 馨怡!! 我在這裏!!
PAGE 1
壹
婊子
貳
她騙我
七十二變
娘啊娘!!
上西南!!
肆
仙
伍
這傢伙根本不會畫畫
雞巴
幹
陸
柒
我一定會下地獄
白
100%
捌
牙膏

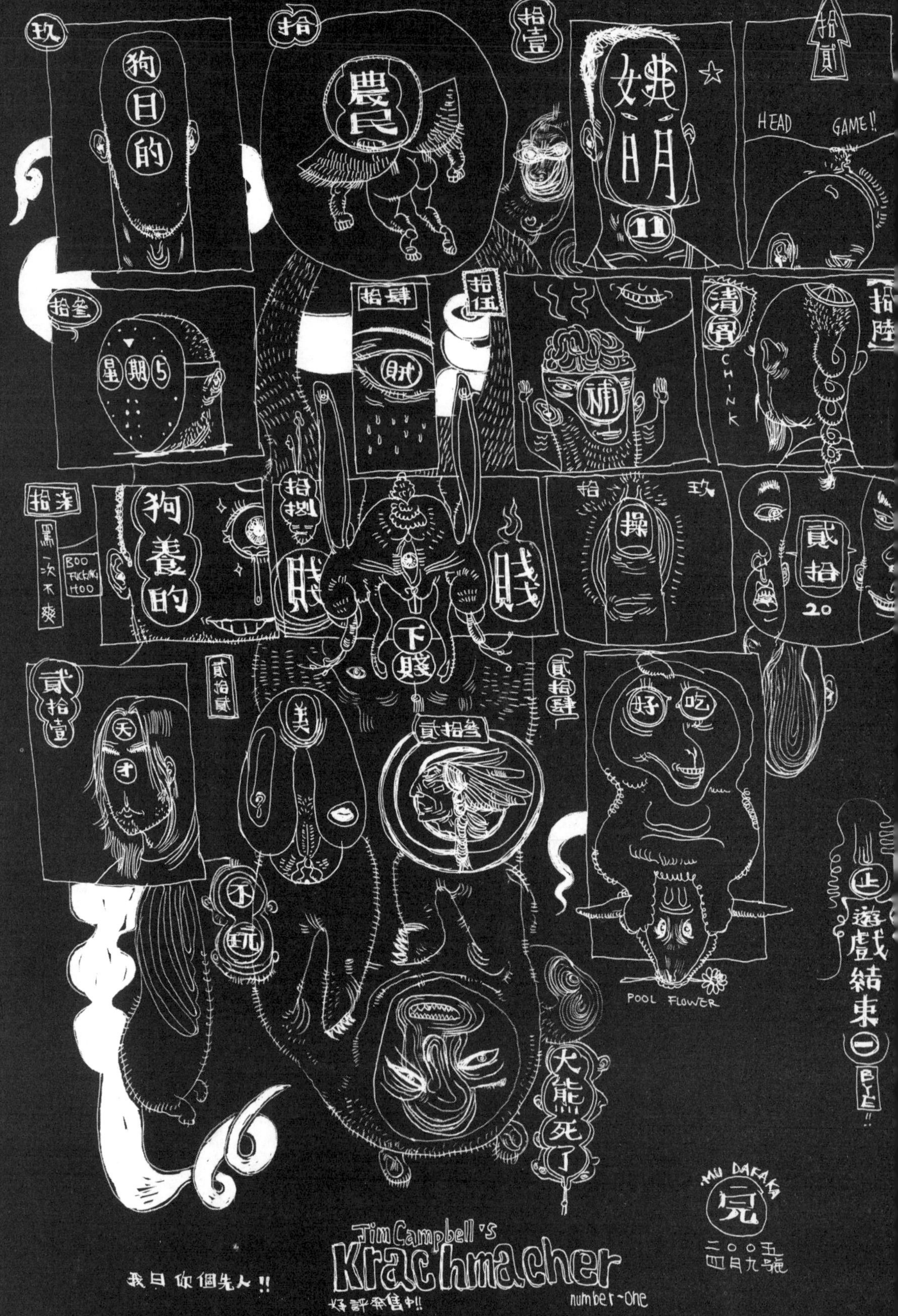

玖
狗日的
拾
農民
拾壹
姚明
11
拾貳
HEAD GAME!!
拾叁
星期5
拾肆
財
拾伍
補
清宮
CHINK
拾陸
拾柒
黑一次不爽
BOO FUCKING HOO
狗養的
拾捌
賤
賤
下賤
拾玖
操
貳拾
20
貳拾壹
天才
貳拾貳
美
貳拾叁
貳拾肆
好吃
不玩
POOL FLOWER
止
遊戲結束
一
BYE!!
大熊死了
MU DAFAKA
完
二〇〇五
四月九號
我日你個先人!!
Jim Campbell's
Krachmacher
number-one
好評発售中!!

Jeffro Kilpatrick

Jeffro Kilpatrick has been a member of
Meathaus since 2001. He is the Cofounder of the
Philadelphia Cartoonist Society. His work has also
been published by Baboon Books (Petey, Bunch of
Baboons, PCS Book One); Dark Horse Comics
(Strip Search); the Prophecy Anthology; and
several other magazines.

Jeffro devotes a lot of time volunteering his art
for charities in Philly (Fishtown Cartoon Camp,
Children's Crisis Treatment Center, Philadelphia
Committee to End Homelessness).
He lives in Fishtown, a small Philly neighborhood
where he was born and raised. Jeffro teaches
art at his old high school and spends every spare
minute making cartoons and comics.
Email Jeffro: phillytoon@yahoo.com.

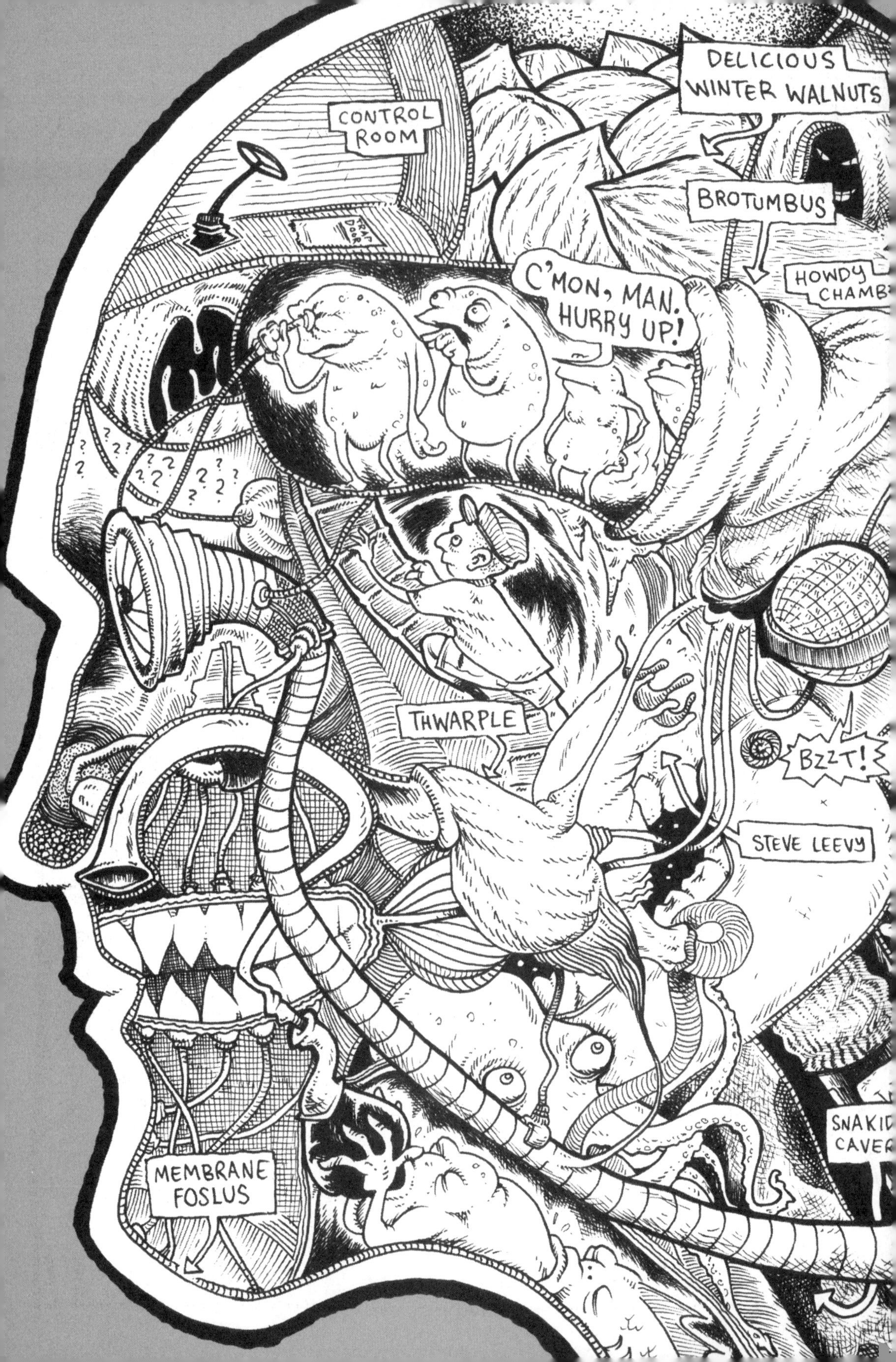
CONTROL ROOM
TRAP DOOR
DELICIOUS WINTER WALNUTS
BROTUMBUS
HOWDY CHAMB
C'MON, MAN. HURRY UP!
THWARPLE
BZZT!
STEVE LEEVY
SNAKID CAVER
MEMBRANE FOSLUS

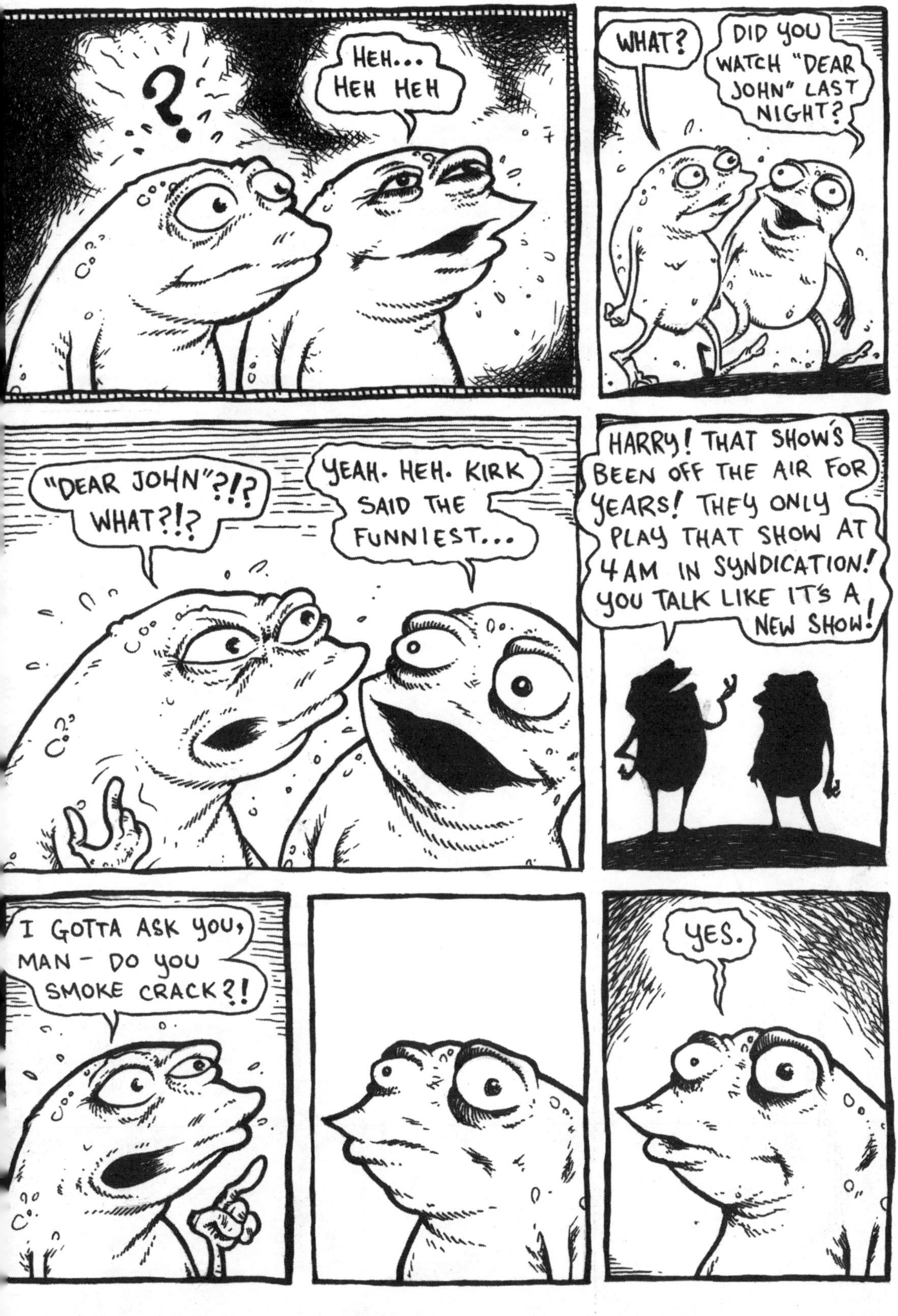
?
HEH... HEH HEH
WHAT?
DID YOU WATCH "DEAR JOHN" LAST NIGHT?
"DEAR JOHN"?!? WHAT?!?
YEAH. HEH. KIRK SAID THE FUNNIEST...
HARRY! THAT SHOW'S BEEN OFF THE AIR FOR YEARS! THEY ONLY PLAY THAT SHOW AT 4AM IN SYNDICATION! YOU TALK LIKE IT'S A NEW SHOW!
I GOTTA ASK YOU, MAN - DO YOU SMOKE CRACK?!
YES.

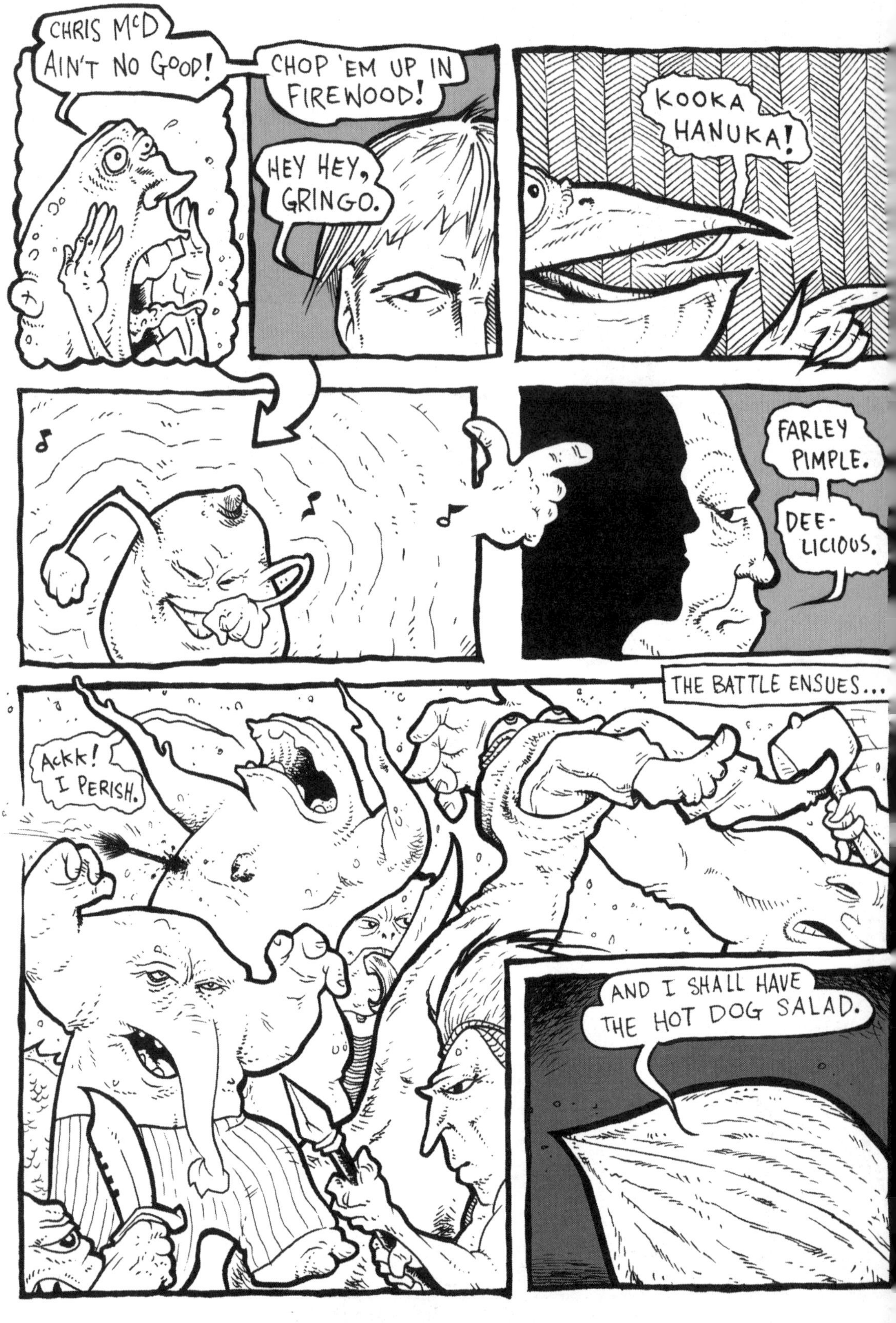
CHRIS McD AIN'T NO GOOD!
CHOP 'EM UP IN FIREWOOD!
HEY HEY, GRINGO.
KOOKA HANUKA!
FARLEY PIMPLE.
DEE-LICIOUS.
THE BATTLE ENSUES...
Ackk! I PERISH.
AND I SHALL HAVE THE HOT DOG SALAD.

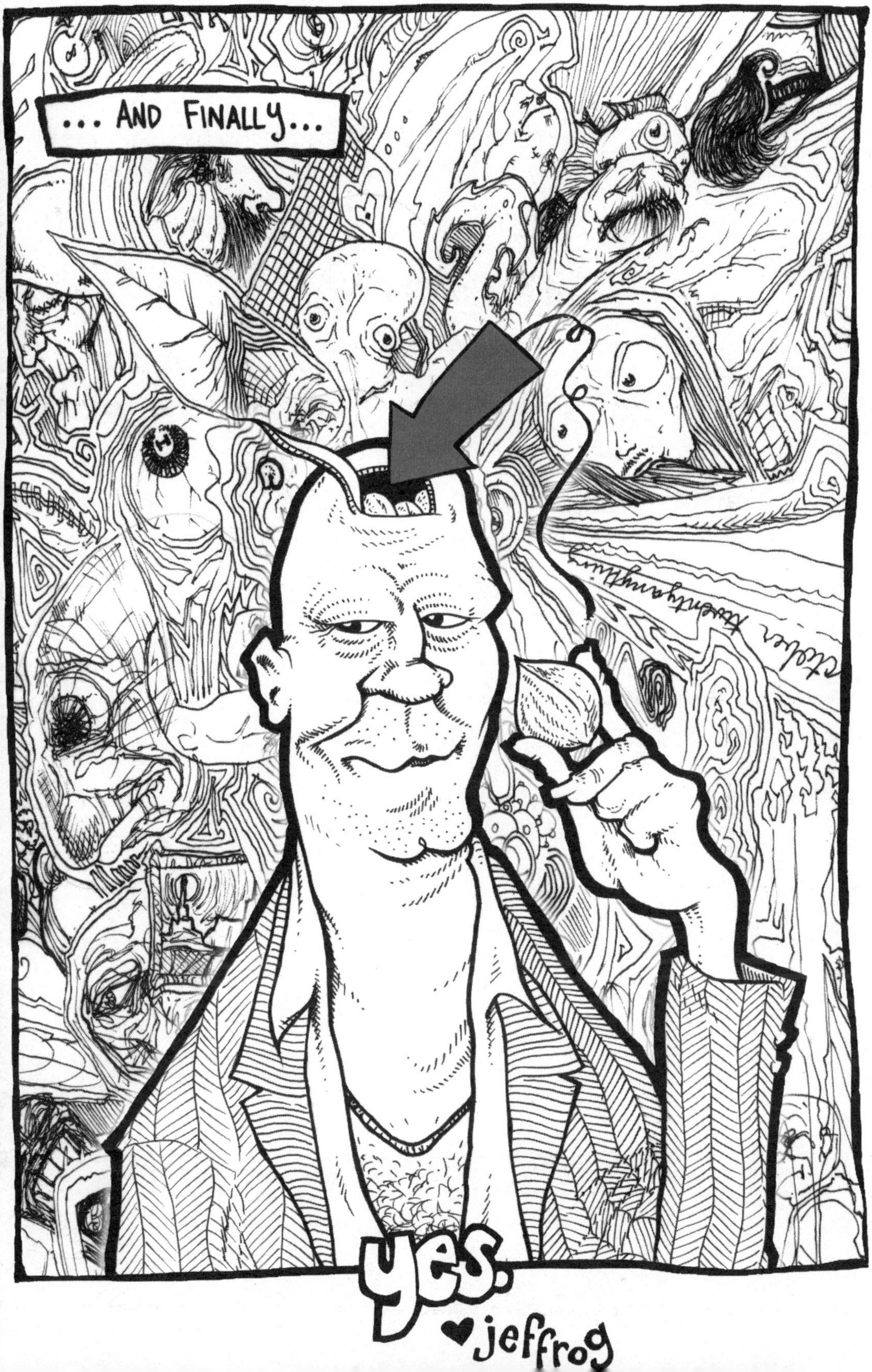
... AND FINALLY ...
yes.
jeffrog

Keith Graham

Keith Graham divides his time between an apartment in Brooklyn, New York and a shotgun shack in Bend, Oregon. He is currently building a totally awesome vehicle for the next Paping Soap Box Derby and plotting a trip around the world.
email: domelogistics@gmail.com
site: www.brothersgraham.com

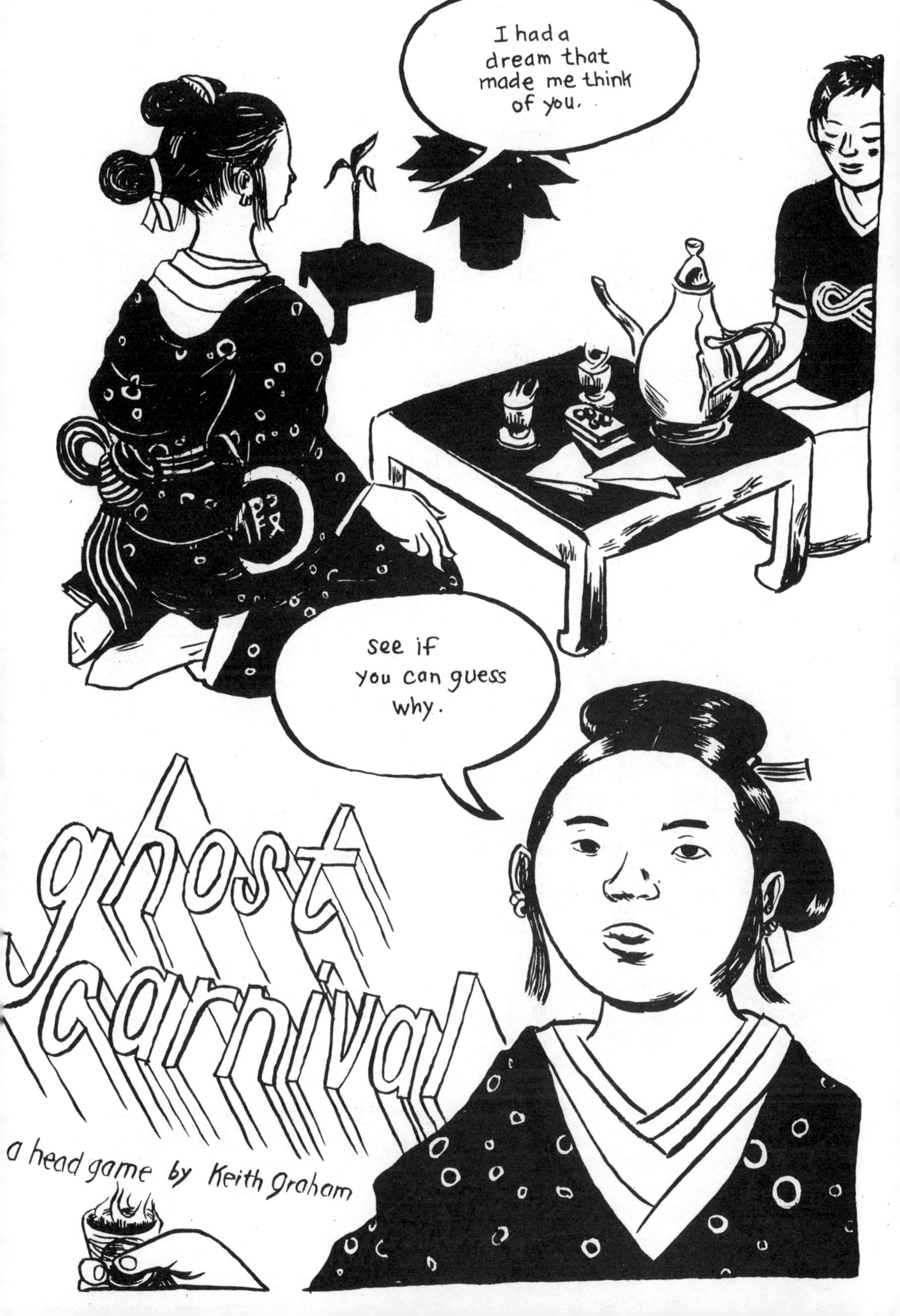
I had a dream that made me think of you.
see if you can guess why.
ghost carnival
a head game by Keith Graham

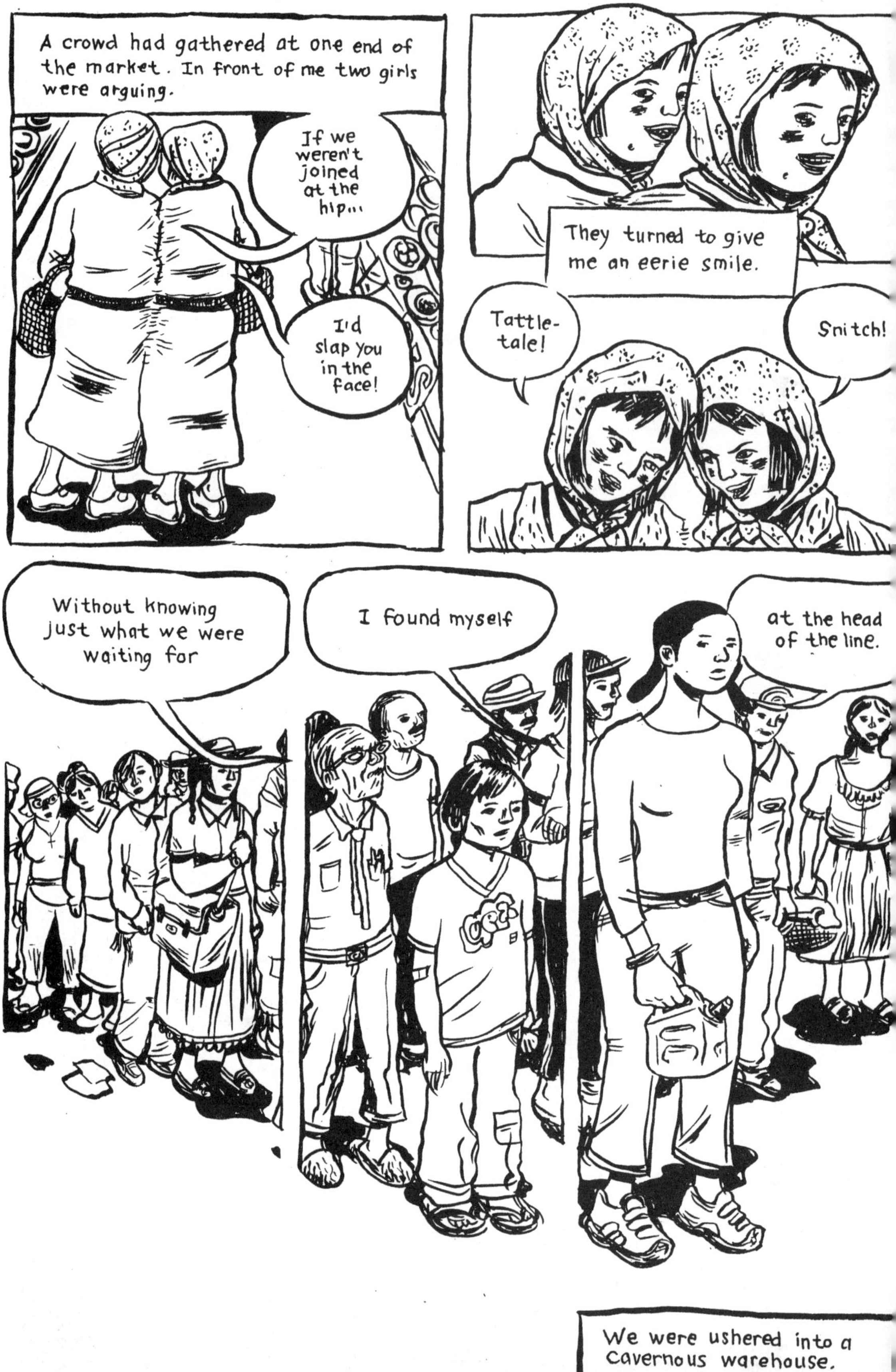

A crowd had gathered at one end of the market. In front of me two girls were arguing.
If we weren't joined at the hip...
I'd slap you in the face!
They turned to give me an eerie smile.
Tattle-tale!
Snitch!
Without knowing just what we were waiting for
I found myself
at the head of the line.
We were ushered into a cavernous warehouse.

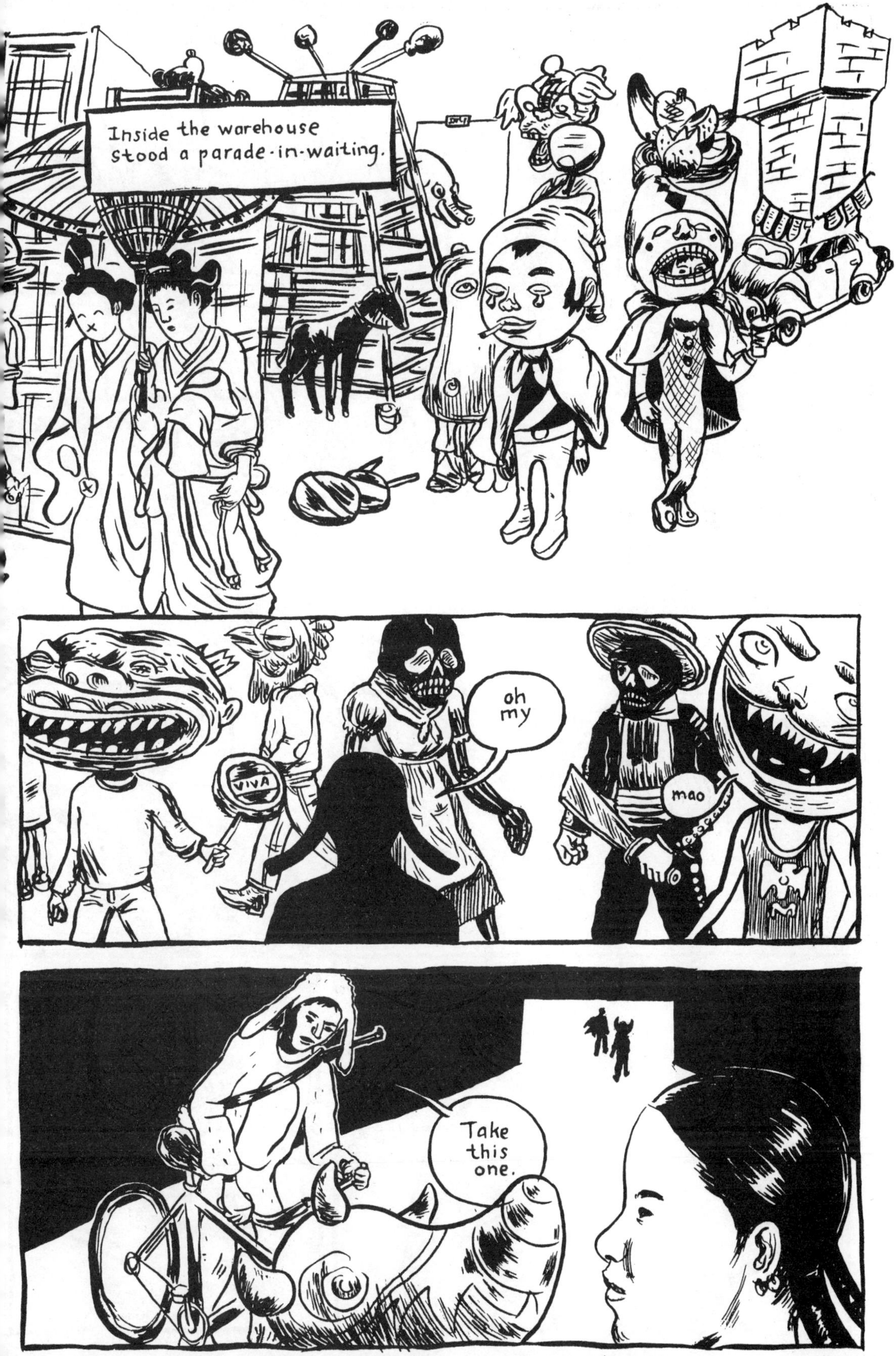
Inside the warehouse stood a parade-in-waiting.
VIVA
oh my
mao
Take this one.

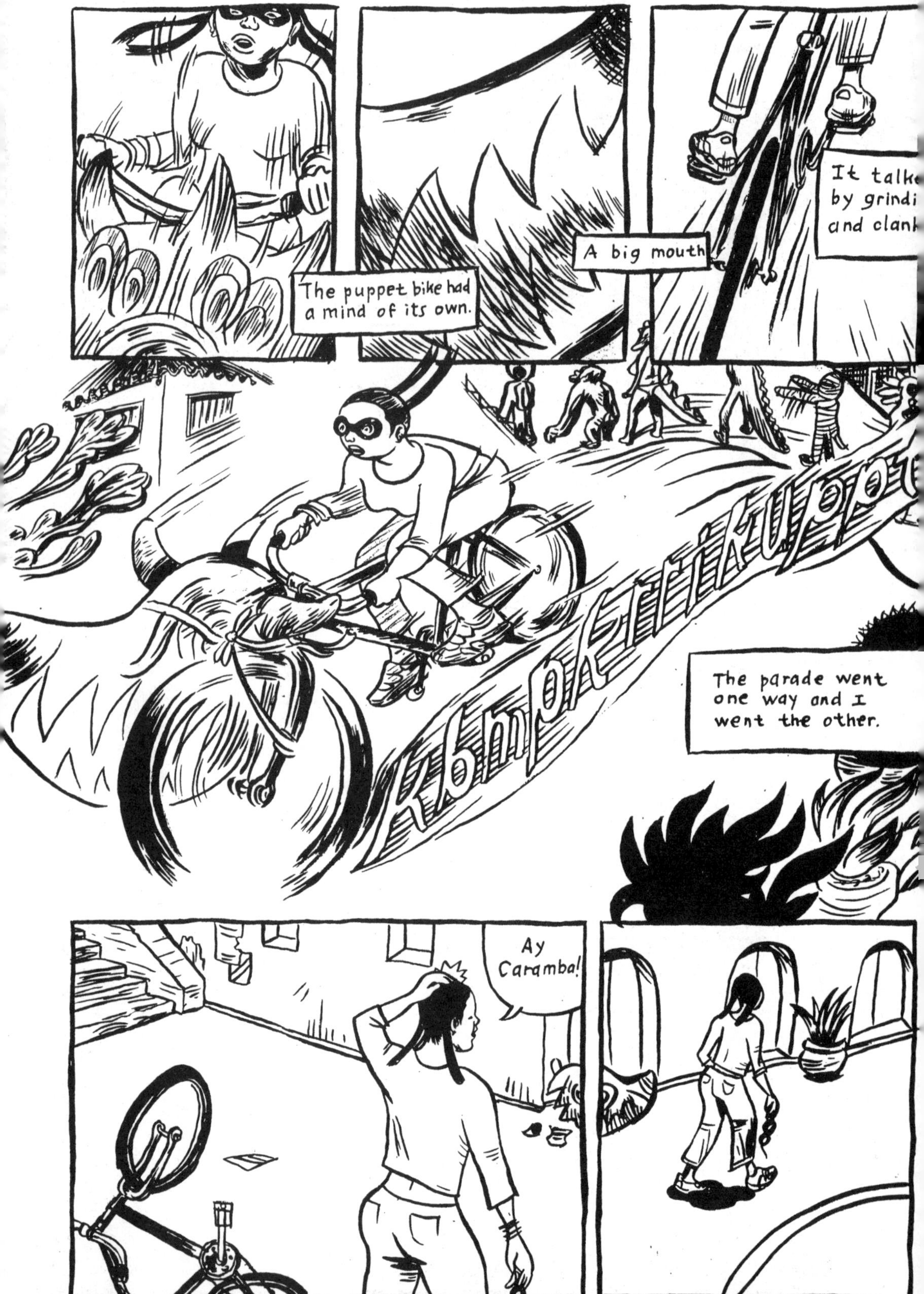
The puppet bike had a mind of its own.
A big mouth
It talke by grindi and clank
KbmpKrrrikupp
The parade went one way and I went the other.
Ay Caramba!

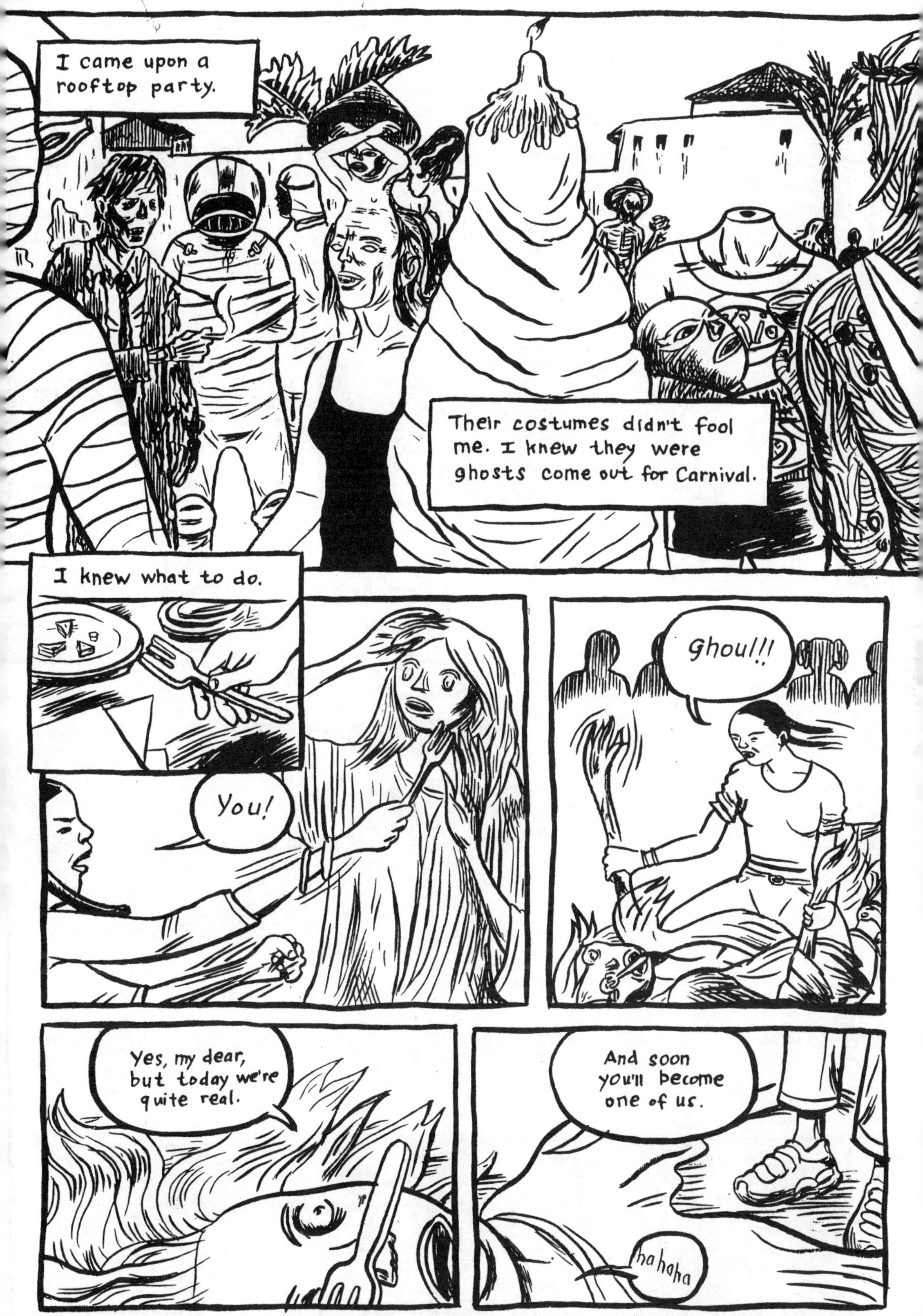
I came upon a rooftop party.
Their costumes didn't fool me. I knew they were ghosts come out for Carnival.
I knew what to do.
You!
Ghoul!!
Yes, my dear, but today we're quite real.
And soon you'll become one of us.
hahaha

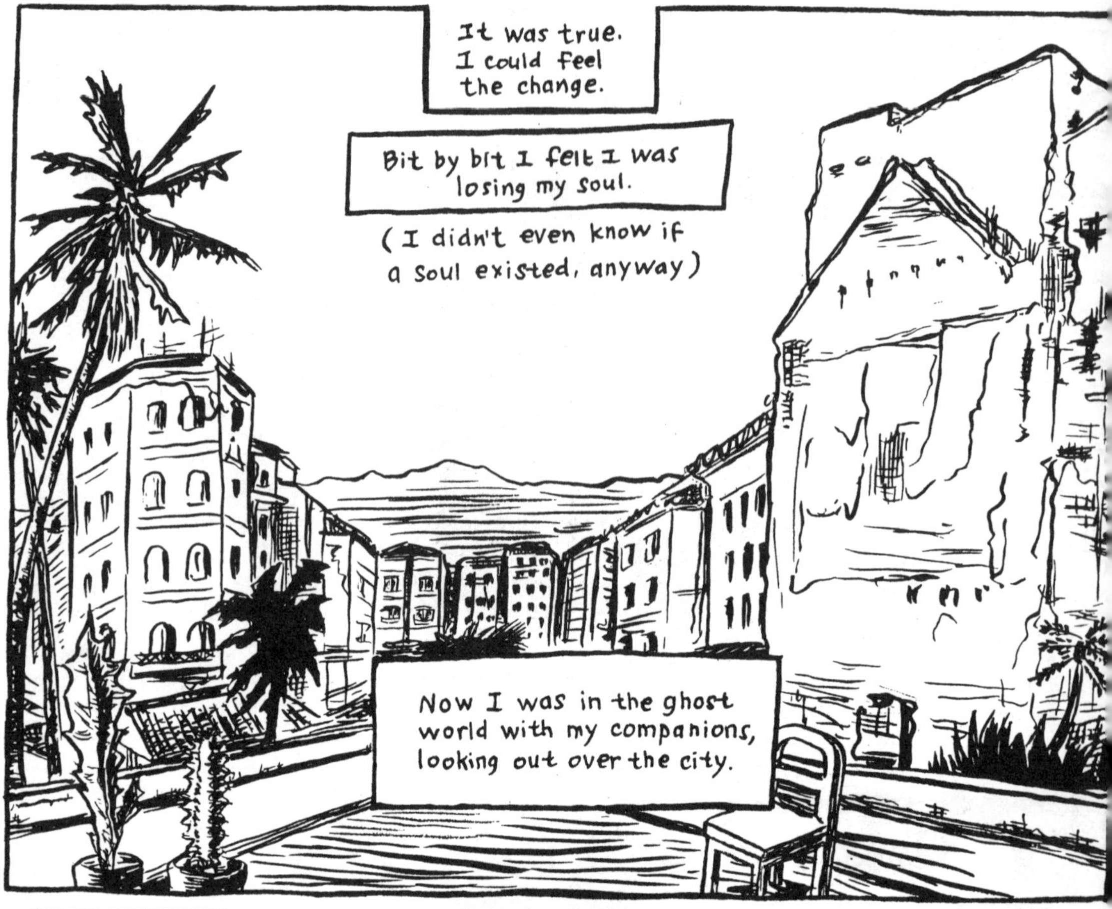
It was true. I could feel the change.
Bit by bit I felt I was losing my soul.
(I didn't even know if a soul existed, anyway)
Now I was in the ghost world with my companions, looking out over the city.

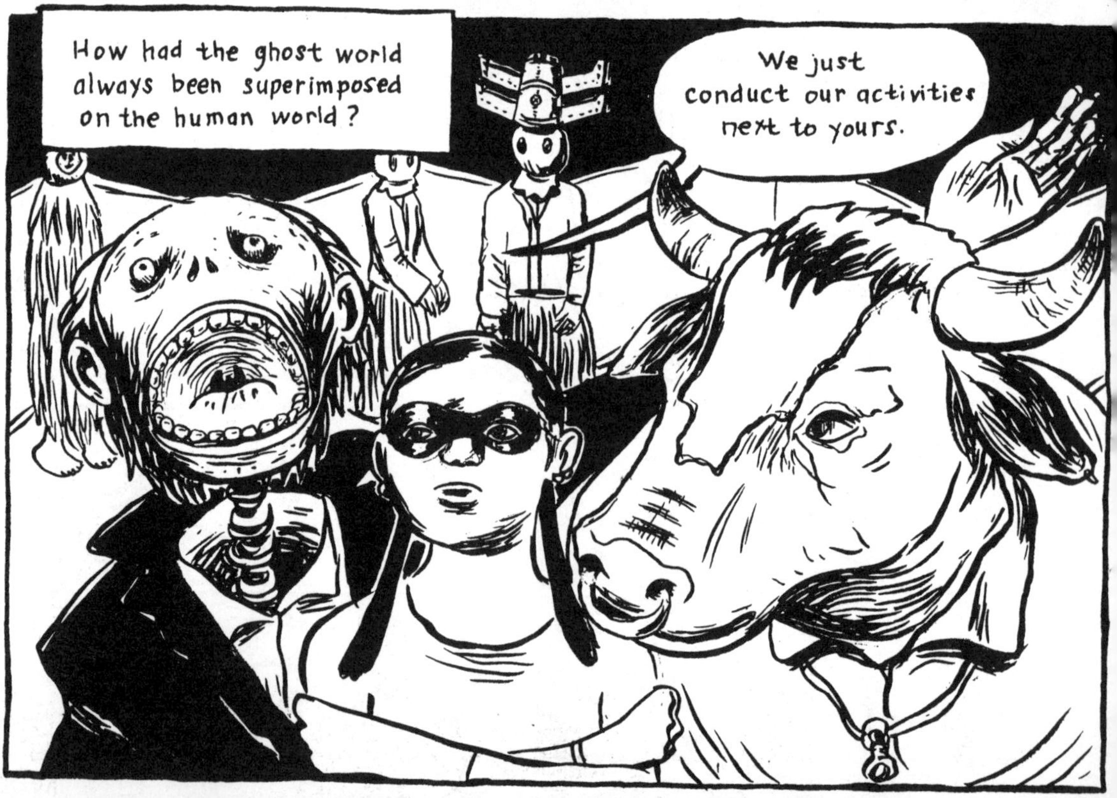
How had the ghost world always been superimposed on the human world?
We just conduct our activities next to yours.

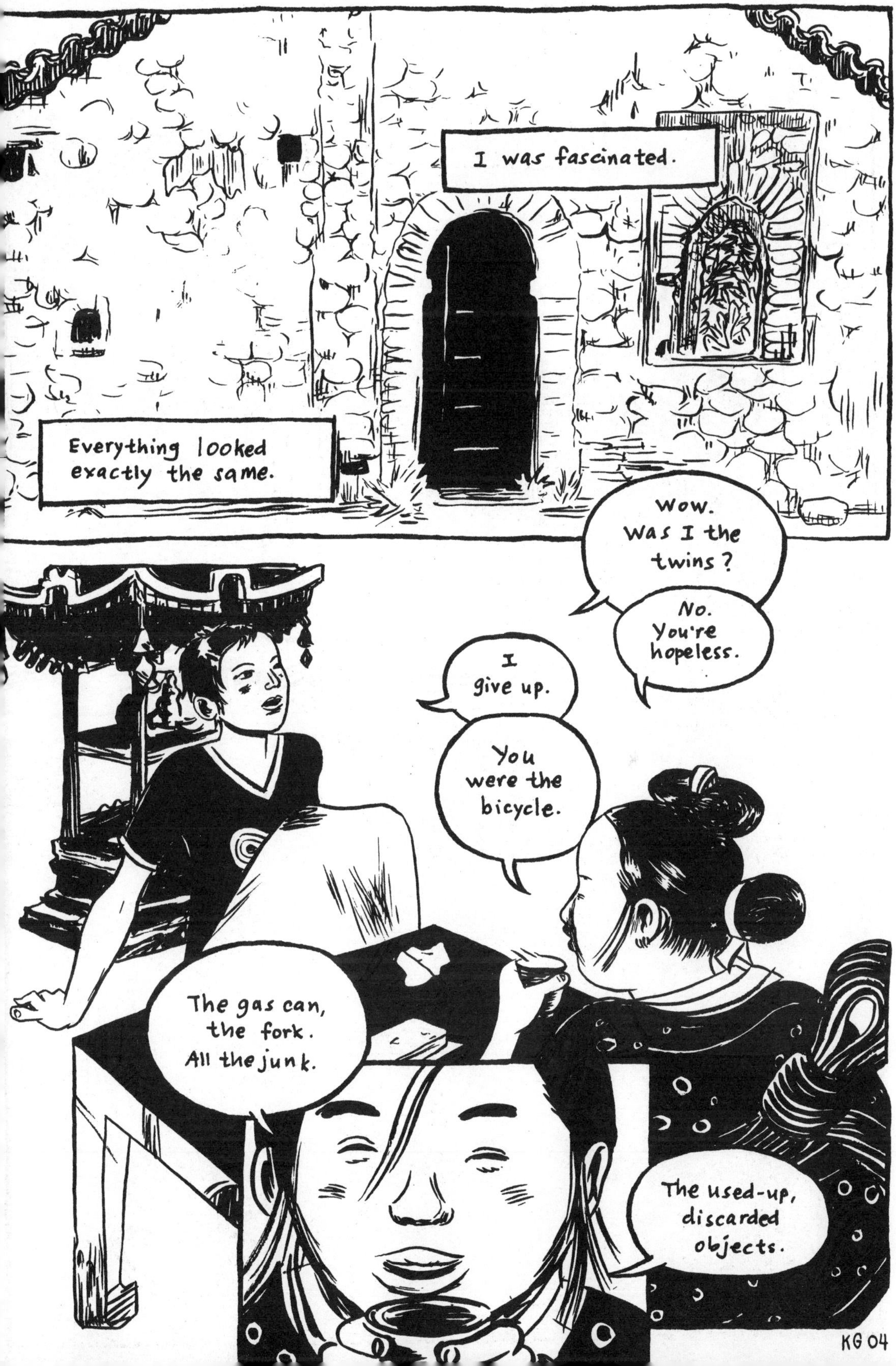
I was fascinated.
Everything looked exactly the same.
Wow. Was I the twins?
No. You're hopeless.
I give up.
You were the bicycle.
The gas can, the fork. All the junk.
The used-up, discarded objects.
KG 04

Jay Sacher

Jay Sacher is the author of And My Also and a long-time Meathaus contributor. He lives in the San Francisco Bay Area.
jaytsacher@gmail.com

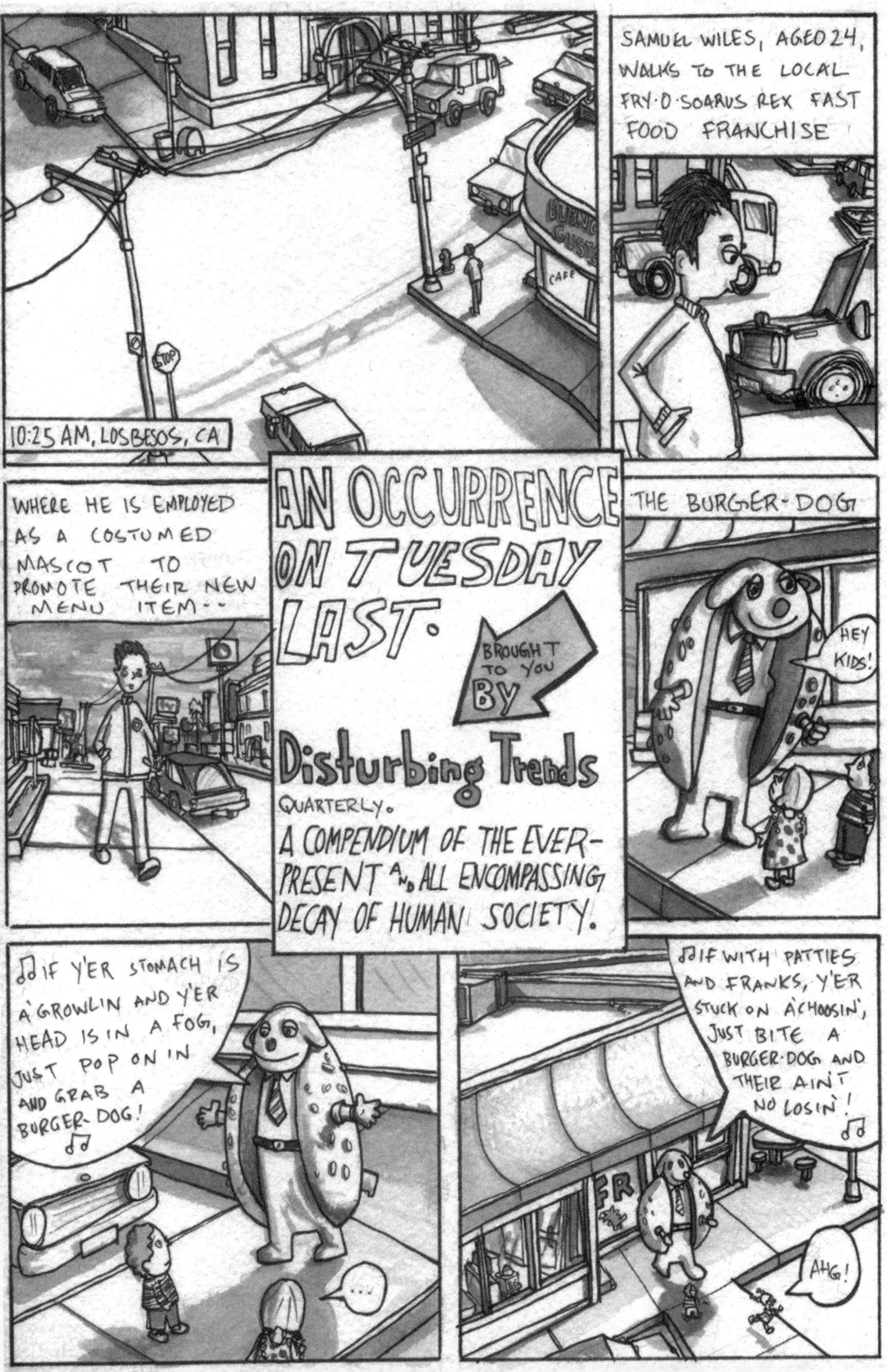
10:25 AM, LOSBESOS, CA
SAMUEL WILES, AGED 24, WALKS TO THE LOCAL FRY-O-SOARUS REX FAST FOOD FRANCHISE
AN OCCURRENCE ON TUESDAY LAST.
BROUGHT TO YOU BY
Disturbing Trends QUARTERLY.
A COMPENDIUM OF THE EVER-PRESENT AND ALL ENCOMPASSING DECAY OF HUMAN SOCIETY.
WHERE HE IS EMPLOYED AS A COSTUMED MASCOT TO PROMOTE THEIR NEW MENU ITEM--
THE BURGER-DOG
HEY KIDS!
IF Y'ER STOMACH IS A'GROWLIN AND Y'ER HEAD IS IN A FOG, JUST POP ON IN AND GRAB A BURGER-DOG!
IF WITH PATTIES AND FRANKS, Y'ER STUCK ON A'CHOOSIN', JUST BITE A BURGER-DOG AND THEIR AIN'T NO LOSIN'!
AHG!

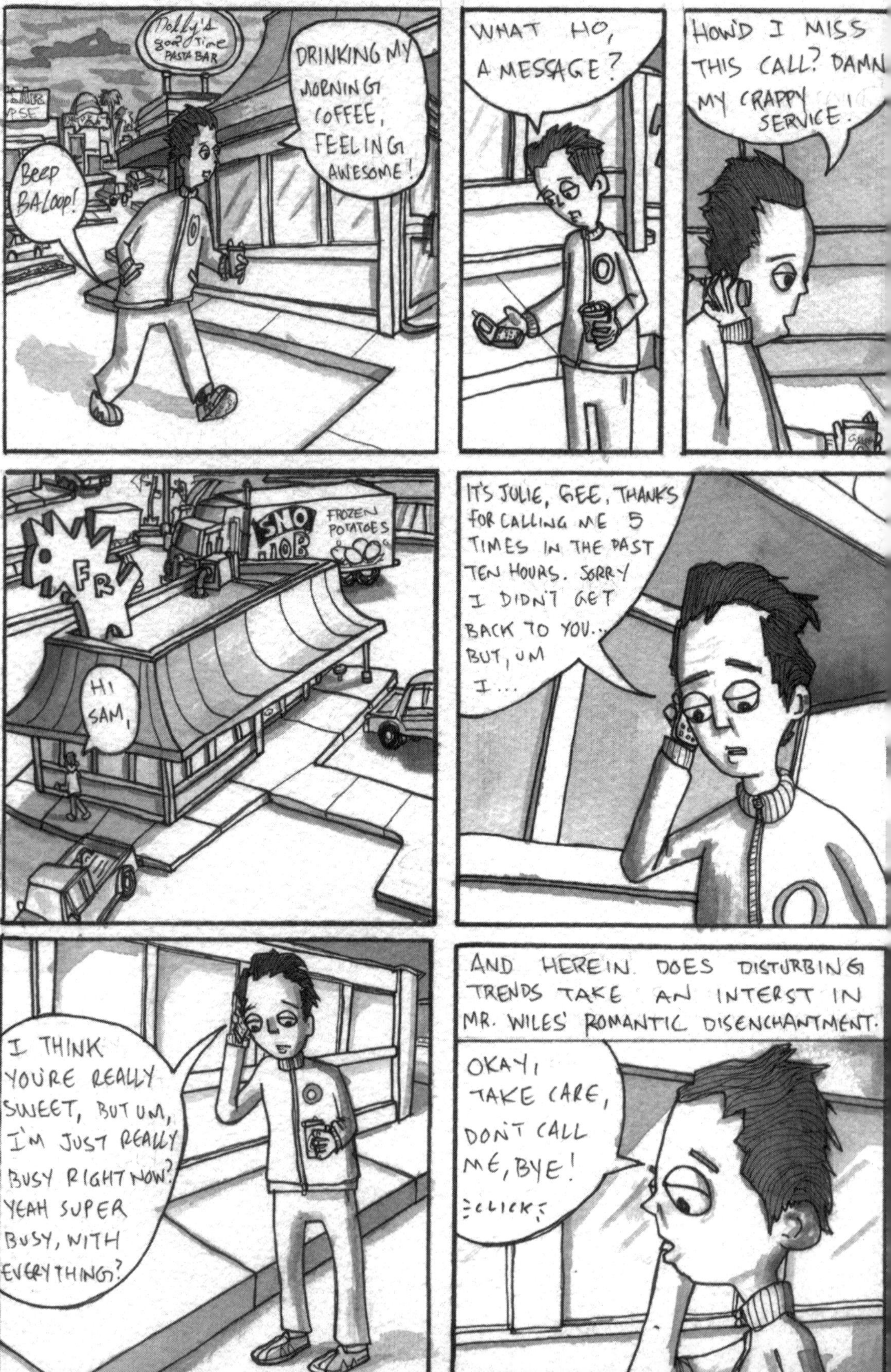
Dolly's good time PASTA BAR
DRINKING MY MORNING COFFEE, FEELING AWESOME!
BEEP BALOOP!
WHAT HO, A MESSAGE?
HOW'D I MISS THIS CALL? DAMN MY CRAPPY SERVICE!
SNO JOB
FROZEN POTATOES
HI SAM,
IT'S JULIE, GEE, THANKS FOR CALLING ME 5 TIMES IN THE PAST TEN HOURS. SORRY I DIDN'T GET BACK TO YOU... BUT, UM I...
I THINK YOU'RE REALLY SWEET, BUT UM, I'M JUST REALLY BUSY RIGHT NOW? YEAH SUPER BUSY, WITH EVERYTHING?
AND HEREIN DOES DISTURBING TRENDS TAKE AN INTERST IN MR. WILES' ROMANTIC DISENCHANTMENT.
OKAY, TAKE CARE, DON'T CALL ME, BYE!
CLICK

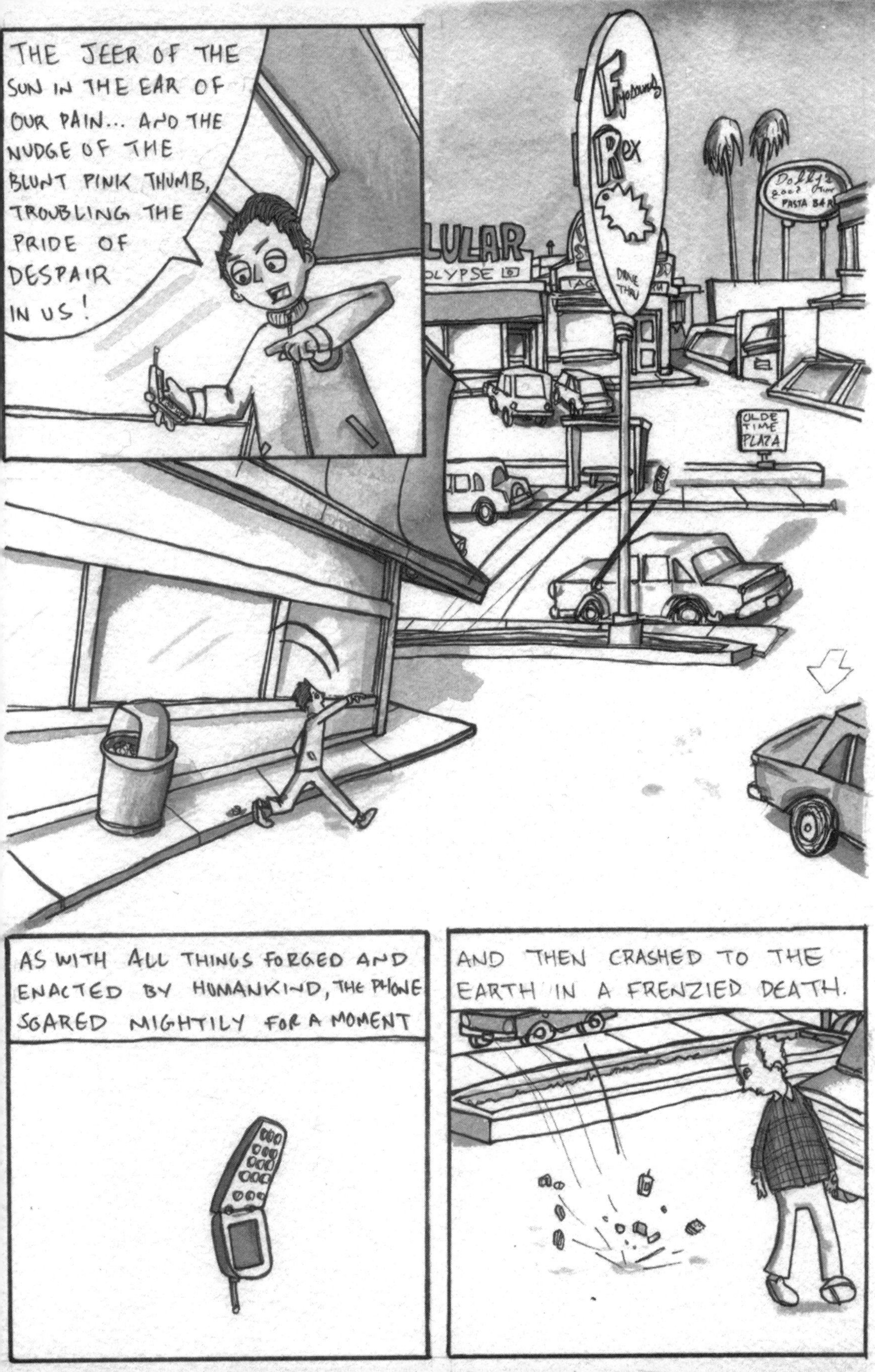
THE JEER OF THE SUN IN THE EAR OF OUR PAIN... AND THE NUDGE OF THE BLUNT PINK THUMB, TROUBLING THE PRIDE OF DESPAIR IN US!
LULAR
Rex
OLDE TIME PLAZA
PASTA BAR
AS WITH ALL THINGS FORGED AND ENACTED BY HUMANKIND, THE PHONE SOARED MIGHTILY FOR A MOMENT
AND THEN CRASHED TO THE EARTH IN A FRENZIED DEATH.

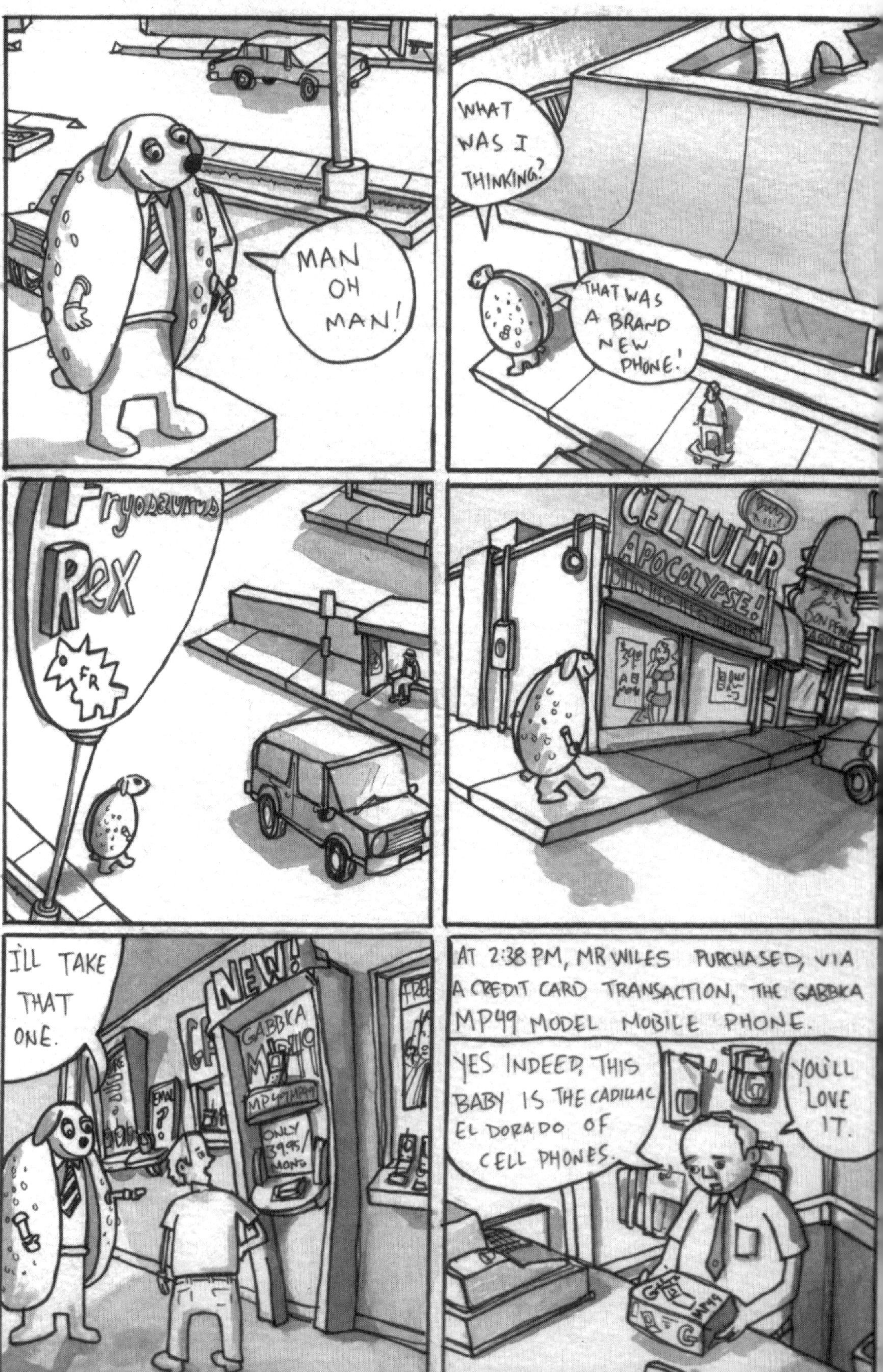
MAN
OH
MAN!
WHAT
WAS I
THINKING?
THAT WAS
A BRAND
NEW
PHONE!
Fryosaurus
Rex
FR
CELLULAR
APOCOLYPSE!
I'LL TAKE
THAT
ONE.
NEW!
GABBKA
MP49
ONLY
39.95/
MONTH
AT 2:38 PM, MR WILES PURCHASED, VIA
A CREDIT CARD TRANSACTION, THE GABBKA
MP49 MODEL MOBILE PHONE.
YES INDEED, THIS
BABY IS THE CADILLAC
EL DORADO OF
CELL PHONES.
YOU'LL
LOVE
IT.
MP49

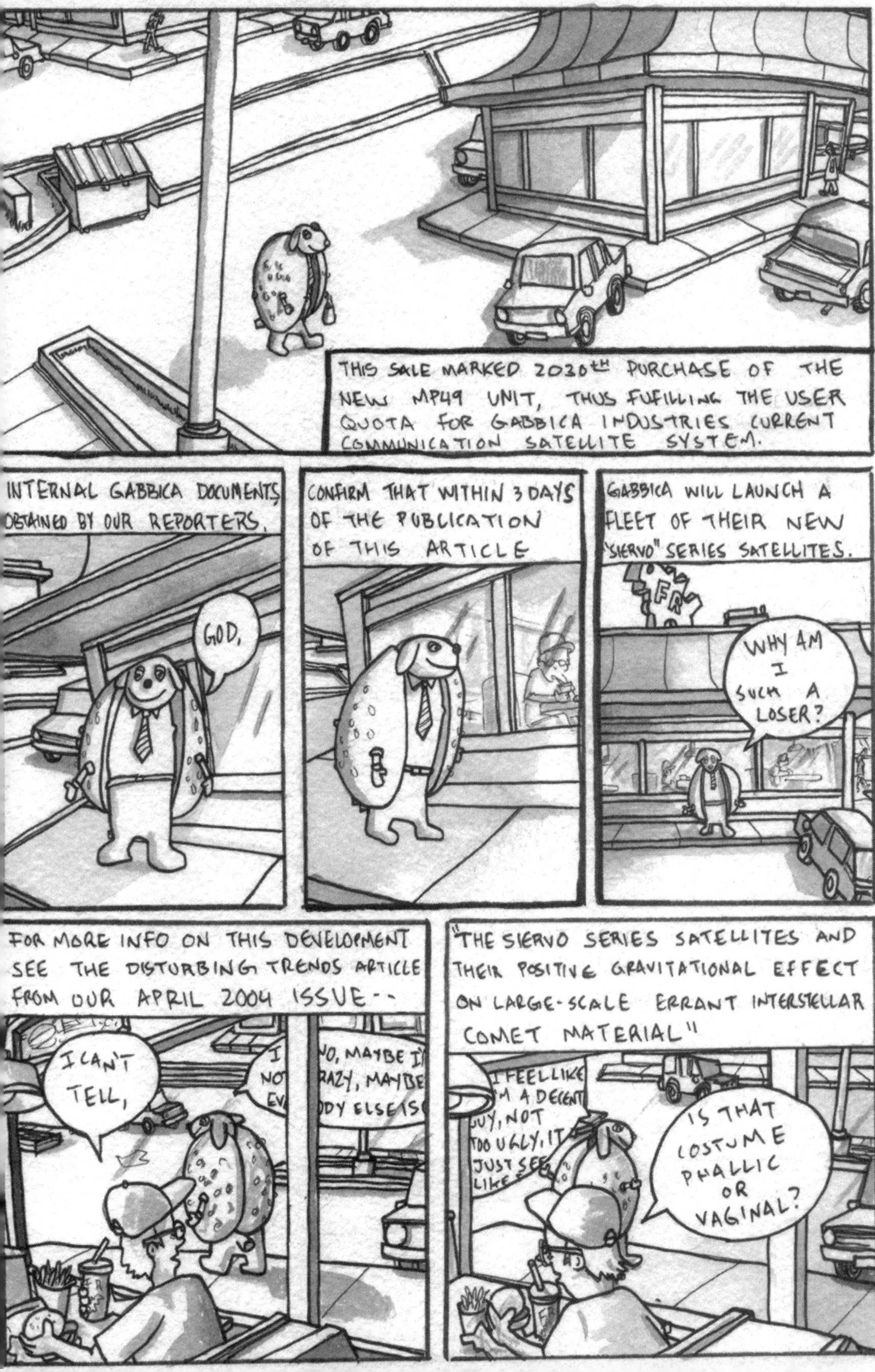
THIS SALE MARKED 2030TH PURCHASE OF THE NEW MP49 UNIT, THUS FUFILLING THE USER QUOTA FOR GABBICA INDUSTRIES CURRENT COMMUNICATION SATELLITE SYSTEM.
INTERNAL GABBICA DOCUMENTS, OBTAINED BY OUR REPORTERS,
GOD,
CONFIRM THAT WITHIN 3 DAYS OF THE PUBLICATION OF THIS ARTICLE
GABBICA WILL LAUNCH A FLEET OF THEIR NEW "SIERVO" SERIES SATELLITES.
WHY AM I SUCH A LOSER?
FOR MORE INFO ON THIS DEVELOPMENT SEE THE DISTURBING TRENDS ARTICLE FROM OUR APRIL 2004 ISSUE--
I CAN'T TELL,
I NO, MAYBE I
NO RAZY, MAYBE
EV DDY ELSE IS
"THE SIERVO SERIES SATELLITES AND THEIR POSITIVE GRAVITATIONAL EFFECT ON LARGE-SCALE ERRANT INTERSTELLAR COMET MATERIAL"
I FEEL LIKE
M A DECENT
UY, NOT
TOO UGLY, IT
JUST SE
LIKE
IS THAT COSTUME PHALLIC OR VAGINAL?

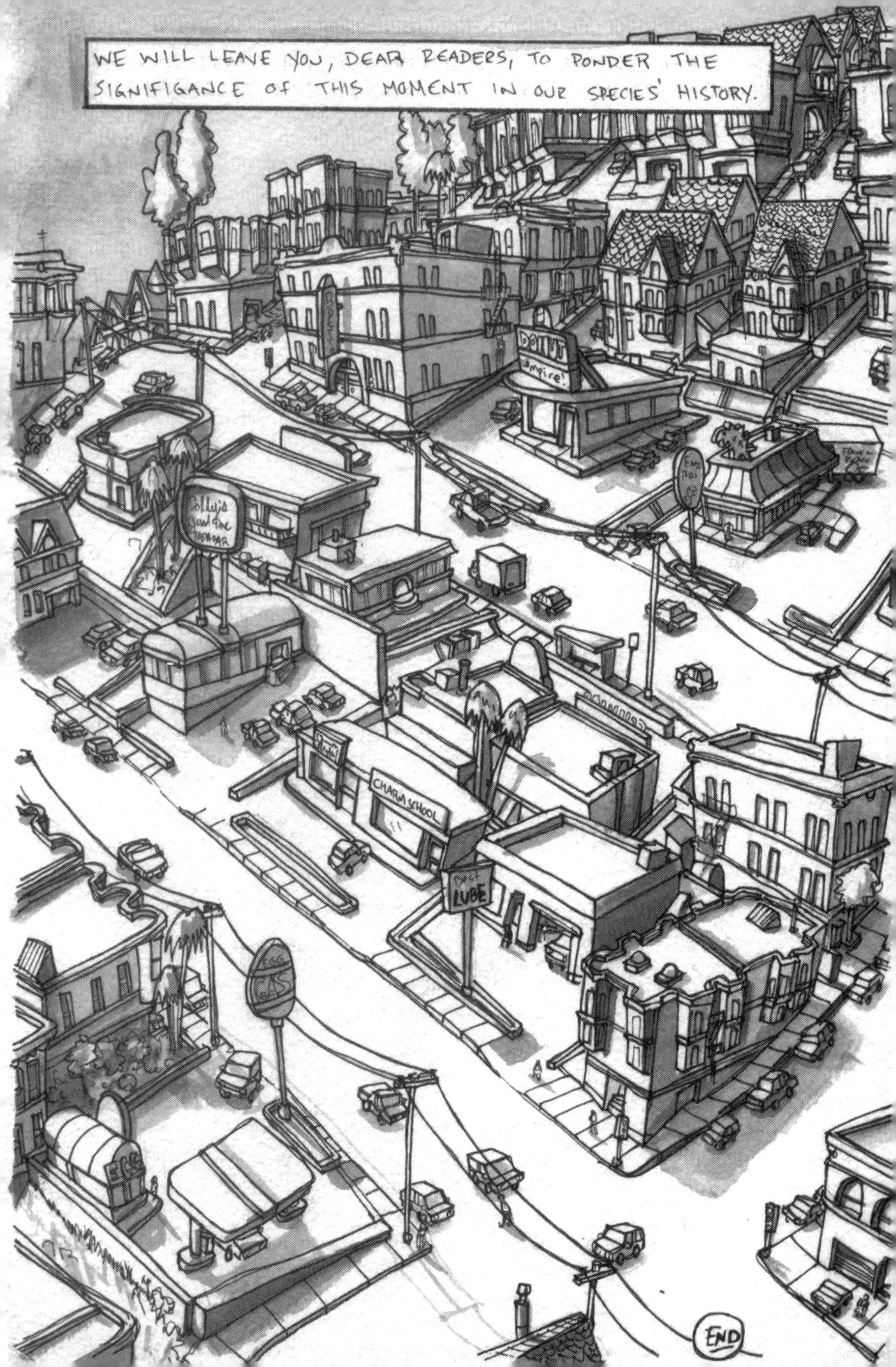
WE WILL LEAVE YOU, DEAR READERS, TO PONDER THE SIGNIFIGANCE OF THIS MOMENT IN OUR SPECIES' HISTORY.
DONUT
Empire!
CHARM SCHOOL
LUBE
GAS
END

INTELLIGENT DESIGN

or: Hyper tension for fun and profit BY JAY SACHER

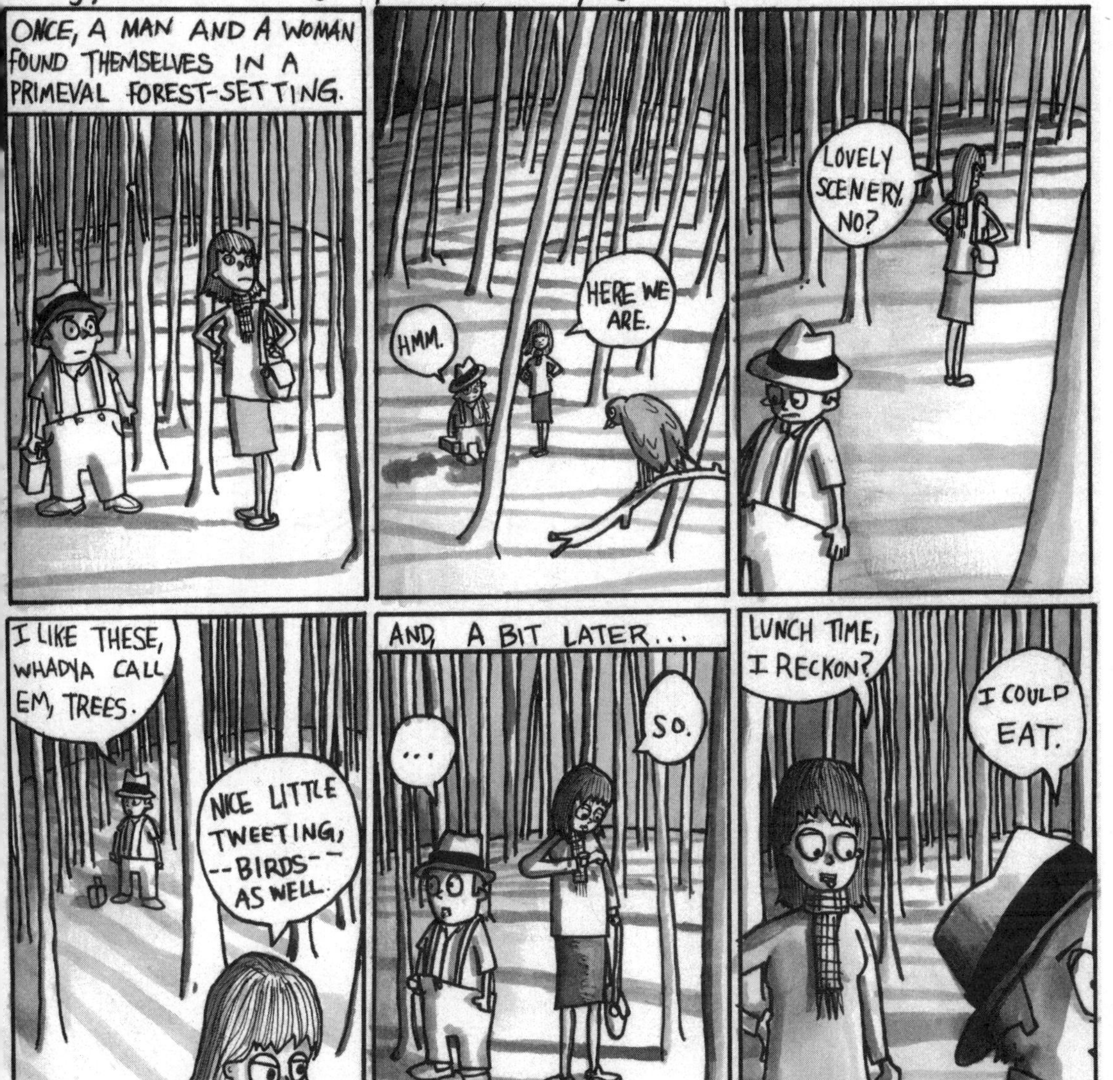

ONCE, A MAN AND A WOMAN FOUND THEMSELVES IN A PRIMEVAL FOREST-SETTING.
HMM.
HERE WE ARE.
LOVELY SCENERY, NO?
I LIKE THESE, WHADYA CALL EM, TREES.
NICE LITTLE TWEETING, --BIRDS-- AS WELL.
AND, A BIT LATER...
...
SO.
LUNCH TIME, I RECKON?
I COULD EAT.

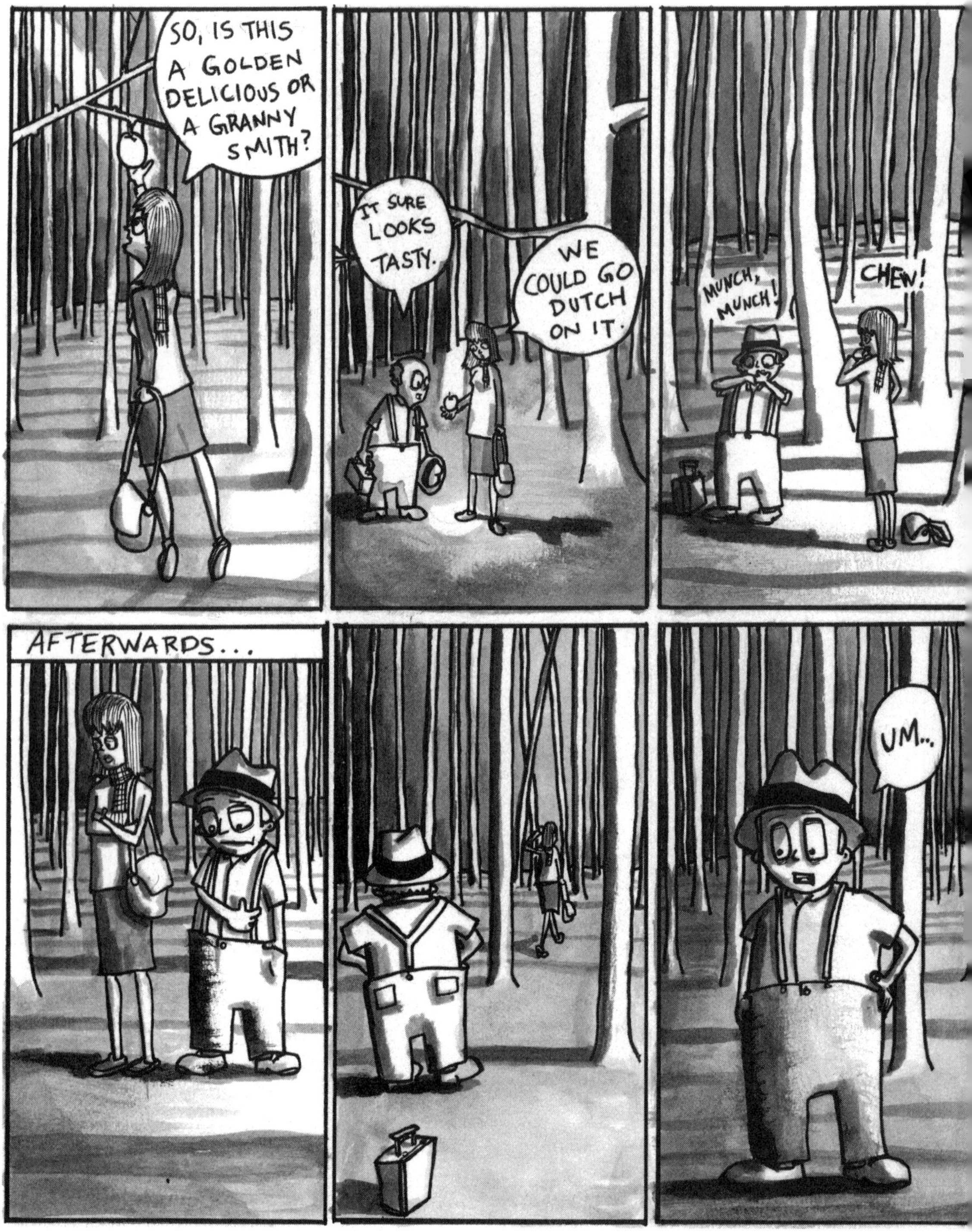

SO, IS THIS A GOLDEN DELICIOUS OR A GRANNY SMITH?
IT SURE LOOKS TASTY.
WE COULD GO DUTCH ON IT.
MUNCH, MUNCH!
CHEW!
AFTERWARDS...
UM...

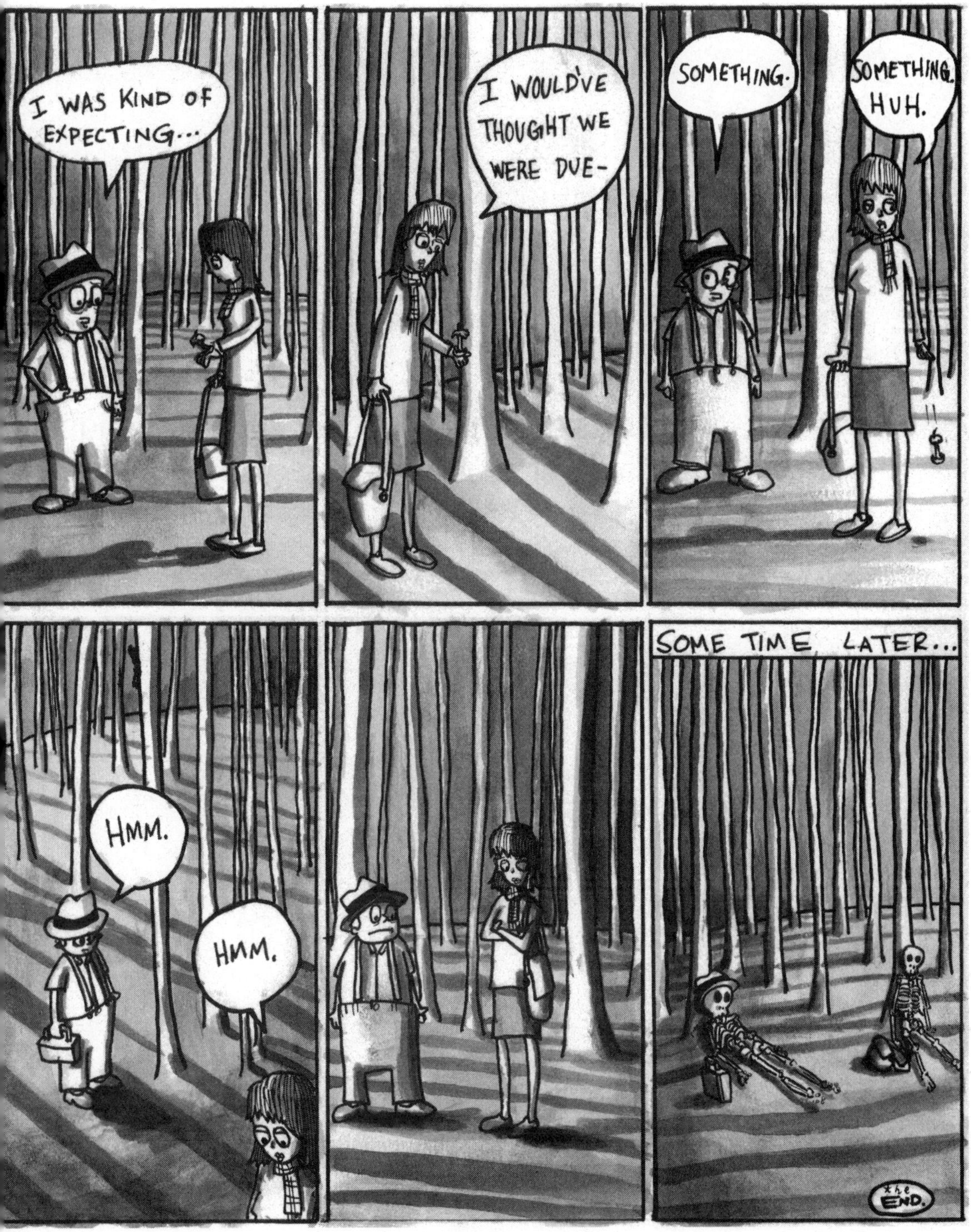
I WAS KIND OF EXPECTING...
I WOULD'VE THOUGHT WE WERE DUE-
SOMETHING.
SOMETHING. HUH.
HMM.
HMM.
SOME TIME LATER...
THE END.

Jennie Yim

Jennie Yim currently lives in Philadelphia and just quit her job in administration. She judges neighborhoods by how close a bowl of Pho soup is. Her e-mail is jennieyim@yahoo.com.

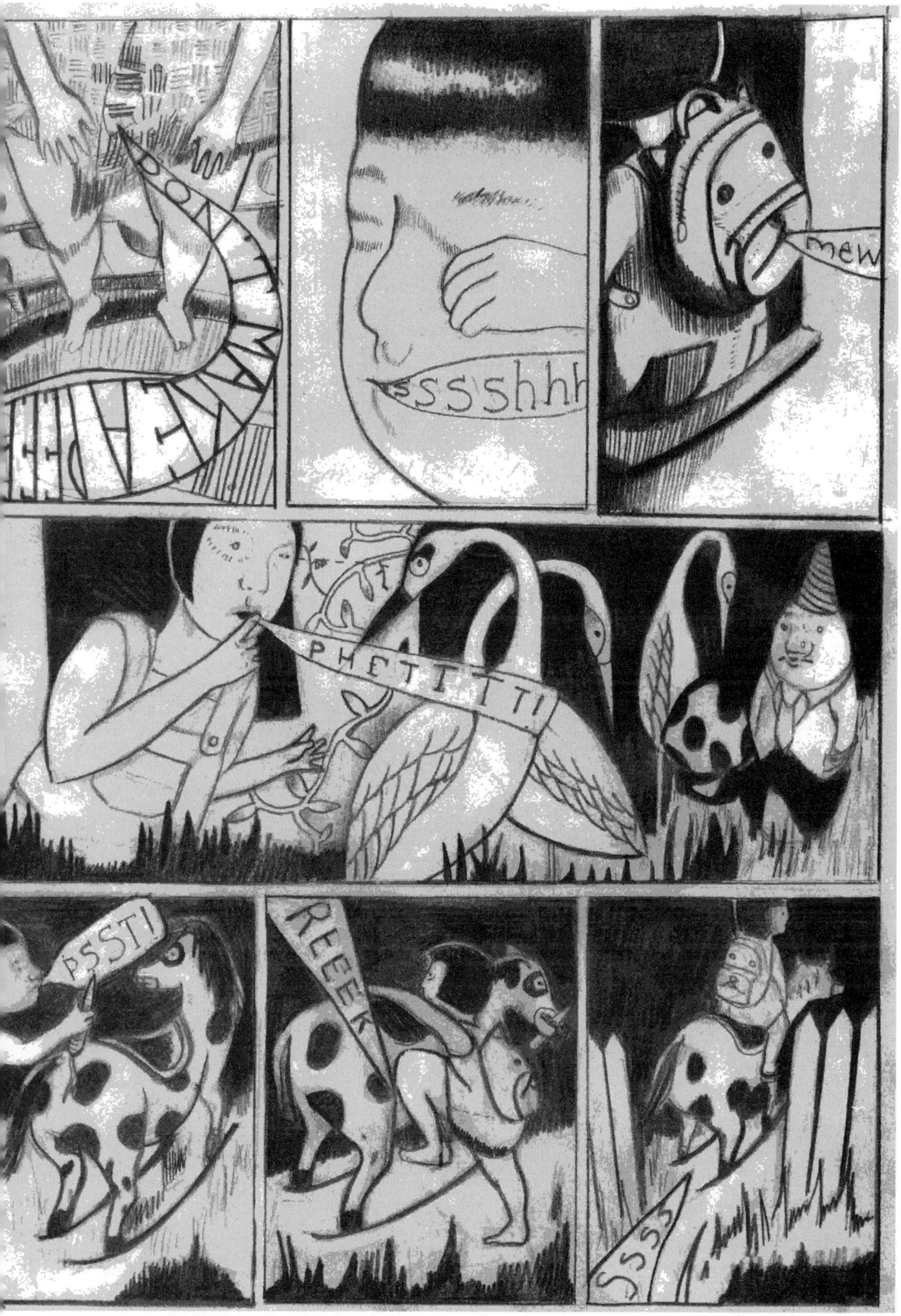
DON'T
sssshhh
mew
PHETTTT!
PSST!
REEEK
SSSS

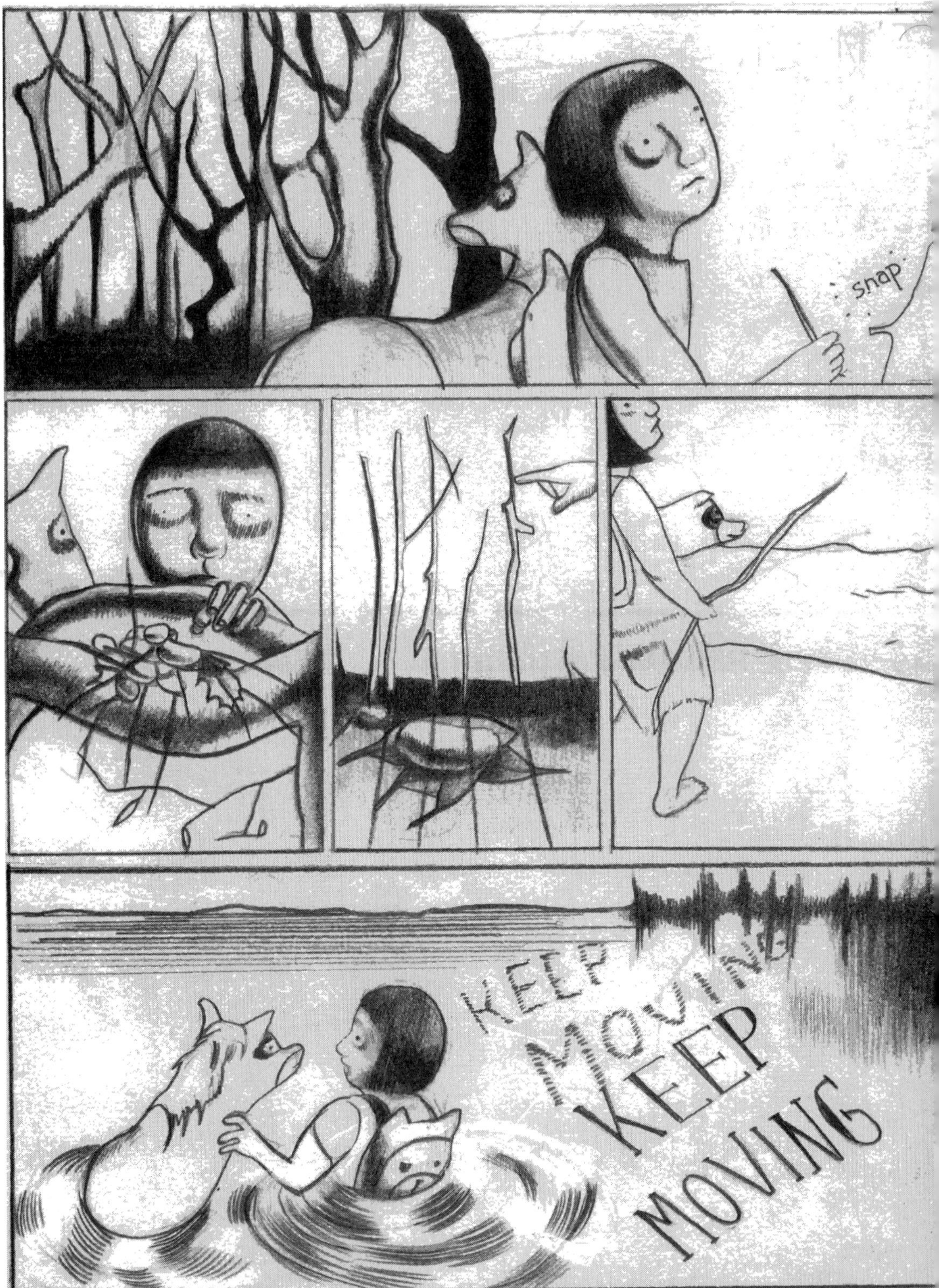
snap
KEEP MOVIN
KEEP MOVING

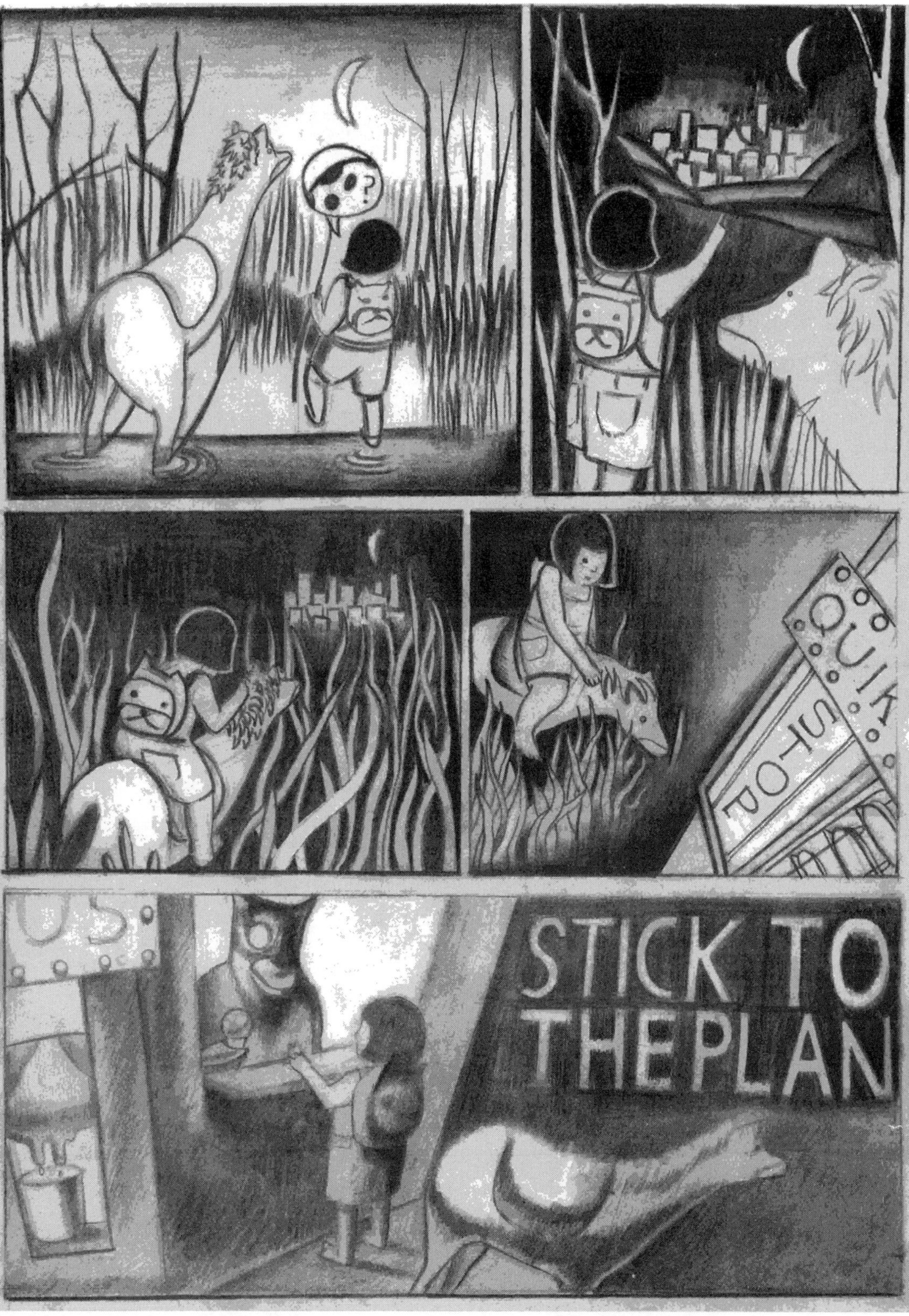
?
QUIK SHOP
STICK TO
THEPLAN

Jim Rugg

Jim Rugg lives in Pittsburgh with his wife and their cat. He co-created Street Angel, published by Slave Labor Graphics.
www.streetangelcomics.com

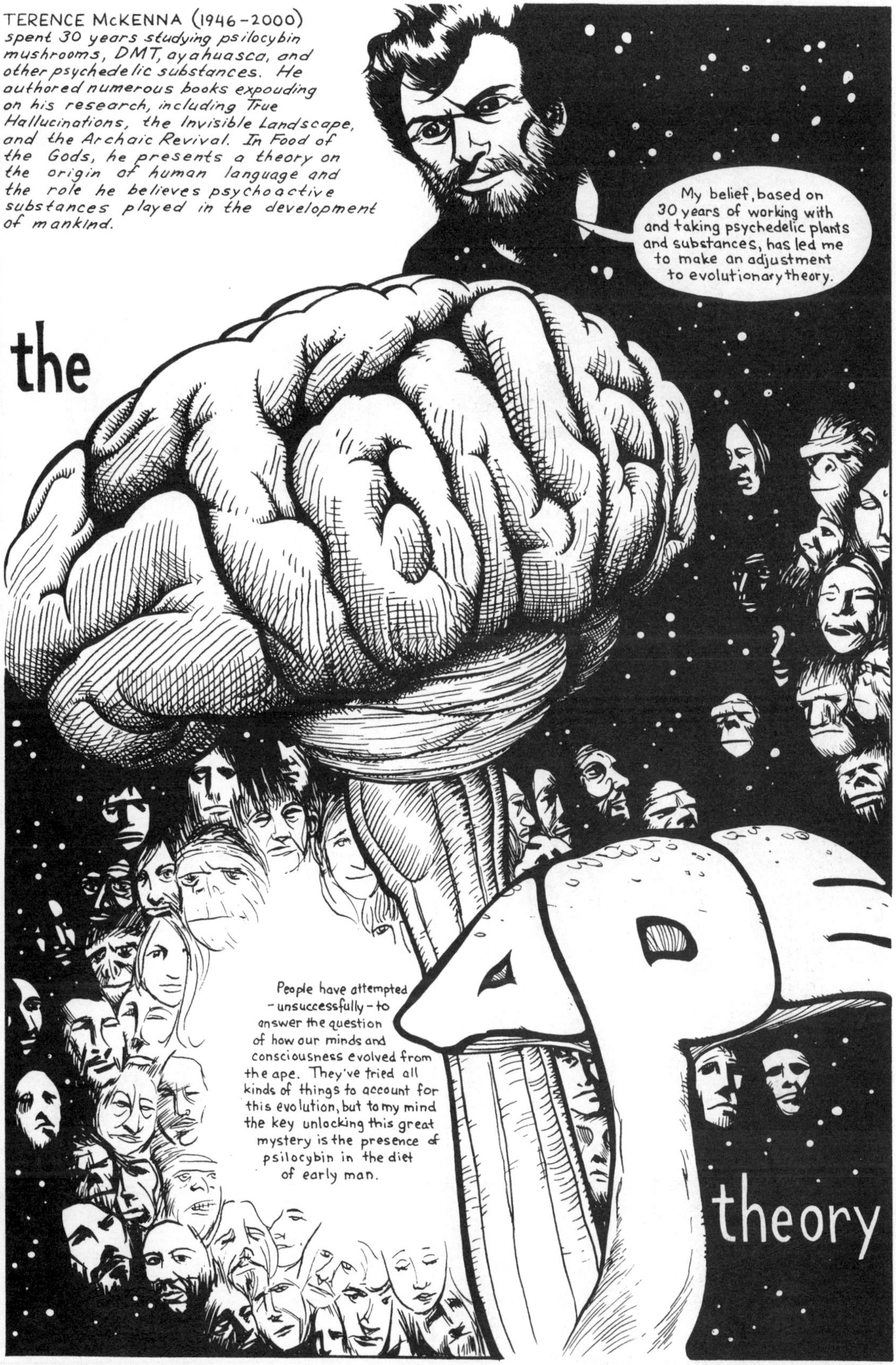
TERENCE McKENNA (1946-2000) spent 30 years studying psilocybin mushrooms, DMT, ayahuasca, and other psychedelic substances. He authored numerous books expouding on his research, including True Hallucinations, the Invisible Landscape, and the Archaic Revival. In Food of the Gods, he presents a theory on the origin of human language and the role he believes psychoactive substances played in the development of mankind.
My belief, based on 30 years of working with and taking psychedelic plants and substances, has led me to make an adjustment to evolutionary theory.
the
theory
People have attempted -unsuccessfully- to answer the question of how our minds and consciousness evolved from the ape. They've tried all kinds of things to account for this evolution, but to my mind the key unlocking this great mystery is the presence of psilocybin in the diet of early man.

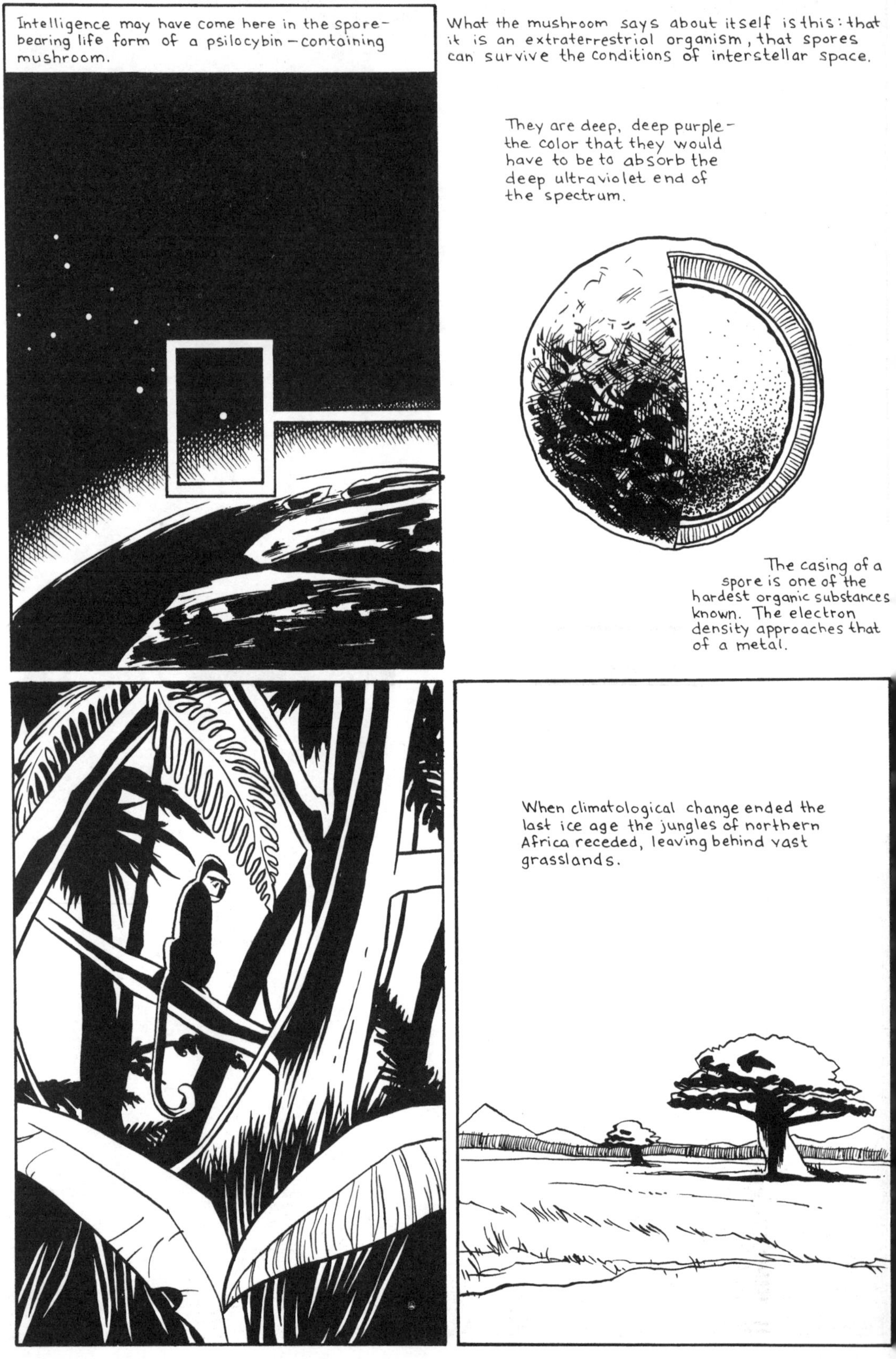
Intelligence may have come here in the spore-bearing life form of a psilocybin-containing mushroom.
What the mushroom says about itself is this: that it is an extraterrestrial organism, that spores can survive the conditions of interstellar space.
They are deep, deep purple-the color that they would have to be to absorb the deep ultraviolet end of the spectrum.
The casing of a spore is one of the hardest organic substances known. The electron density approaches that of a metal.
When climatological change ended the last ice age the jungles of northern Africa receded, leaving behind vast grasslands.

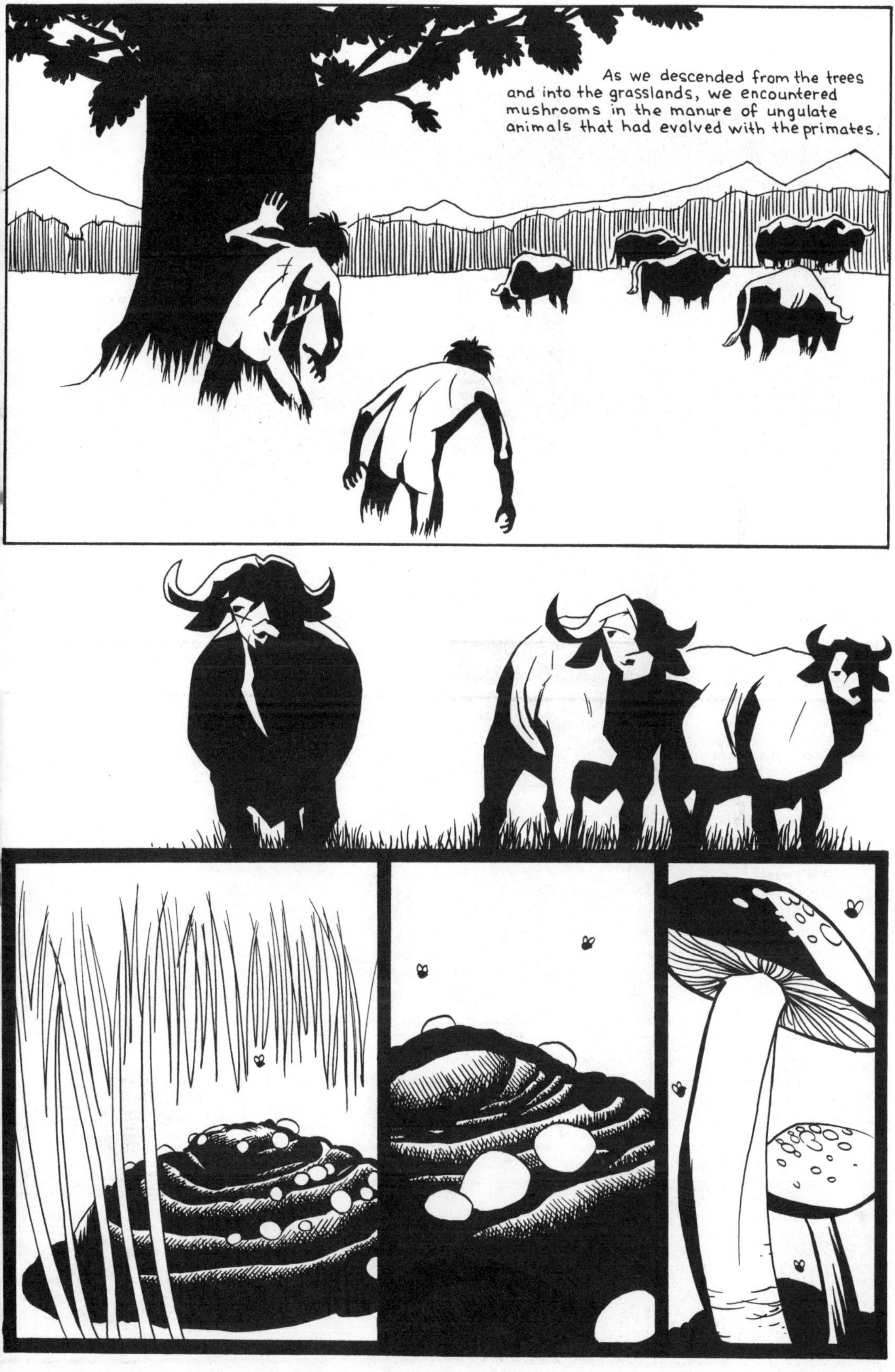
As we descended from the trees and into the grasslands, we encountered mushrooms in the manure of ungulate animals that had evolved with the primates.

The mushroom acted as a tremendous force for directing the evolution of human beings away from that of the rest of the anthropoid apes and toward the unique adaptation that we see as special to human beings today. It did this through a series of self-reinforcing tendencies.

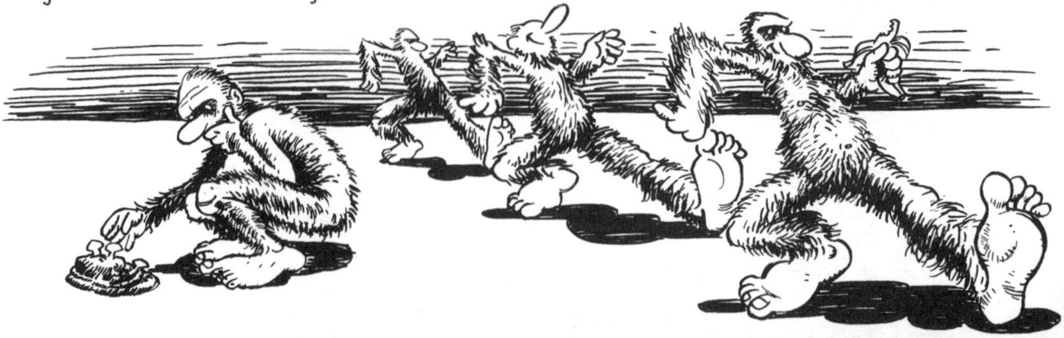

1. Lab work shows that psilocybin eaten in amounts so small that it can't be detected, as an experience, increases visual accuity – increased visual acuity means increased success at getting food.

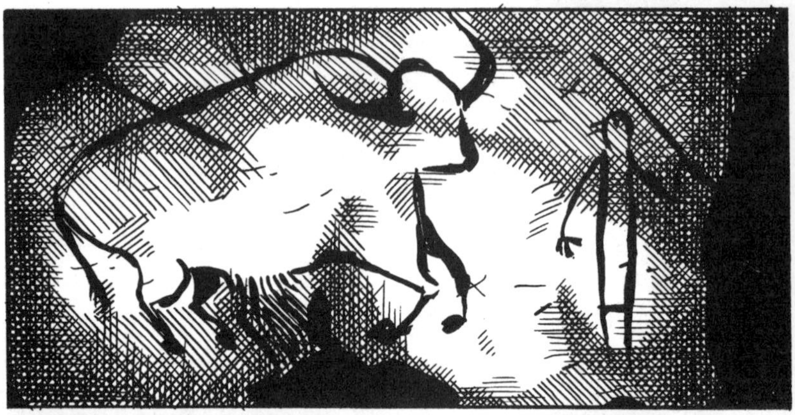

2. At slightly higher doses of psilocybin there is sexual arousal, a factor which would increase reproductive success. So the mushroom-using population will tend to outbreed the non-mushroom population.

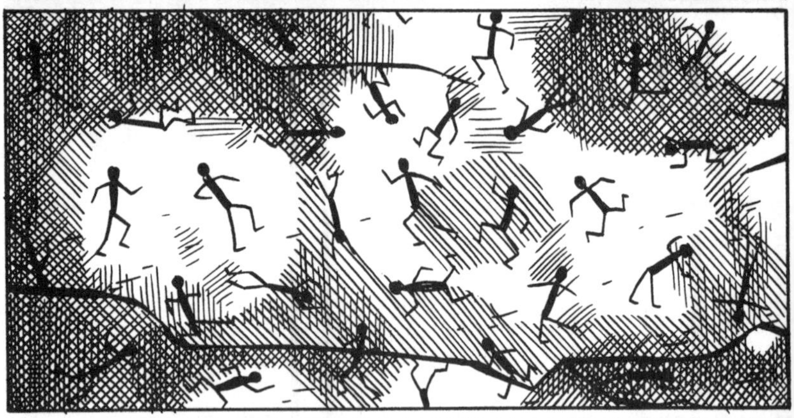

3. The third and final factor, which pushed these mushroom-using primates into a position of ascendancy, is that psilocybin at the psychedelic dose level actually stimulates the areas of the brain that are concerned with the production of language.

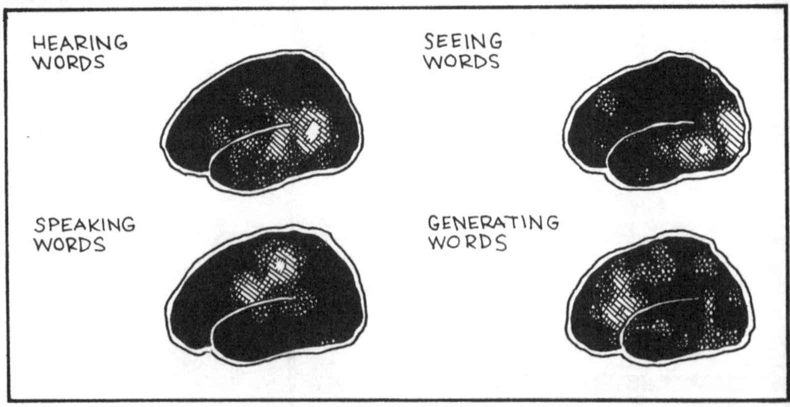
HEARING WORDS
SEEING WORDS
SPEAKING WORDS
GENERATING WORDS

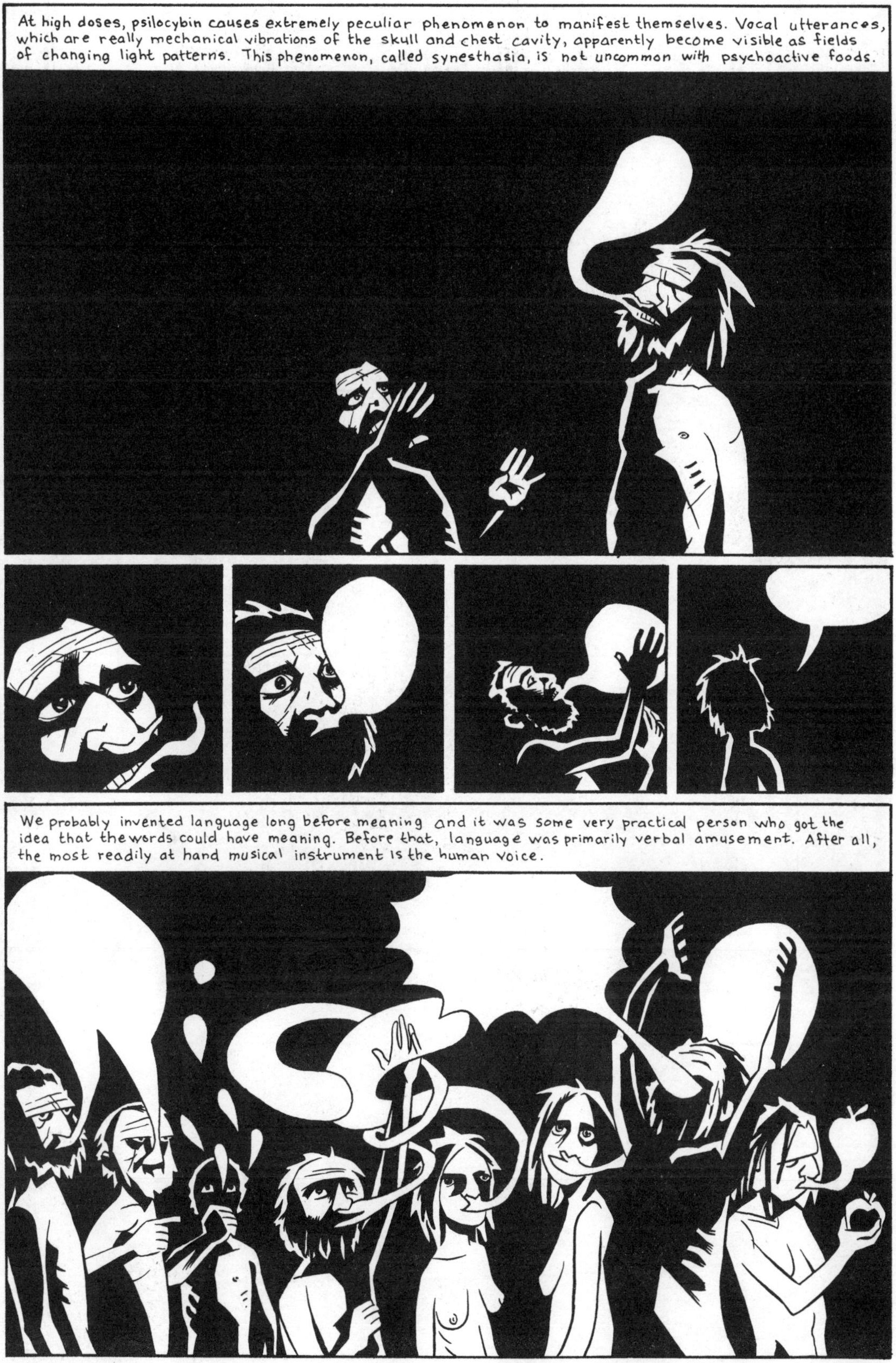
At high doses, psilocybin causes extremely peculiar phenomenon to manifest themselves. Vocal utterances, which are really mechanical vibrations of the skull and chest cavity, apparently become visible as fields of changing light patterns. This phenomenon, called synesthasia, is not uncommon with psychoactive foods.
We probably invented language long before meaning and it was some very practical person who got the idea that the words could have meaning. Before that, language was primarily verbal amusement. After all, the most readily at hand musical instrument is the human voice.

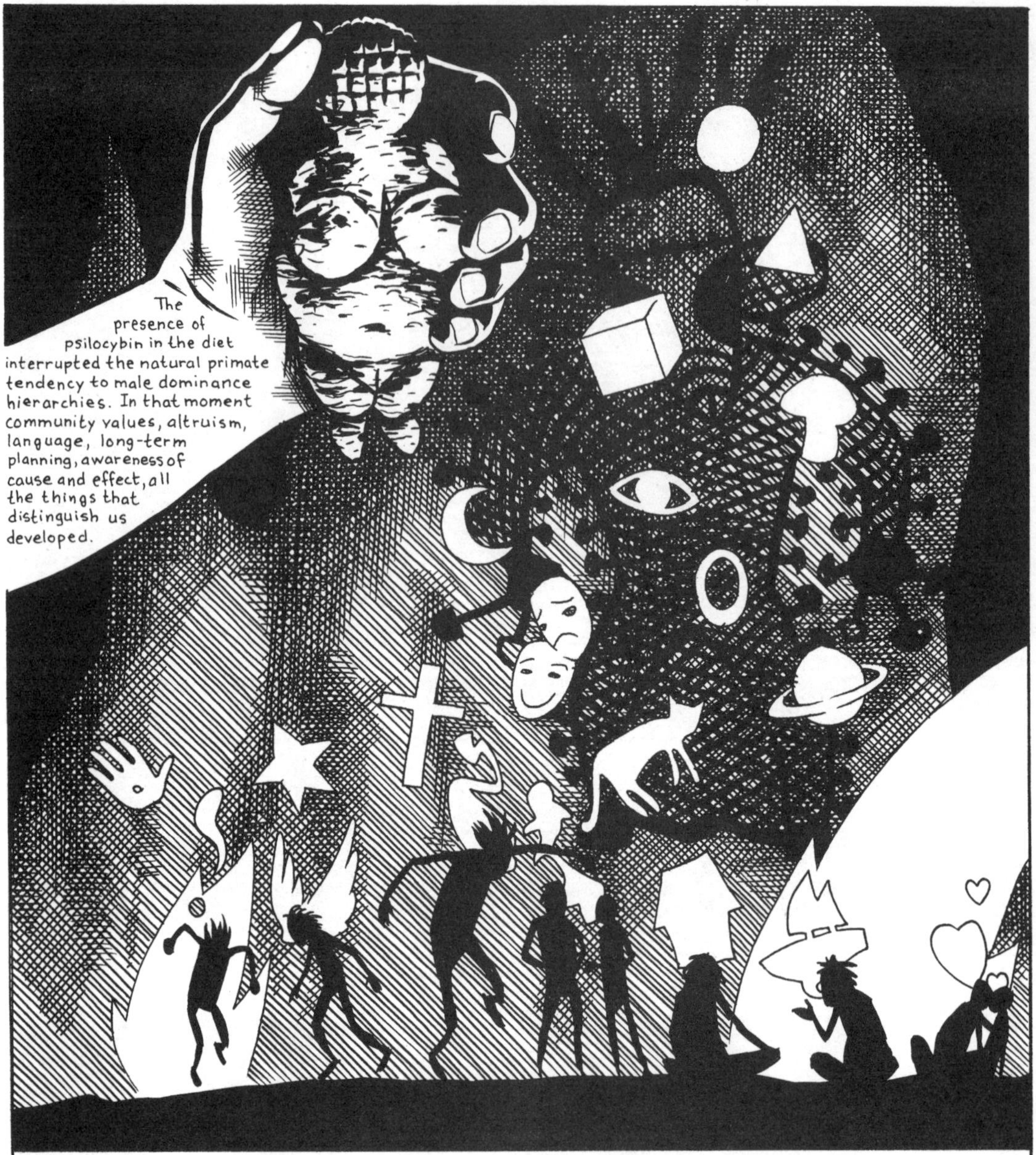
The presence of psilocybin in the diet interrupted the natural primate tendency to male dominance hierarchies. In that moment community values, altruism, language, long-term planning, awareness of cause and effect, all the things that distinguish us developed.
For a very long time, as we evolved out of the animal nature, perhaps a hundred thousand years, psilocybin was a part of our diet and our rituals and our religion.

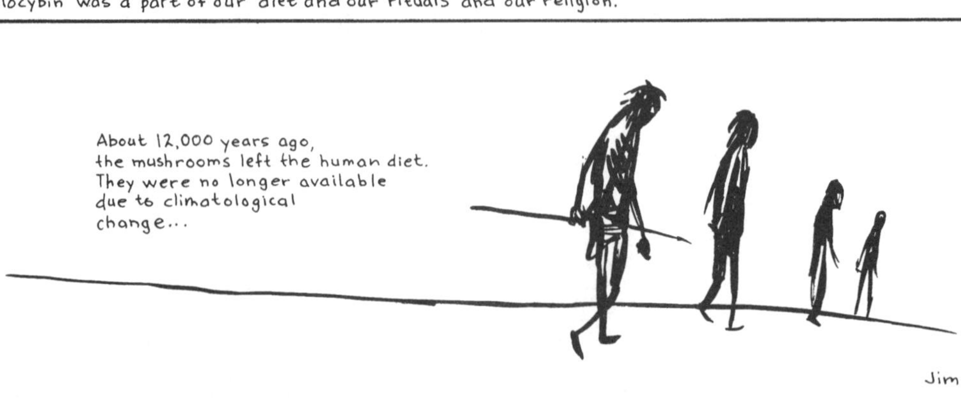
About 12,000 years ago, the mushrooms left the human diet. They were no longer available due to climatological change...

Jim Rugg

Scott Morse

Award-winning storyteller Scott Morse has managed to simultaneously carve out niches in the fields of animation and comics. Recent work includes FRANKENSTEIN from IDW with writer Steve Niles and the forthcoming NOBLE BOY, a tribute to his mentor, Maurice Noble.
http://www.scottmorse.com
and scottmorse.blogspot.com

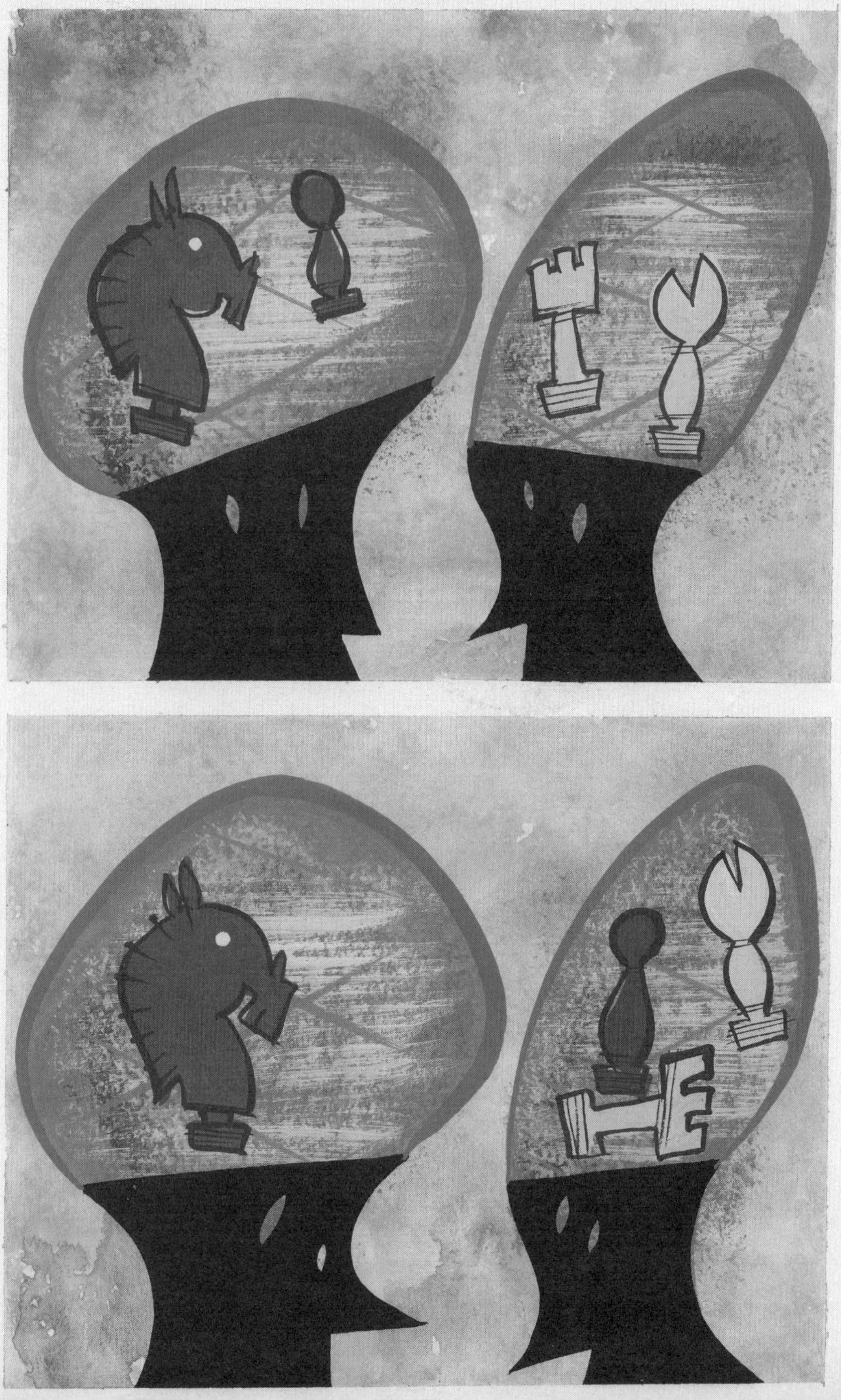

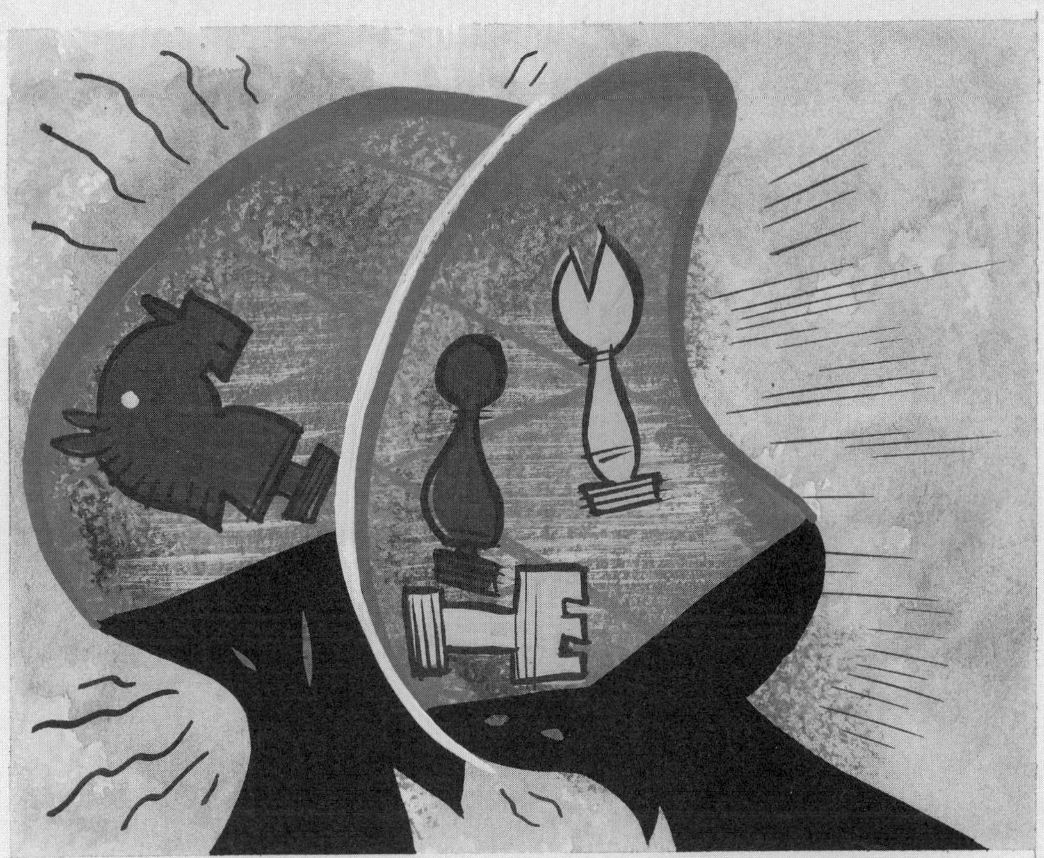

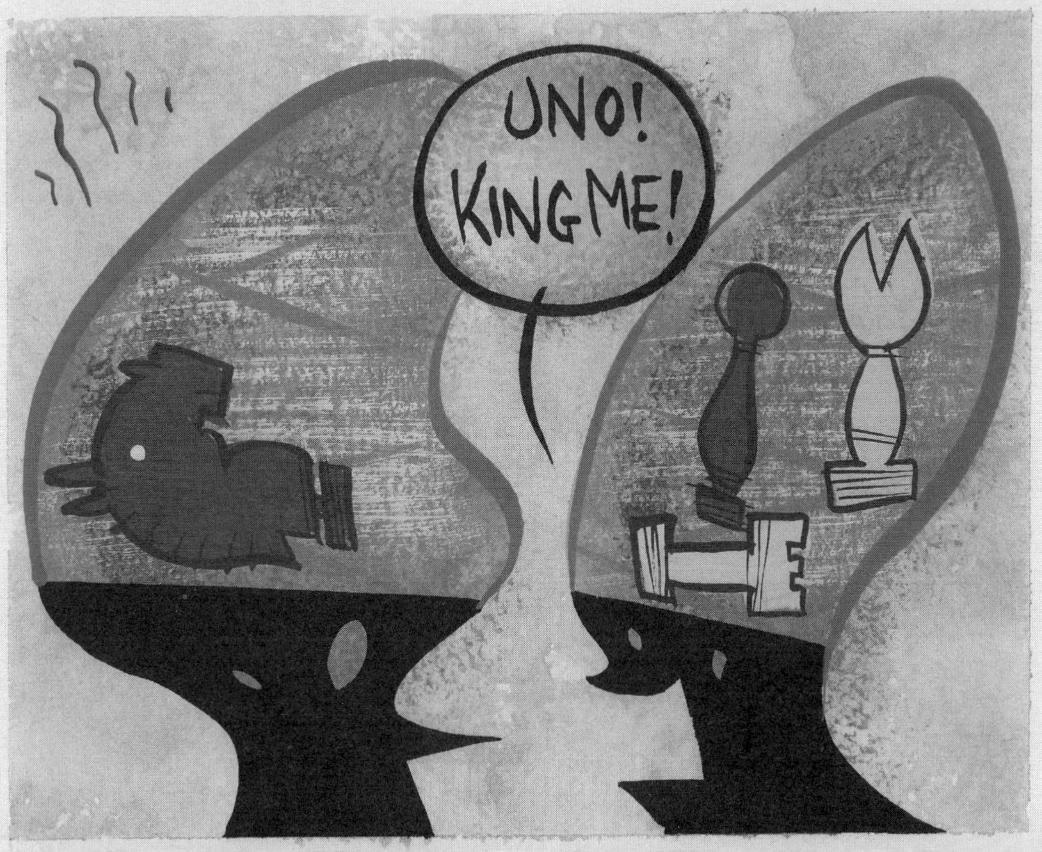
UNO! KING ME!

Jim Mahfood

Jim Mahfood has done some drawings and things. He likes to paint at clubs and drink the sweet liquor. You can view more of his "art" and stuff at www.40ozcomics.com. Thanks

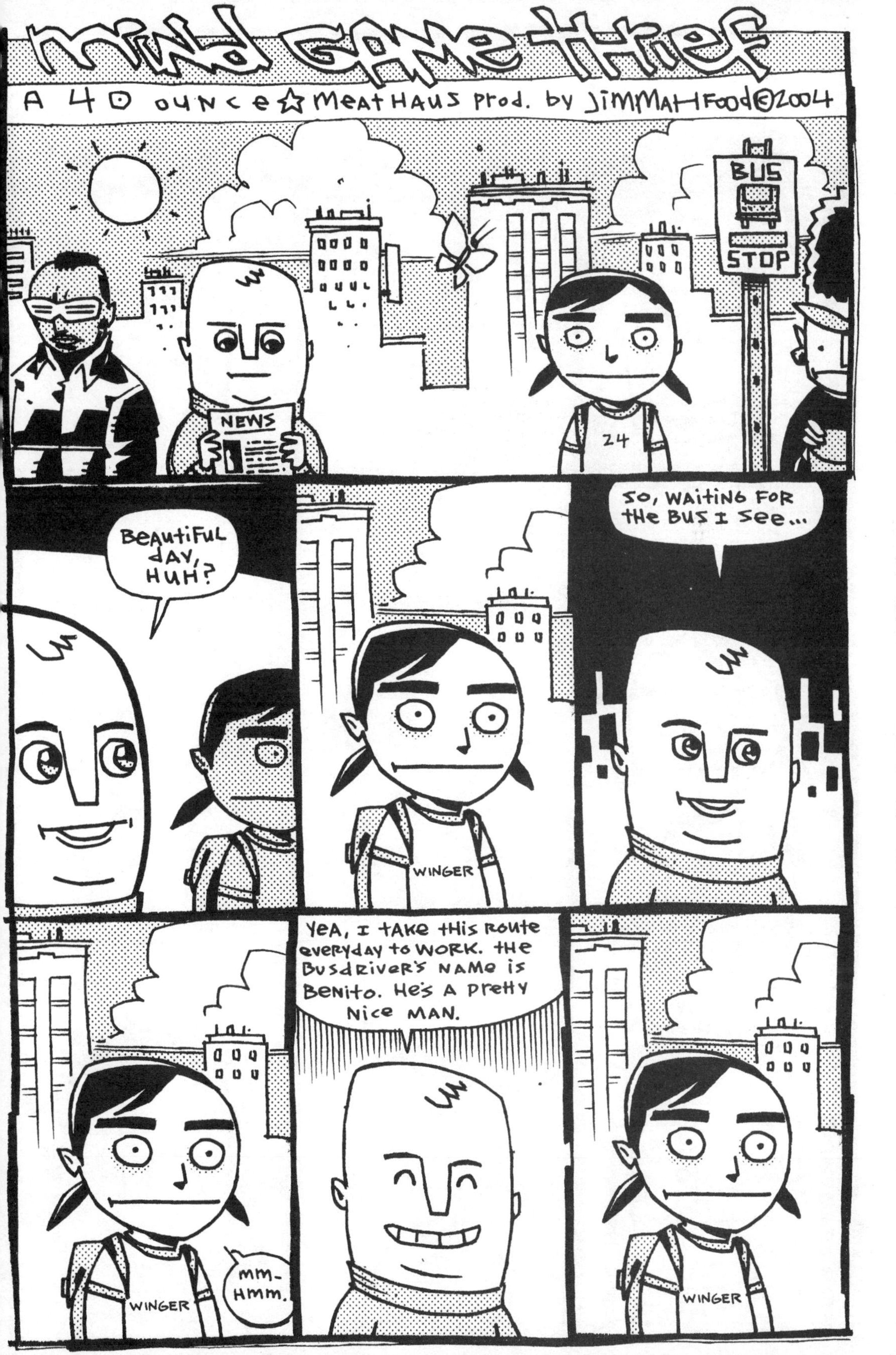
MIND GAME THIEF
A 40 OUNCE☆MEATHAUS PROD. BY JIMMAHFOOD©2004
NEWS
BUS STOP
24
BEAUTIFUL DAY, HUH?
WINGER
SO, WAITING FOR THE BUS I SEE...
WINGER
MM-HMM.
YEA, I TAKE THIS ROUTE EVERYDAY TO WORK. THE BUSDRIVER'S NAME IS BENITO. HE'S A PRETTY NICE MAN.
WINGER

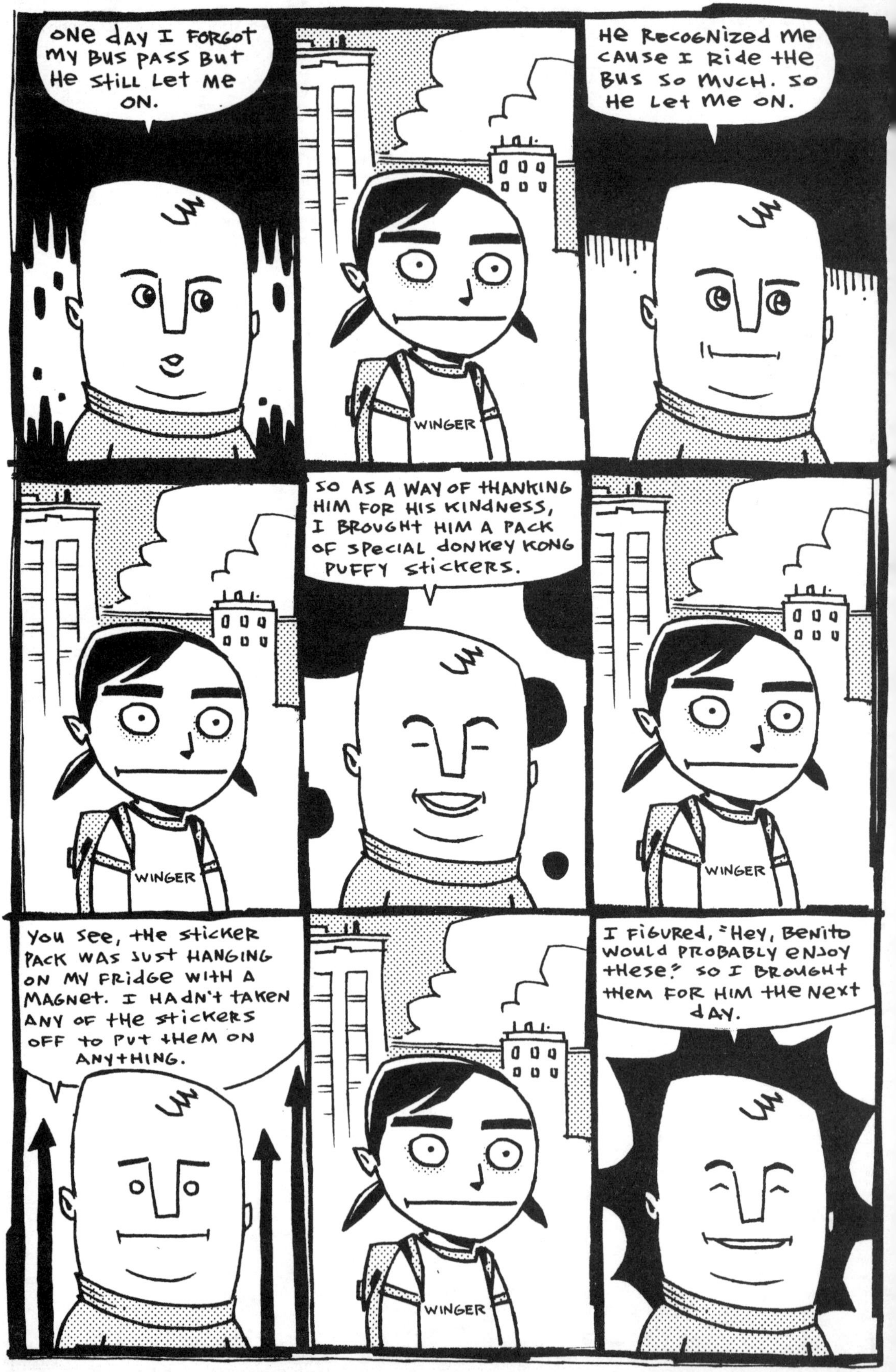
ONE DAY I FORGOT MY BUS PASS BUT HE STILL LET ME ON.
WINGER
HE RECOGNIZED ME CAUSE I RIDE THE BUS SO MUCH. SO HE LET ME ON.
WINGER
SO AS A WAY OF THANKING HIM FOR HIS KINDNESS, I BROUGHT HIM A PACK OF SPECIAL DONKEY KONG PUFFY STICKERS.
WINGER
YOU SEE, THE STICKER PACK WAS JUST HANGING ON MY FRIDGE WITH A MAGNET. I HADN'T TAKEN ANY OF THE STICKERS OFF TO PUT THEM ON ANYTHING.
WINGER
I FIGURED, "HEY, BENITO WOULD PROBABLY ENJOY THESE." SO I BROUGHT THEM FOR HIM THE NEXT DAY.

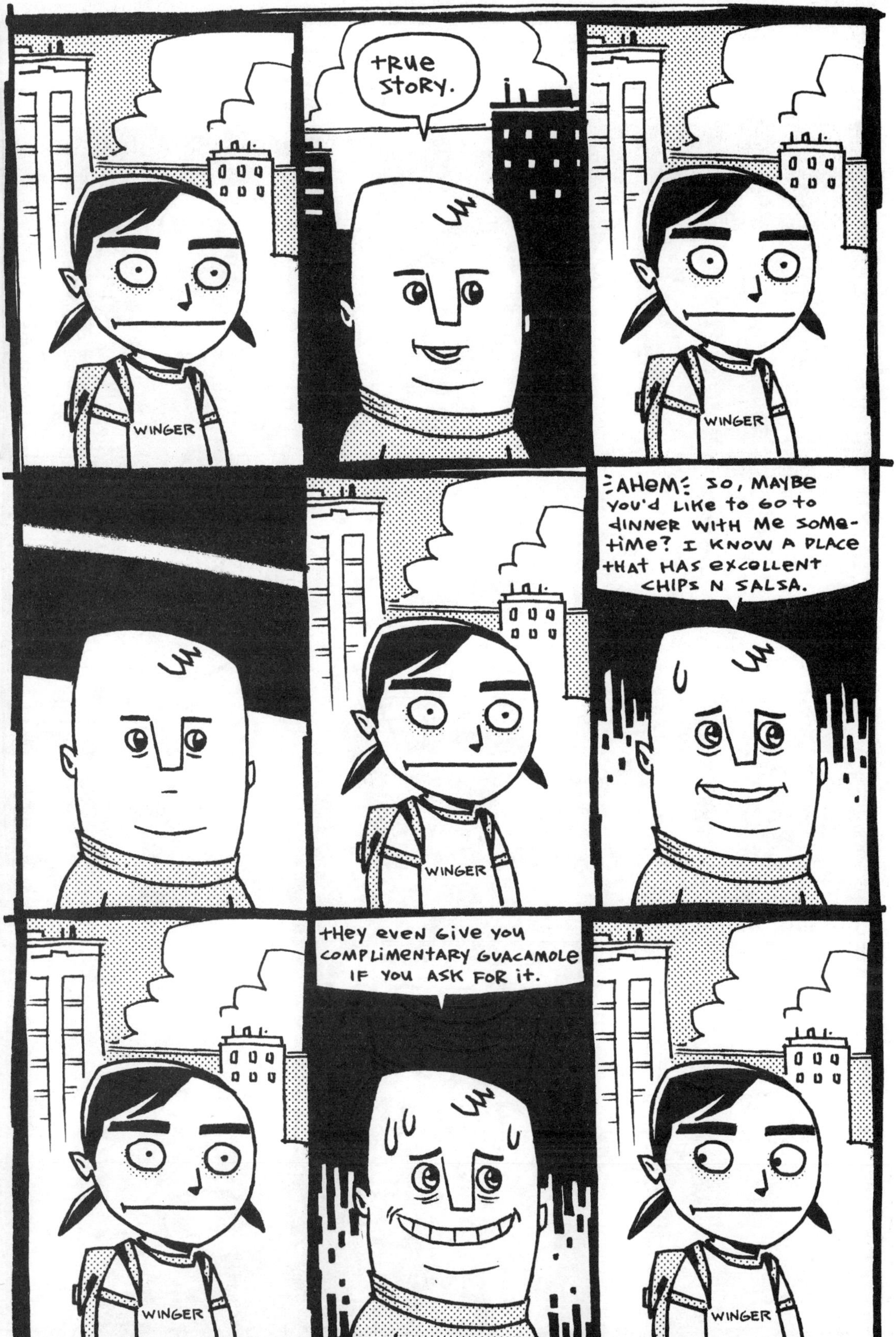
WINGER
true story.
WINGER
WINGER
AHEM SO, MAYBE you'd LIKE to GO to dinner WITH Me SoMetiMe? I KNOW A PLACE that HAS excellent CHIPS N SALSA.
WINGER
they even Give you COMPLIMENTARY GUACAMOLE IF YOU ASK FOR it.
WINGER

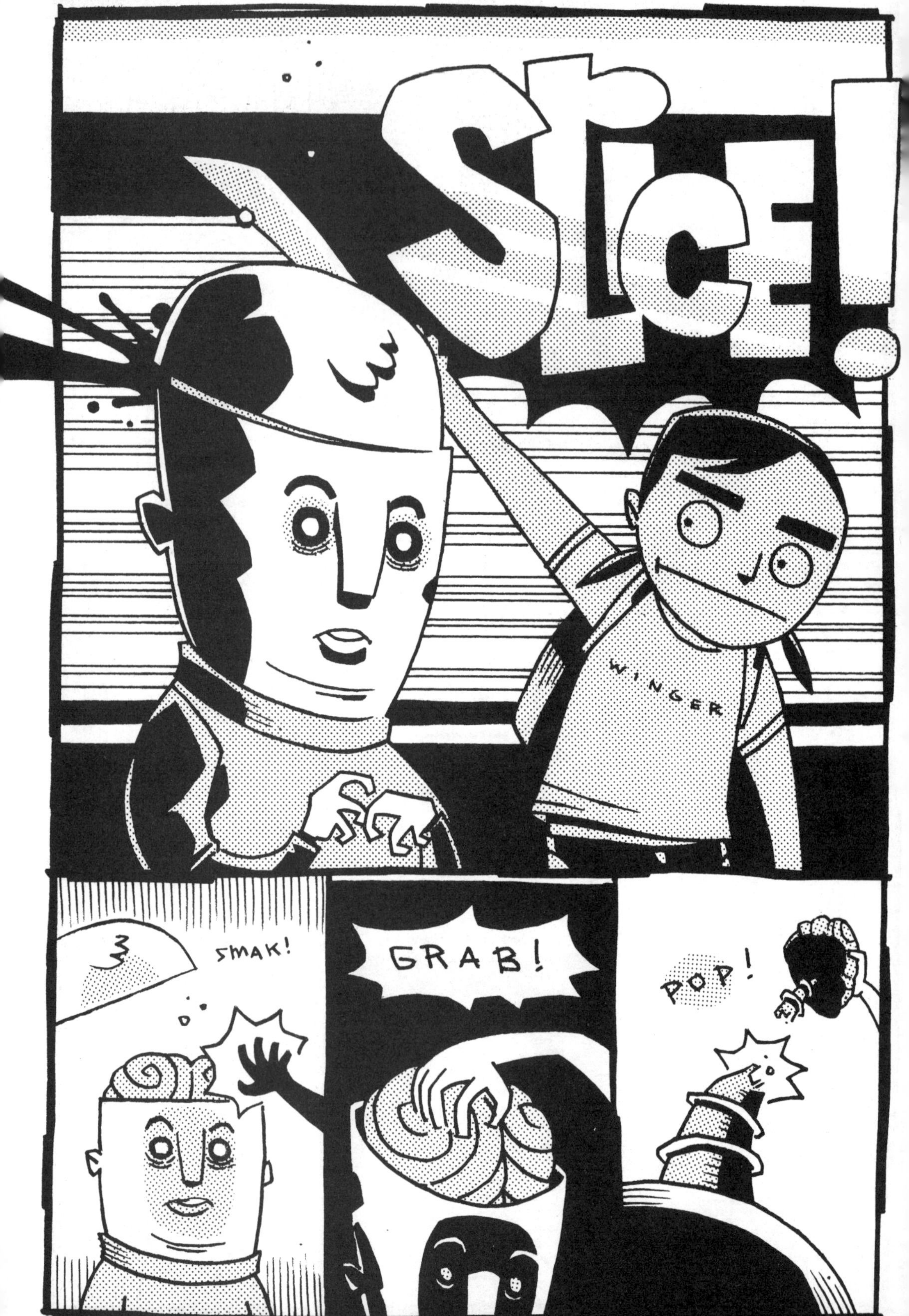
SLICE!
WINGER
SMAK!
GRAB!
POP!

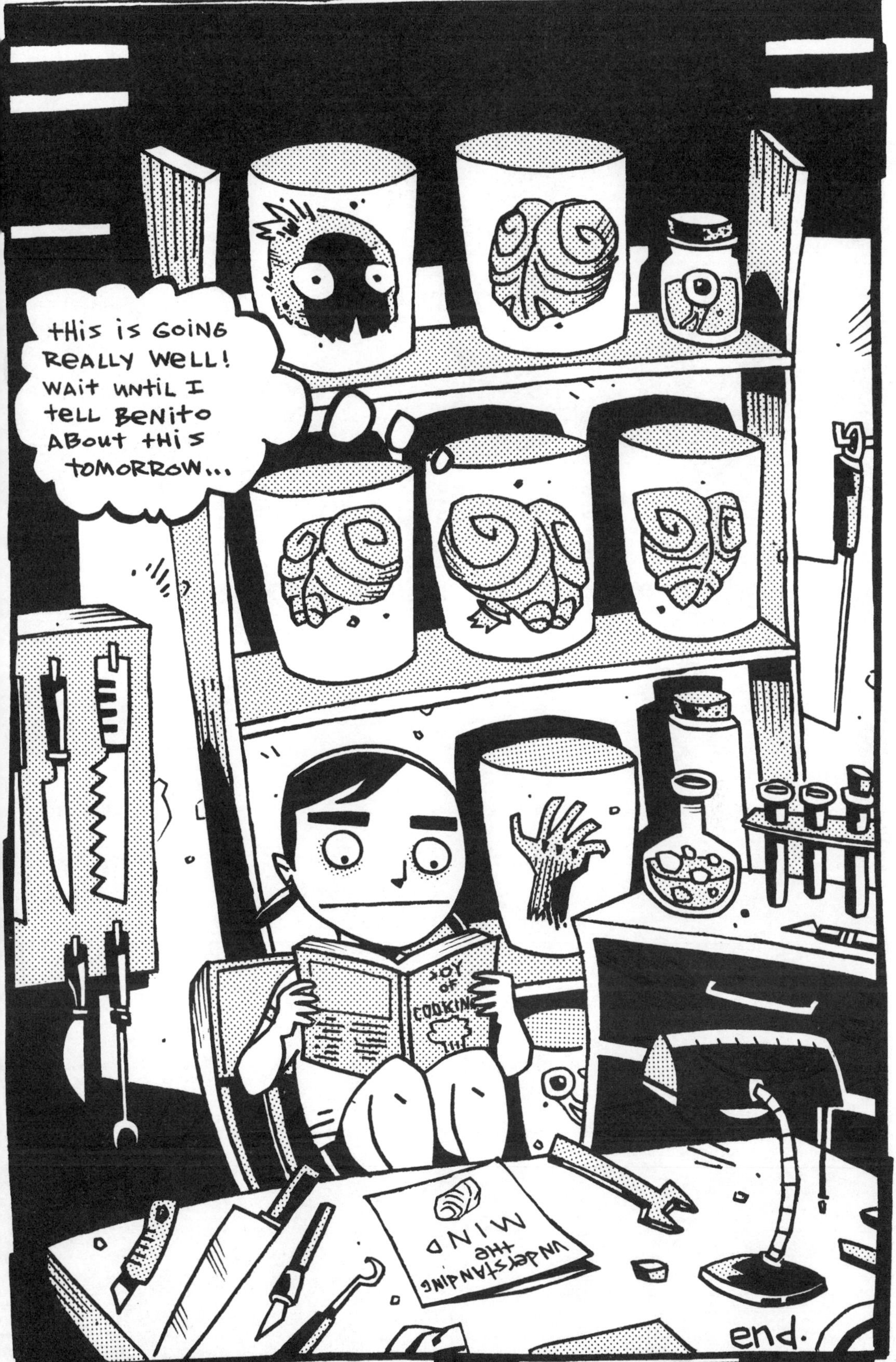
tHIS IS GOING REALLY WELL! WAIT UNTIL I tELL BENItO ABOUt tHIS TOMORROW...
JOY OF COOKING
UNdERSTANdING tHE MIND
end.

Celia Bullwinkel

Celia is a New York based animator who makes comics on the side.
Find out more at: www.celiabullwinkel.com

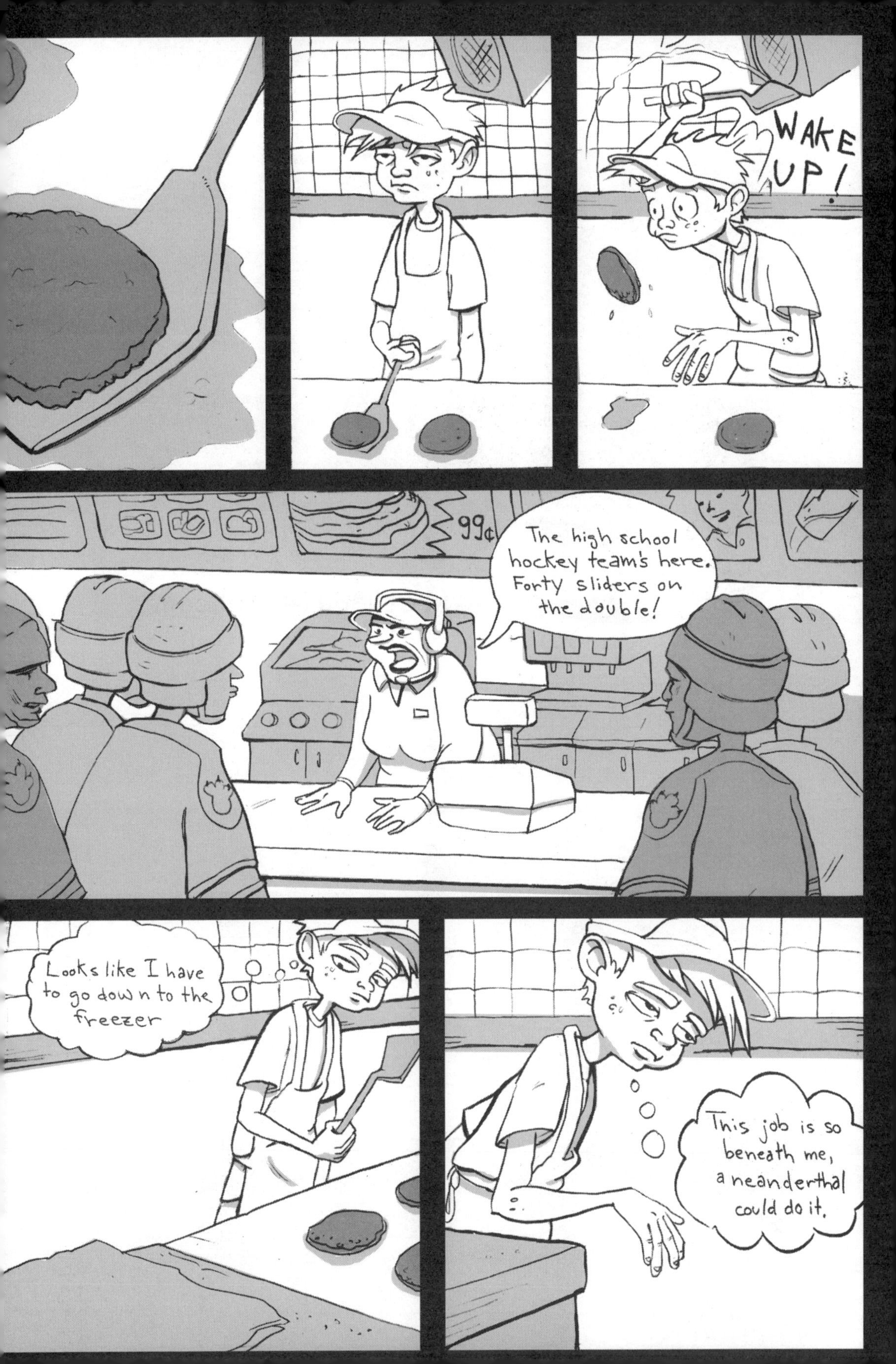
WAKE UP!
99¢
The high school hockey team's here. Forty sliders on the double!
Looks like I have to go down to the freezer
This job is so beneath me, a neanderthal could do it.

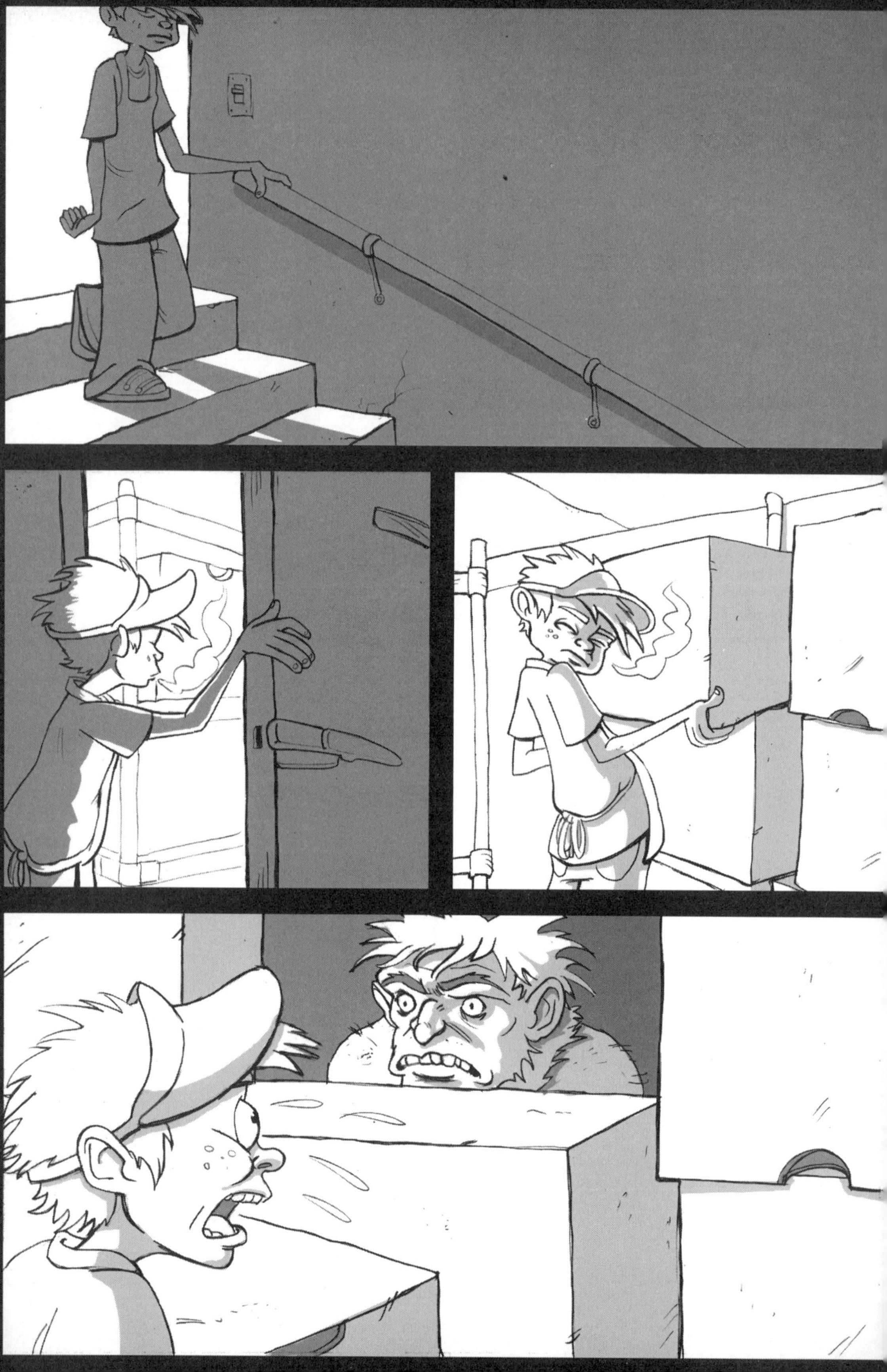

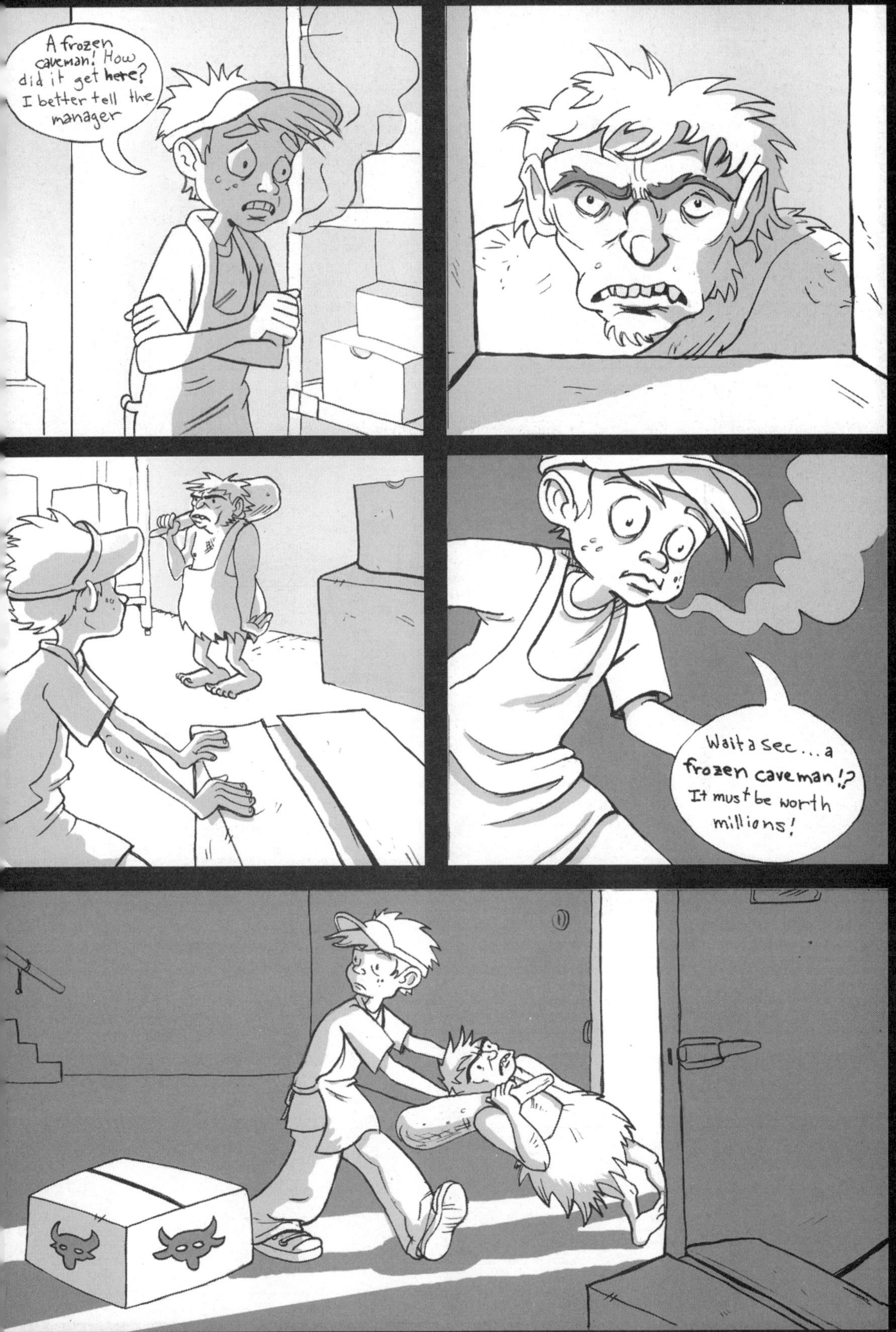
A frozen caveman! How did it get **here**? I better tell the manager
Wait a sec... a **frozen caveman**!? It must be worth millions!

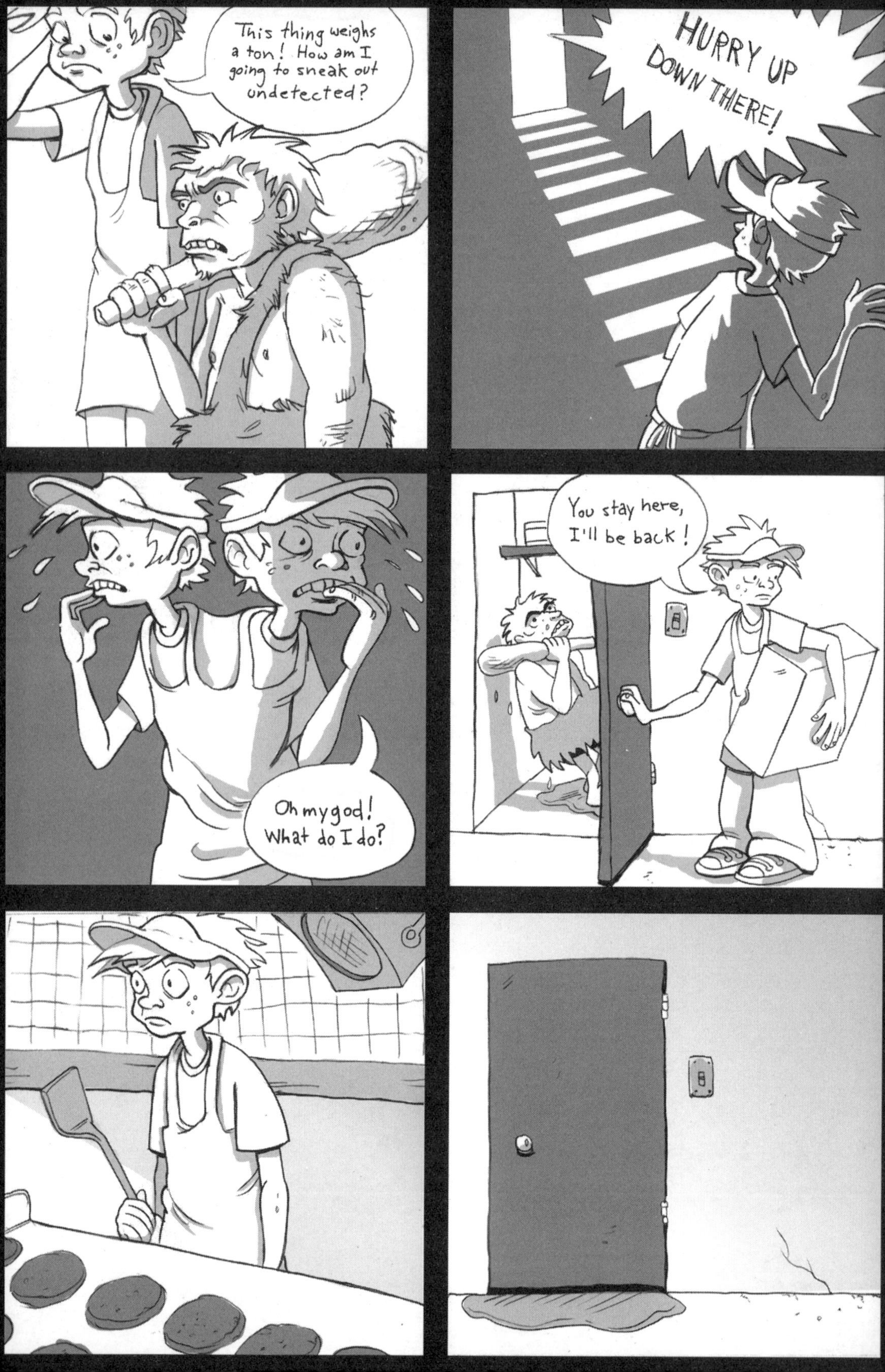
This thing weighs a ton! How am I going to sneak out undetected?
HURRY UP DOWN THERE!
Oh my god! What do I do?
You stay here, I'll be back!

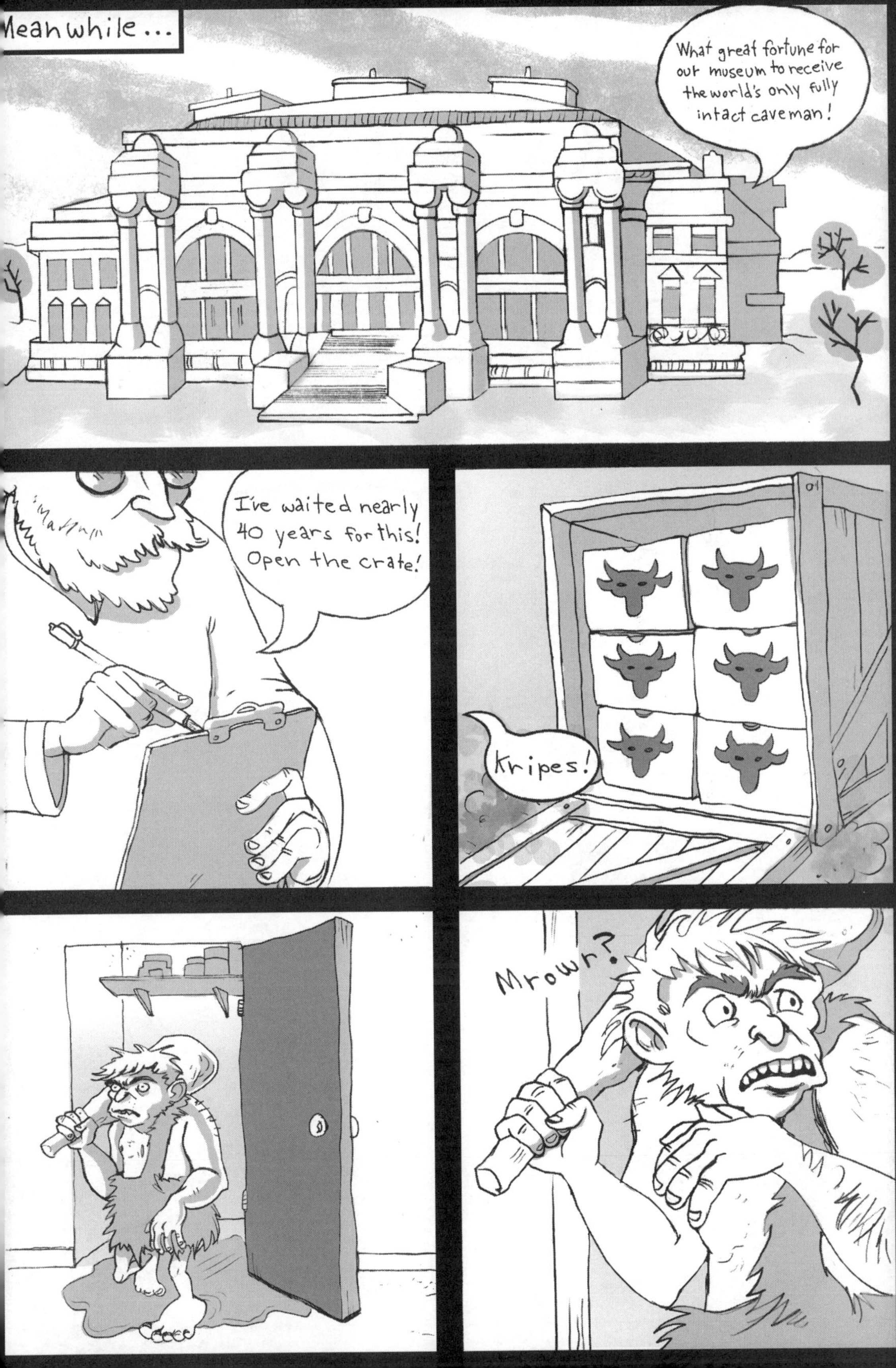
Meanwhile...
What great fortune for our museum to receive the world's only fully intact caveman!
I've waited nearly 40 years for this! Open the crate!
Kripes!
Mrowr?

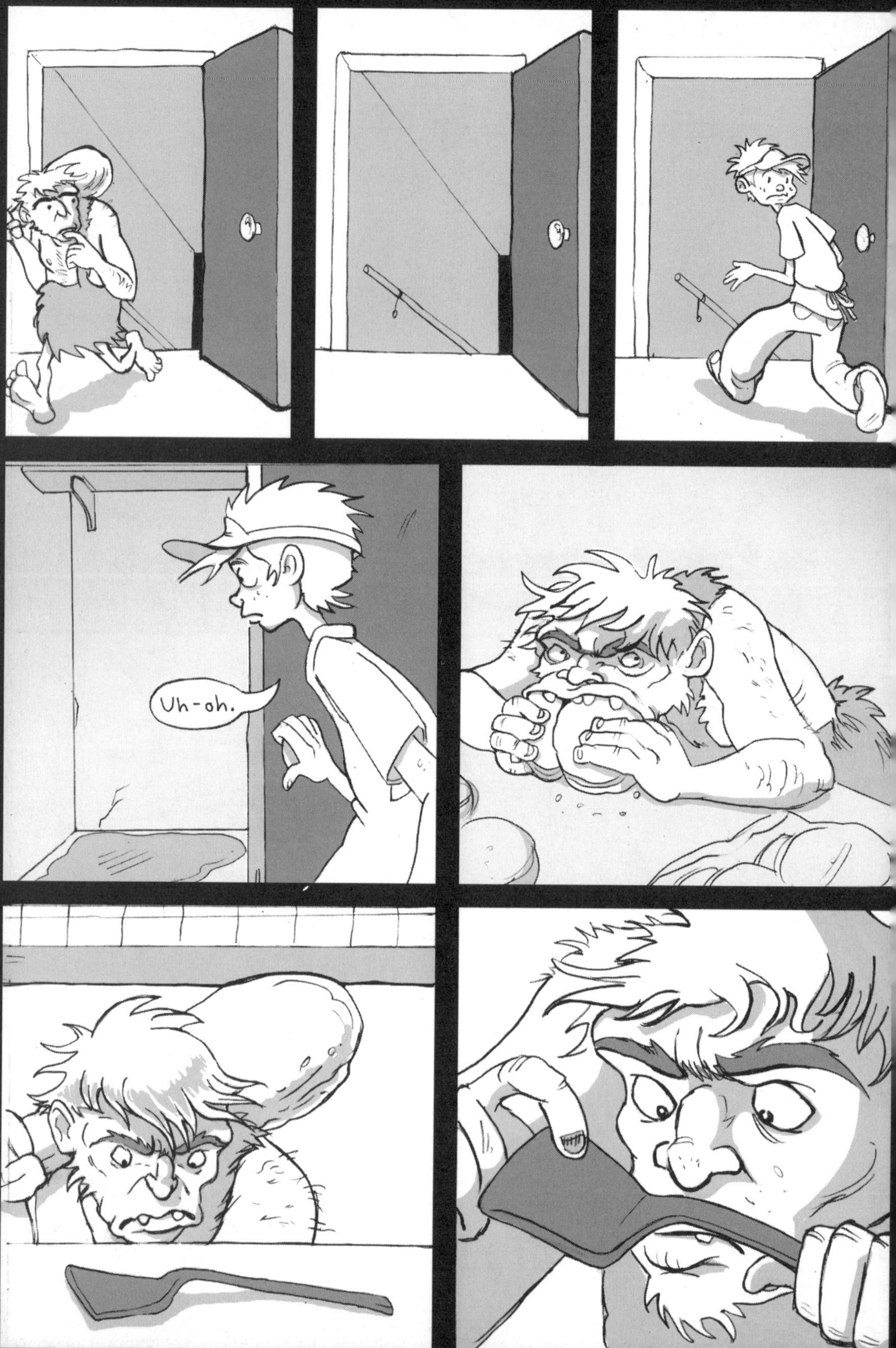
Uh-oh.

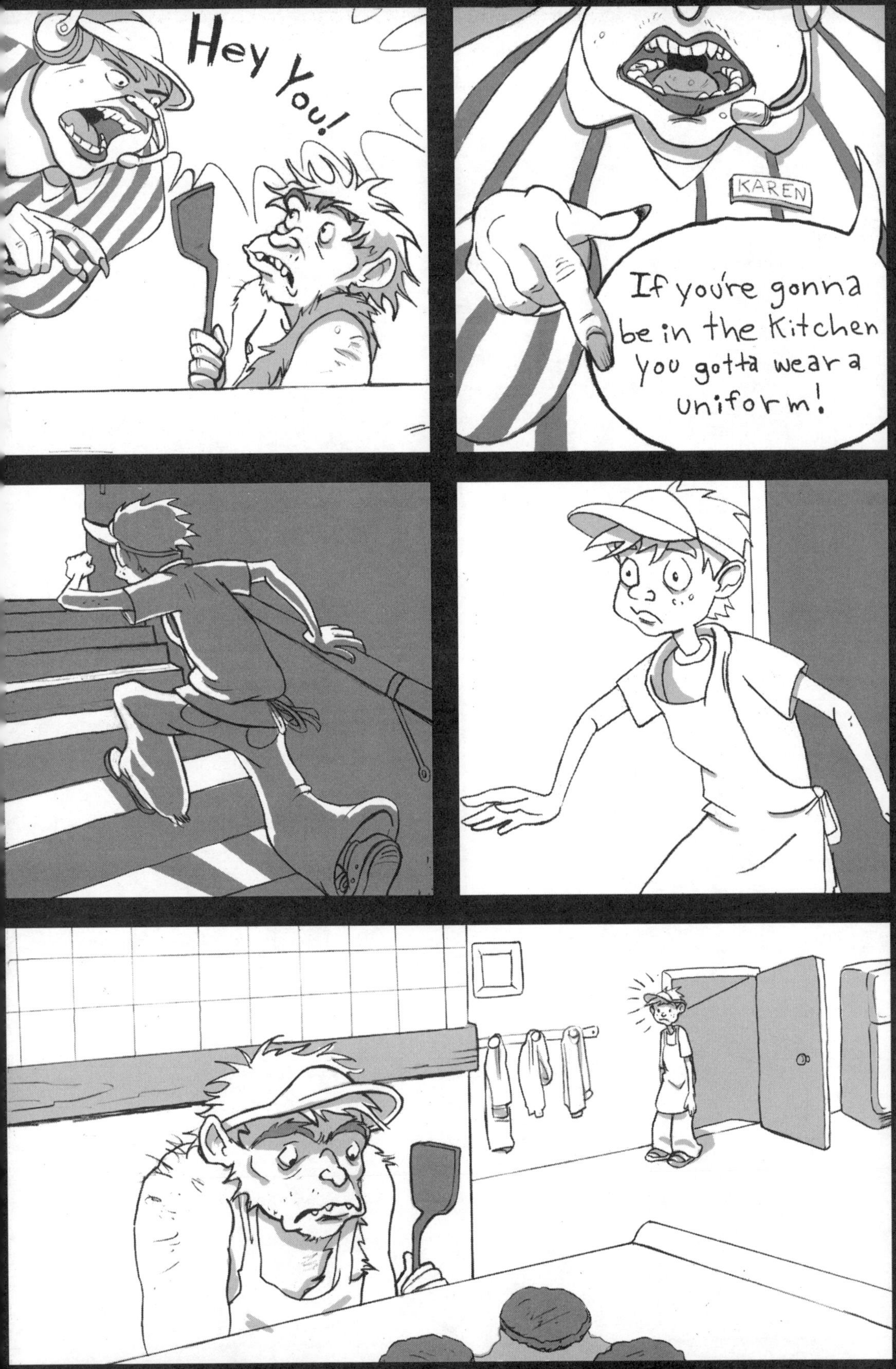
Hey You!
If you're gonna be in the Kitchen you gotta wear a uniform!
KAREN

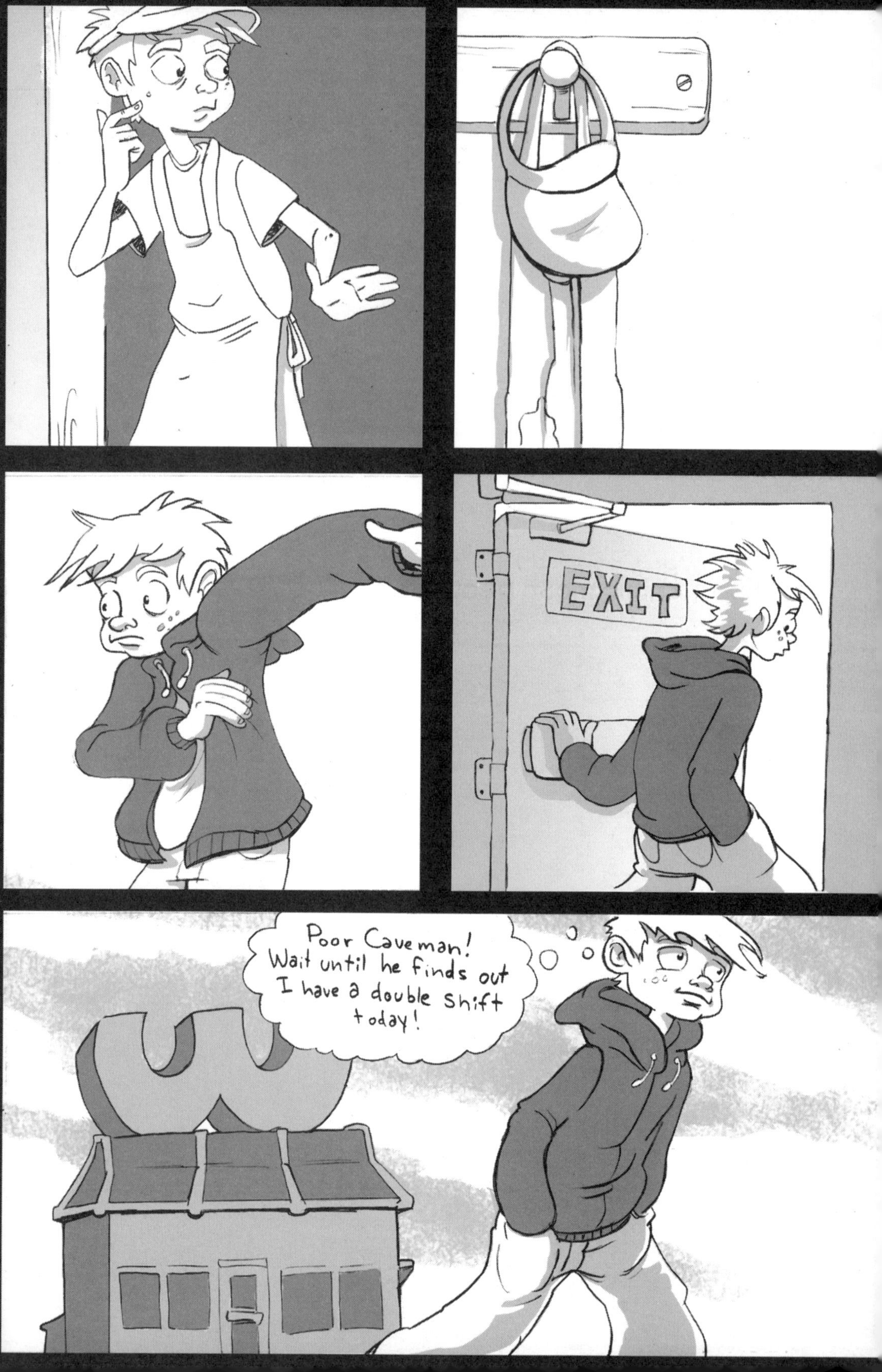
EXIT
Poor Caveman! Wait until he finds out I have a double shift today!

Zachary Flagg

I almost always listen to audiobooks while I'm working. I strongly encourage others to do this. Also I think most people should curse more. Not because they're angry. That makes me uncomfortable. But just as a part of their normal conversation.
www.zacharyflagg.com

meat
the
☺ meatsters beta ®

by Zachary Flagg Baldus
zacharyflagg.com

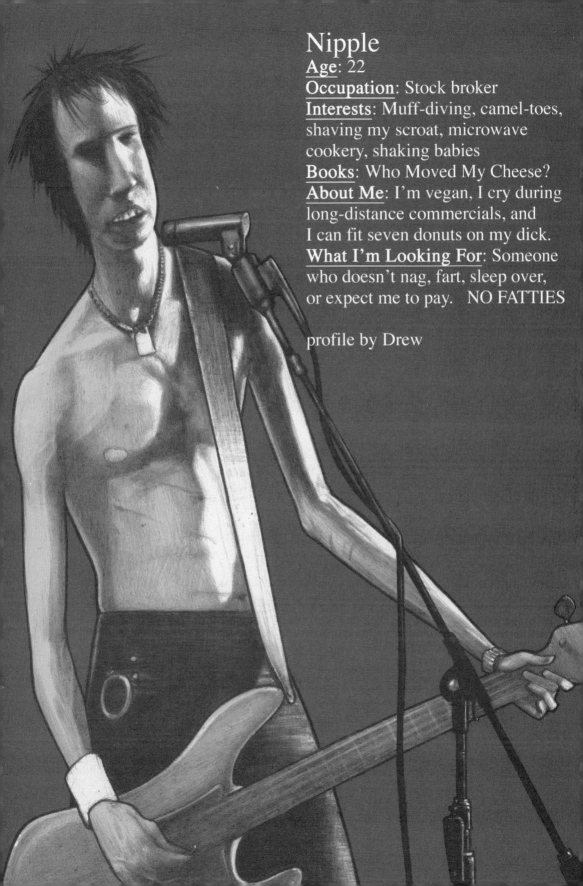

Nipple

Age: 22

Occupation: Stock broker

Interests: Muff-diving, camel-toes, shaving my scroat, microwave cookery, shaking babies

Books: Who Moved My Cheese?

About Me: I'm vegan, I cry during long-distance commercials, and I can fit seven donuts on my dick.

What I'm Looking For: Someone who doesn't nag, fart, sleep over, or expect me to pay. NO FATTIES

profile by Drew

Meat Mitts

Gender: american
Occupation: Retired.
Affiliations: Theres a bar downstairs from where I live.
Favorite music: I was the drummer in a beach band. Called ourselves 'the Tuff Customers'. The songs were all about how lousy the service was in these different restaurants.
Favorite books: Anything with a tit or a smile.
Favorite movies: I like anything where the gal shows her pal her locale in the corral!
About me: If you showed me a picture of a robot with human body parts glued onto it, I wouldn't say 'what the hell is that thing there?!"
Who I want to meat: Any sort of woman, I guess.

profile by Andy Bodor

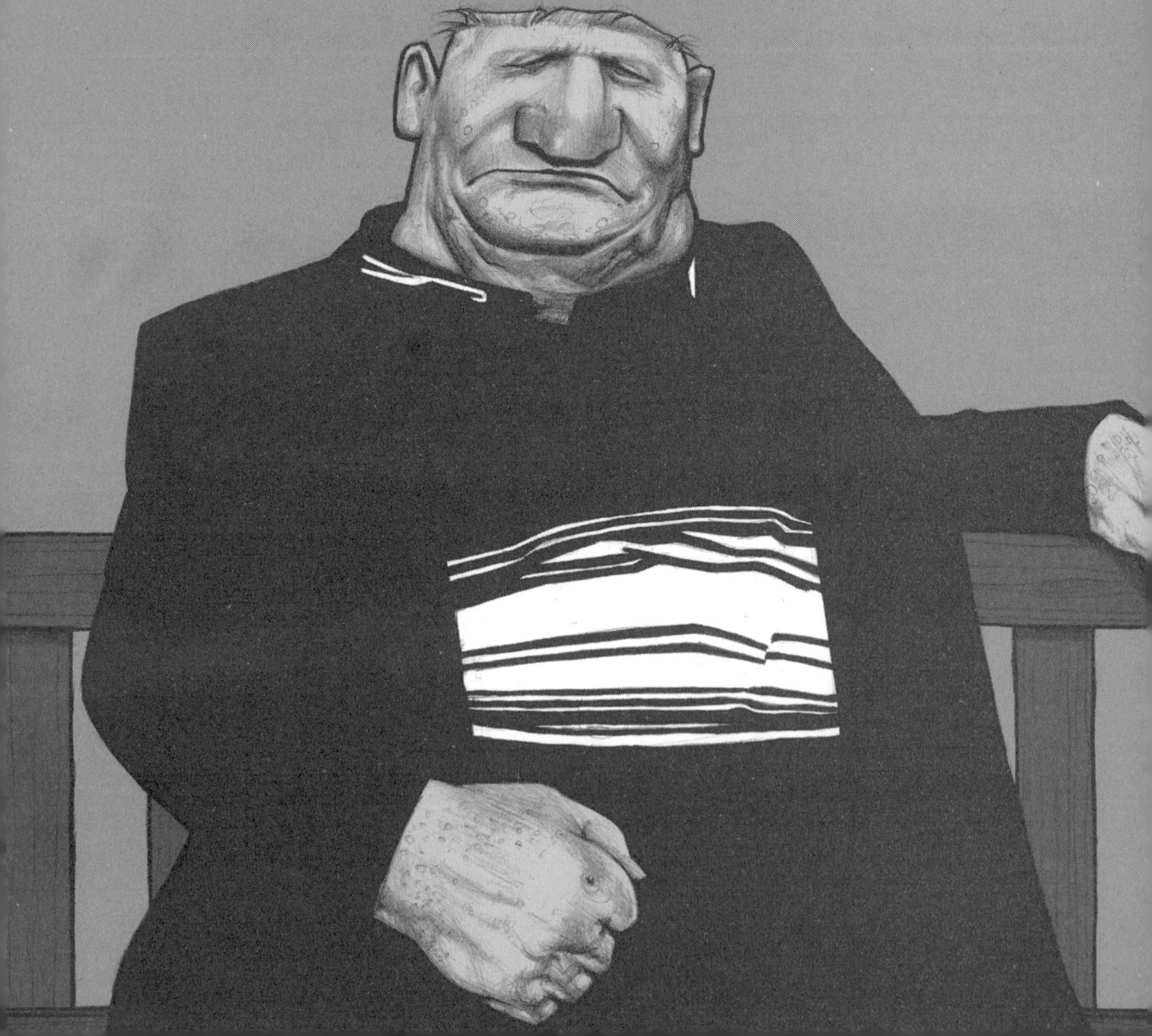

Meat Gowls

Gender: as male as they get
Occupation: RR construction (retired)
Interests: sowing the seed the good lord gave me, praying for the evil baby killers
Affiliations: our good lord's home
Favorite Music: psalms 43 and 44
Favorite Books: the good book
Favorite Movies: Taxi Driver, Raising Arizona

Who I want to meat: a woman with good, strong child-bearing hips and is willing to put them to the test by having several of my babies

profile by Jessica Liszewski

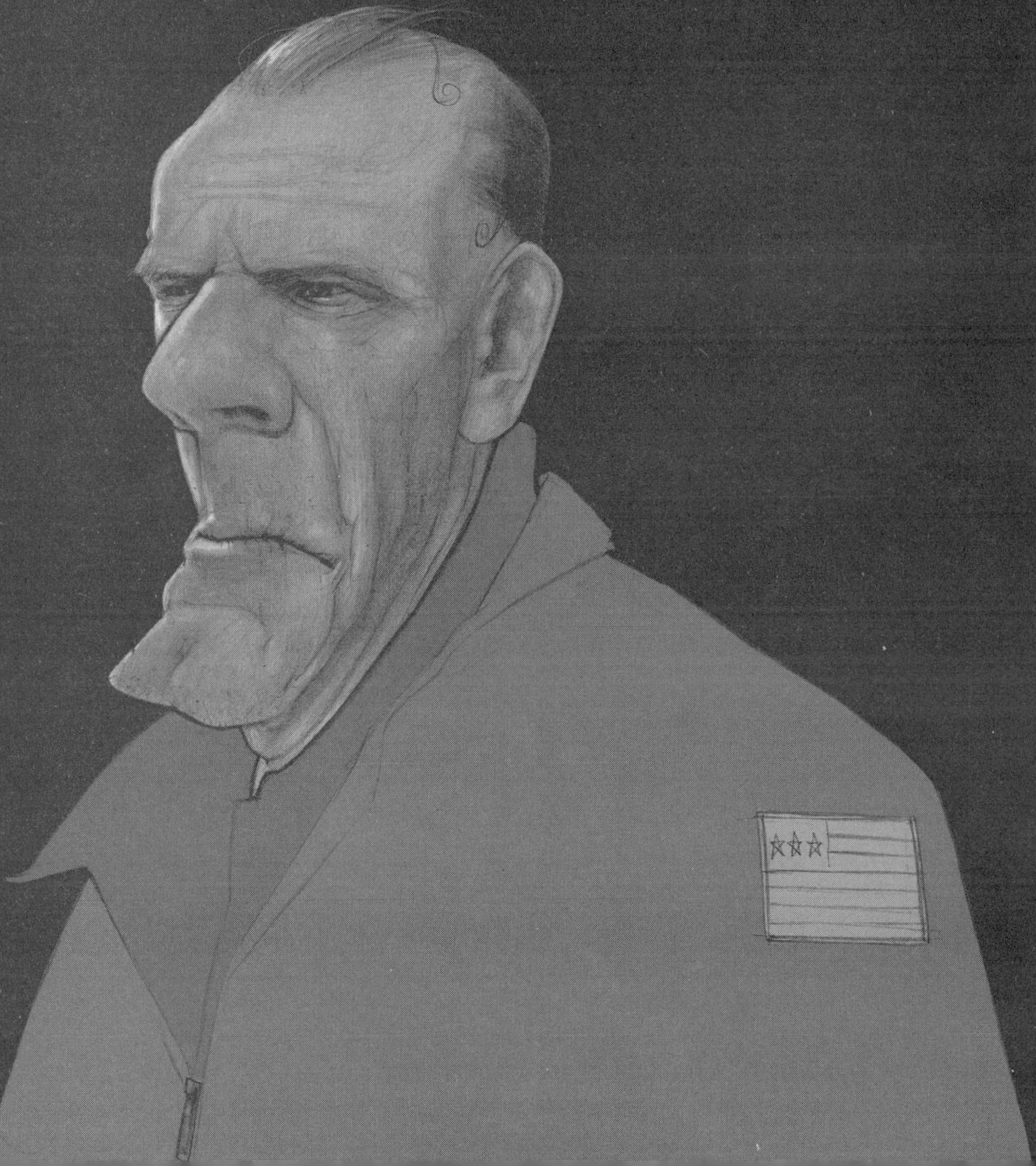

Meat Hook

Gender: All man, ladies (well hung).
Interested in meating people for:
Just hooking up.
Age: 30-ish
Occupation: Personal Trainer/
Events/Catering
Favorite Music: I don't play
music... but I hear it at night
behind the dark curtain that
is my conscious mind.
Favorite Movies: Tremors
1 - 3 (not #4 or the TV show)
About Me: I live in an unlit
cave surrounded by the
bones of human female
sacrifices, I've been ordered
to execute by the voices
nside my broken TV
Who I want to meat: Gotta
be a woman with
recognizable female genitalia.
Gotta have a good heart.
And other organs should
be good too.

profile by endsim

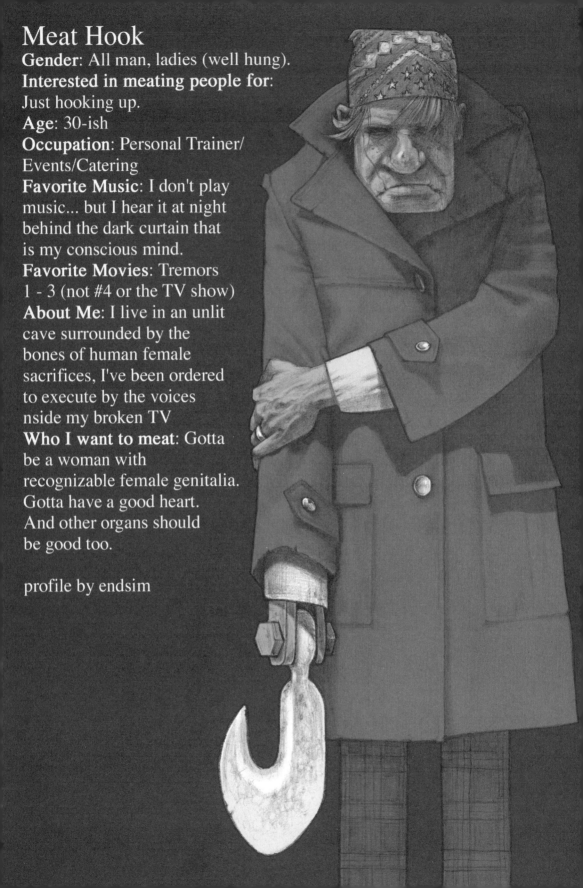

Meater Maid

Gender: Female
Occupation: I sure miss those cute kids and kittie katz.
Location: Miami
Interests: my stuffed cat, oujia board.
Affiliations: Sisters Unite.
Favorite TV Shows: Highway To Heaven
Favorite Movies: Musicals, if in Espanol I will cry sooner. There I go again...
About Me: I have several
Who I want to meat: I like chicken tenders.

profile by rogerhumanbeing

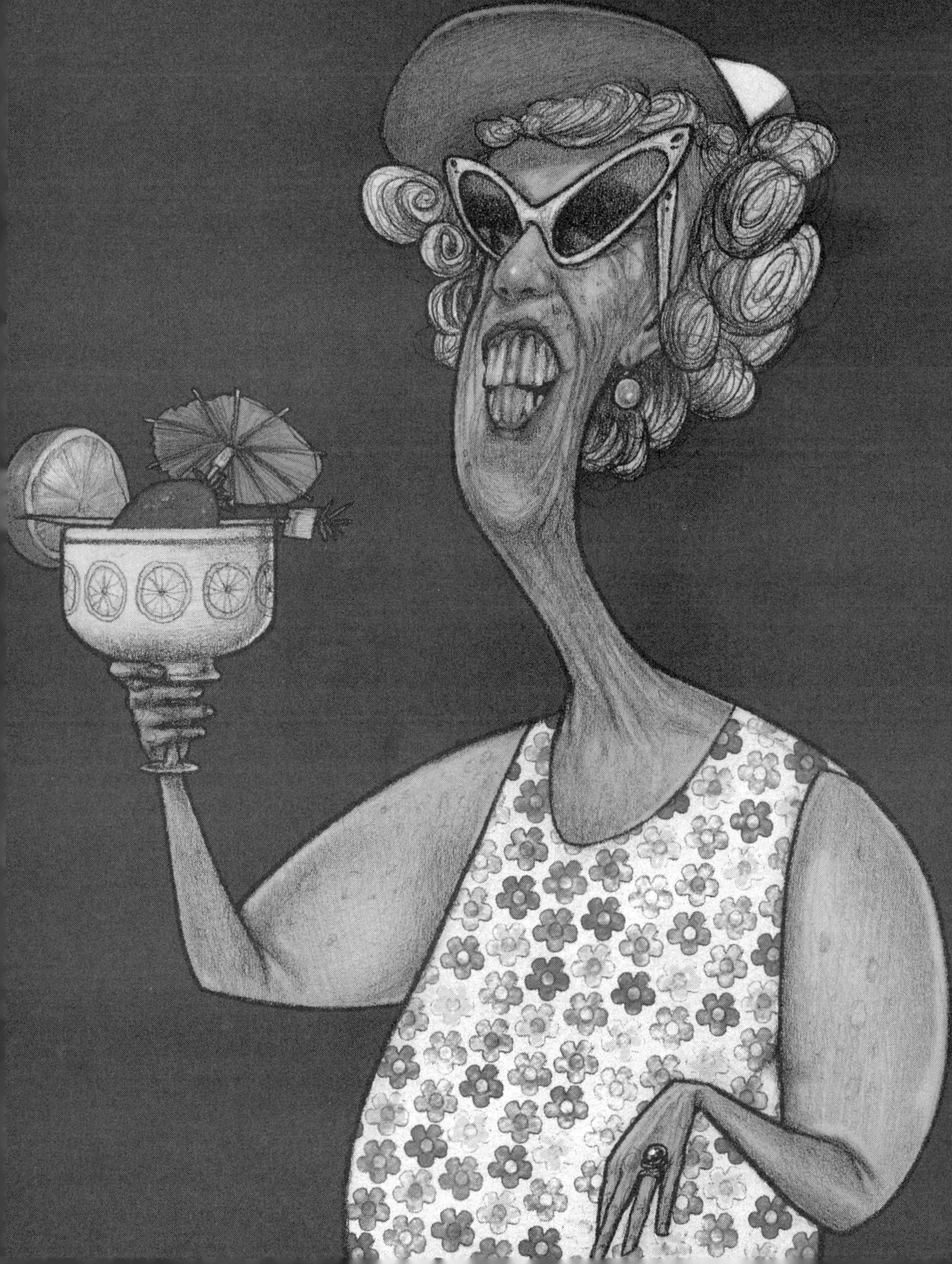

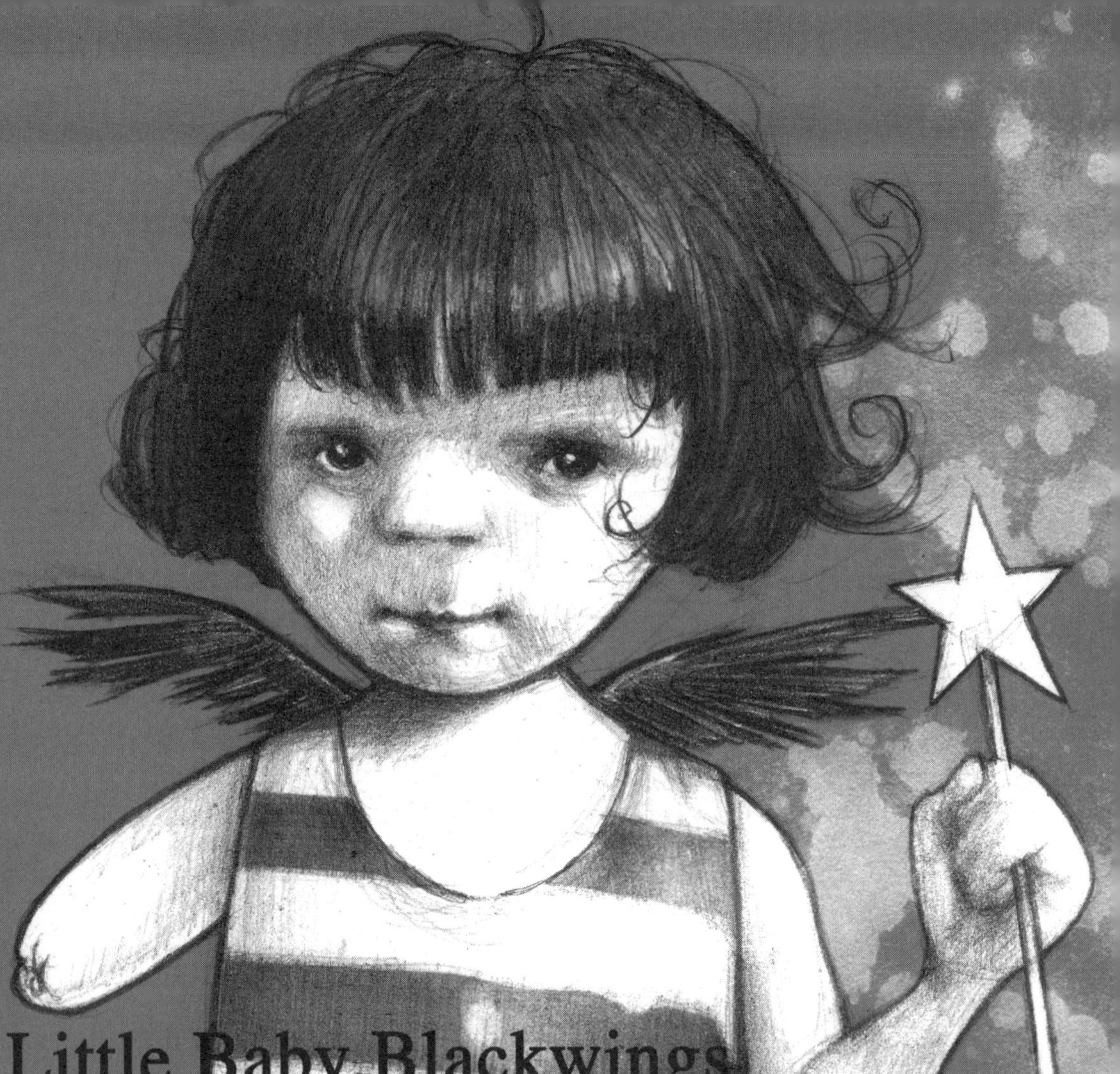

Little Baby Blackwings

Gender: female
Location: Candy Cowboyland
Hometown: Harmonica
Occupation: makes candy for people
Interests: candy things that make you go upside down
Favorite Music: Fox
Favorite Books: Mary had a little lamb, I was stuck in a forest and like a million miles away.
Favorite Movies: I feel different about me, I went on a trip and then I can't find the way back home, I like it that way and don't stop, I se something weird, I like something but not that brilliant
About me: I had something weird

profile by Maguire Baldus (age 6)

Troy Nixey

Troy Nixey lives in Canada. He's been drawing
comics for fifteen years. He's now shifted his
attention to movies. Look for his short film,
LATCHKEY'S LAMENT, coming soon. Check out a
couple production stills at meathaus.com.

VINEGAR TEETH

by Troy Nixey

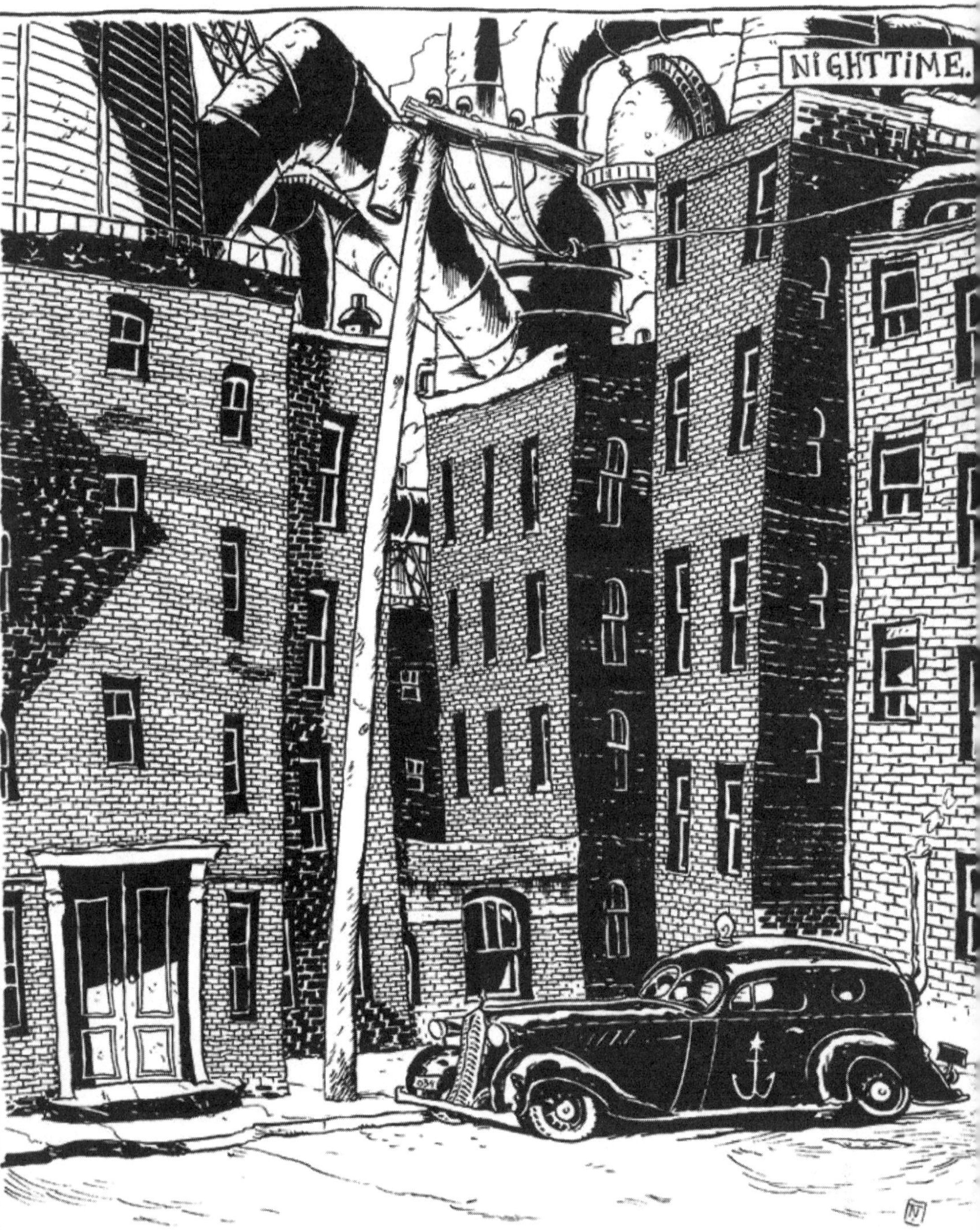
NIGHTTIME.

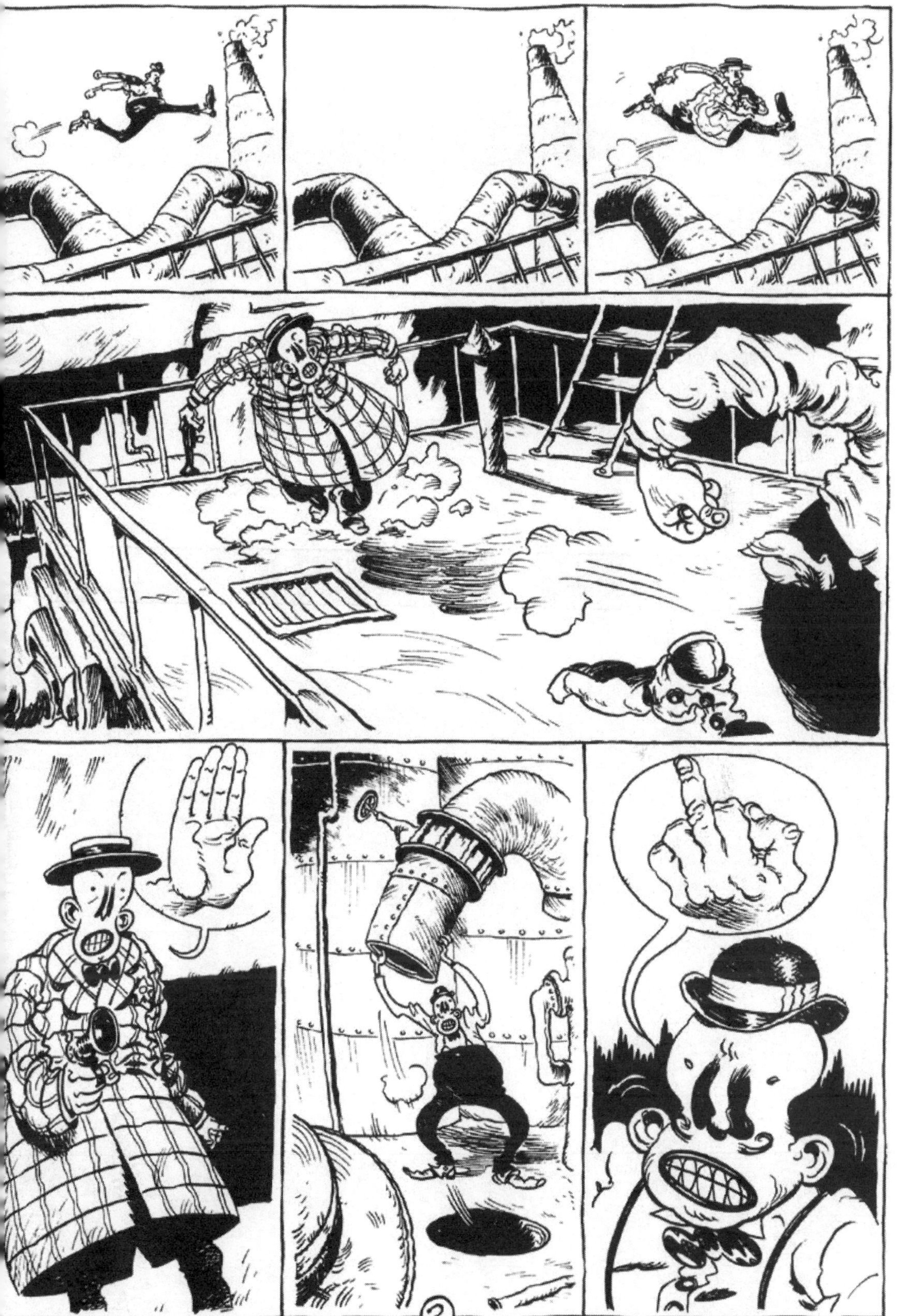

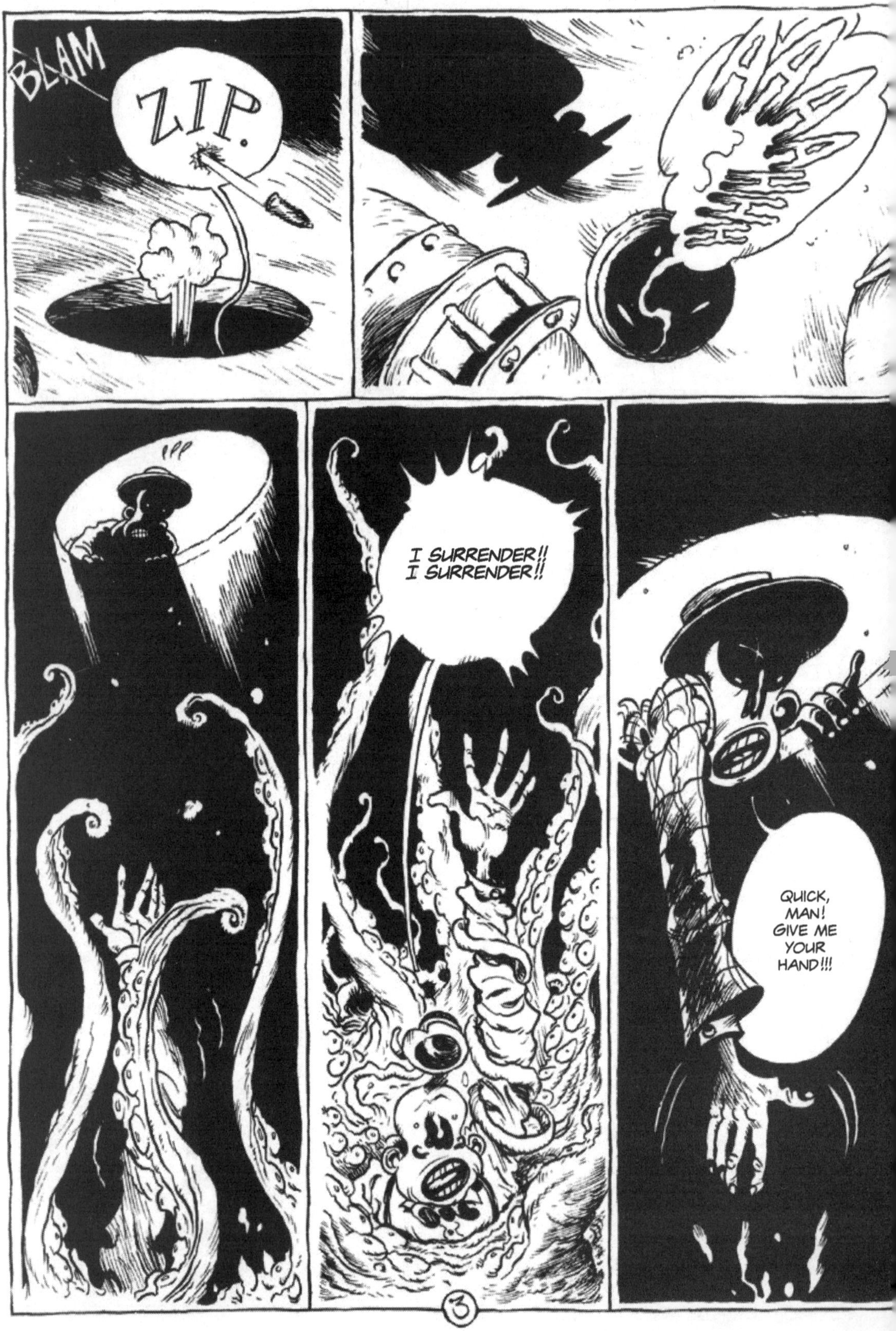
BLAM
ZIP.
HAHAHAHA
I SURRENDER!!
I SURRENDER!!
QUICK, MAN! GIVE ME YOUR HAND!!!

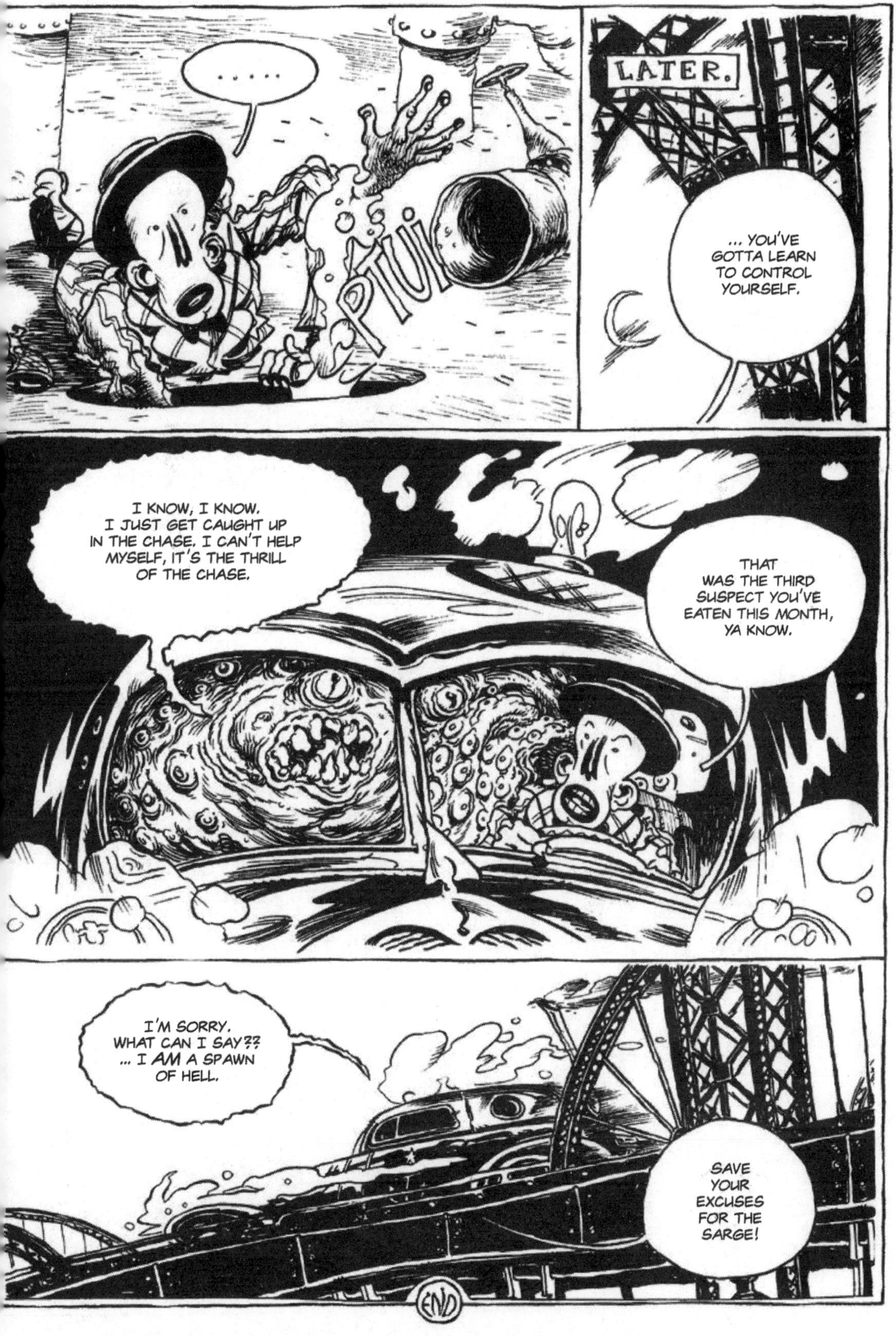
. . . . .
PTUI
LATER.
... YOU'VE GOTTA LEARN TO CONTROL YOURSELF.
I KNOW, I KNOW. I JUST GET CAUGHT UP IN THE CHASE. I CAN'T HELP MYSELF, IT'S THE THRILL OF THE CHASE.
THAT WAS THE THIRD SUSPECT YOU'VE EATEN THIS MONTH, YA KNOW.
I'M SORRY. WHAT CAN I SAY?? ... I AM A SPAWN OF HELL.
SAVE YOUR EXCUSES FOR THE SARGE!
END

Tony Sandoval

I was born in the desert of Sonora Mexico, in 1973. In 1997 I started self-publishing comics with Nocturno#1; 1998, Nocturno#3; 1998, las mania-codesventuras de rodo y poly (short edition). In 2000, I started working for Shibalba Press, drawing Tinieblas and Alushe. In 2001 I self-published comic Blacky; 2004, participated with a short story, The Wardrobe, in the Urban Dreams compilation; Lluvia in Pulpo Comics recompilation; 2005, participated with a short story, Paseo Vespertino, in Cosecuencias compilation; the art for Vieille Amerique for Editions Paquet; The art for Jhonny Caronte and The Gun for Alias Enterprises and Recerca Editorial. You can find some of my stuff on-line at:
nocturno.tk

a wave of you

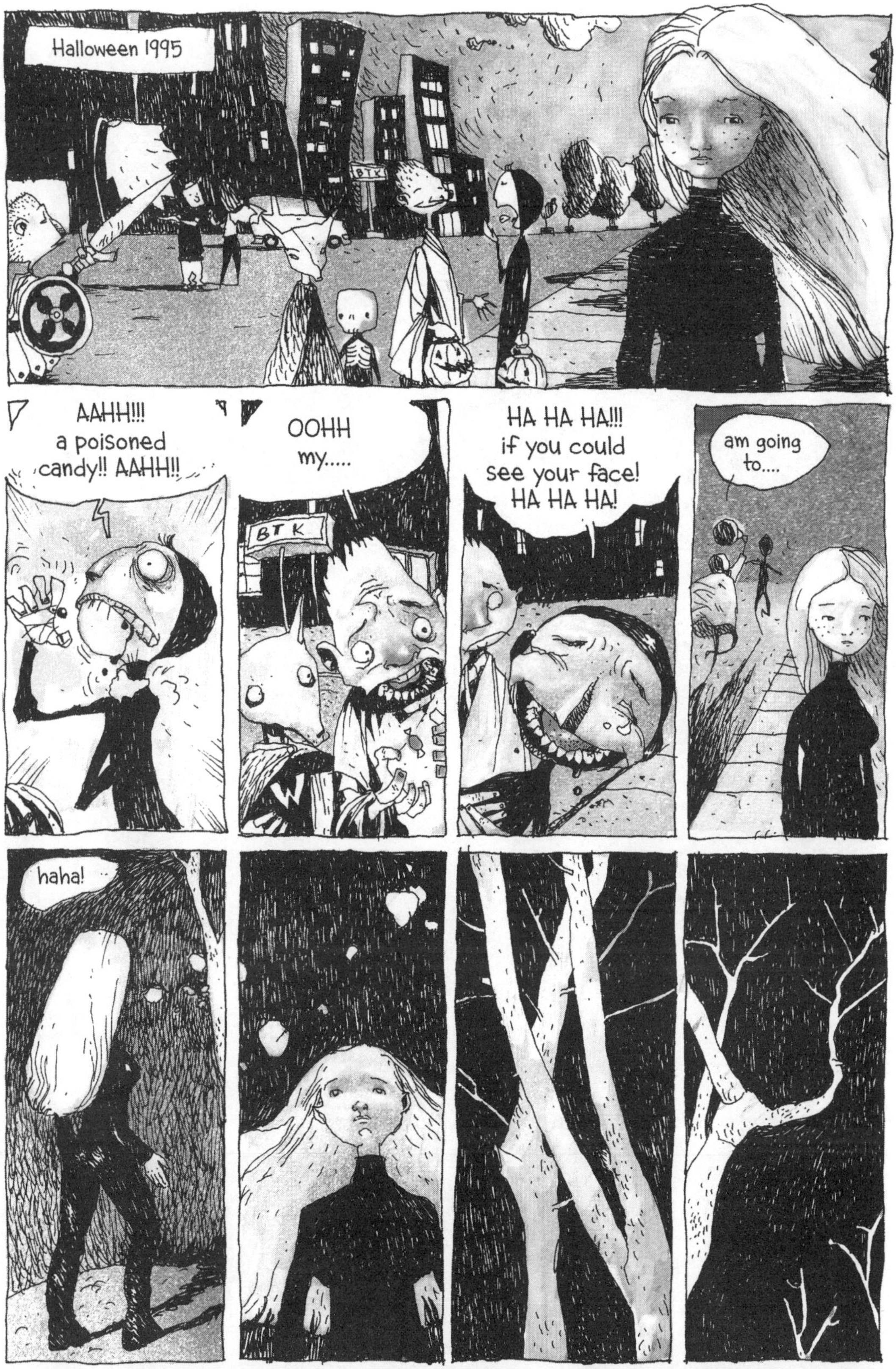

Halloween 1995
AAHH!!! a poisoned candy!! AAHH!!
OOHH my.....
HA HA HA!!! if you could see your face! HA HA HA!
am going to....
haha!

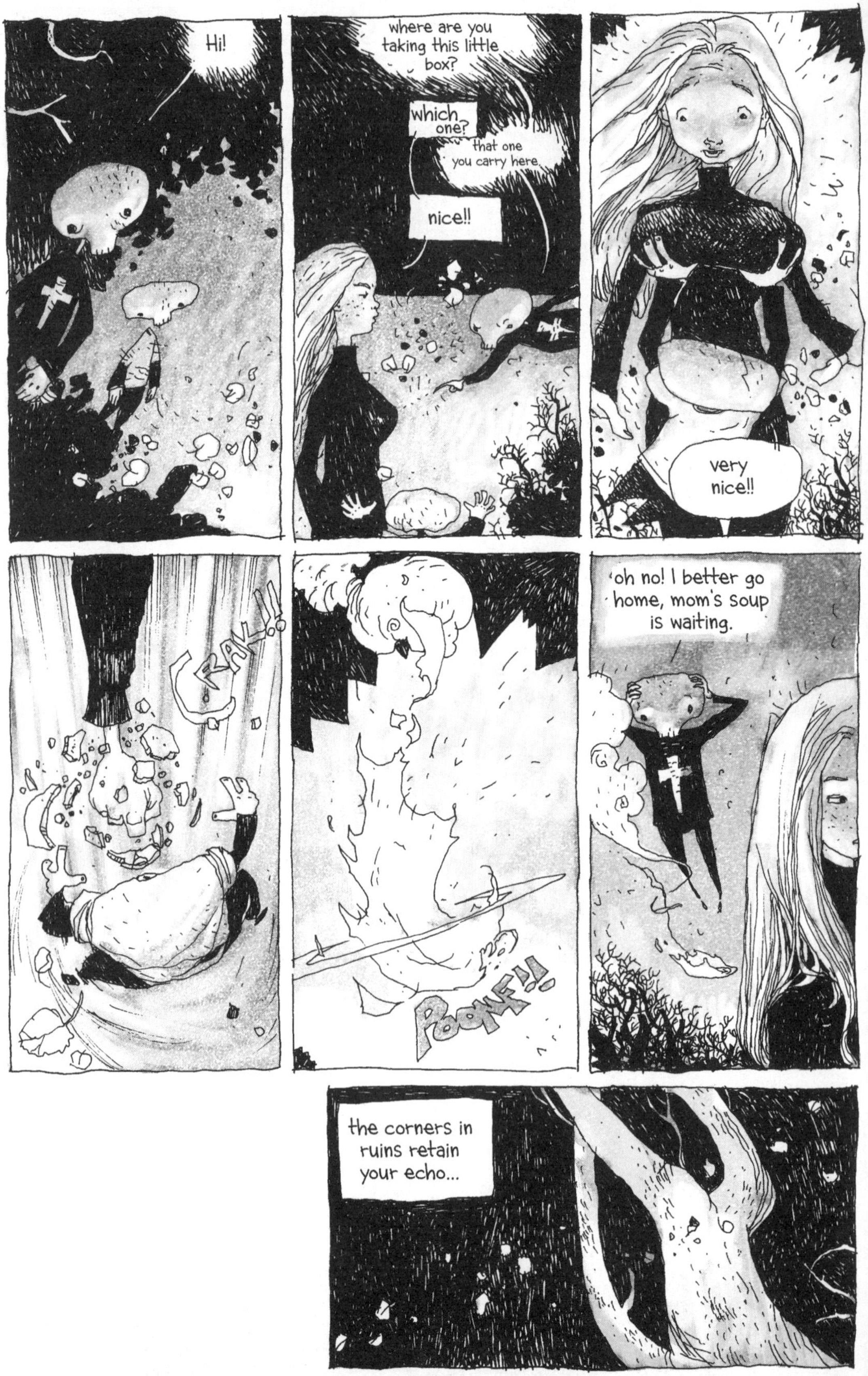
Hi!
where are you taking this little box?
which one?
that one you carry here.
nice!!
very nice!!
CRAK!!
POOF!!
oh no! I better go home, mom's soup is waiting.
the corners in ruins retain your echo...

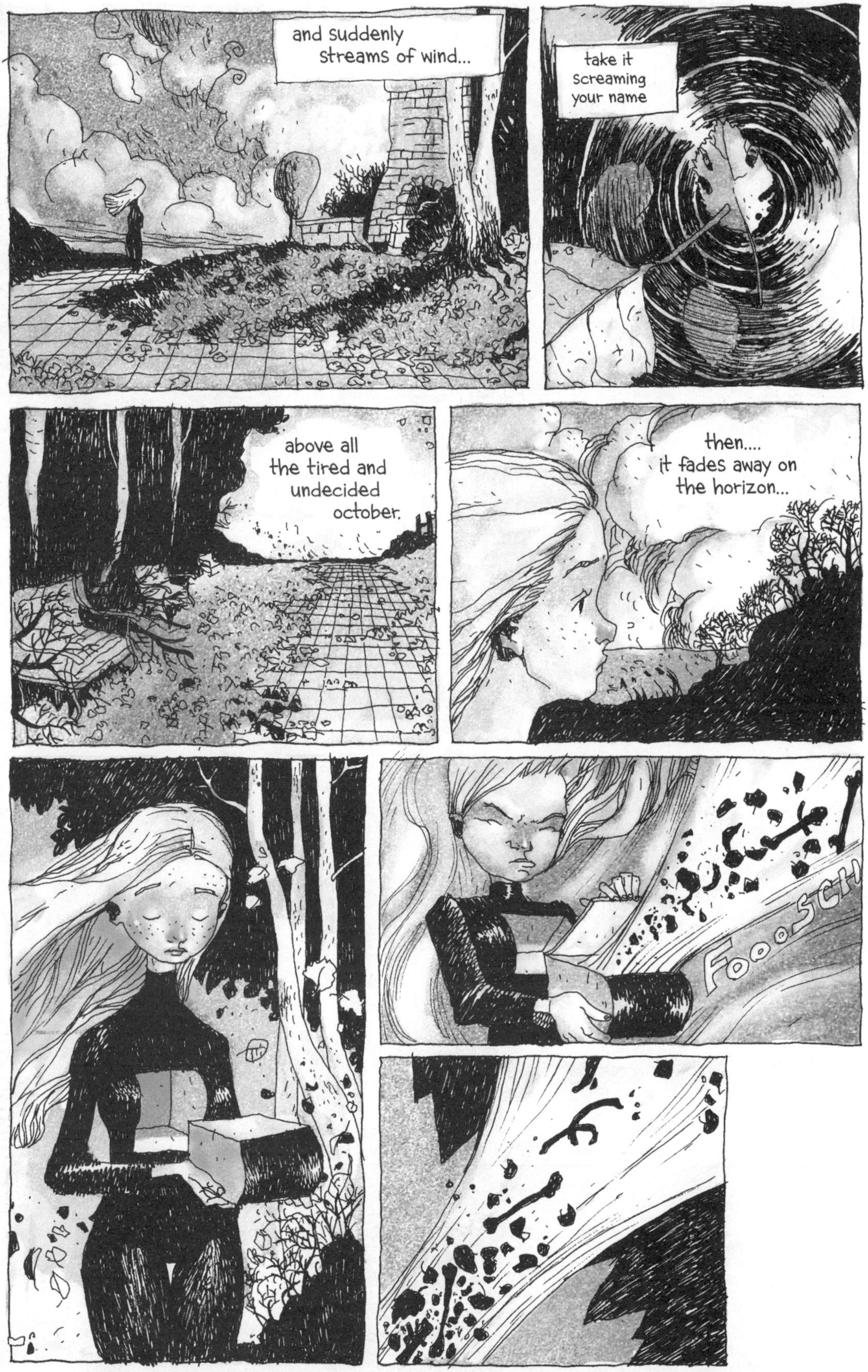
and suddenly
streams of wind...
take it
screaming
your name
above all
the tired and
undecided
october.
then....
it fades away on
the horizon...
FoooSCH

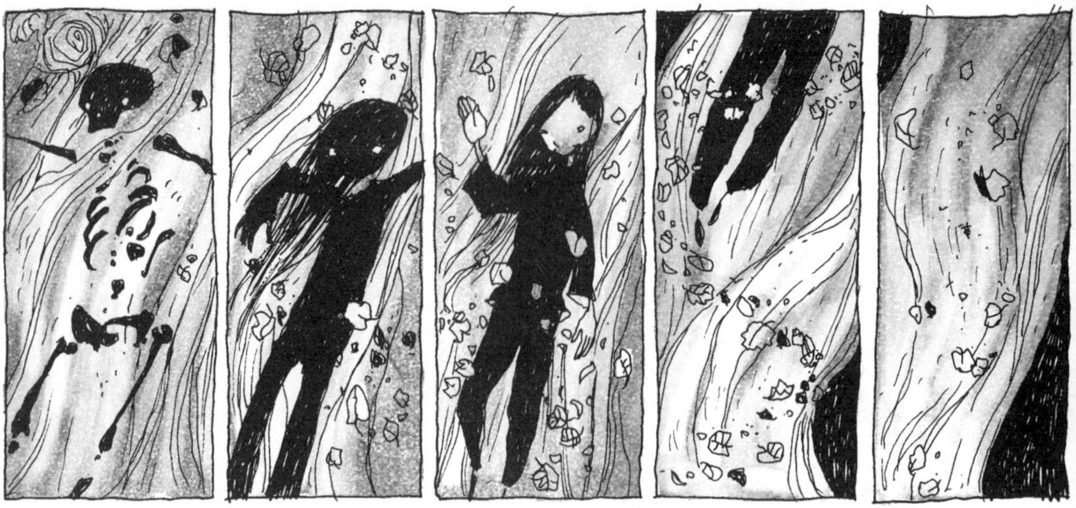

and I let go of the last breath
that was trapped inside the
ribs of my extinct memory.

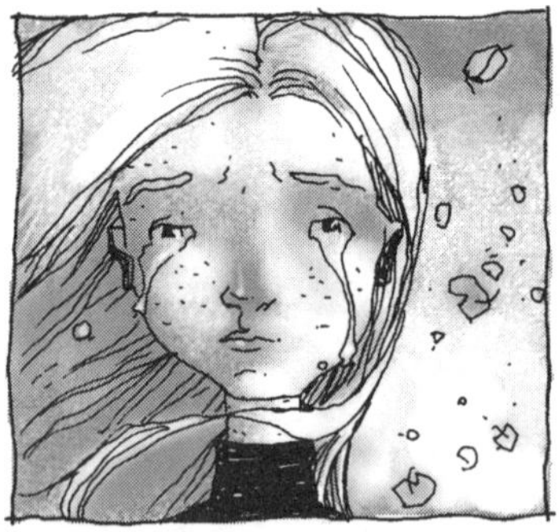

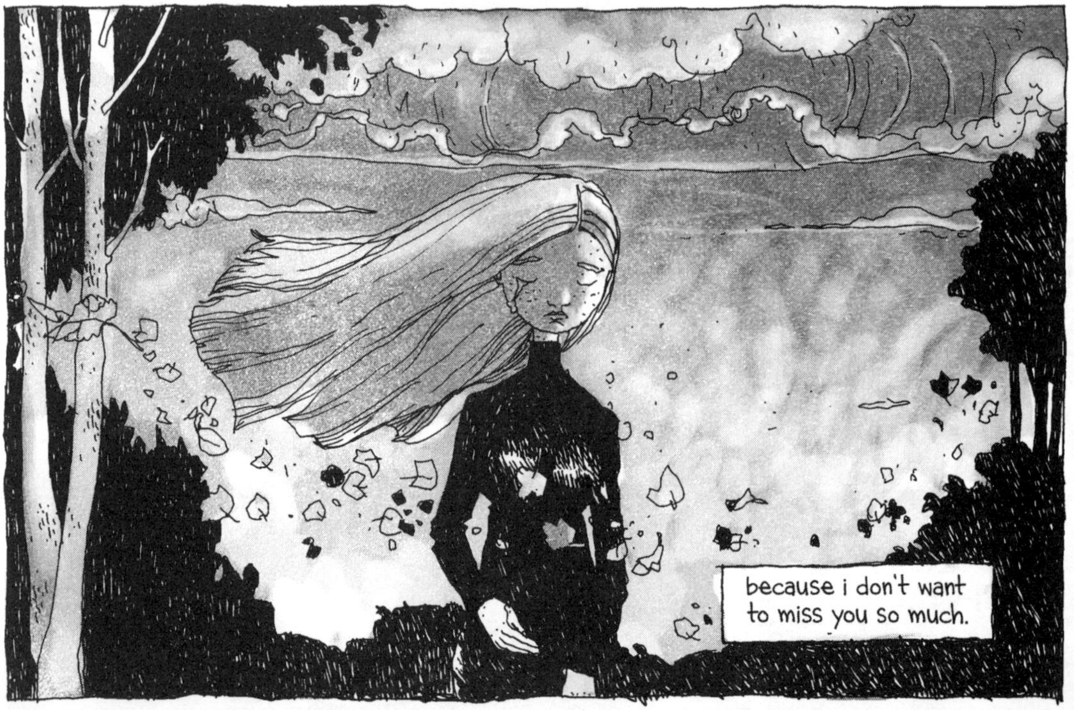
because i don't want
to miss you so much.

Tomer Hanuka

Tomer Hanuka is an illustrator and a cartoonist. He regularly works for publications such as The New Yorker, The New York Times, Time Magazine, New York Magazine and others. he is one half of Bipolar, an experimental comic co-created with his twin brother Asaf.

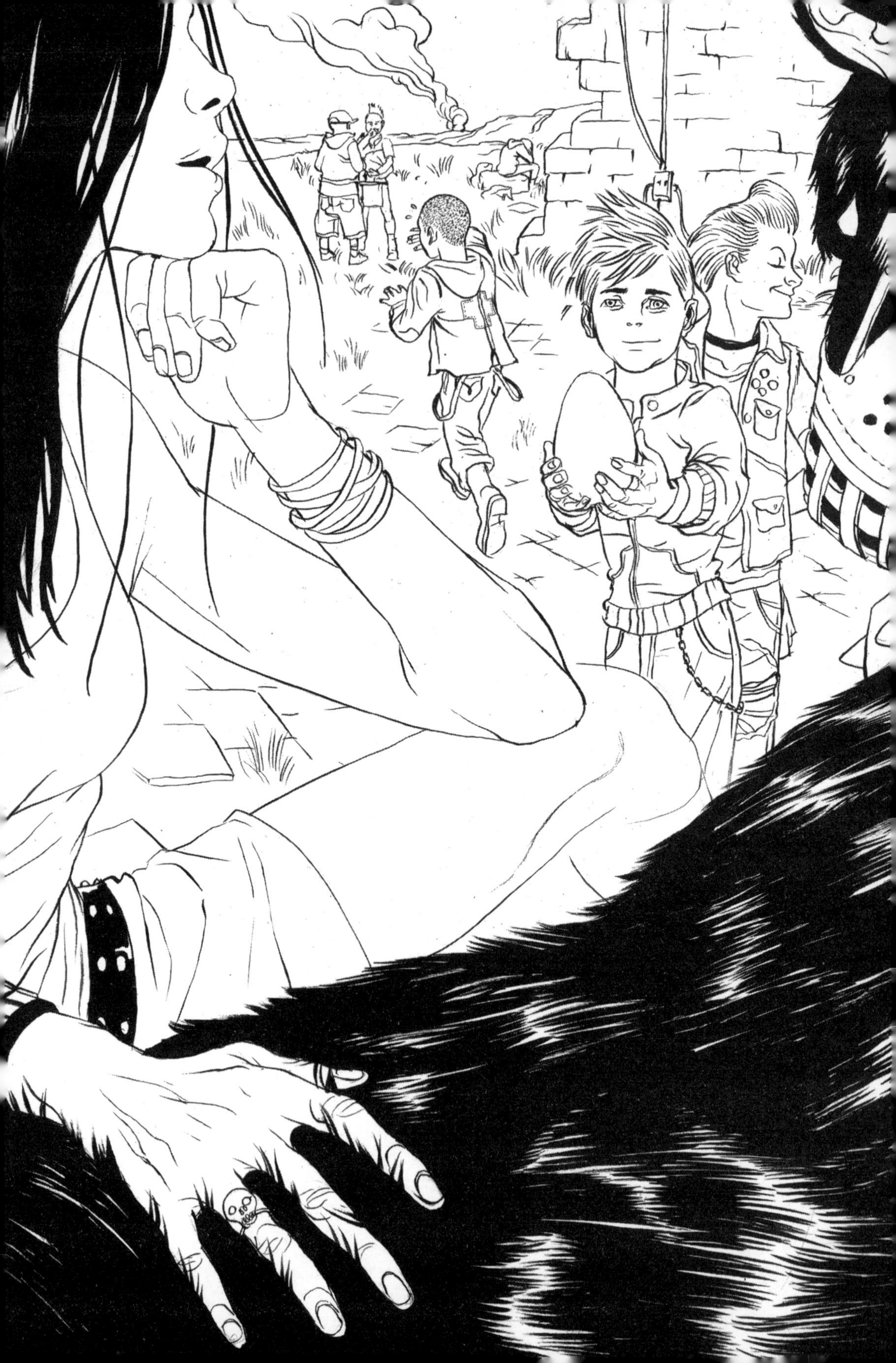

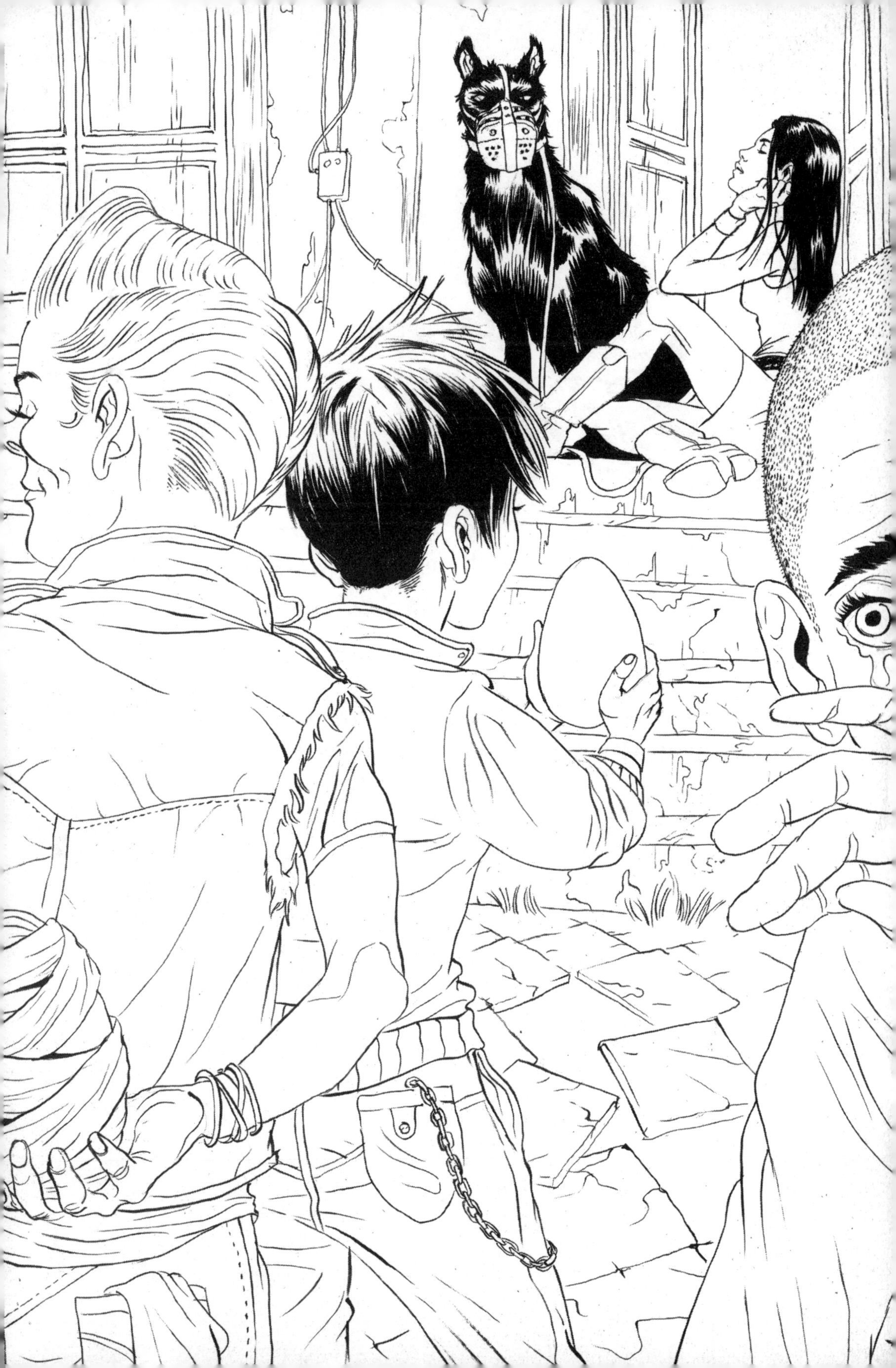

Jim Campbell

Jim Campbell has been very distracted lately playing rock and roll, working in advertising, doing some flash animation, and coloring other people's comics. Somehow he has found time to publish his first solo book Krachmacher Number One (in which the story of Cedrick and Mr. Pork Roast continue) with some help from the Xeric Foundation. The second issue will be available in a store near you soon from Alternative Comics.

IN CASE YOU MISSED IT, "FIREFOX 45" FROM MEATHAUS 7 HAS BEEN CONTINUED IN MY BOOK KRACHMACHER AVAILABLE AT COMIC SHOPS AND AT KRACHMACHER.ORG, NOW HERE'S...

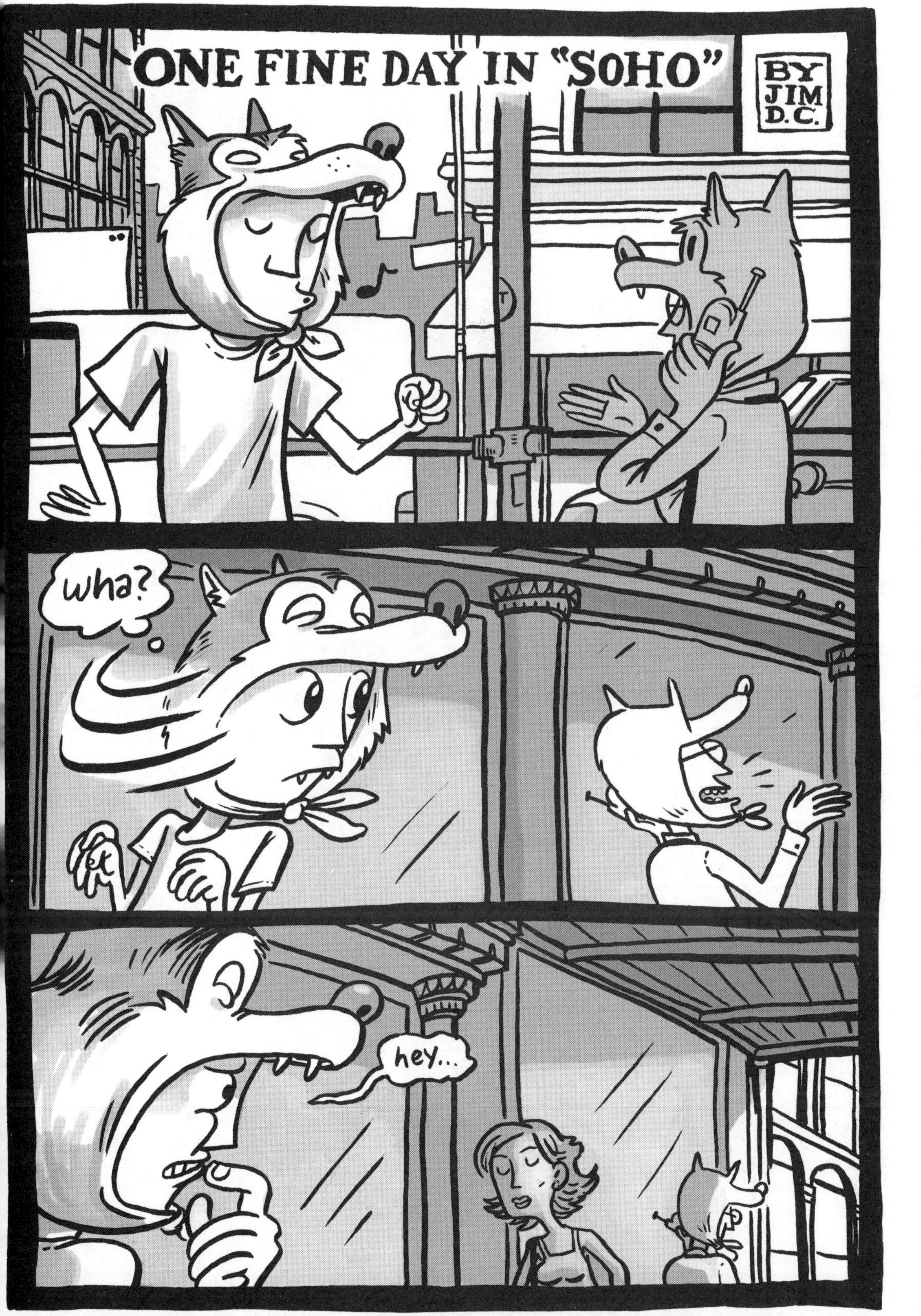

ONE FINE DAY IN "SOHO"
BY JIM D.C.
wha?
hey...

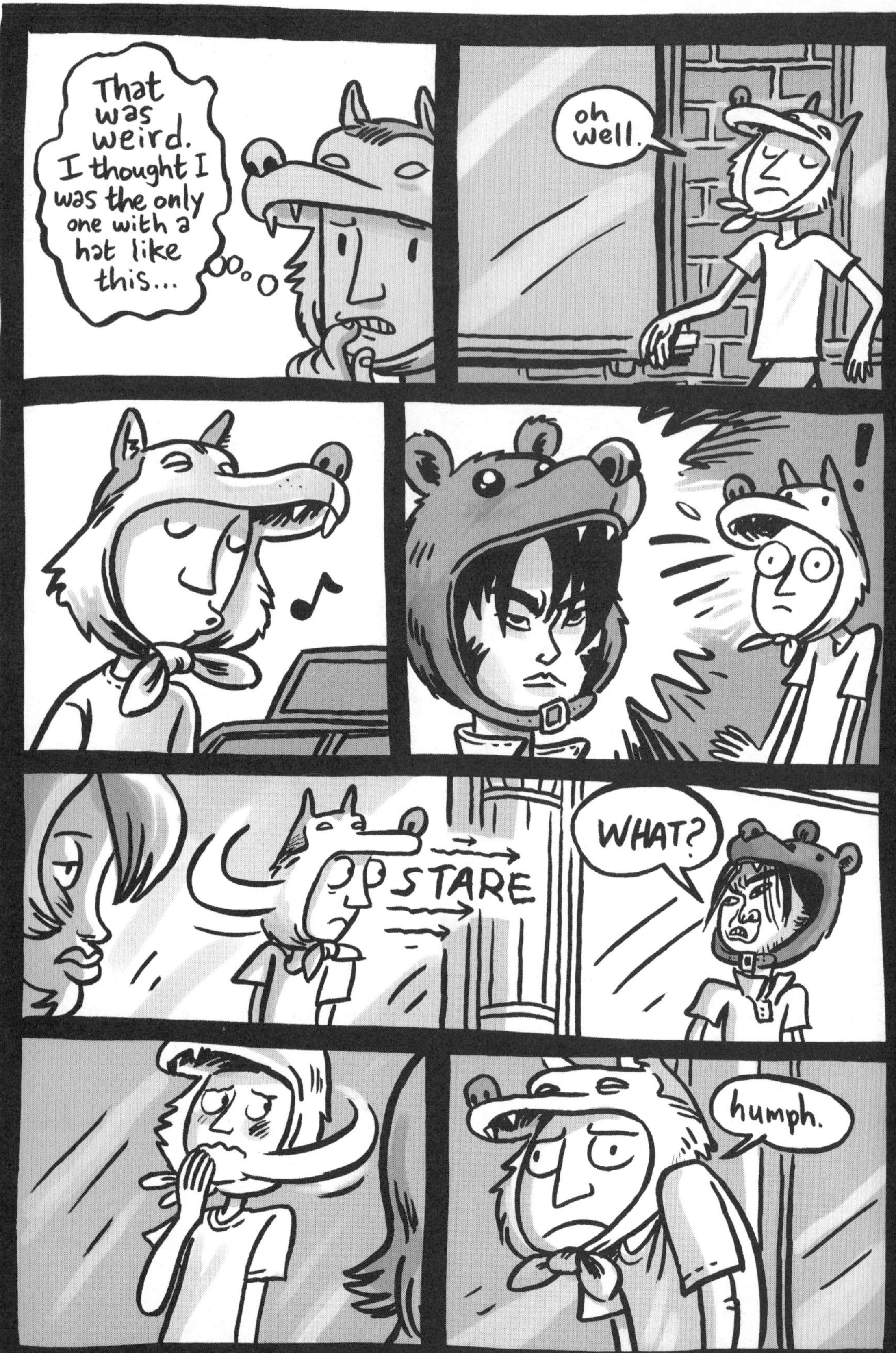
That was weird. I thought I was the only one with a hat like this...
oh well.
!
STARE
WHAT?
humph.

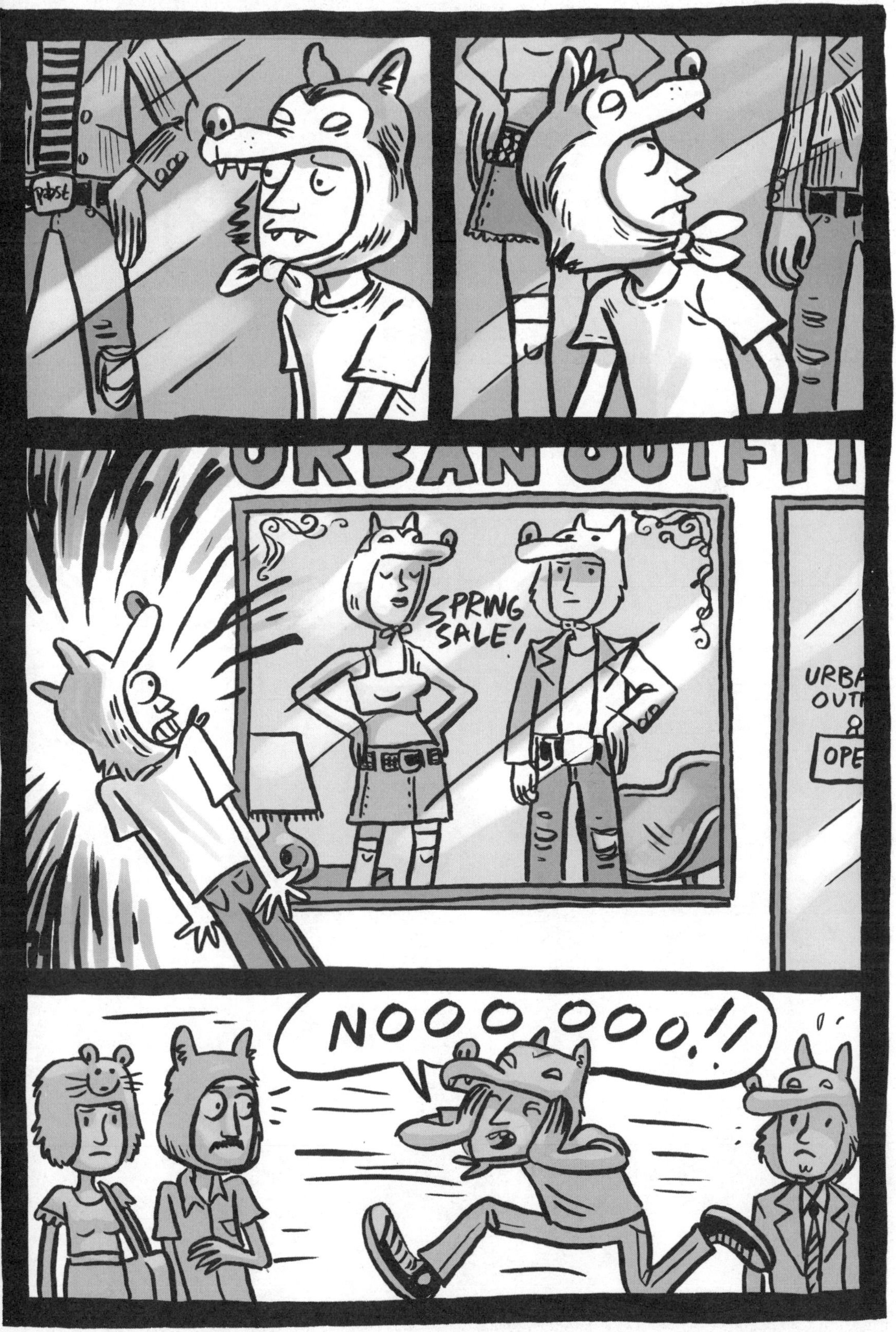
pabst
URBAN OUTFIT
SPRING SALE!
URBA OUTF
OPE
NOOO OOOO!!

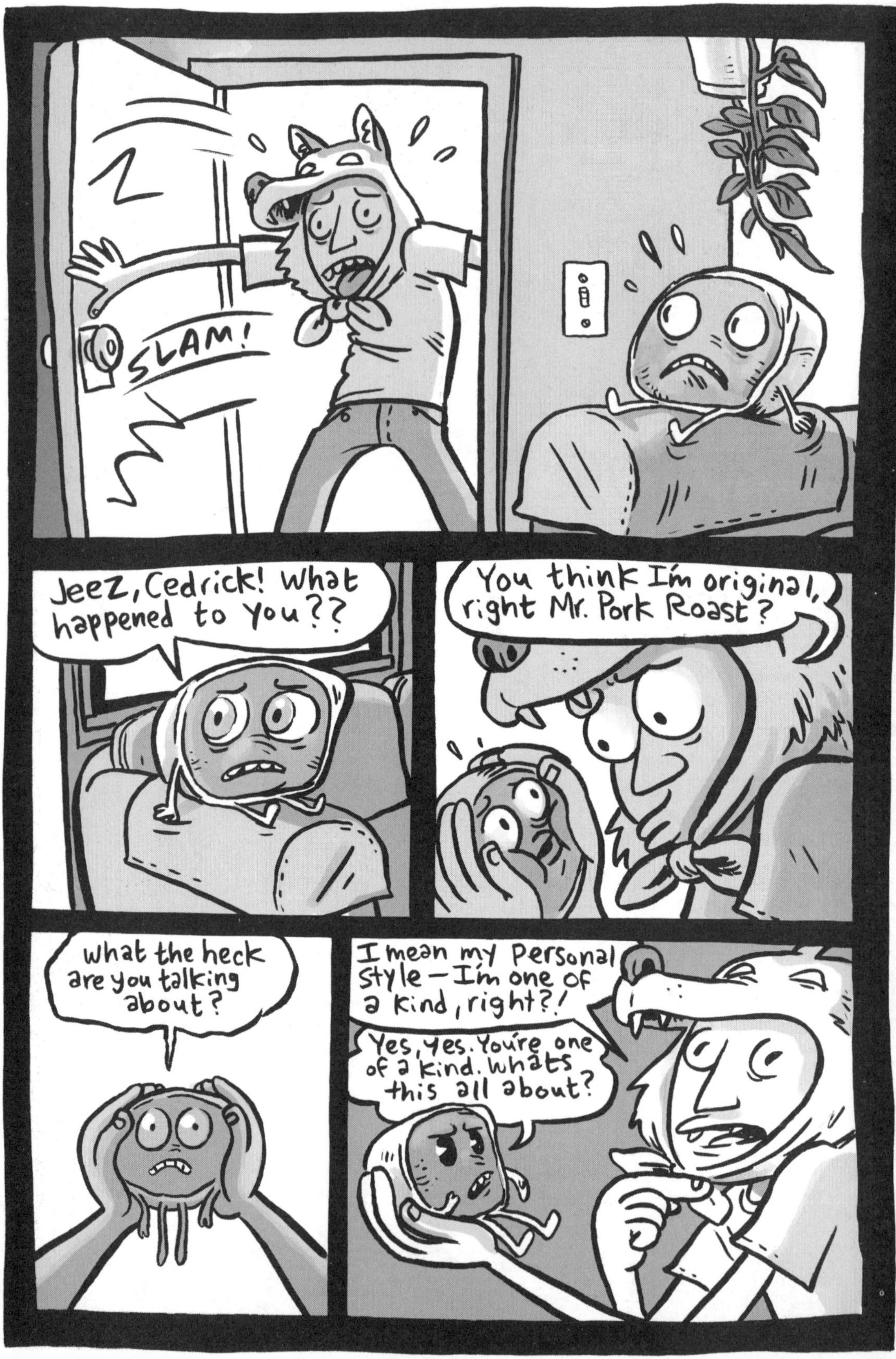
SLAM!
Jeez, Cedrick! What happened to You??
You think I'm original, right Mr. Pork Roast?
what the heck are you talking about?
I mean my Personal style—I'm one of a kind, right?!
Yes, Yes. You're one of a kind. What's this all about?

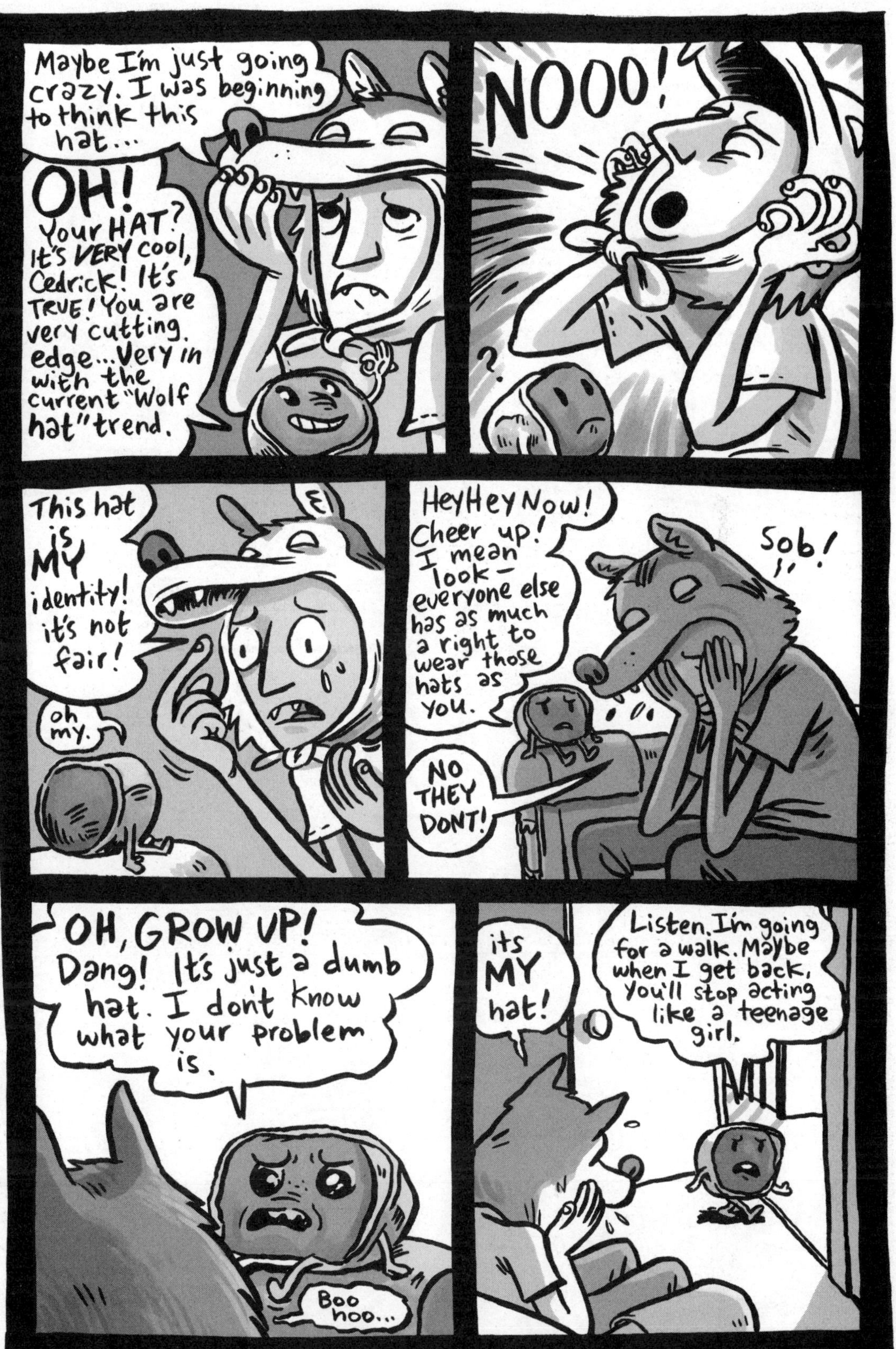
Maybe I'm just going crazy. I was beginning to think this hat...
OH! Your HAT? It's VERY cool, Cedrick! It's TRUE! You are very cutting edge... Very in with the current "Wolf hat" trend.
NOOO!
?
This hat is MY identity! it's not fair!
oh my.
HeyHey Now! Cheer up! I mean look— everyone else has as much a right to wear those hats as you.
Sob!
NO THEY DONT!
OH, GROW UP! Dang! It's just a dumb hat. I don't know what your problem is.
Boo hoo...
its MY hat!
Listen. I'm going for a walk. Maybe when I get back, you'll stop acting like a teenage girl.

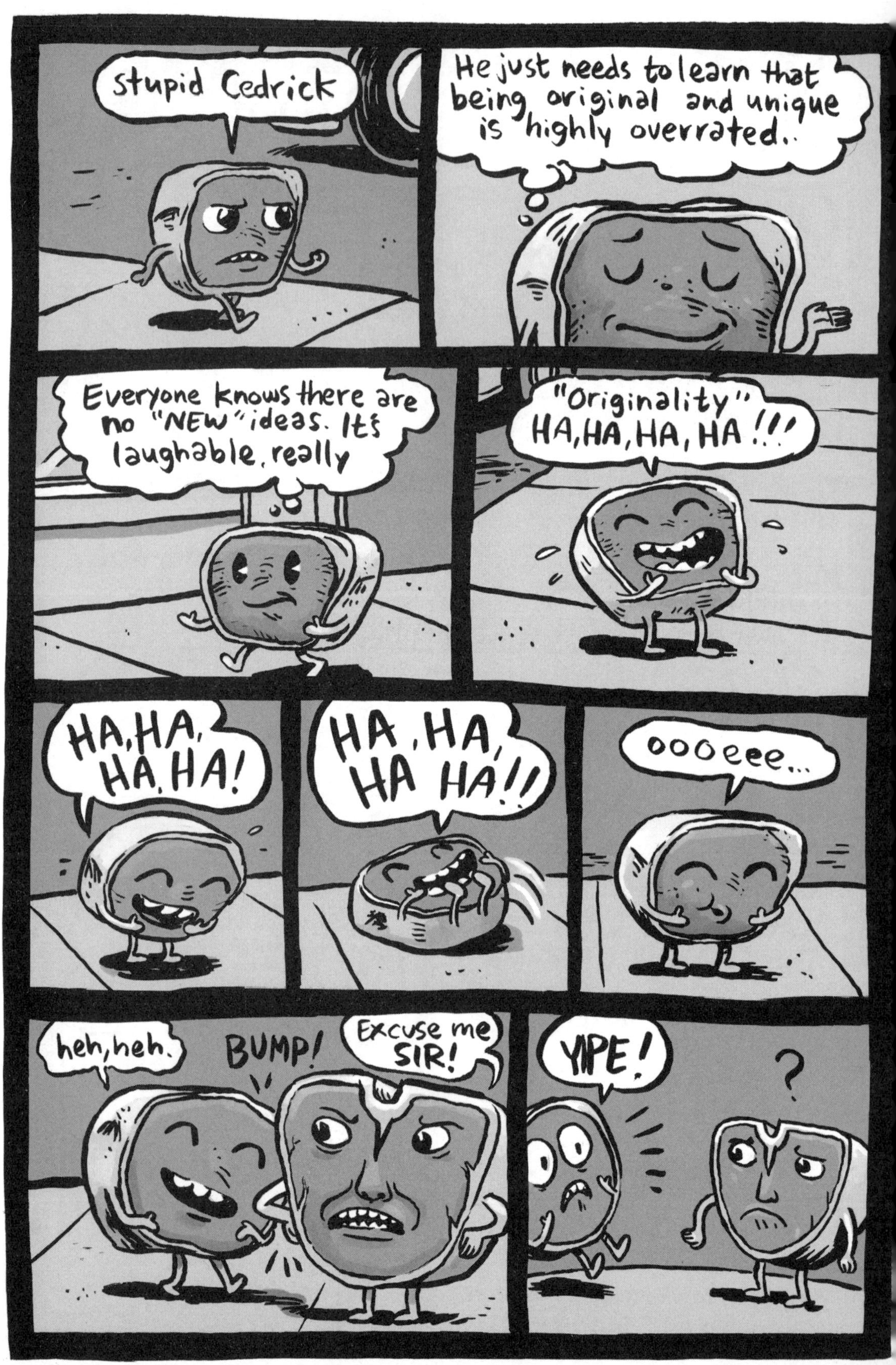
stupid Cedrick
He just needs to learn that being original and unique is highly overrated..
Everyone knows there are no "NEW" ideas. It's laughable, really
"Originality" HA, HA, HA, HA!!!
HA, HA, HA, HA!
HA, HA, HA HA!!
oooeee...
heh, heh.
BUMP!
Excuse me SIR!
YIPE!
?

Vincent Stall

King MIni International aka Vincent Stall recently accepted his horrid lot in life with the passion and vigor of a true optimist. Coffee and donuts served 24/7 at www.kingmini.com

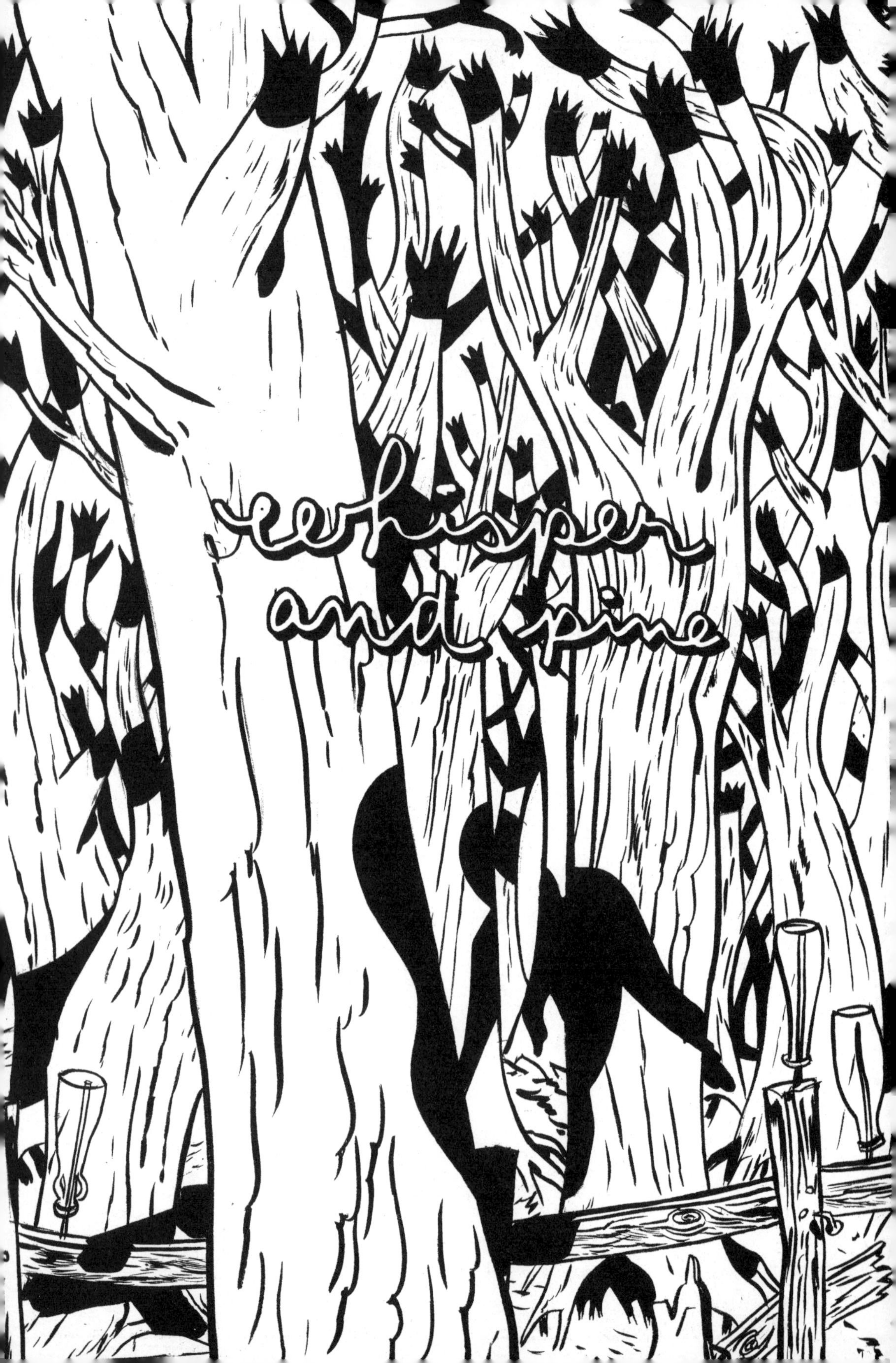
whisper
and pine

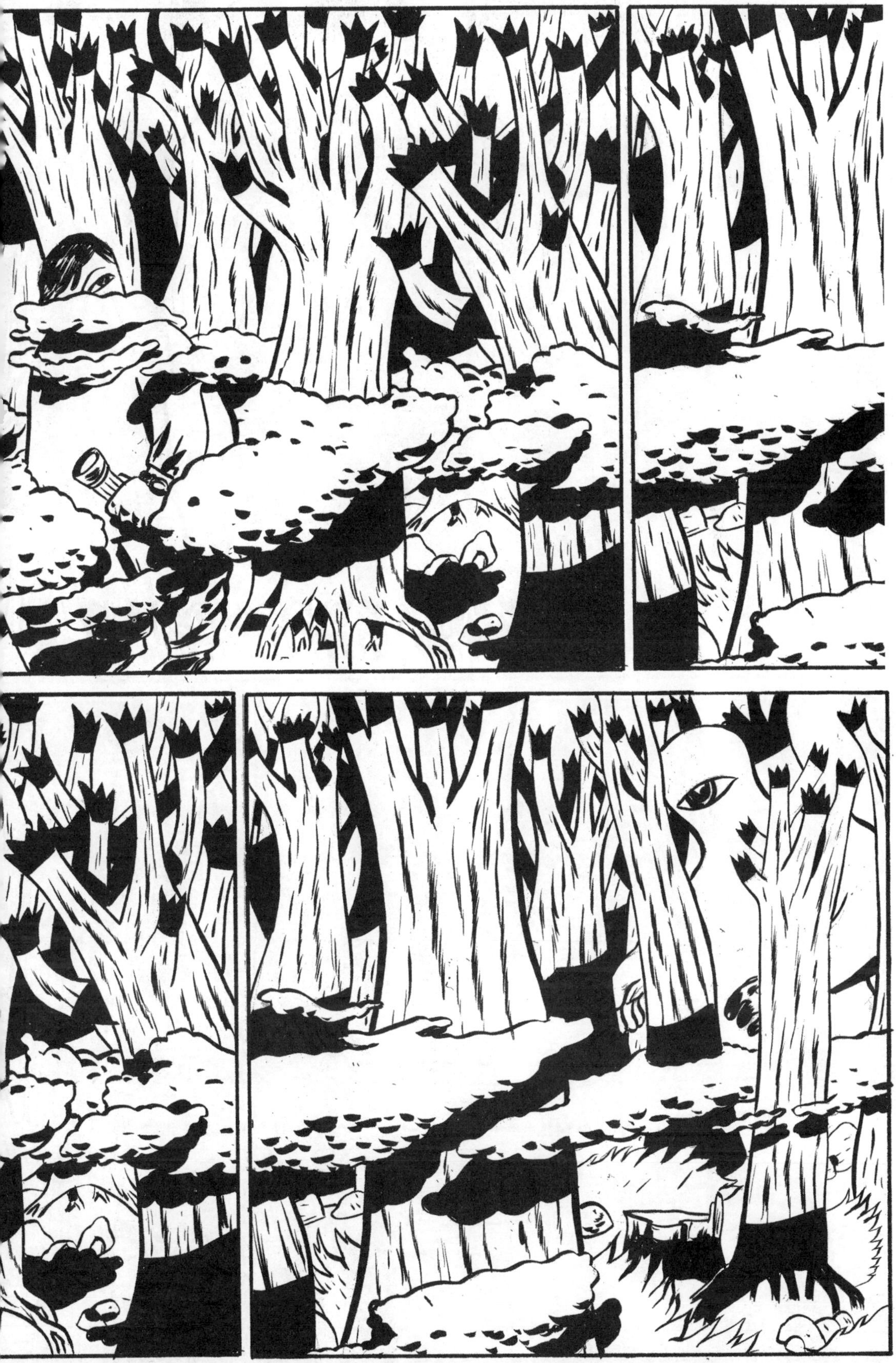

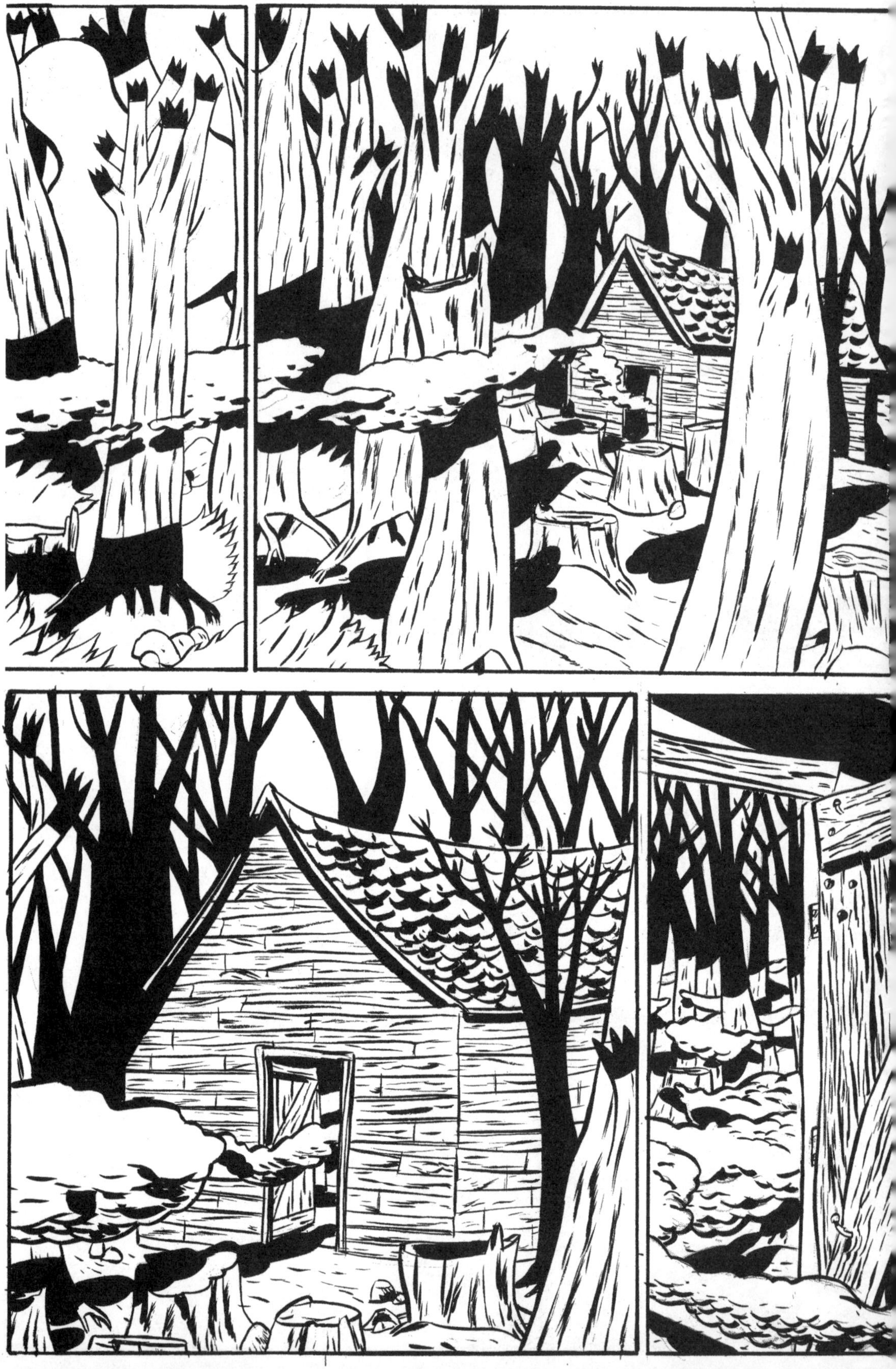

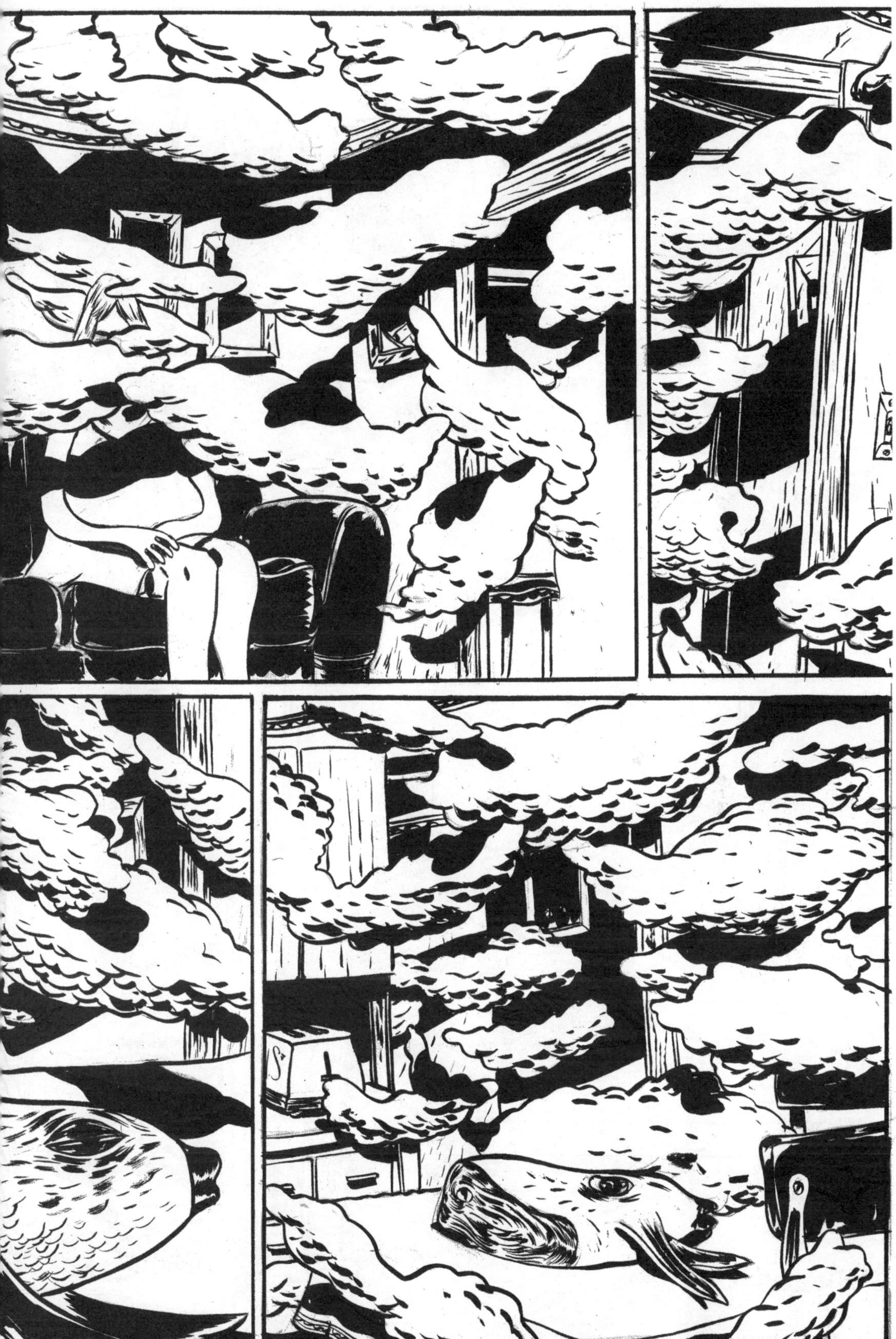

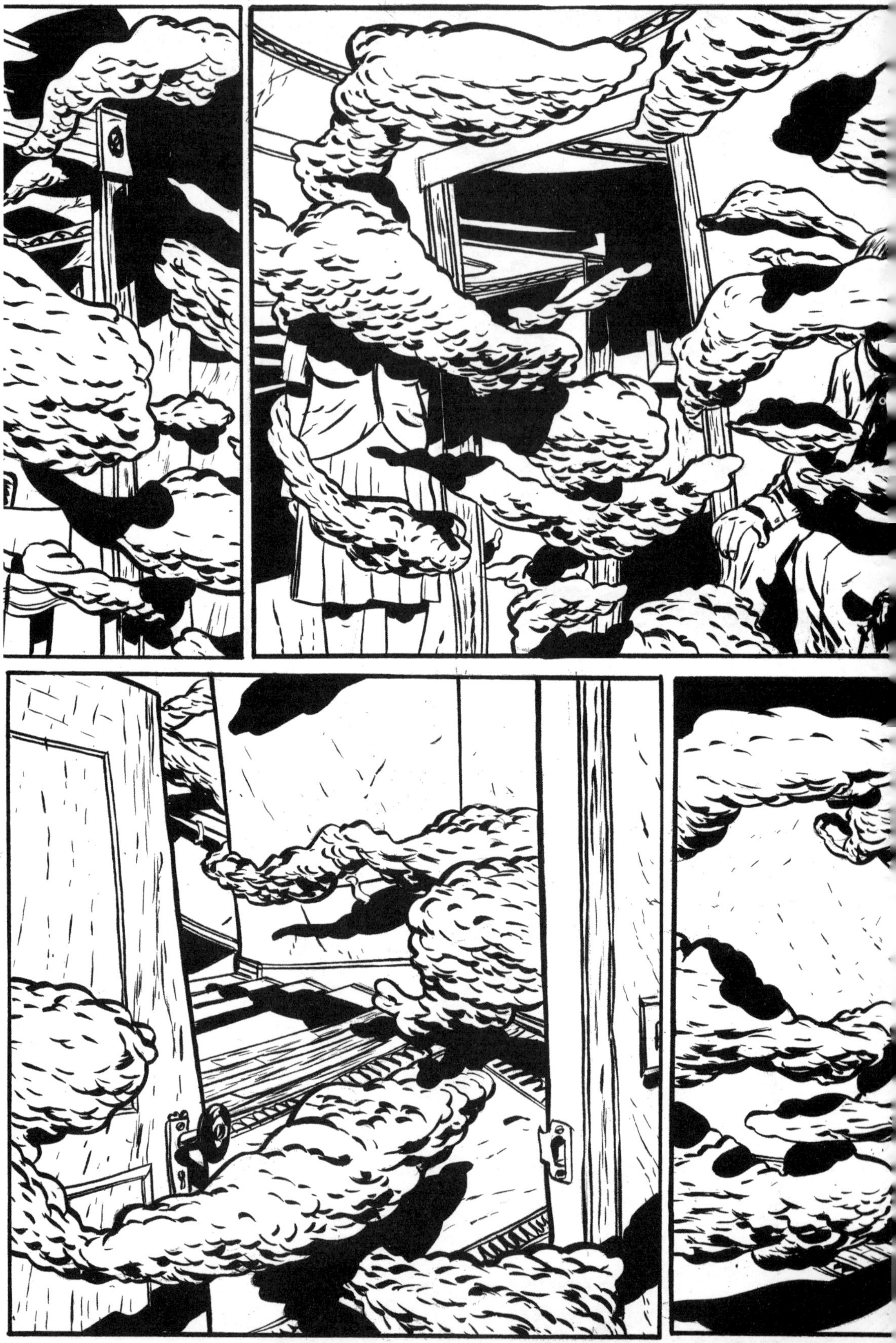

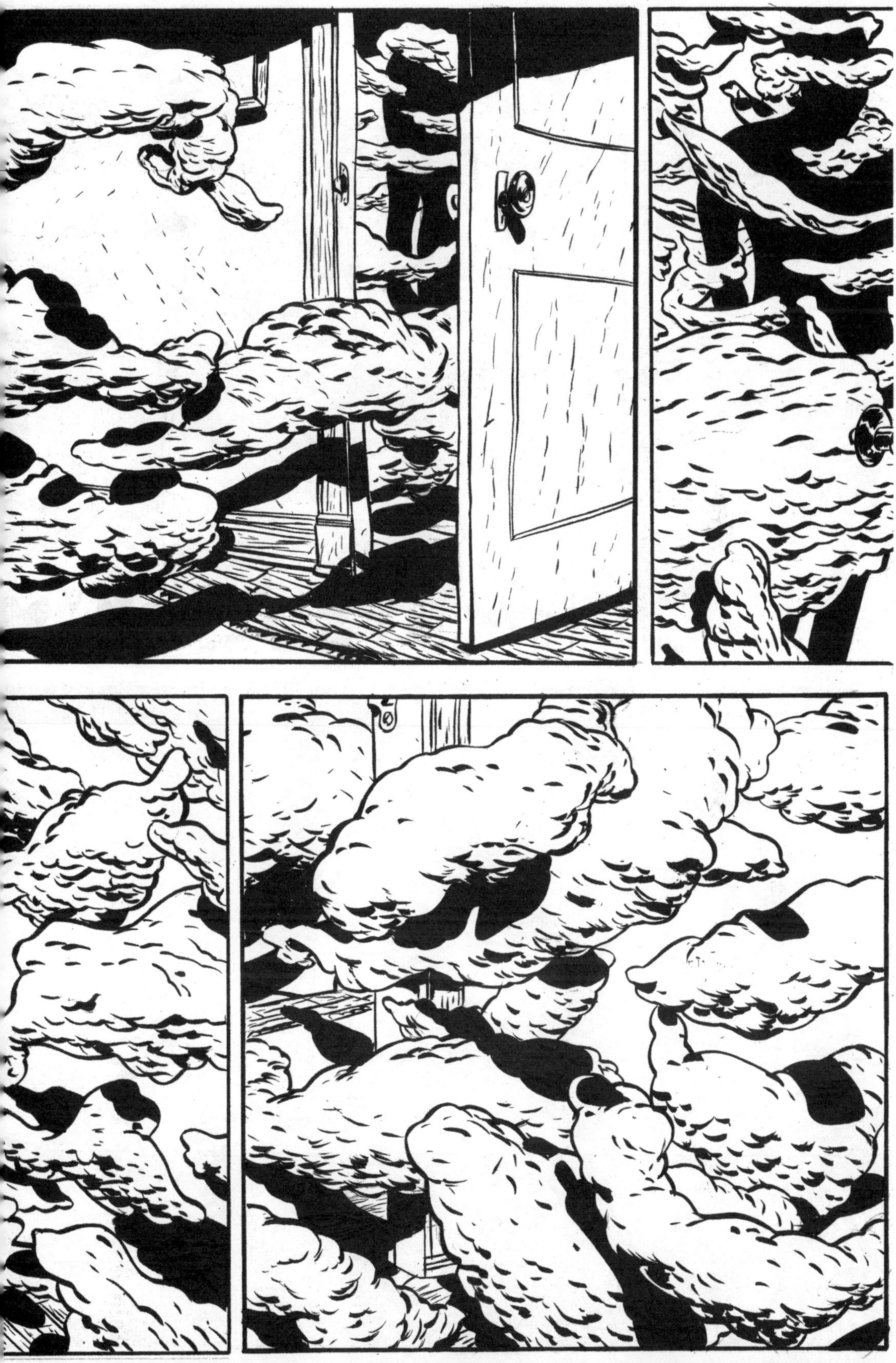

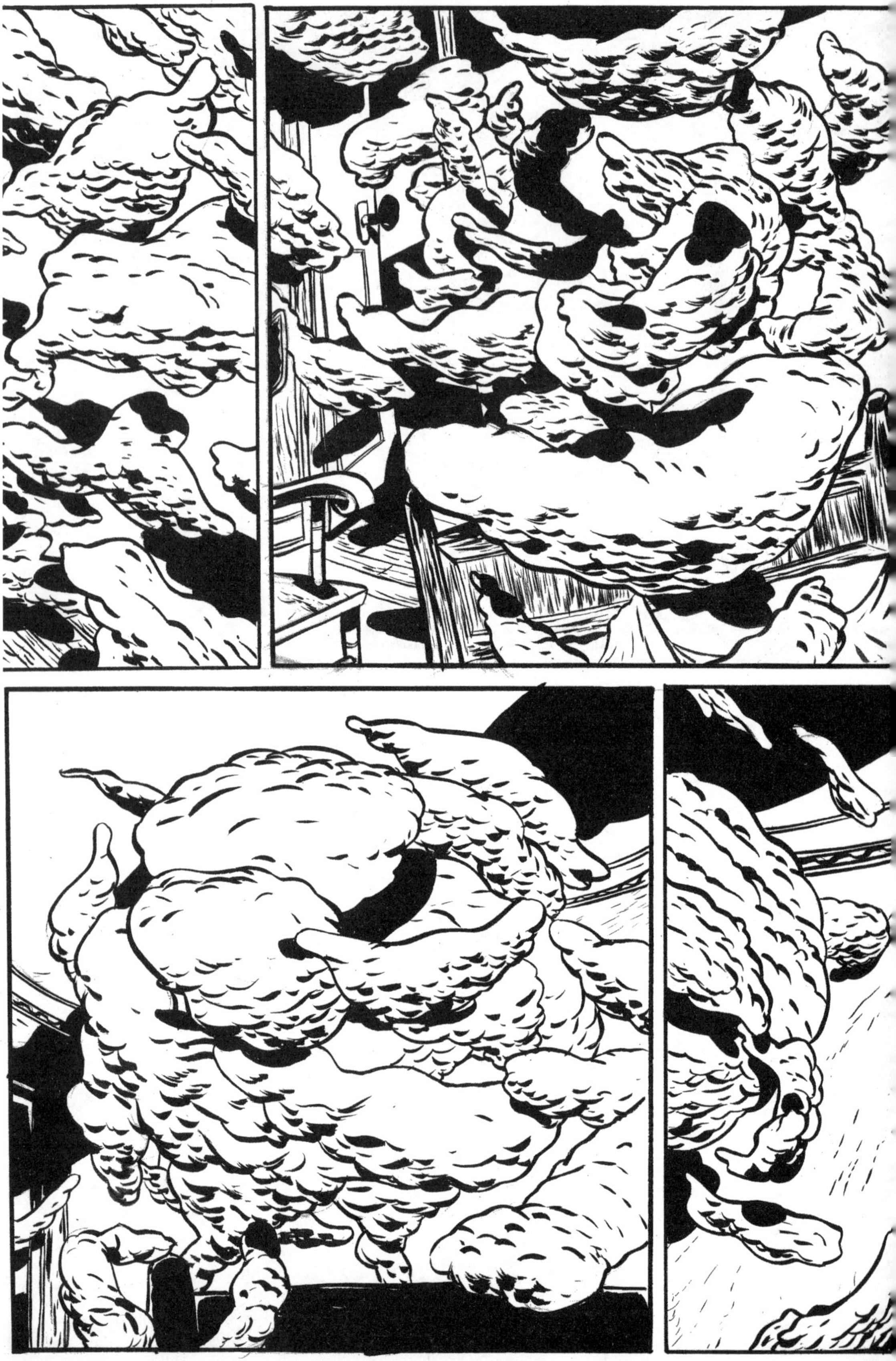

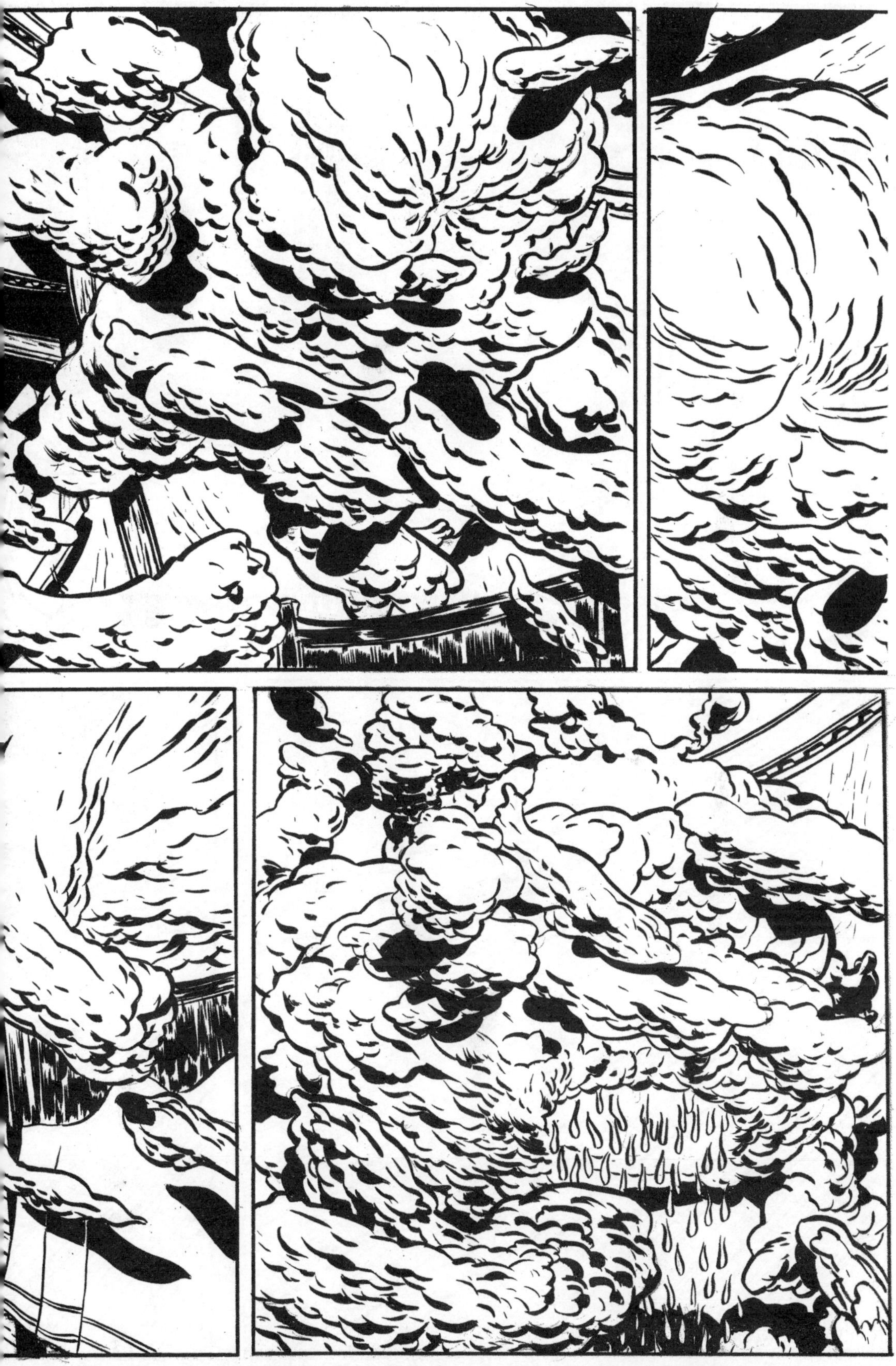

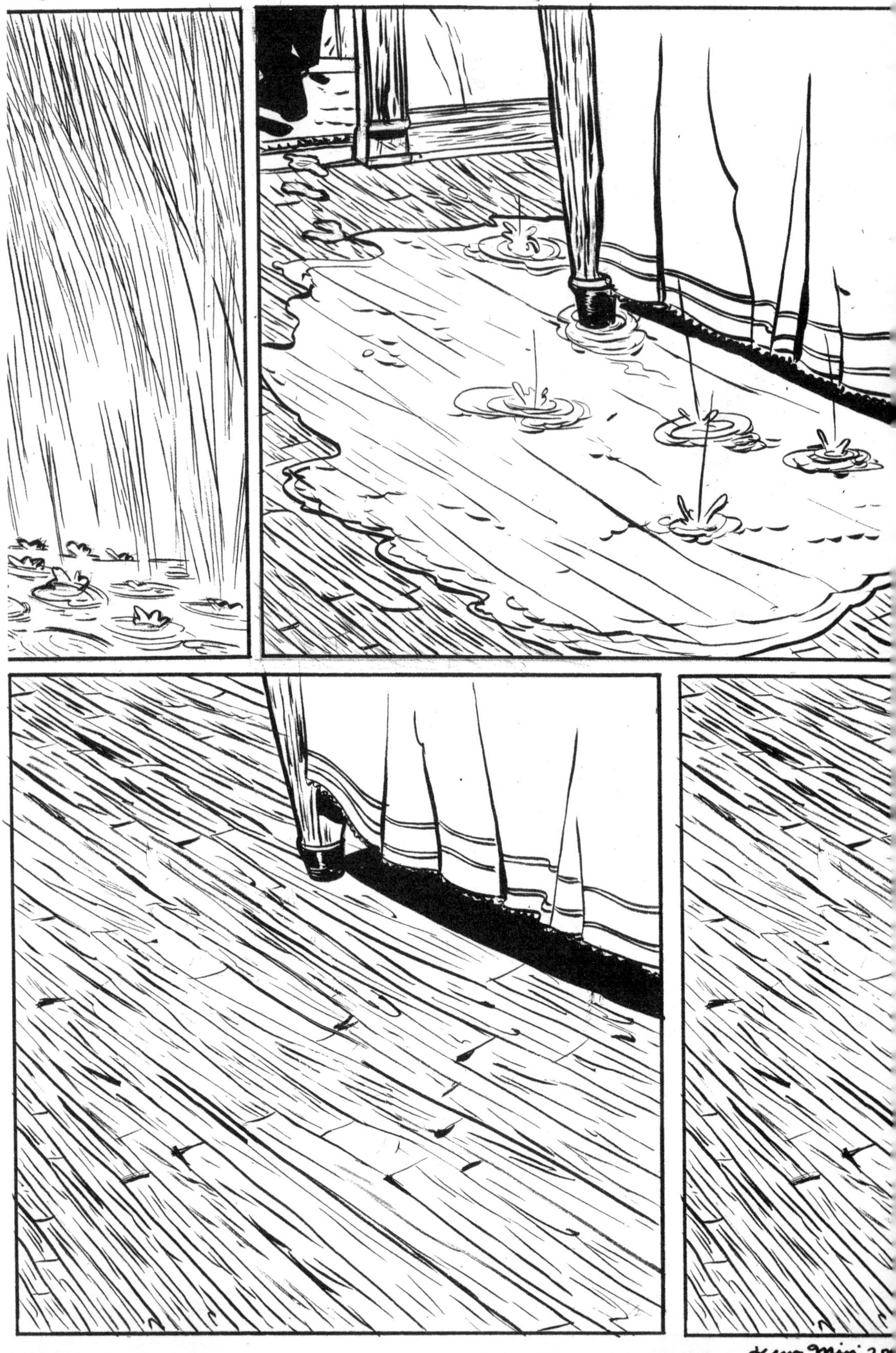

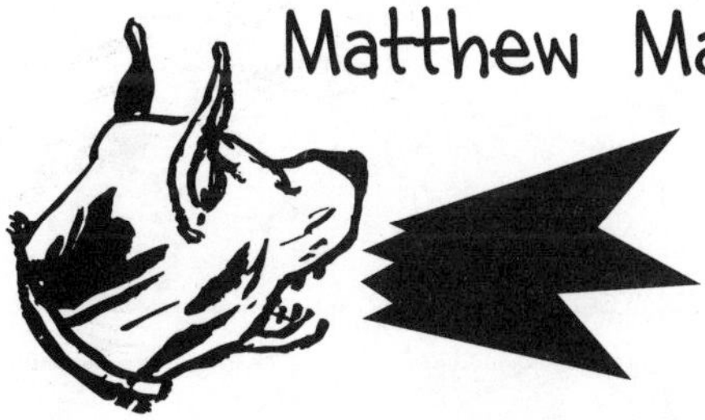

Matthew Manning and Robert Donnelly

An Ohio expatriate living on borrowed time and fast women, Matthew K. Manning has written for the likes of DC and Marvel Comics as well as for literary magazines like Rosebud and Writers' Journal. For a virtual tour of his life of missed opportunities, visit www.matthewkmanning.com. For more on the characters Winston Golden and Wendy St. Claire, visit your local thrift mart and purchase the Meathaus special entitled For Best Results: Do Not Open. And then go treat yourself to a frosted malt. It's on the house.

Robert Donnelly
I have accomplished very little in my life so far. I have a succinct feeling however, that this year will be a winner. See more of my work at Robdraw.com

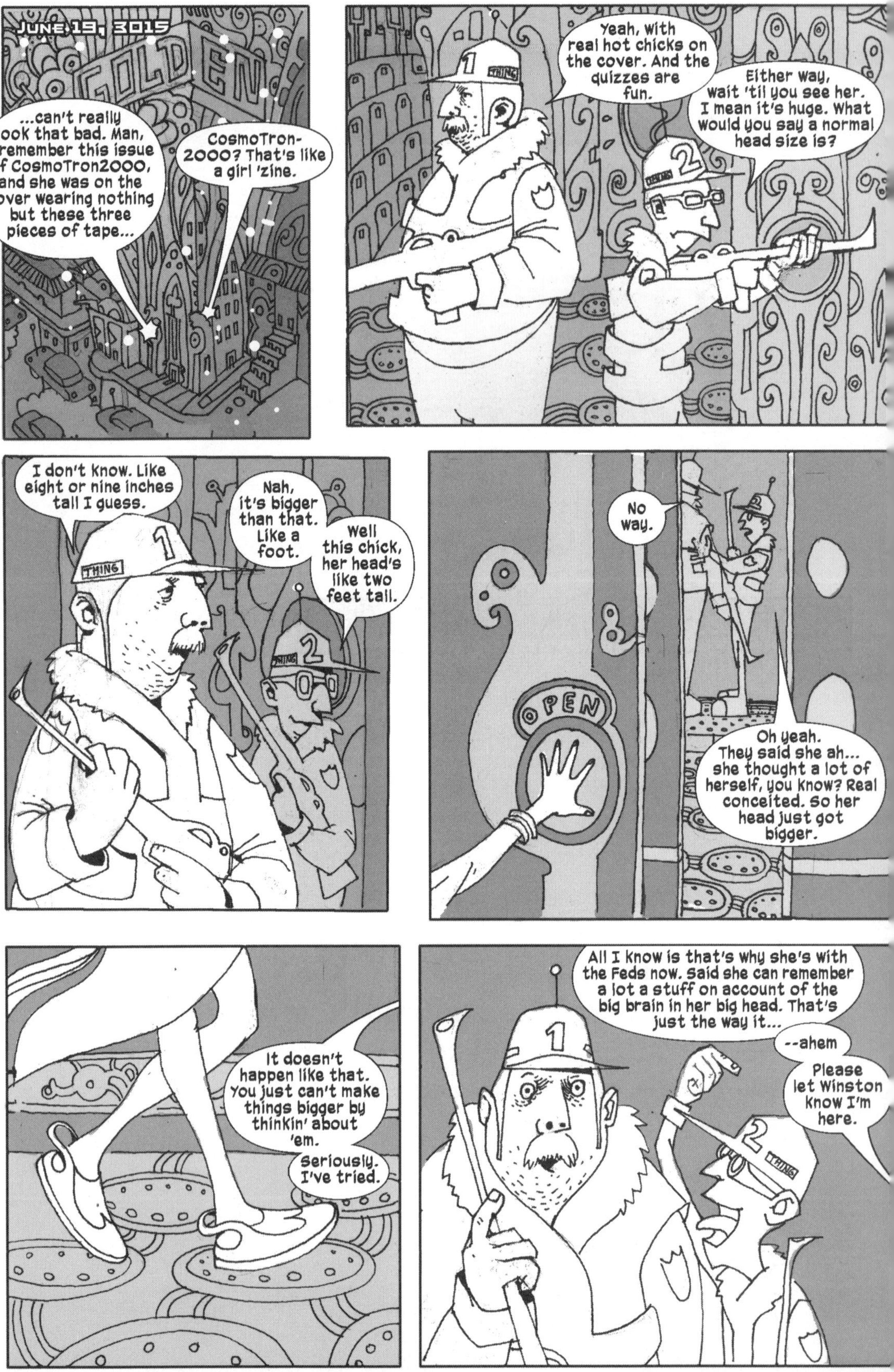
JUNE 19, 3015
GOLDEN
...can't really look that bad. Man, I remember this issue of CosmoTron2000, and she was on the cover wearing nothing but these three pieces of tape...
CosmoTron-2000? That's like a girl 'zine.
Yeah, with real hot chicks on the cover. And the quizzes are fun.
Either way, wait 'til you see her. I mean it's huge. What would you say a normal head size is?
I don't know. Like eight or nine inches tall I guess.
Nah, it's bigger than that. Like a foot.
Well this chick, her head's like two feet tall.
No way.
OPEN
Oh yeah. They said she ah... she thought a lot of herself, you know? Real conceited. So her head just got bigger.
It doesn't happen like that. You just can't make things bigger by thinkin' about 'em.
Seriously. I've tried.
All I know is that's why she's with the Feds now. Said she can remember a lot a stuff on account of the big brain in her big head. That's just the way it...
--ahem
Please let Winston know I'm here.

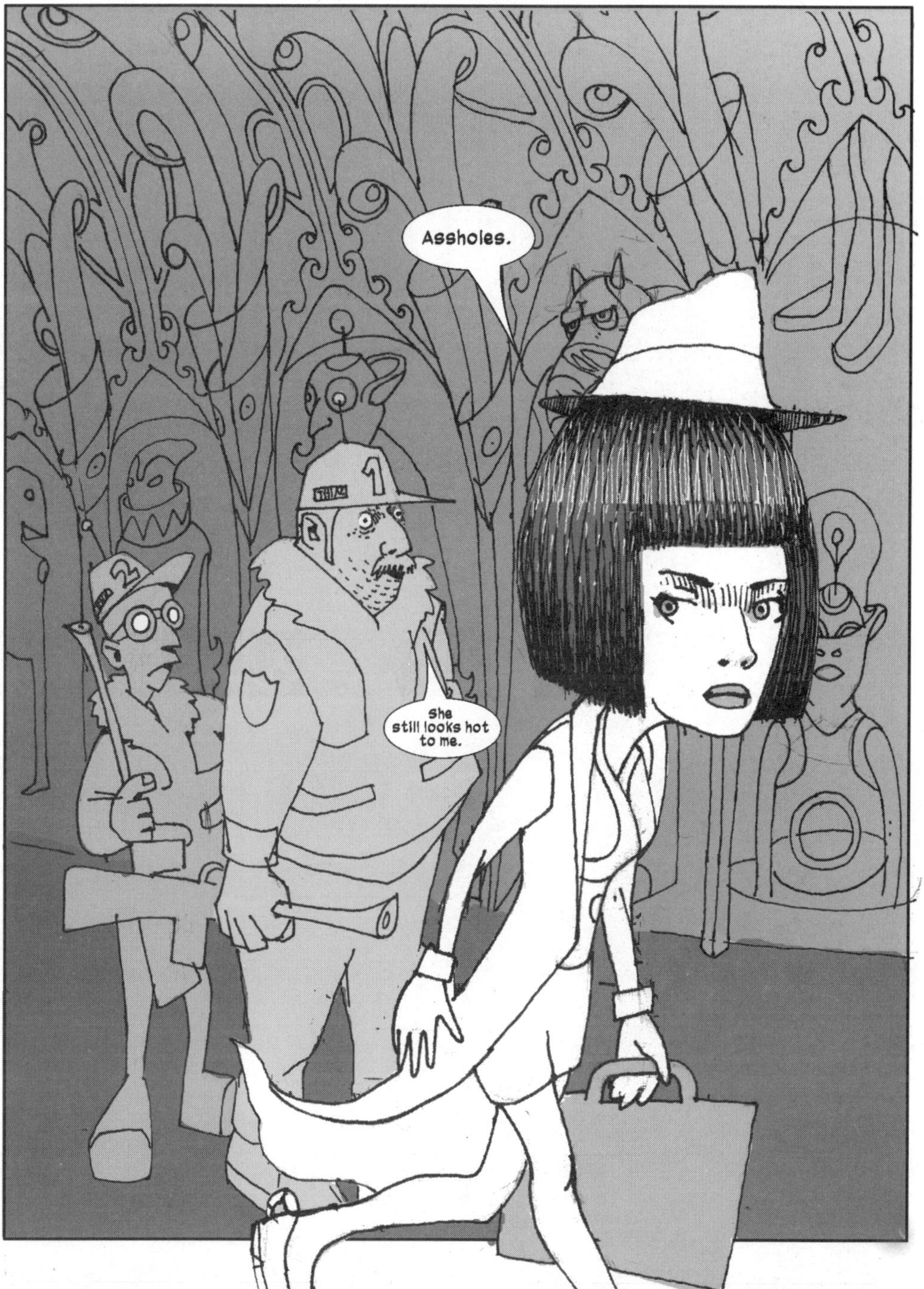

Assholes.
She still looks hot to me.

false advertising

WRITTEN BY MATTHEW K. MANNING
ILLUSTRATED BY ROBERT DONNELLY
LETTERED BY CORY PETIT

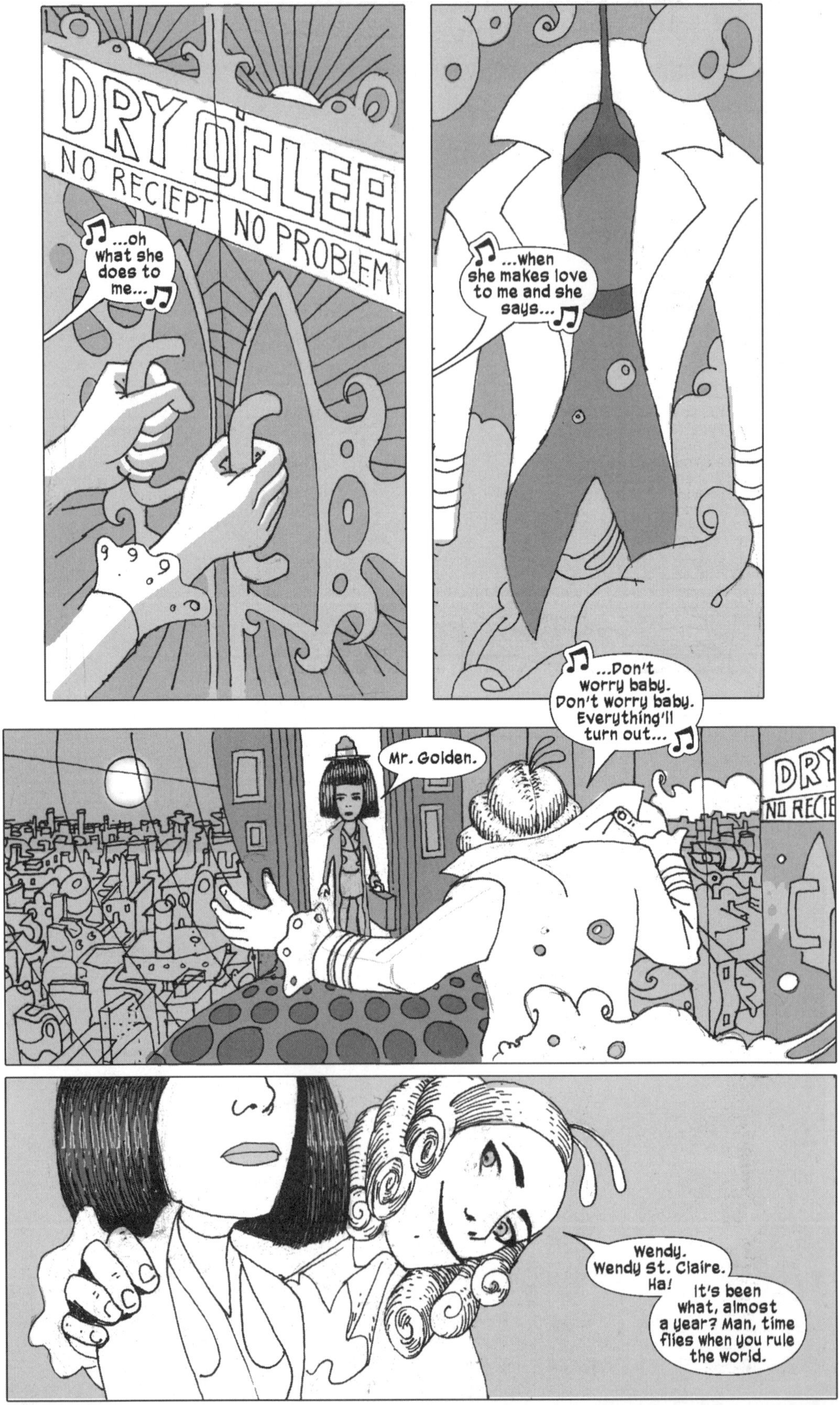
DRY O'CLEA
NO RECIEPT NO PROBLEM
...oh what she does to me...
...when she makes love to me and she says...
...Don't worry baby. Don't worry baby. Everything'll turn out...
Mr. Golden.
DRY
NO RECIE
Wendy. Wendy St. Claire. Ha!
It's been what, almost a year? Man, time flies when you rule the world.

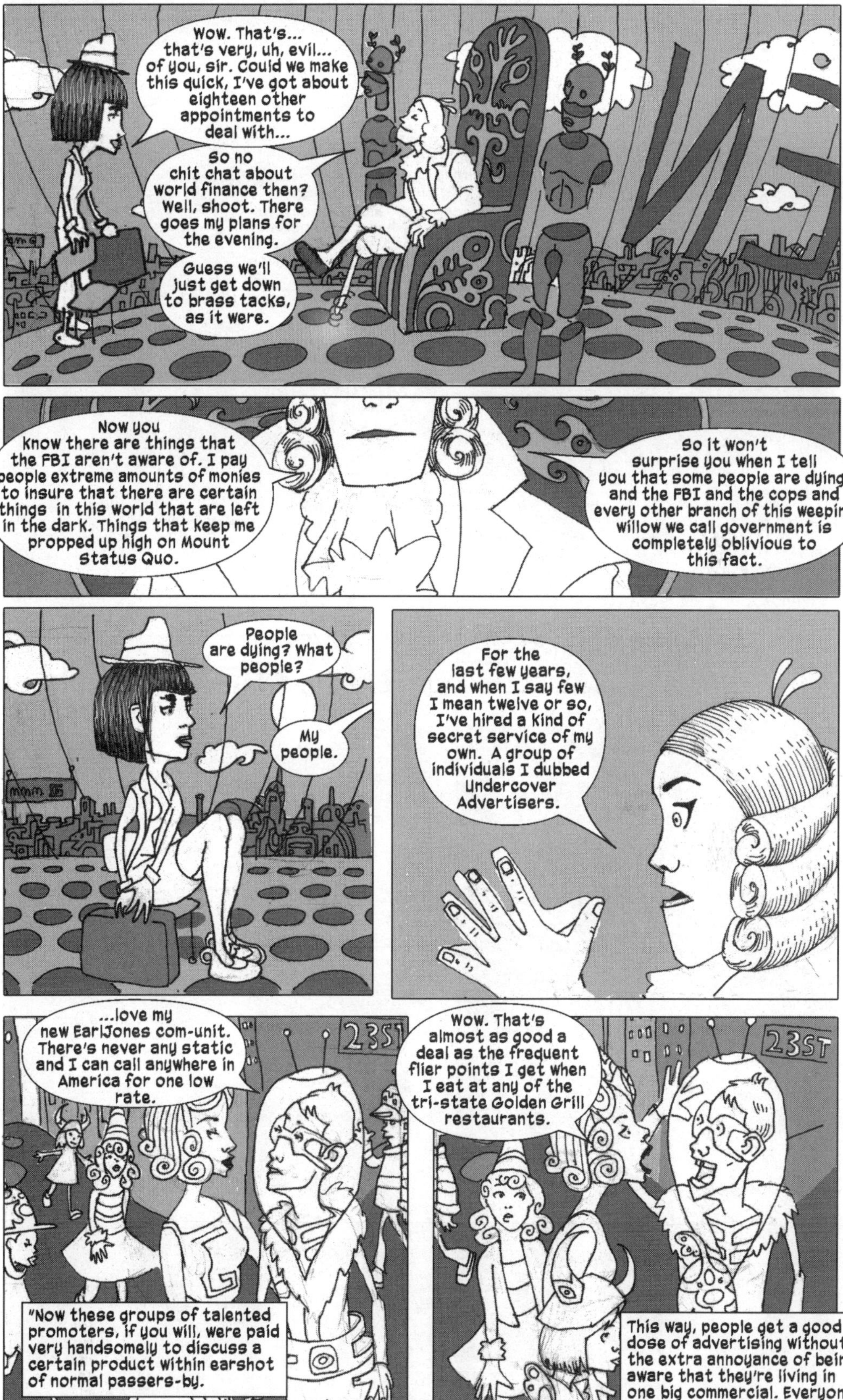
Wow. That's... that's very, uh, evil... of you, sir. Could we make this quick, I've got about eighteen other appointments to deal with...
So no chit chat about world finance then? Well, shoot. There goes my plans for the evening.
Guess we'll just get down to brass tacks, as it were.
Now you know there are things that the FBI aren't aware of. I pay people extreme amounts of monies to insure that there are certain things in this world that are left in the dark. Things that keep me propped up high on Mount Status Quo.
So it won't surprise you when I tell you that some people are dying, and the FBI and the cops and every other branch of this weeping willow we call government is completely oblivious to this fact.
People are dying? What people?
My people.
For the last few years, and when I say few I mean twelve or so, I've hired a kind of secret service of my own. A group of individuals I dubbed Undercover Advertisers.
...love my new EarlJones com-unit. There's never any static and I can call anywhere in America for one low rate.
"Now these groups of talented promoters, if you will, were paid very handsomely to discuss a certain product within earshot of normal passers-by.
23ST
Wow. That's almost as good a deal as the frequent flier points I get when I eat at any of the tri-state Golden Grill restaurants.
23ST
This way, people get a good dose of advertising without the extra annoyance of being aware that they're living in one big commercial. Everyone wins.
Especially me.

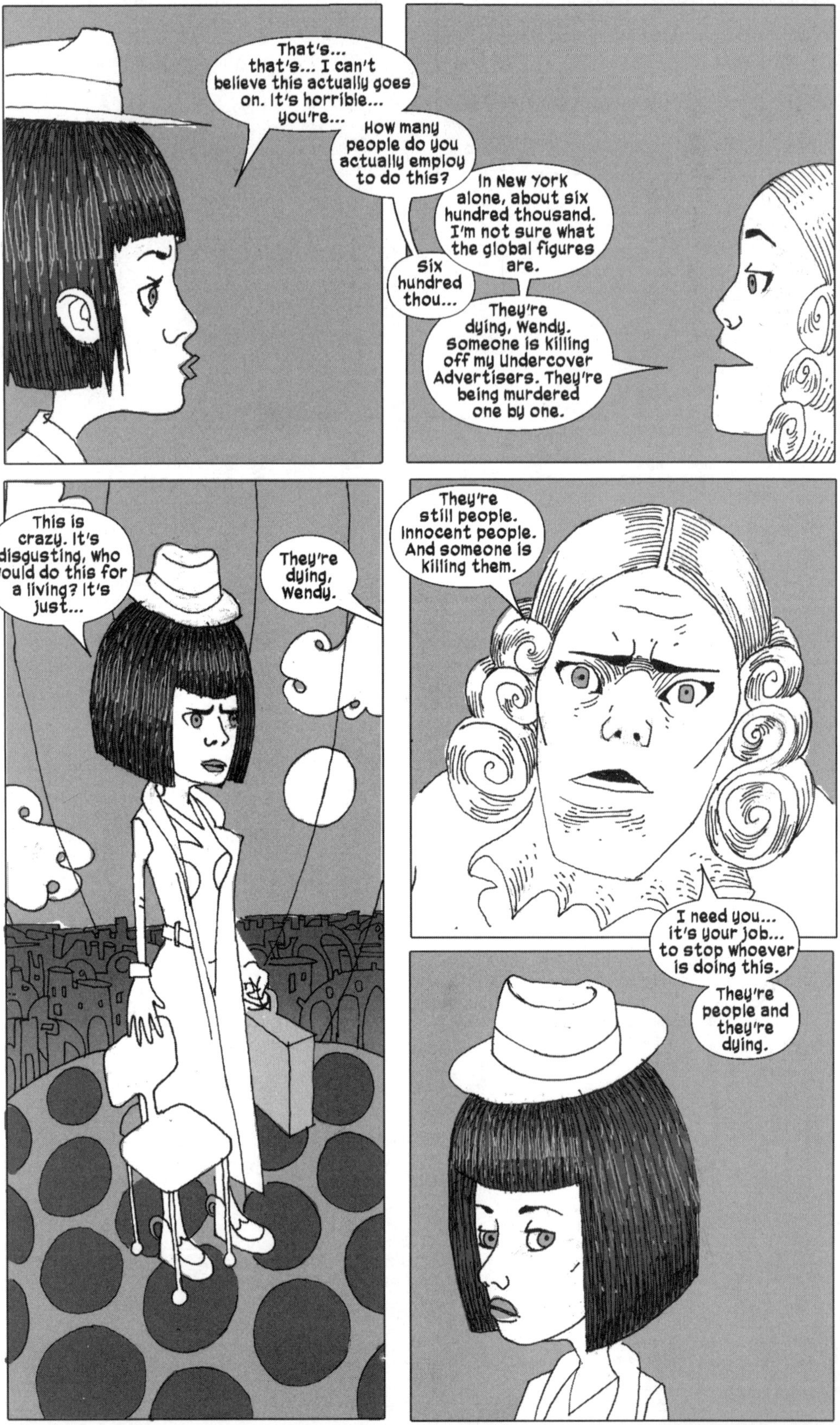
That's... that's... I can't believe this actually goes on. It's horrible... you're...
How many people do you actually employ to do this?
In New York alone, about six hundred thousand. I'm not sure what the global figures are.
Six hundred thou...
They're dying, Wendy. Someone is killing off my Undercover Advertisers. They're being murdered one by one.
This is crazy. It's disgusting, who would do this for a living? It's just...
They're dying, Wendy.
They're still people. Innocent people. And someone is killing them.
I need you... it's your job... to stop whoever is doing this.
They're people and they're dying.

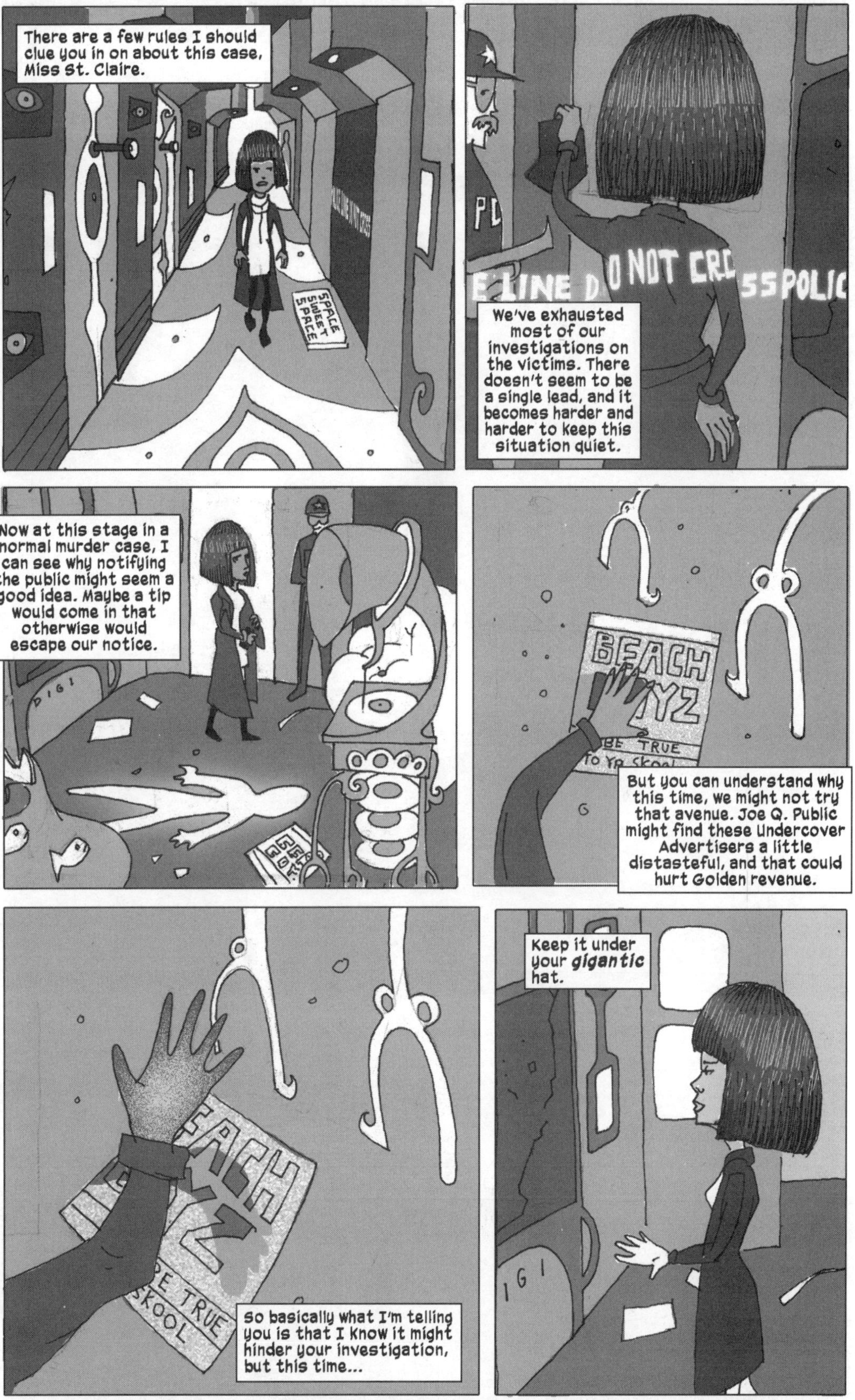
There are a few rules I should clue you in on about this case, Miss St. Claire.
SPACE SWEET SPACE
NOT CRO
55POLIC
We've exhausted most of our investigations on the victims. There doesn't seem to be a single lead, and it becomes harder and harder to keep this situation quiet.
Now at this stage in a normal murder case, I can see why notifying the public might seem a good idea. Maybe a tip would come in that otherwise would escape our notice.
DIGI
BEACH
BE TRUE
But you can understand why this time, we might not try that avenue. Joe Q. Public might find these Undercover Advertisers a little distasteful, and that could hurt Golden revenue.
BE TRUE
SKOOL
So basically what I'm telling you is that I know it might hinder your investigation, but this time...
Keep it under your *gigantic* hat.
IGI

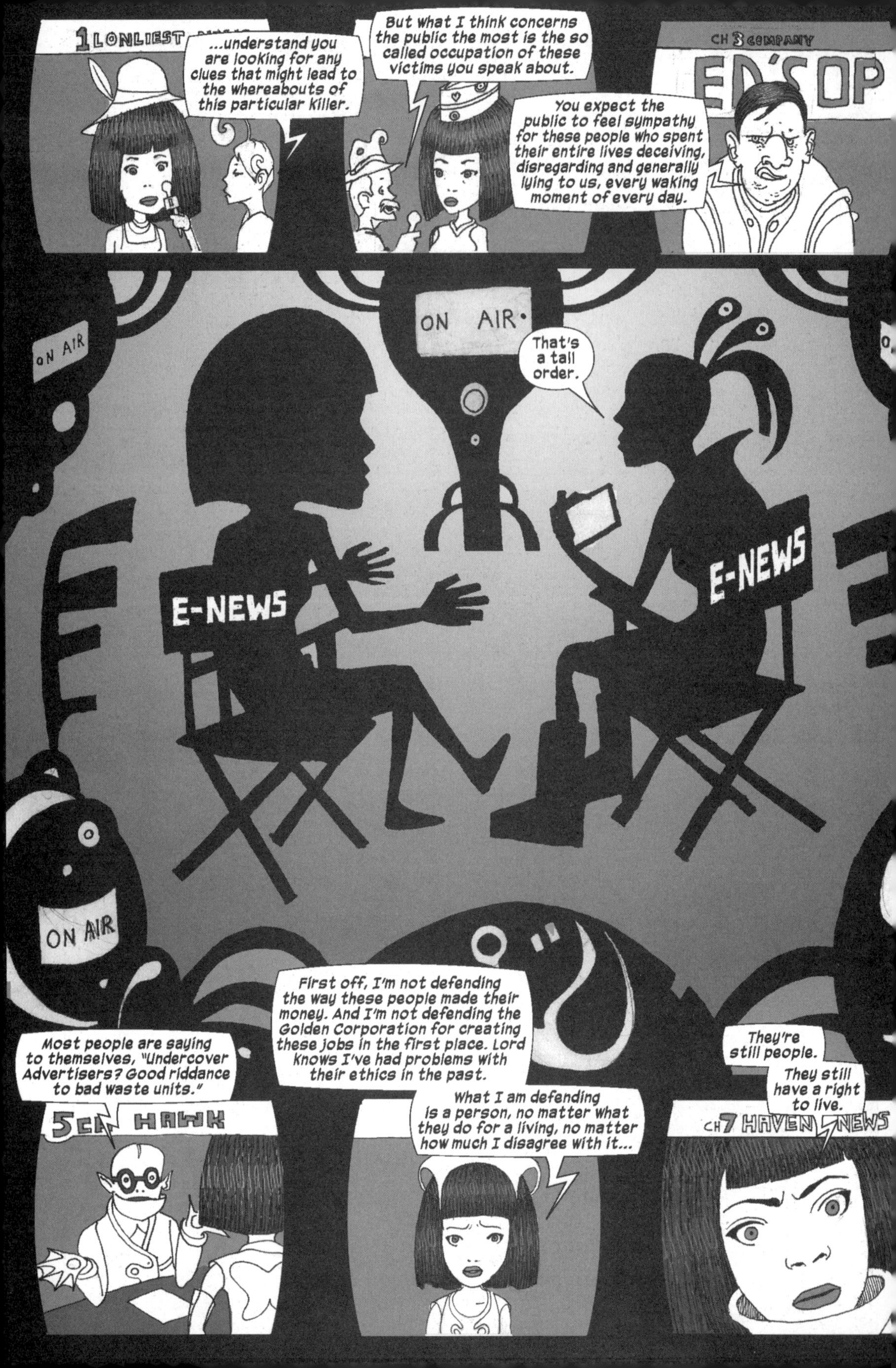
1 LONLIEST
...understand you are looking for any clues that might lead to the whereabouts of this particular killer.
But what I think concerns the public the most is the so called occupation of these victims you speak about.
CH 3 COMPANY
You expect the public to feel sympathy for these people who spent their entire lives deceiving, disregarding and generally lying to us, every waking moment of every day.
ON AIR
ON AIR
That's a tall order.
E-NEWS
E-NEWS
ON AIR
Most people are saying to themselves, "Undercover Advertisers? Good riddance to bad waste units."
HAWK
First off, I'm not defending the way these people made their money. And I'm not defending the Golden Corporation for creating these jobs in the first place. Lord knows I've had problems with their ethics in the past.
What I am defending is a person, no matter what they do for a living, no matter how much I disagree with it...
They're still people.
They still have a right to live.
CH7 HAVEN NEWS

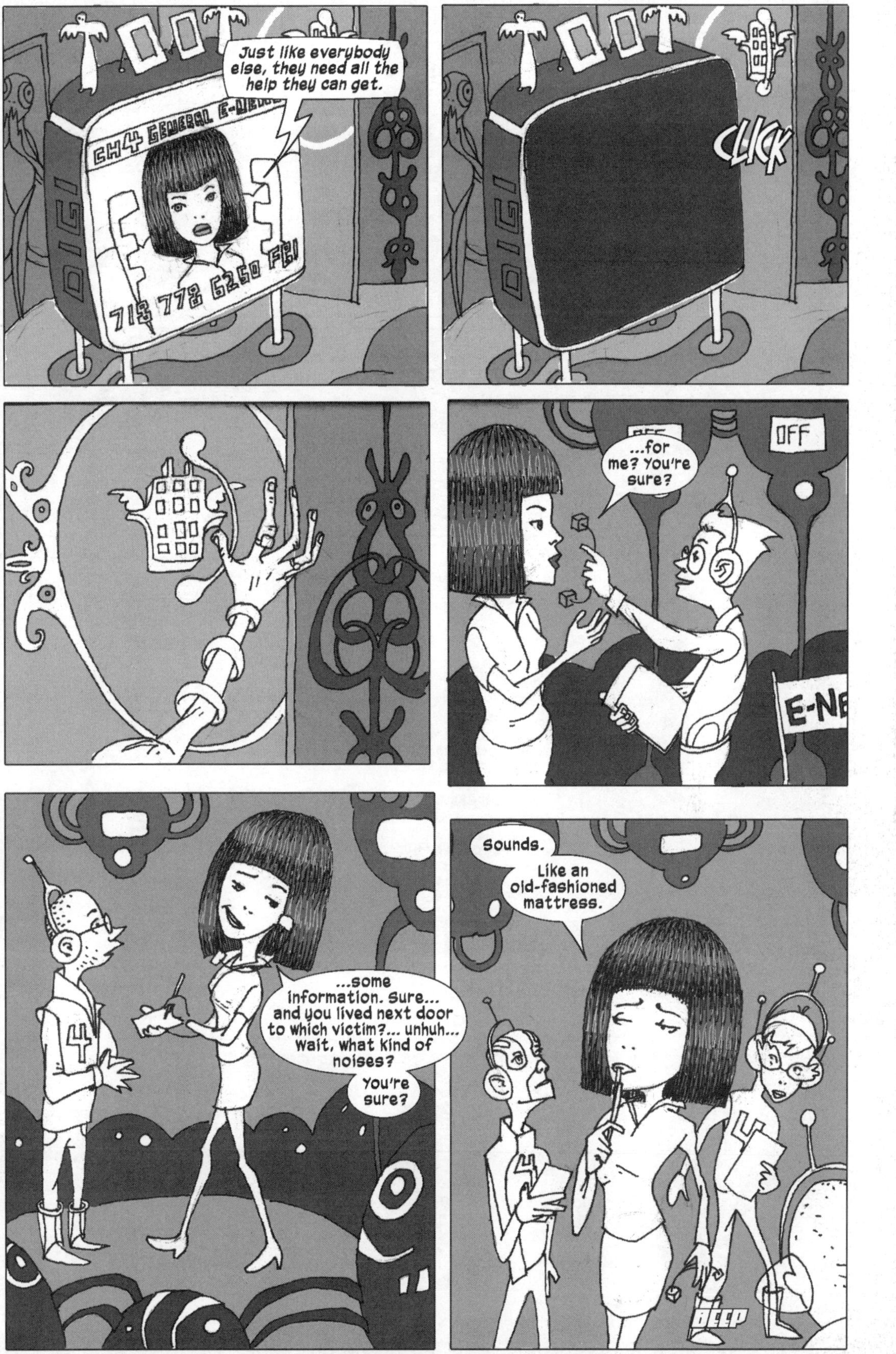
Just like everybody else, they need all the help they can get.
CH4 GENERAL
718 778 6260 FBI
DIGI
DIGI
CLICK
OFF
...for me? You're sure?
...some information. Sure... and you lived next door to which victim?... unhuh... Wait, what kind of noises?
You're sure?
Sounds.
Like an old-fashioned mattress.
BEEP

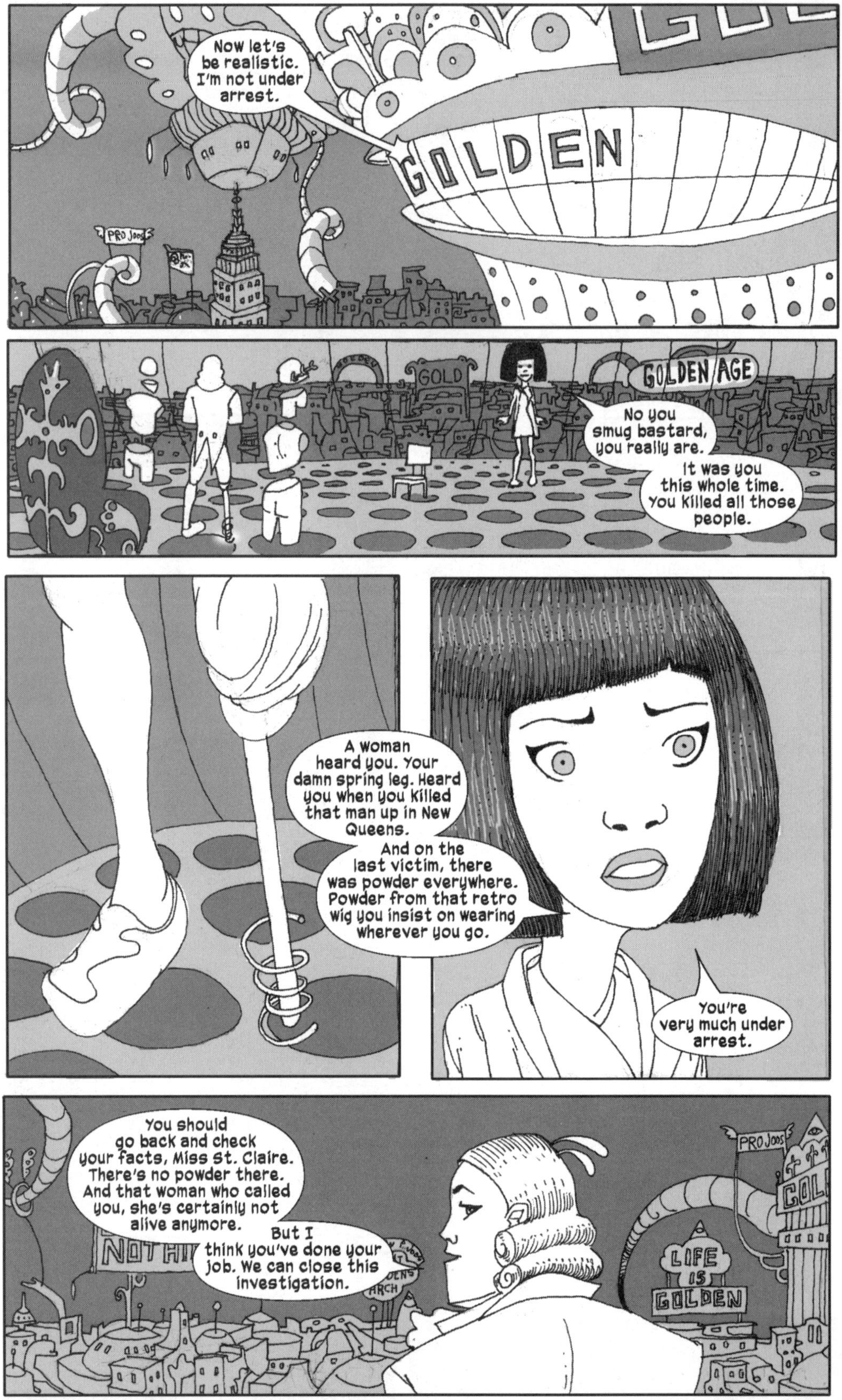
GOLDEN
Now let's be realistic. I'm not under arrest.
PRO JOOS
GOLD
GOLDEN AGE
No you smug bastard, you really are.
It was you this whole time. You killed all those people.
A woman heard you. Your damn spring leg. Heard you when you killed that man up in New Queens.
And on the last victim, there was powder everywhere. Powder from that retro wig you insist on wearing wherever you go.
You're very much under arrest.
You should go back and check your facts, Miss St. Claire. There's no powder there. And that woman who called you, she's certainly not alive anymore.
But I think you've done your job. We can close this investigation.
PRO JOOS
LIFE IS GOLDEN

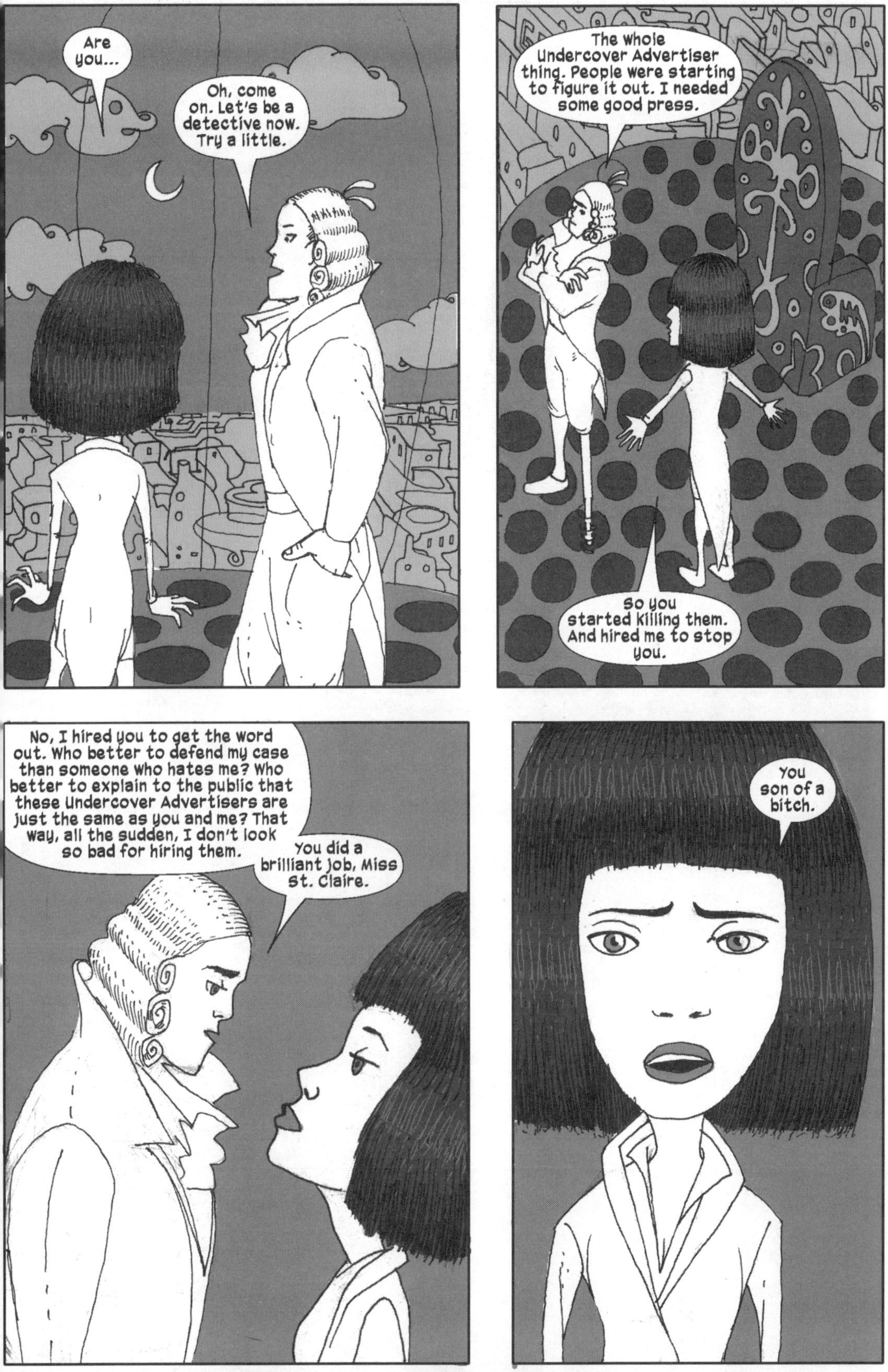
Are you...
Oh, come on. Let's be a detective now. Try a little.
The whole Undercover Advertiser thing. People were starting to figure it out. I needed some good press.
So you started killing them. And hired me to stop you.
No, I hired you to get the word out. Who better to defend my case than someone who hates me? Who better to explain to the public that these Undercover Advertisers are just the same as you and me? That way, all the sudden, I don't look so bad for hiring them.
You did a brilliant job, Miss St. Claire.
You son of a bitch.

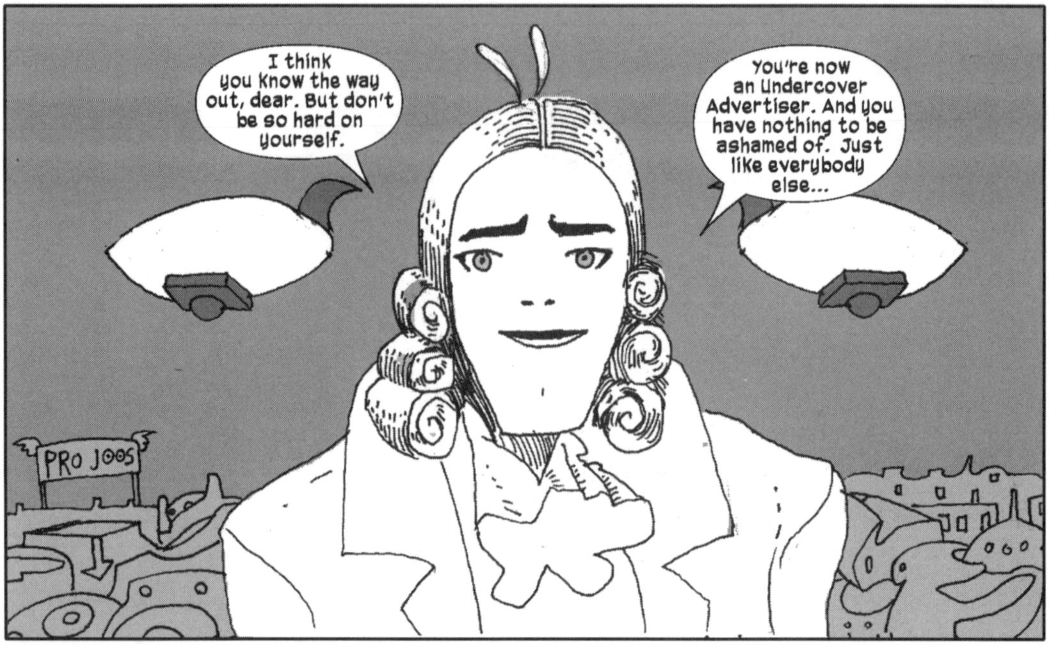
I think you know the way out, dear. But don't be so hard on yourself.
You're now an Undercover Advertiser. And you have nothing to be ashamed of. Just like everybody else...
PRO JOOS

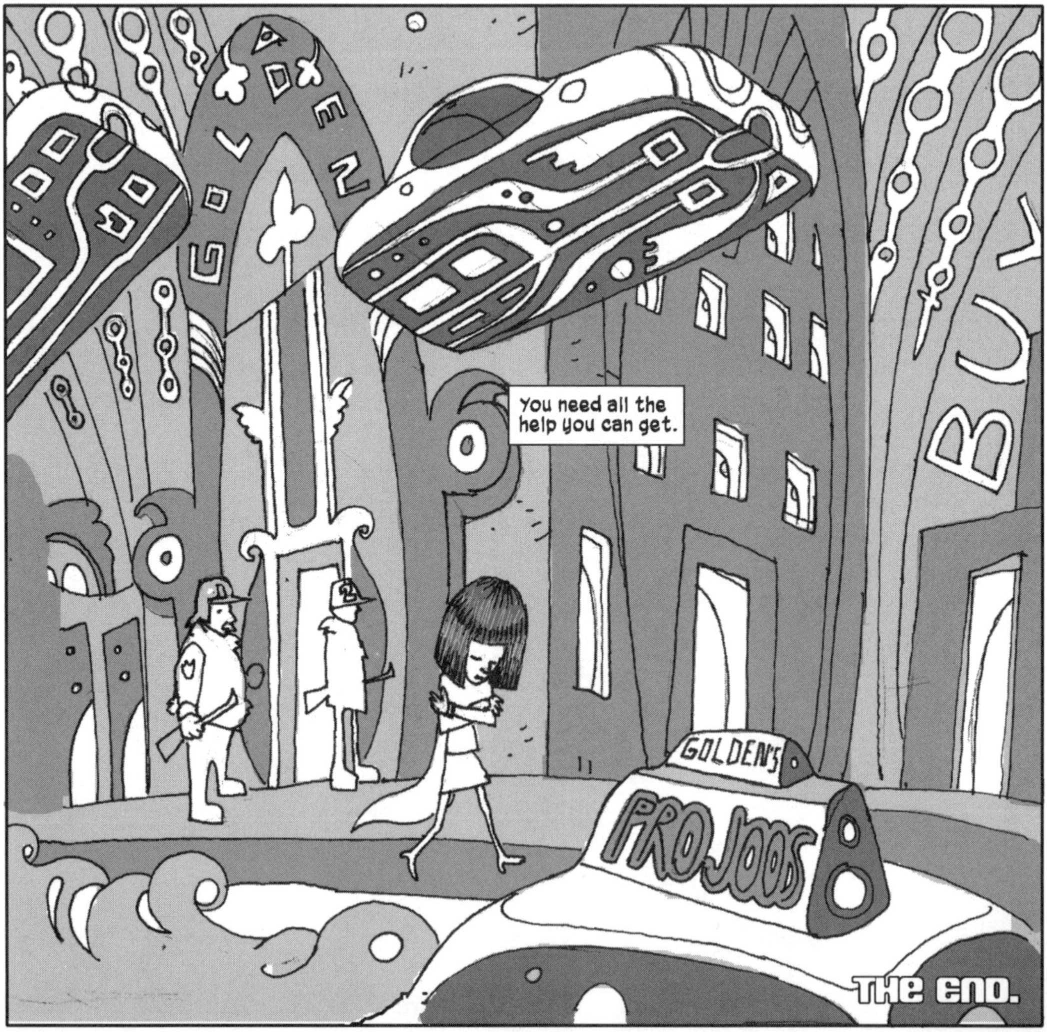
GOLDEN
BUY
You need all the help you can get.
GOLDEN'S
PRO JOOS
THE END.

Mickey Duzyj

Despite frequent, frightening, and fitting comparisons to men 4 times his age, Mickey strongly denies all geriatric fantasies and a reported inclination towards women with unsightly mouths.
mduzyj@hotmail.com
www.mduzyj.com

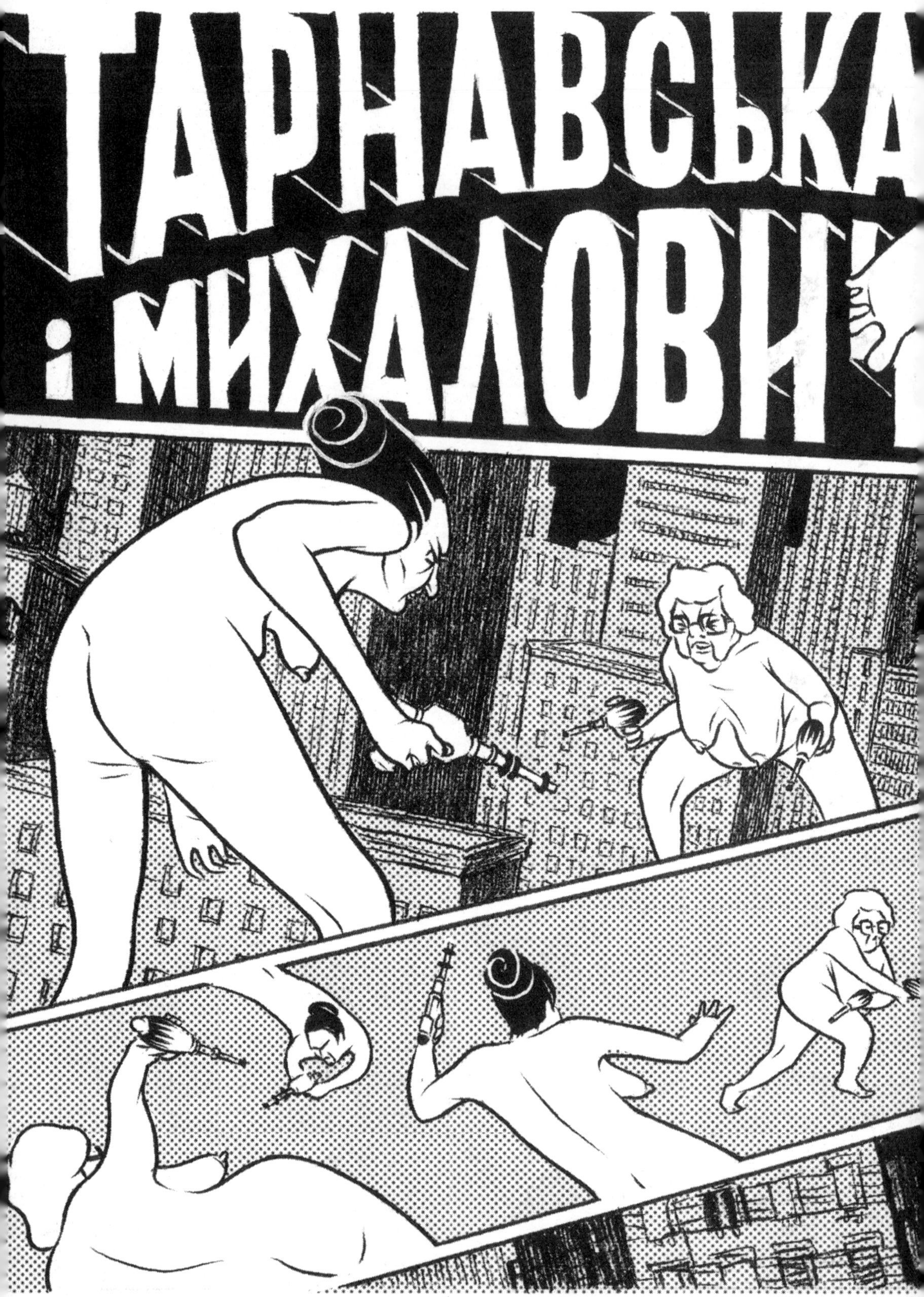
ТАРНАВСЬКА
І МИХАЛОВИ

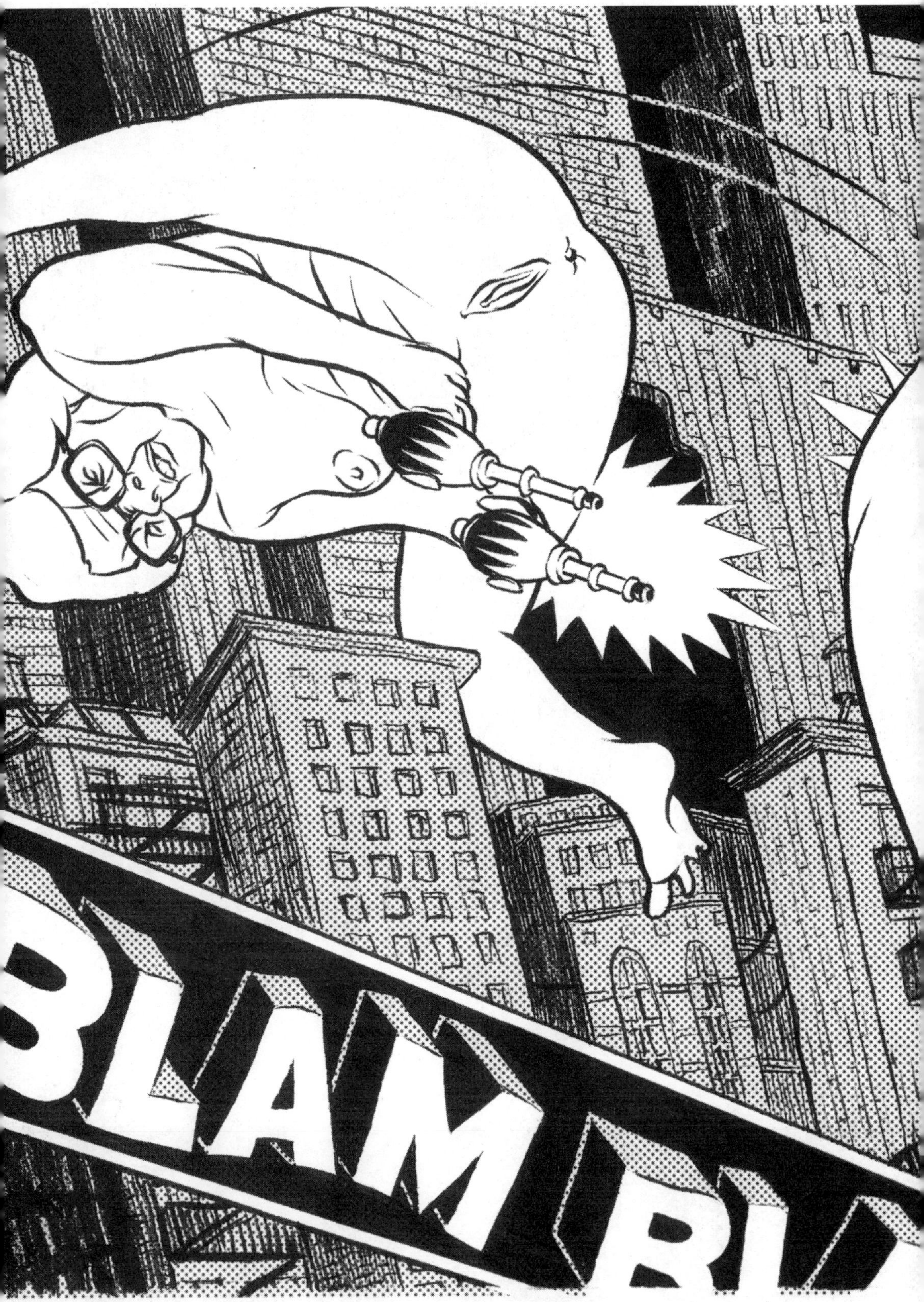
BLAM

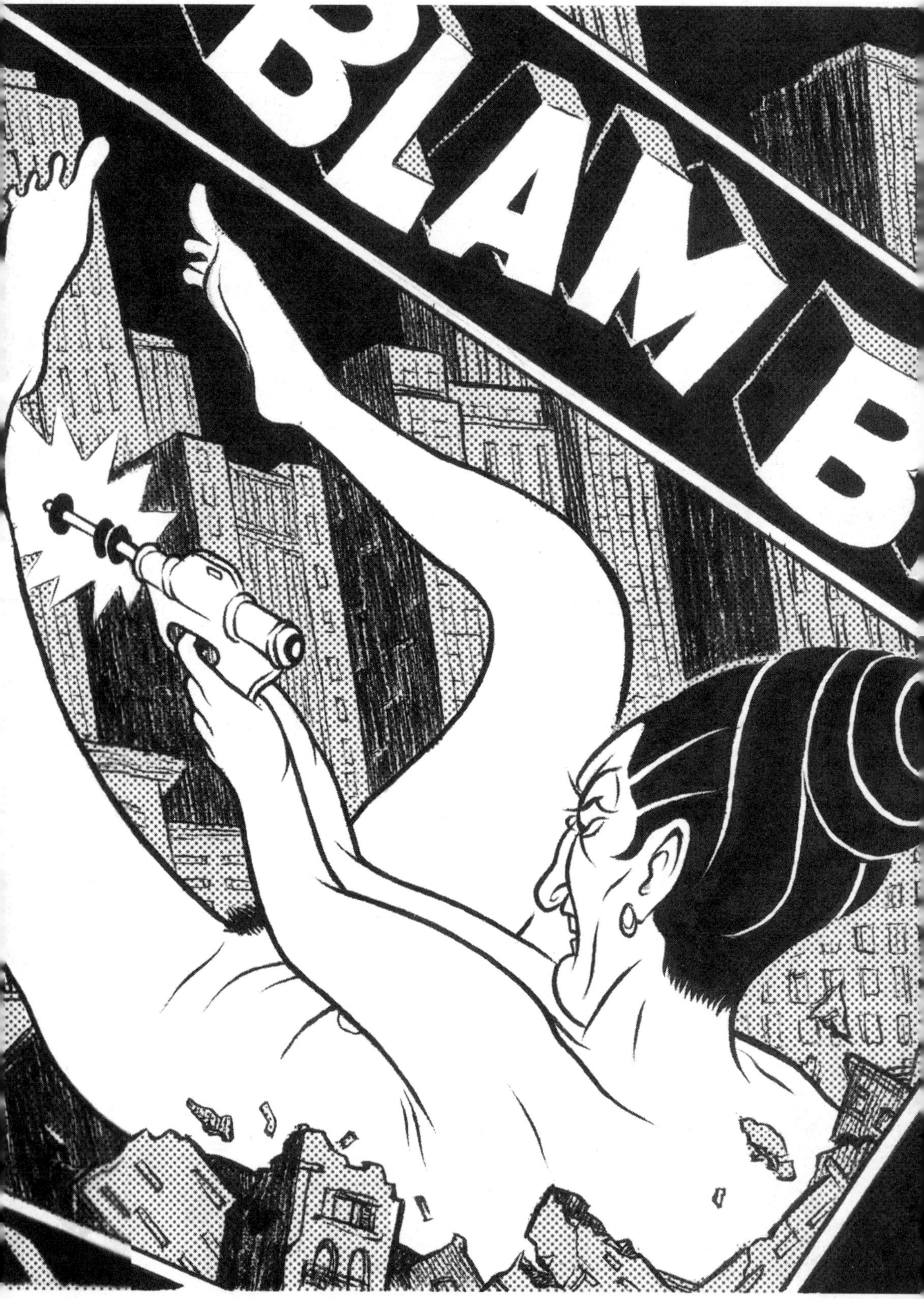
BLAM

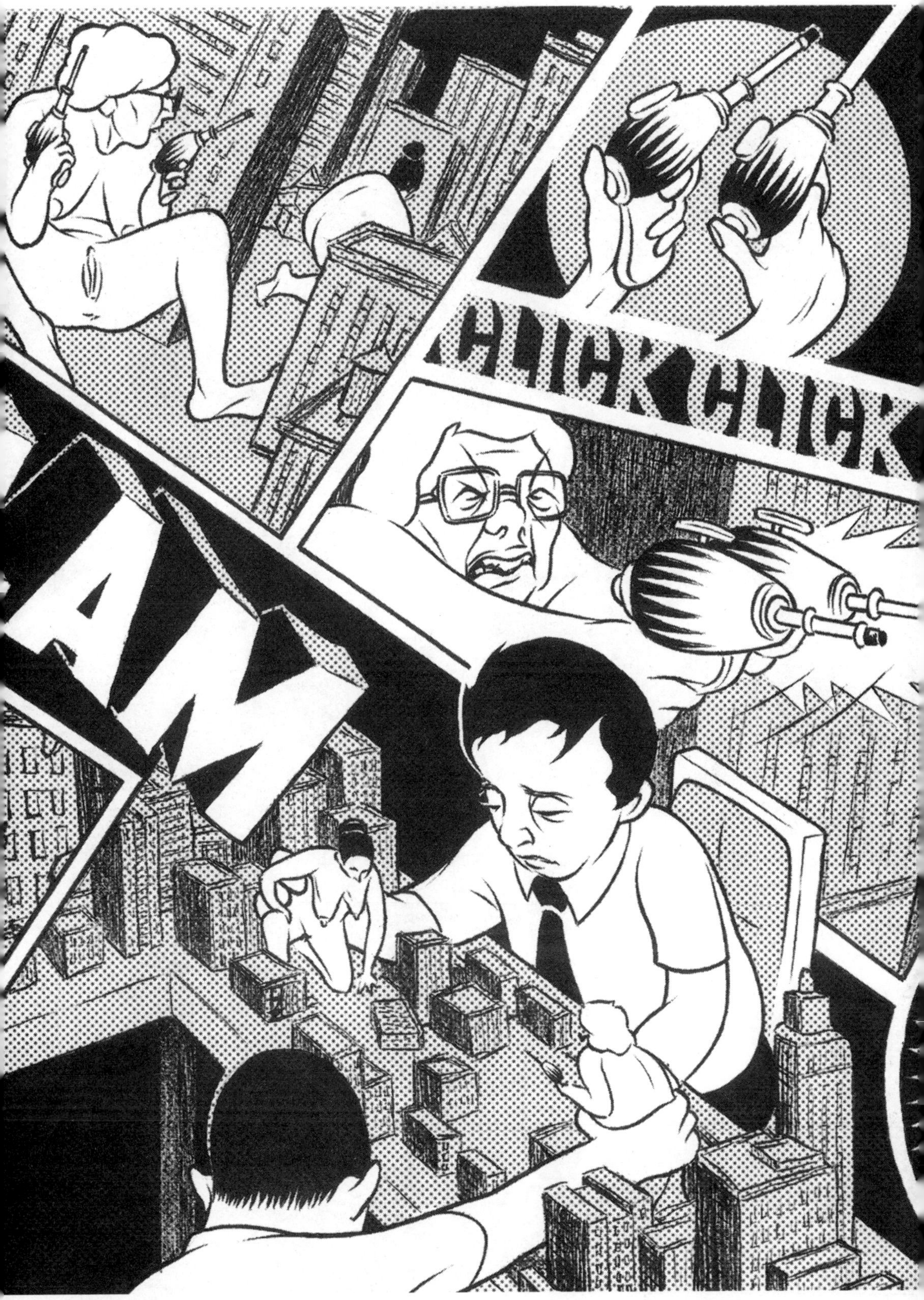
CLICK CLICK
AM

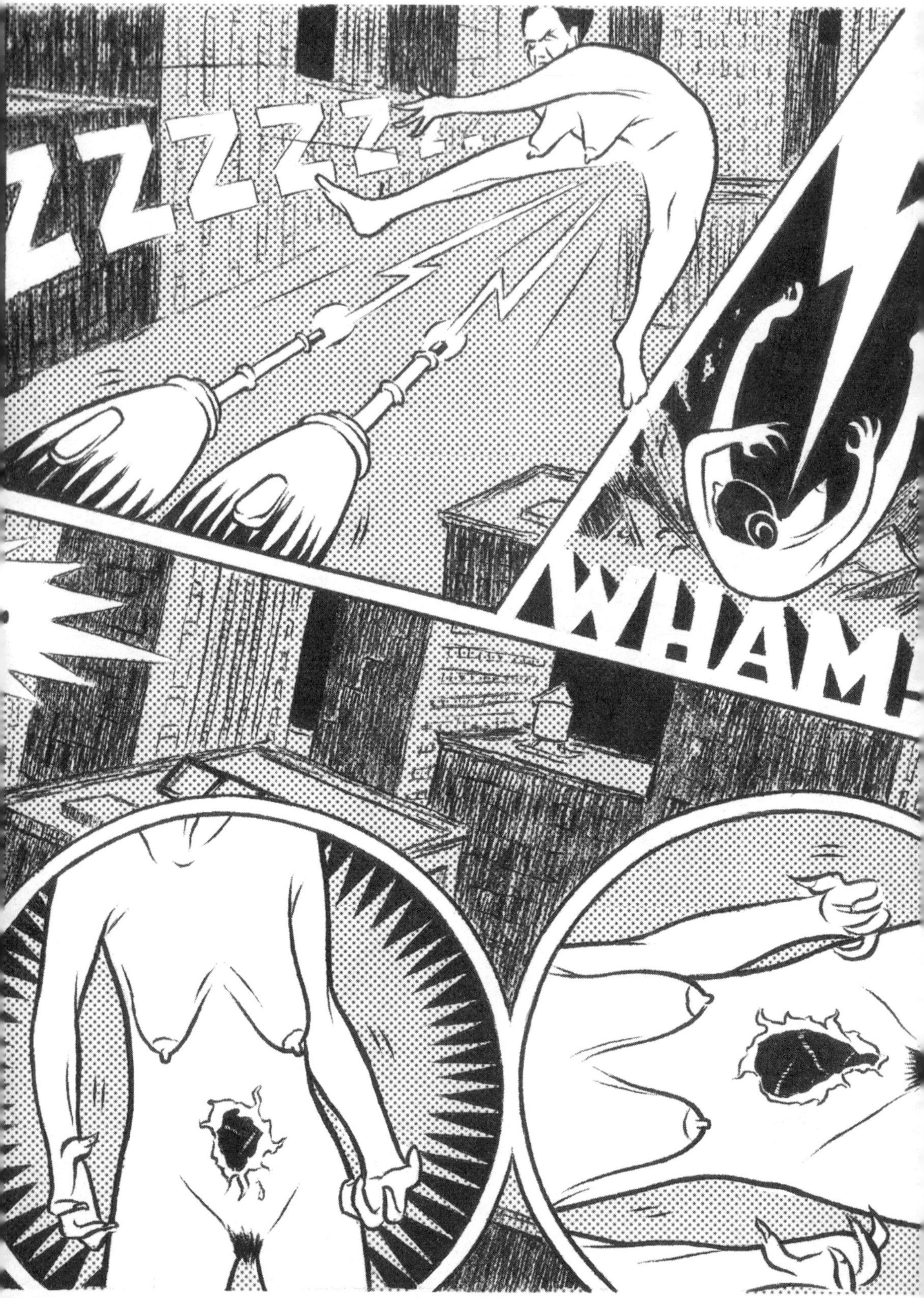
ZZZZZZ
WHAM

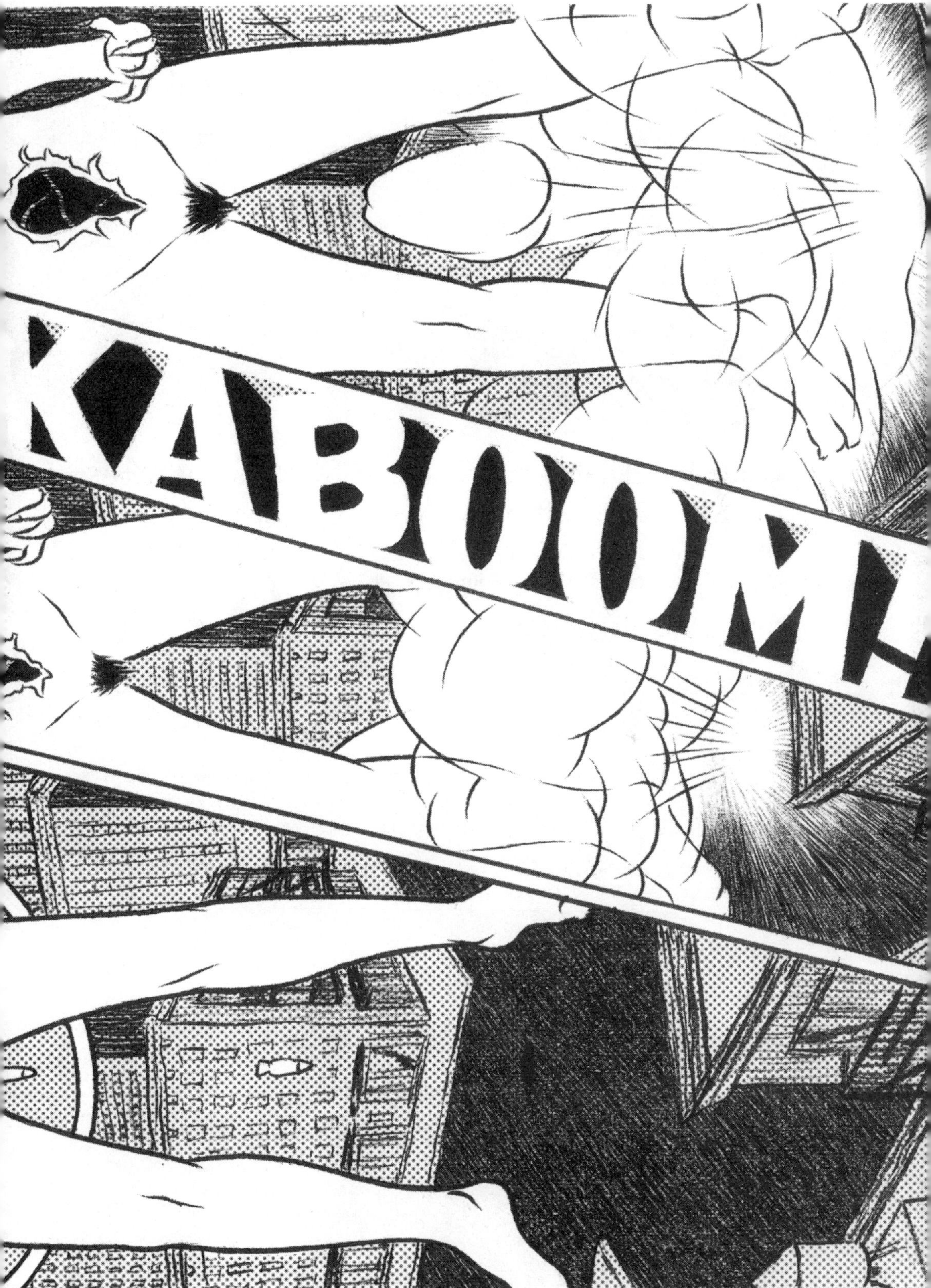
KABOOM!

Phonzie Davis

Columbus Ohio's own Phonzie Davis is the latest of a proud tradition of All-American funny-book makers! He runs the Phreak-Hop Cartoon Factory. Show 'em some love at phizachelli@yahoo.com

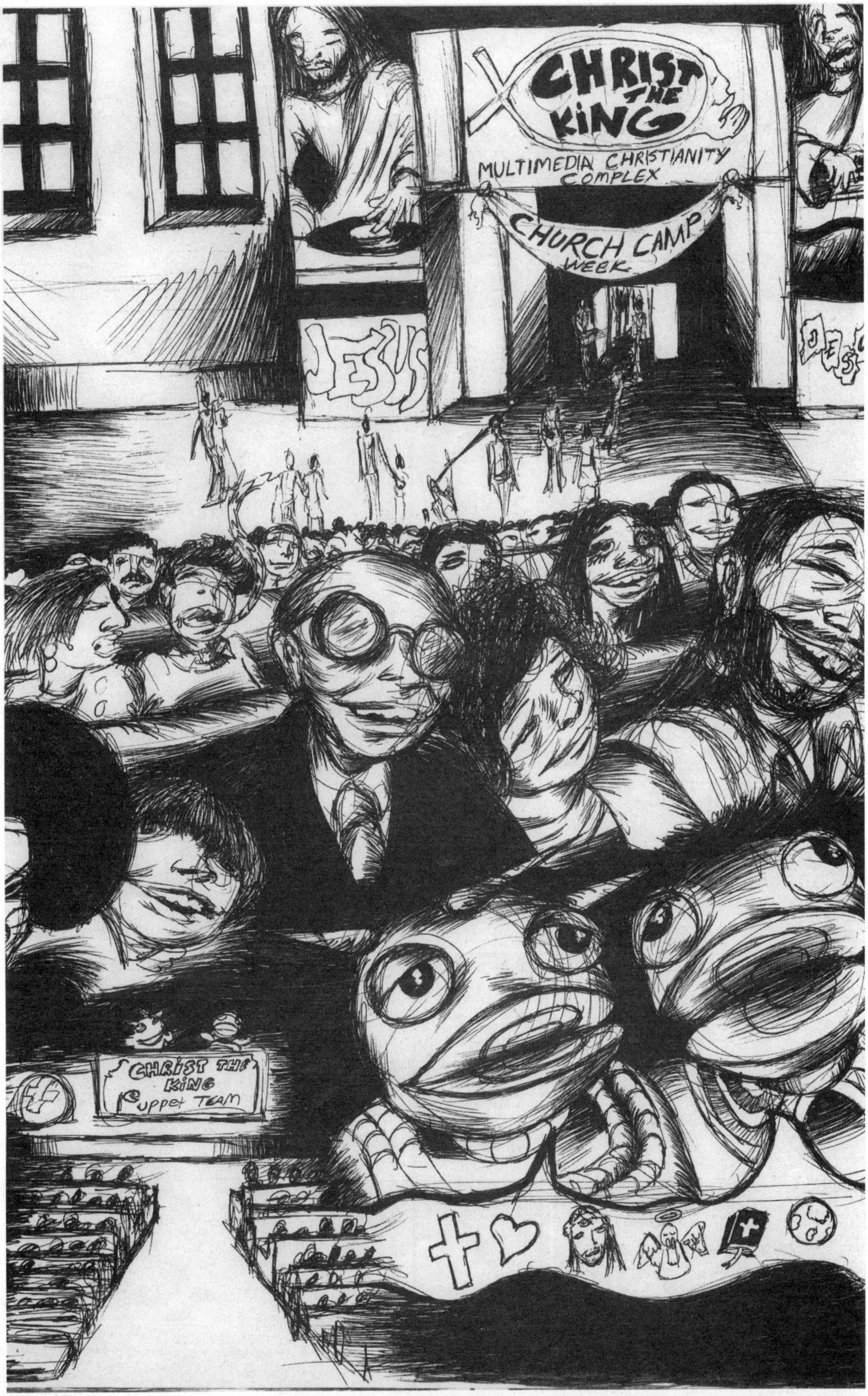
CHRIST THE KING
MULTIMEDIA CHRISTIANITY COMPLEX
CHURCH CAMP WEEK
JESUS
CHRIST THE KING Puppet TEAM

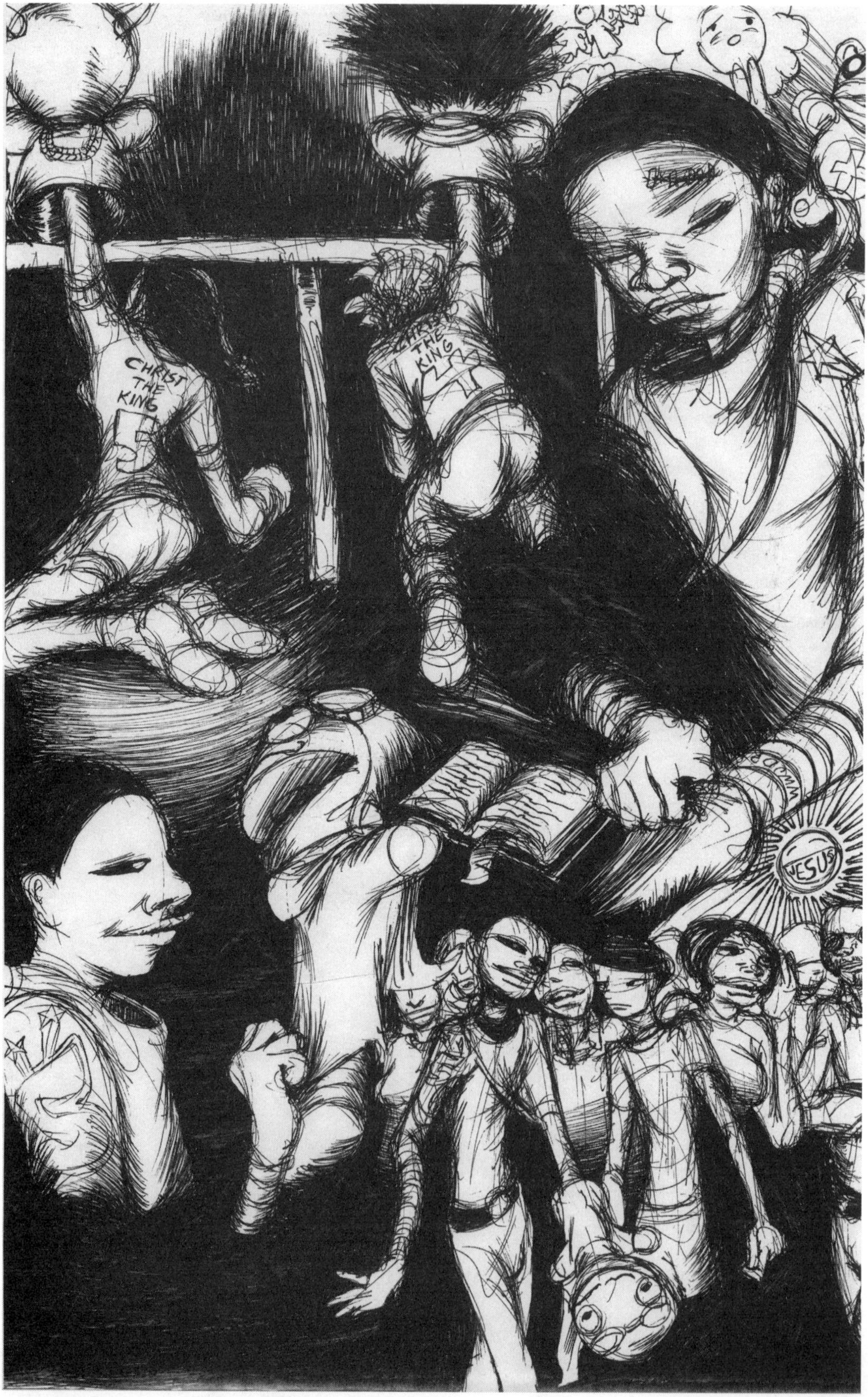
CHRIST THE KING
JESUS

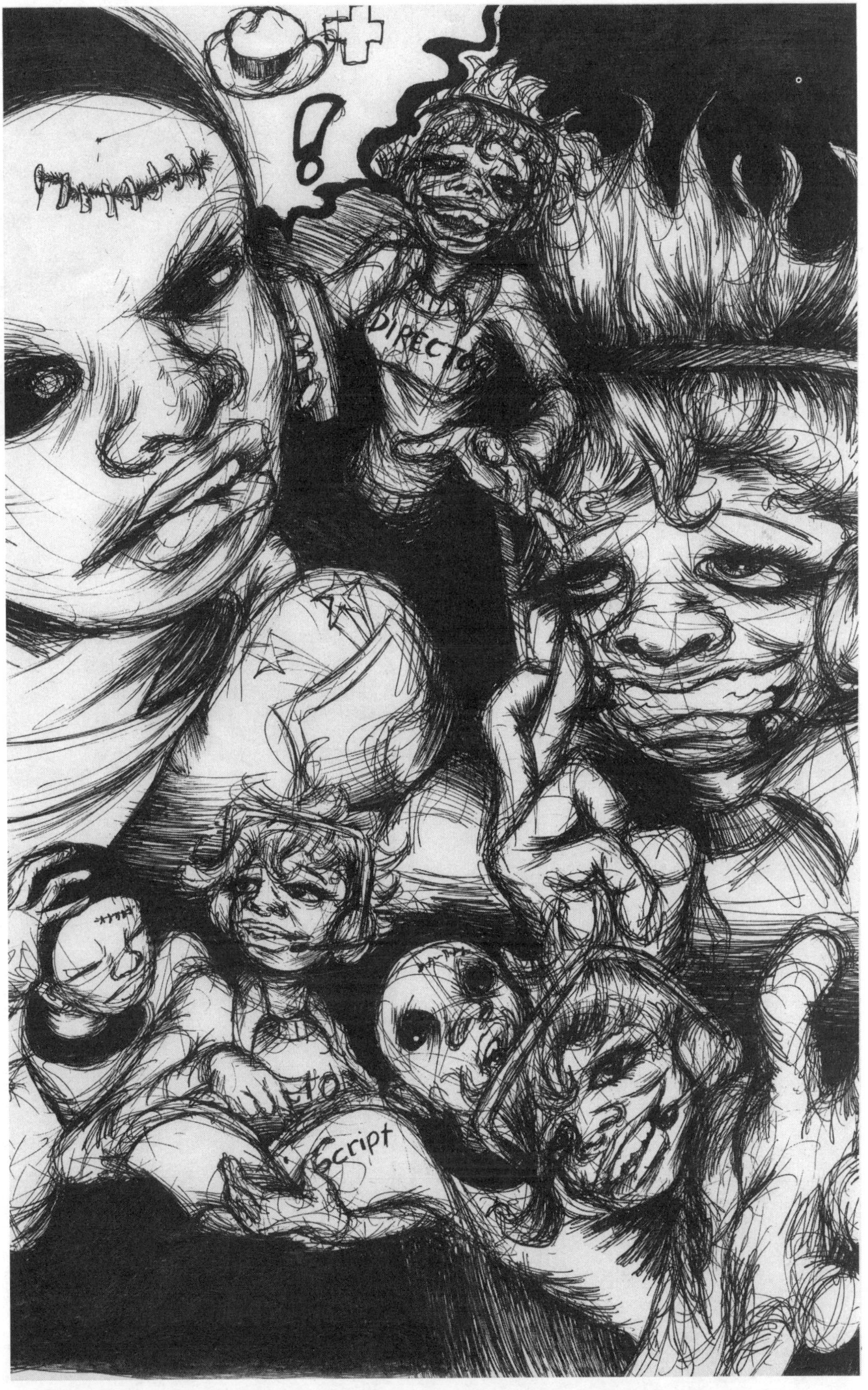
Script

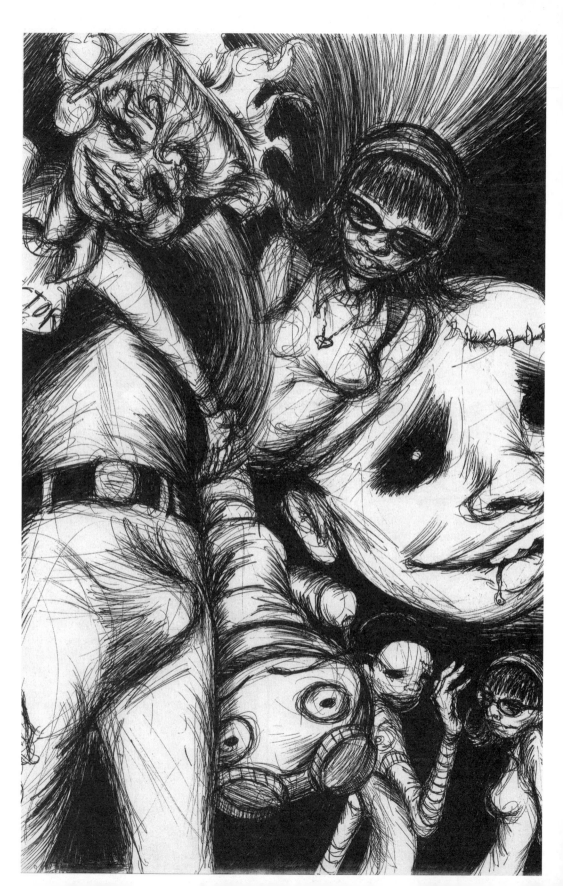

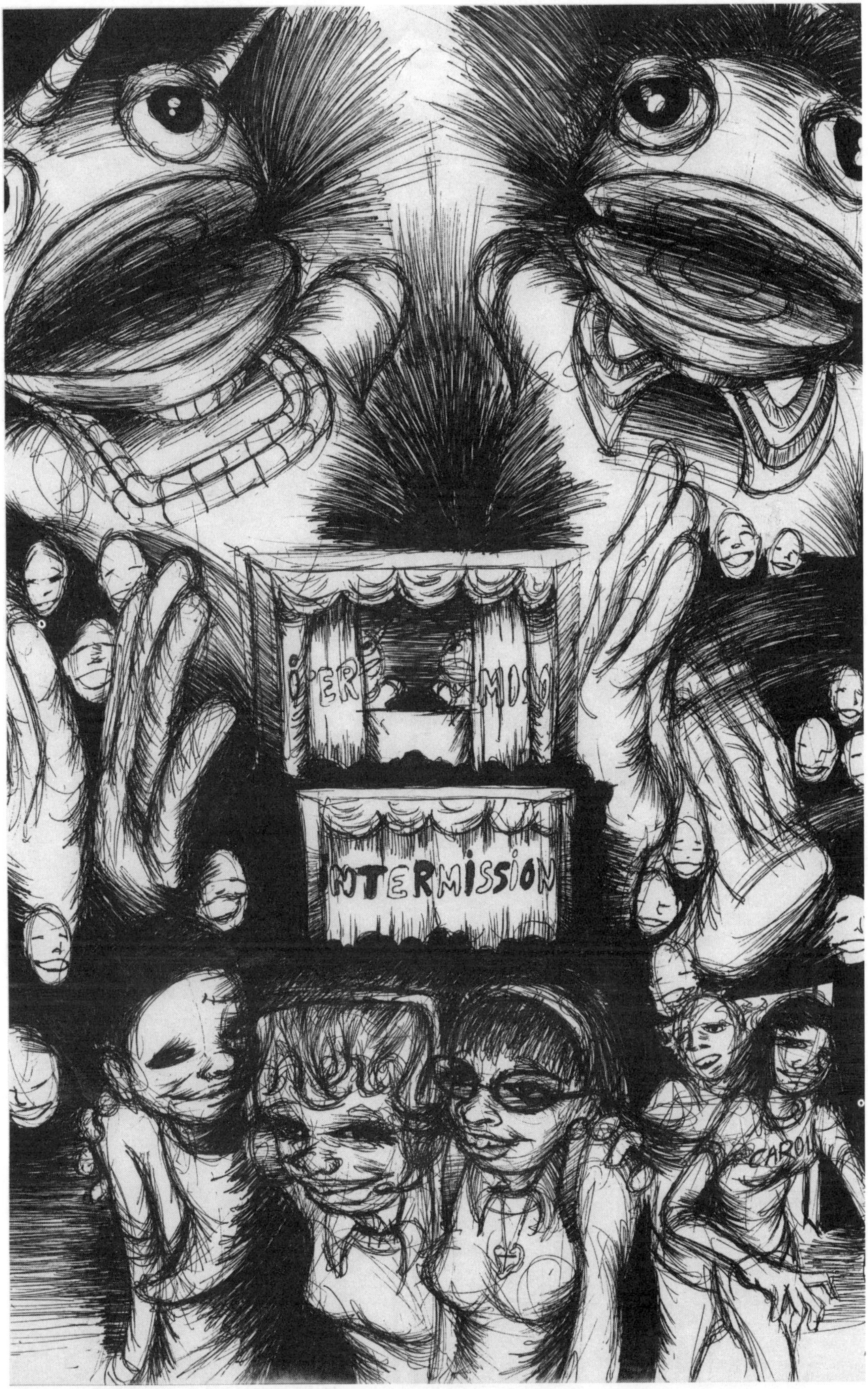
INTERMISSION
CAROL

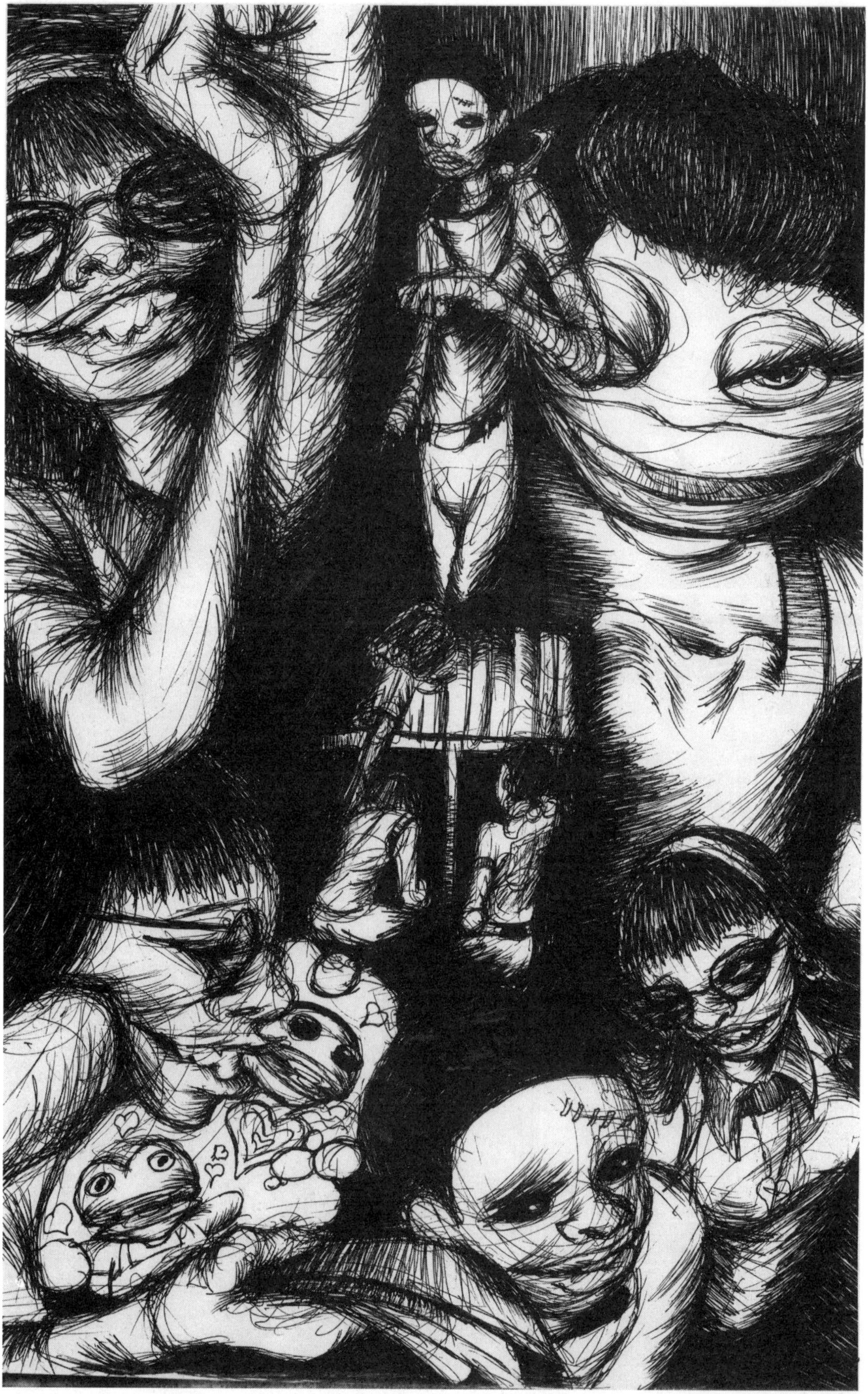

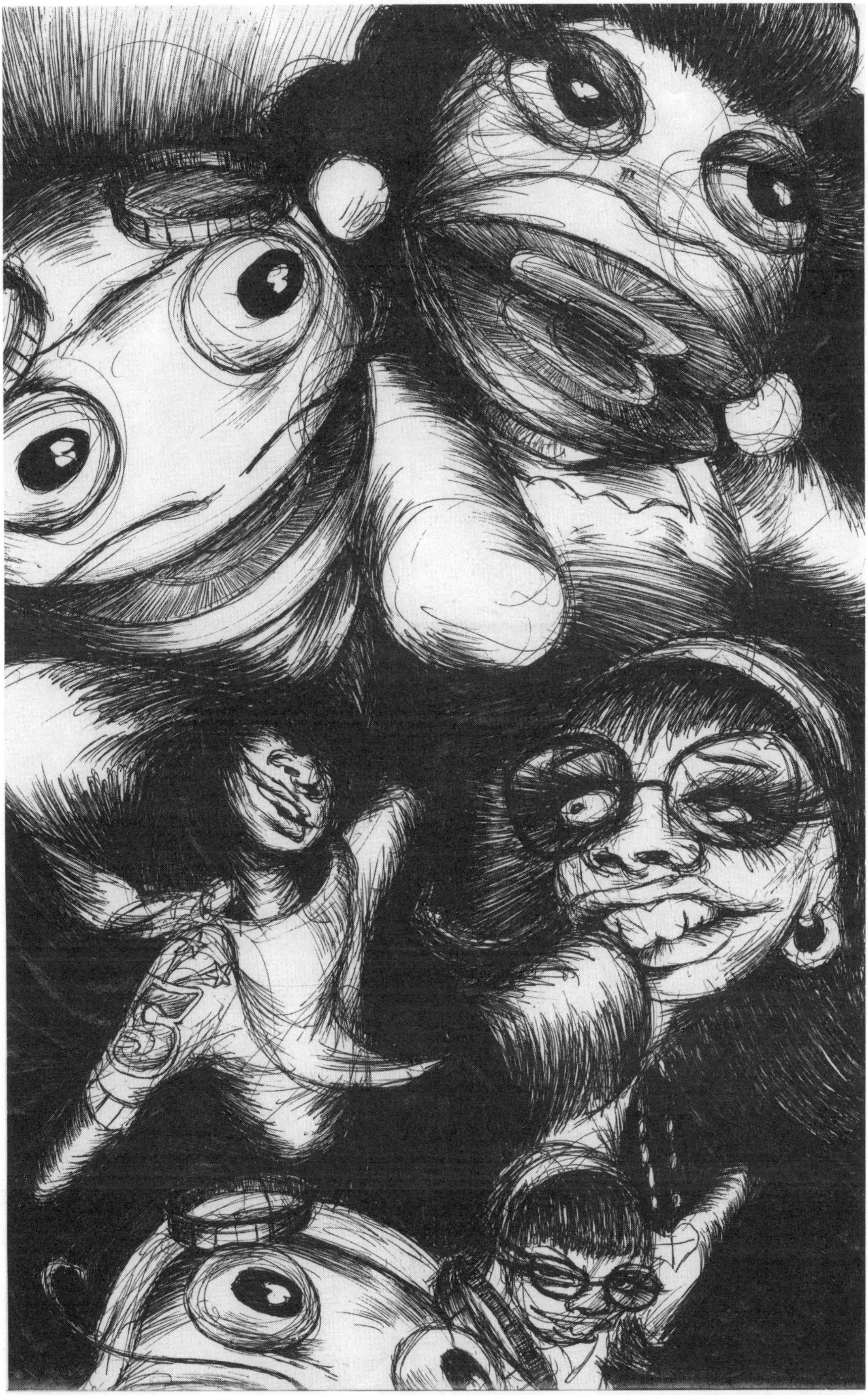

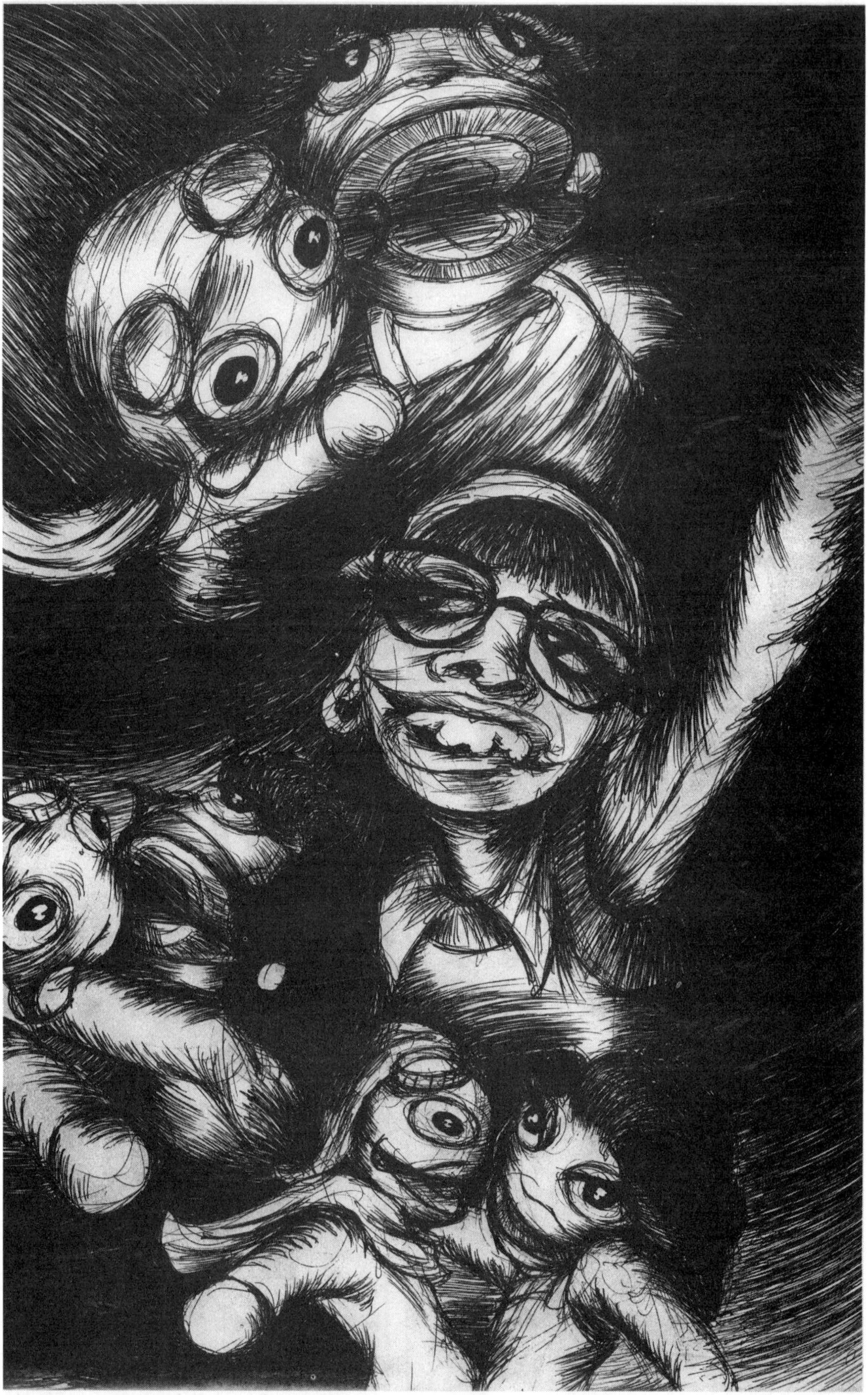

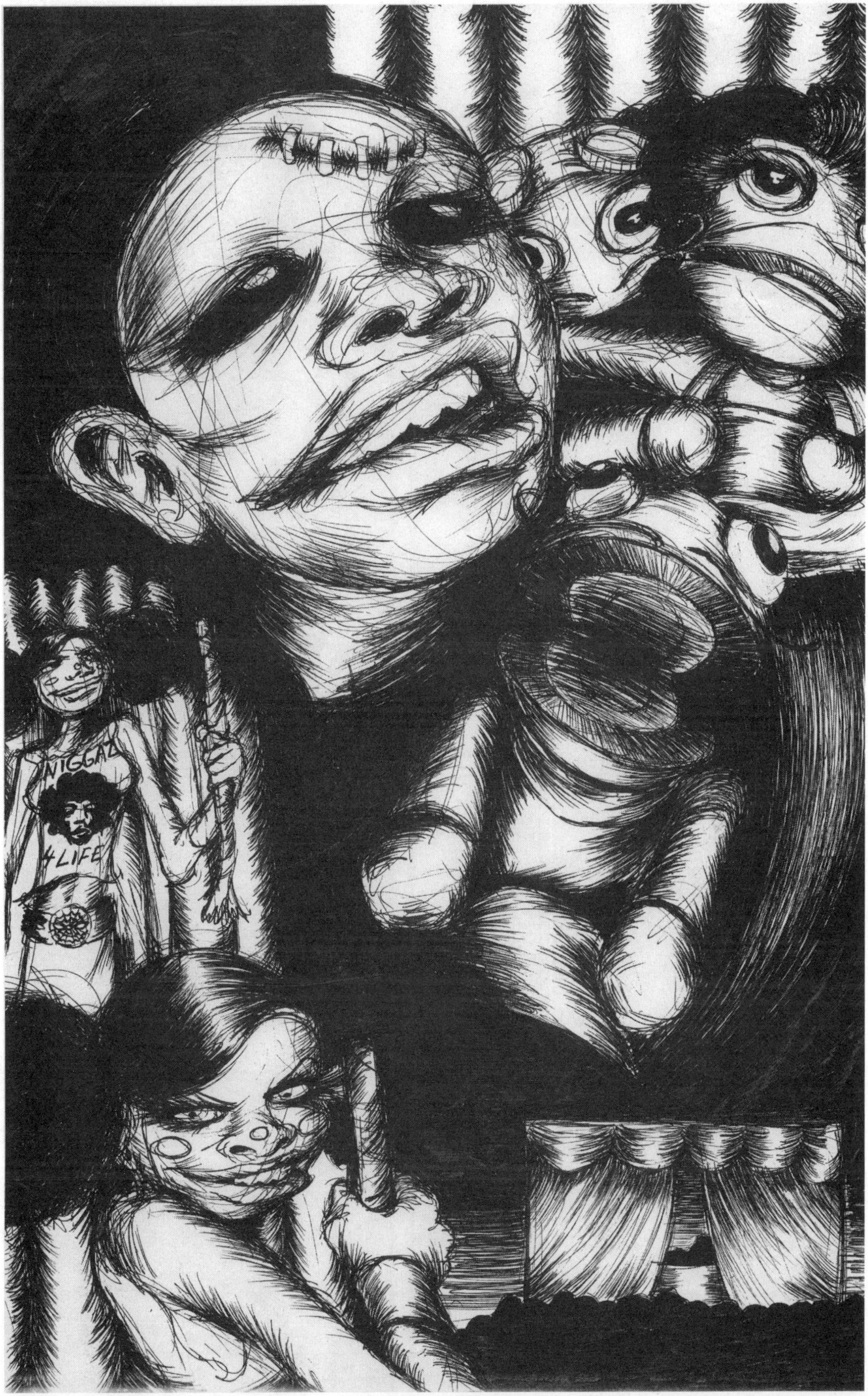
NIGGAZ
4LIFE

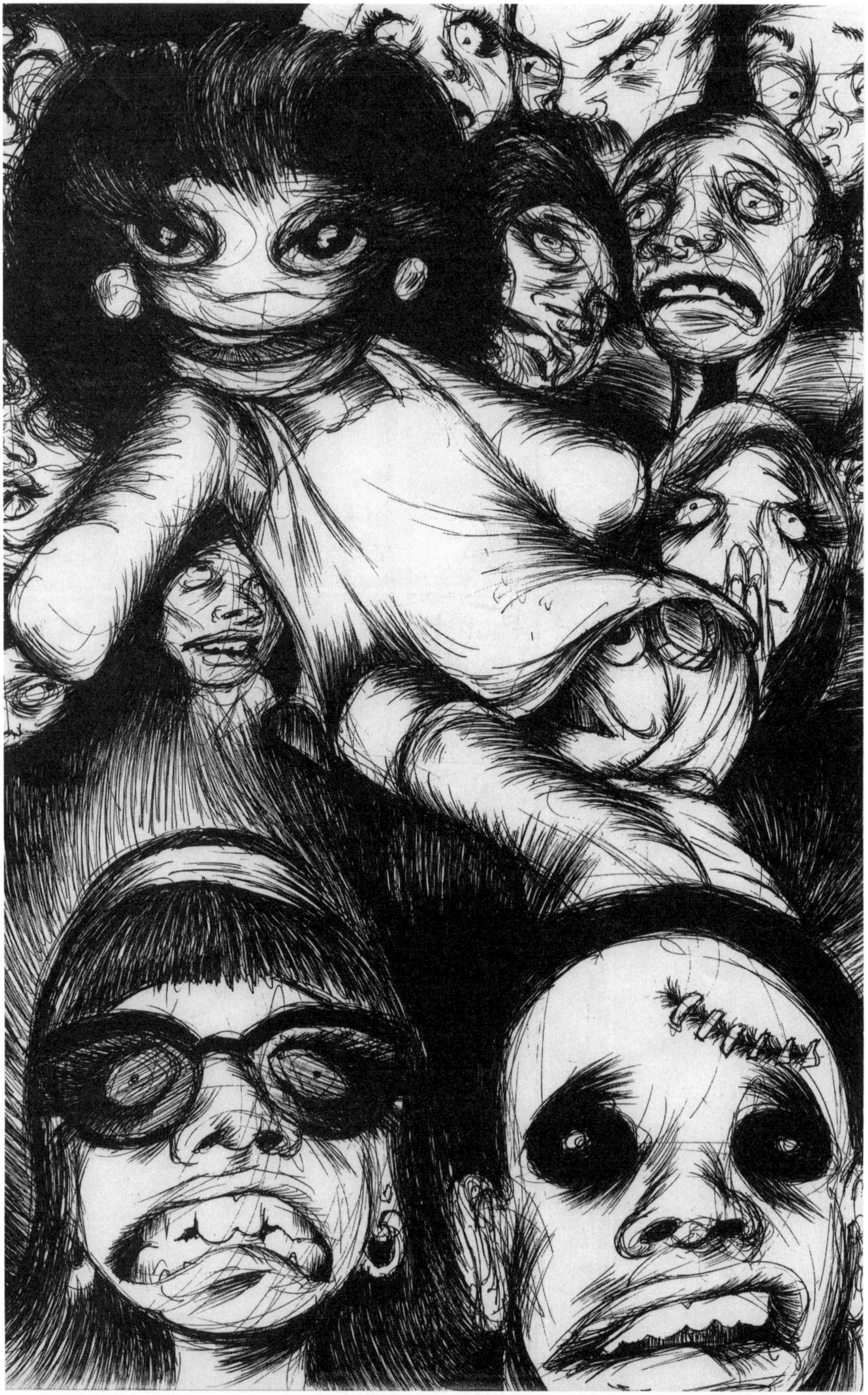

P. Williams

P. Williams fills up a lot of sketchbooks and makes a lot of paintings, some of which he shows in galleries. In general he keeps quite busy. He is quite literal these days and often types in the third person. Look at some of his other work at pwilliamsart.com

THE WEIGHT OF THINGS

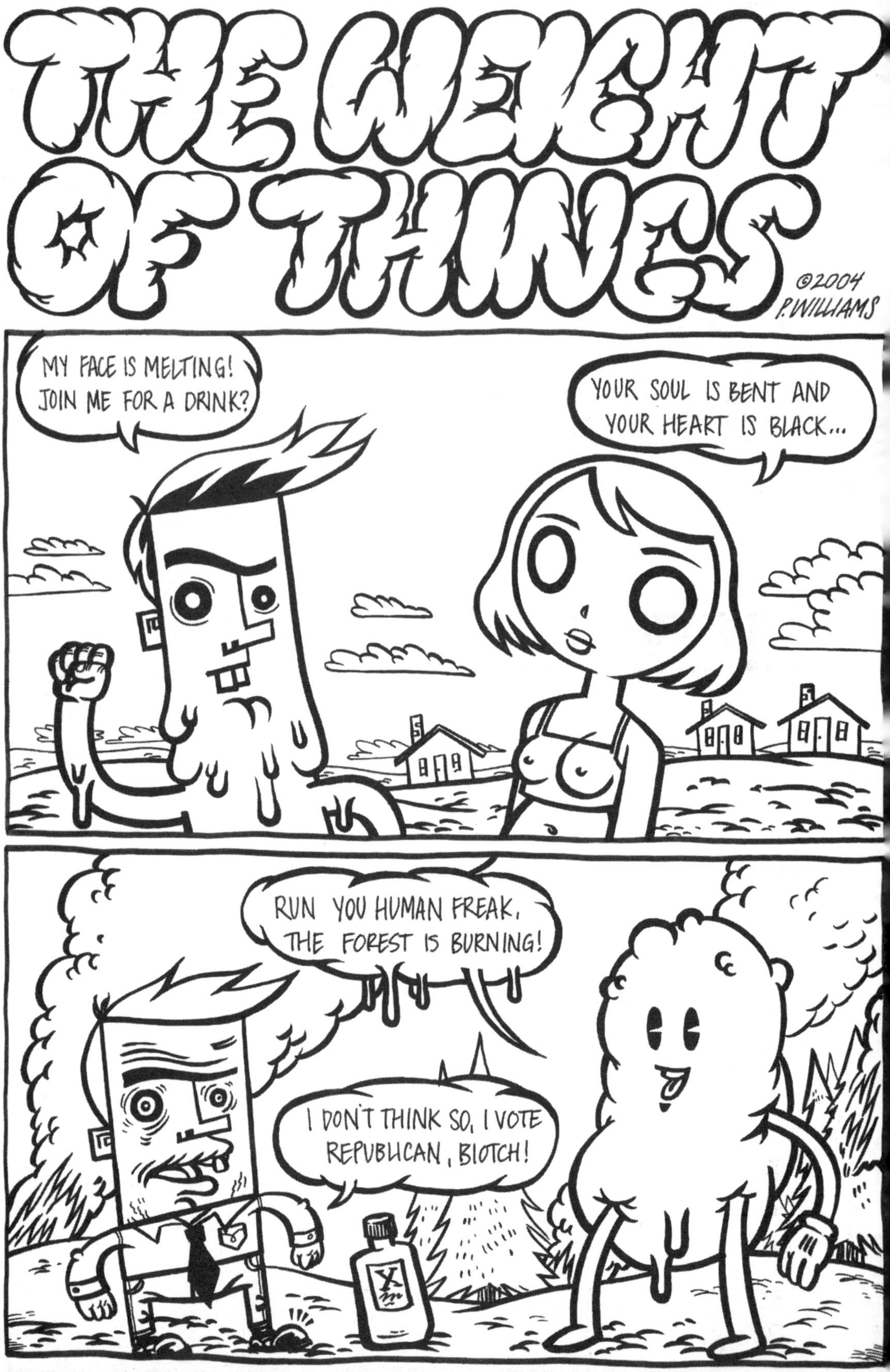
MY FACE IS MELTING! JOIN ME FOR A DRINK?
YOUR SOUL IS BENT AND YOUR HEART IS BLACK...
RUN YOU HUMAN FREAK, THE FOREST IS BURNING!
I DON'T THINK SO, I VOTE REPUBLICAN, BIOTCH!
X

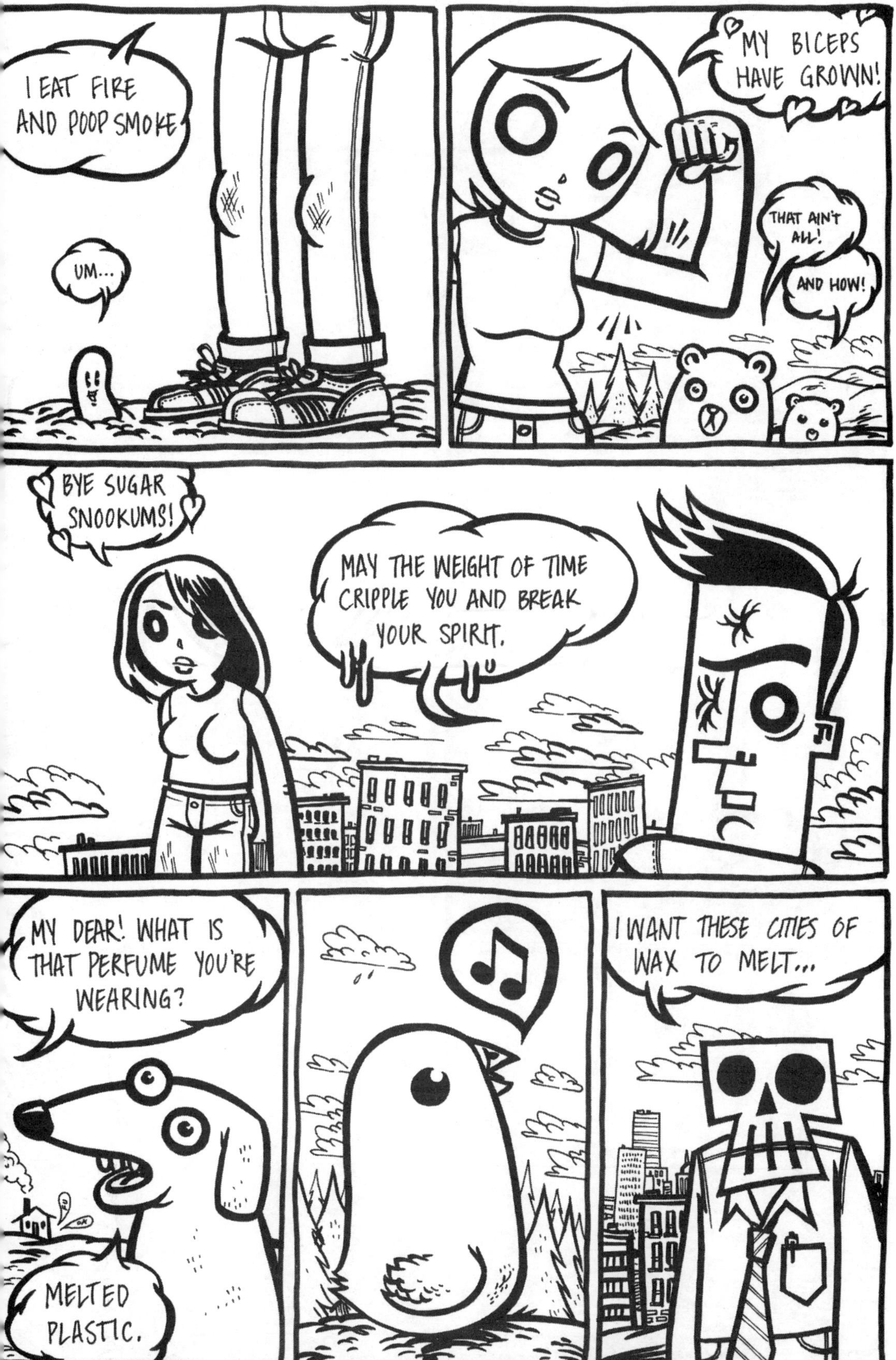
I EAT FIRE AND POOP SMOKE
UM...
MY BICEPS HAVE GROWN!
THAT AIN'T ALL!
AND HOW!
BYE SUGAR SNOOKUMS!
MAY THE WEIGHT OF TIME CRIPPLE YOU AND BREAK YOUR SPIRIT.
MY DEAR! WHAT IS THAT PERFUME YOU'RE WEARING?
MELTED PLASTIC.
I WANT THESE CITIES OF WAX TO MELT...

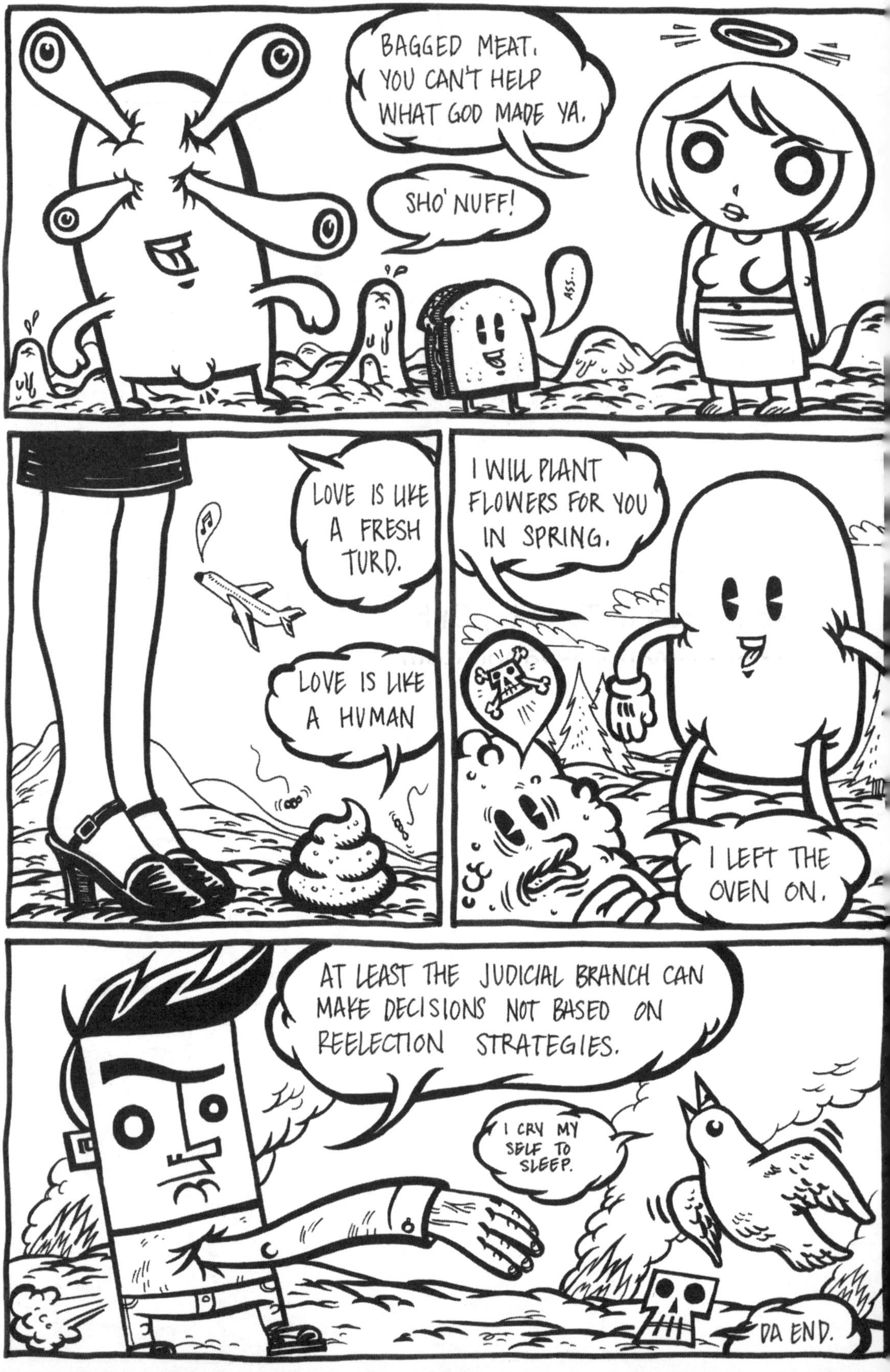
BAGGED MEAT. YOU CAN'T HELP WHAT GOD MADE YA.
SHO' NUFF!
ASS...
LOVE IS LIKE A FRESH TURD.
LOVE IS LIKE A HUMAN
I WILL PLANT FLOWERS FOR YOU IN SPRING.
I LEFT THE OVEN ON.
AT LEAST THE JUDICIAL BRANCH CAN MAKE DECISIONS NOT BASED ON REELECTION STRATEGIES.
I CRY MY SELF TO SLEEP.
DA END.

Theo Edmands

Theo Edmands has a page in Meathaus. He will always refuse chewing gum. He currently occupies approximately a six foot by two foot by one foot area in Toronto, Ontario.
theoedmands@yahoo.com

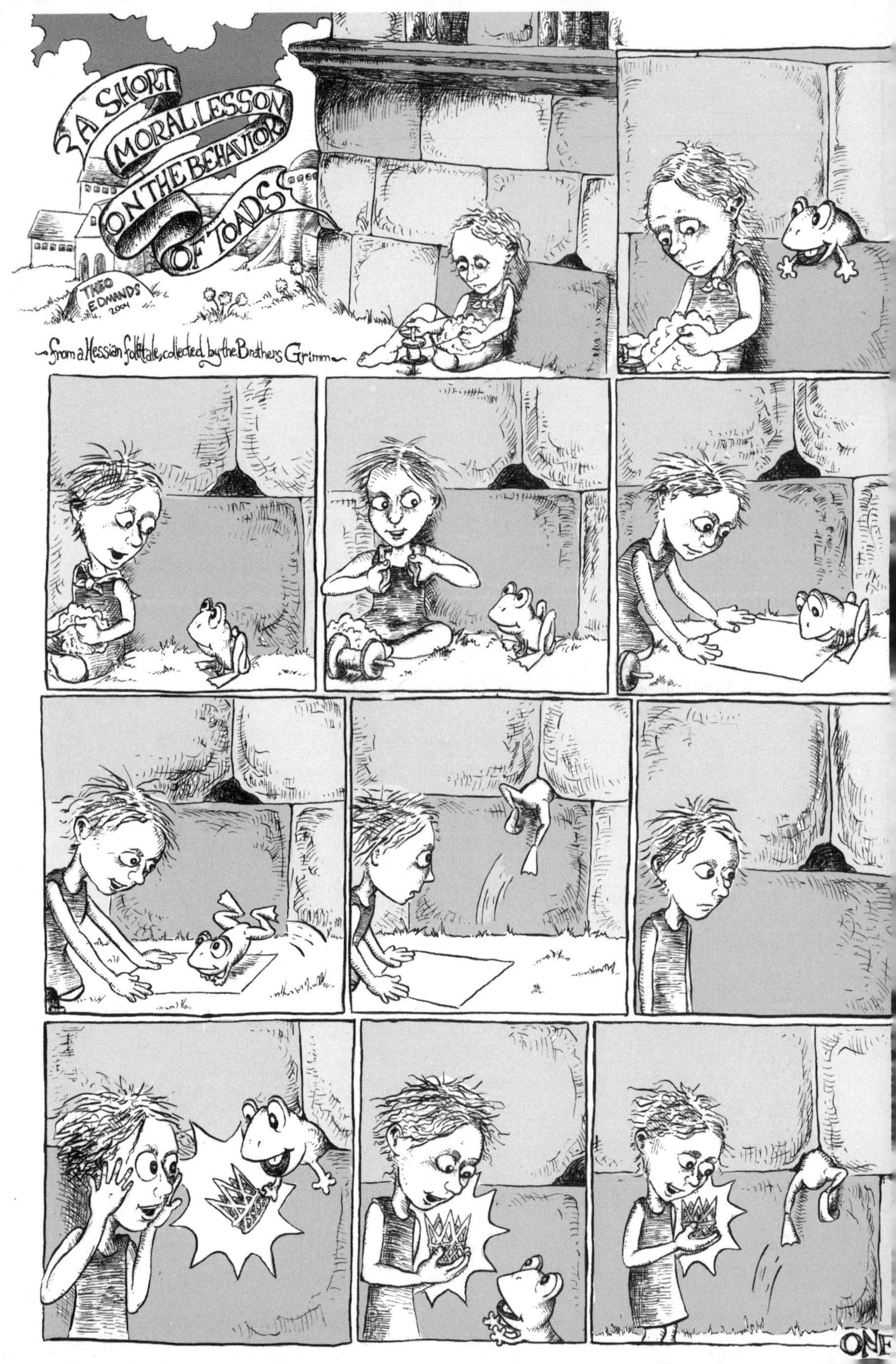

A SHORT MORAL LESSON ON THE BEHAVIOR OF TOADS
THEO EDMANDS 2004
from a Hessian folktale, collected by the Brothers Grimm
ONE

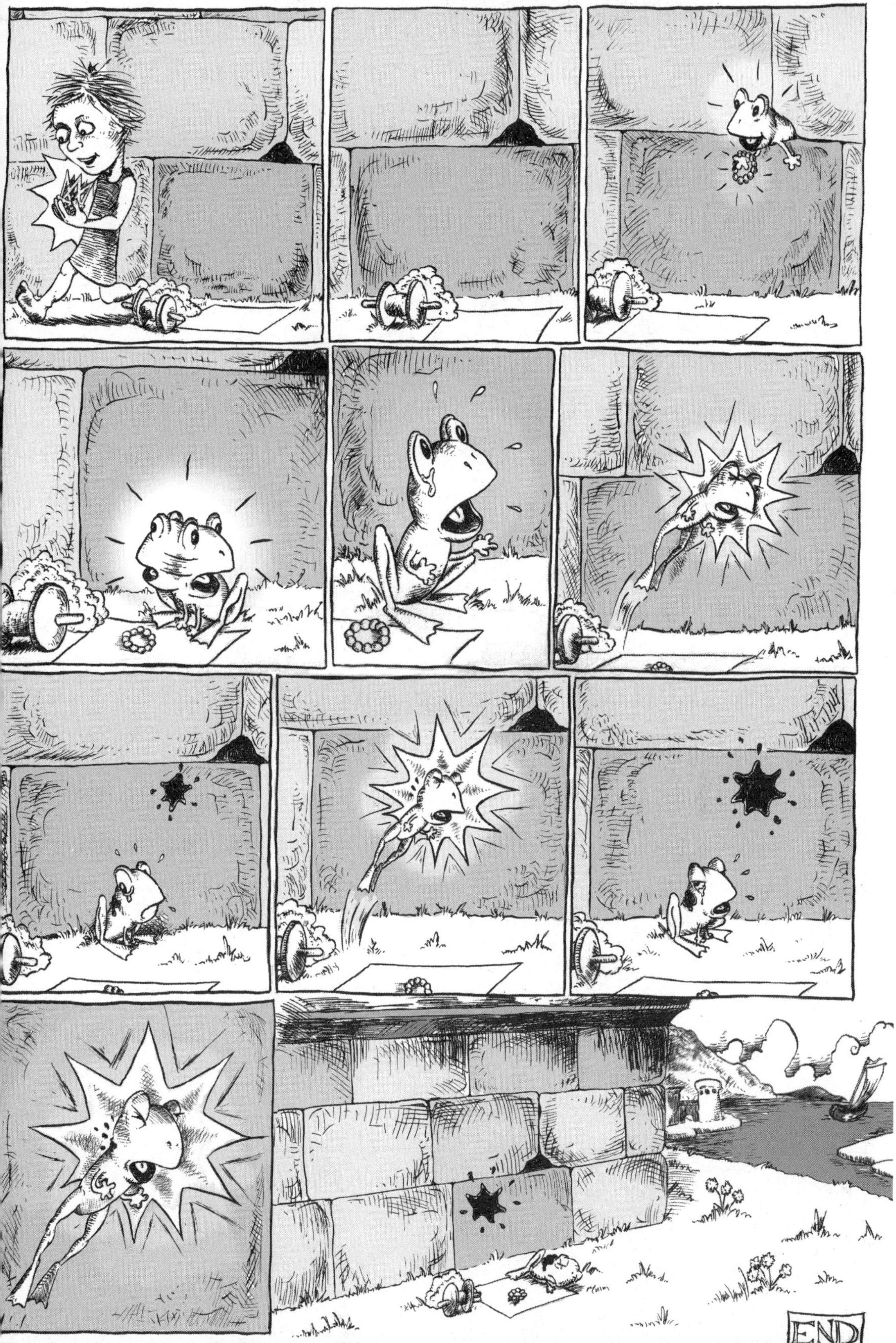
END

Vezun

Vezun loves foreign film, collecting music,
reminiscing on yesteryear's booty and be bustin'
flows sometimes. He put it down with the comics.
But, he feel like people don't read his stuff. This
fool needs some feedback. Tell him something
truthful: v3Zun@yahoo.com

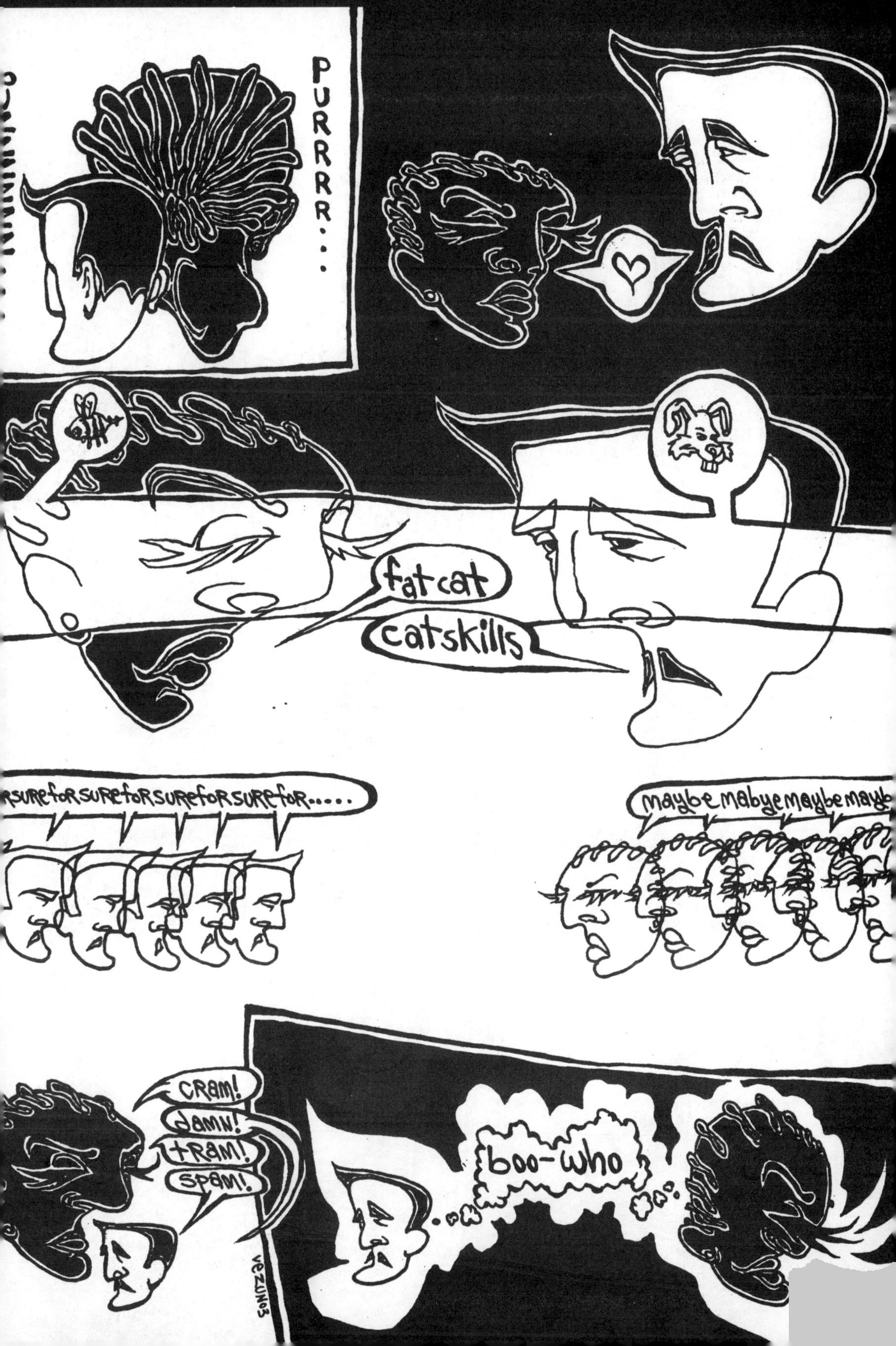
PURRRR...
fatcat
catskills
rsureforsureforsureforsureforsurefor.....
maybemabyemaybemaybemayb
cRam!
damn!
tRam!
spam!
boo-who
VEZUN03

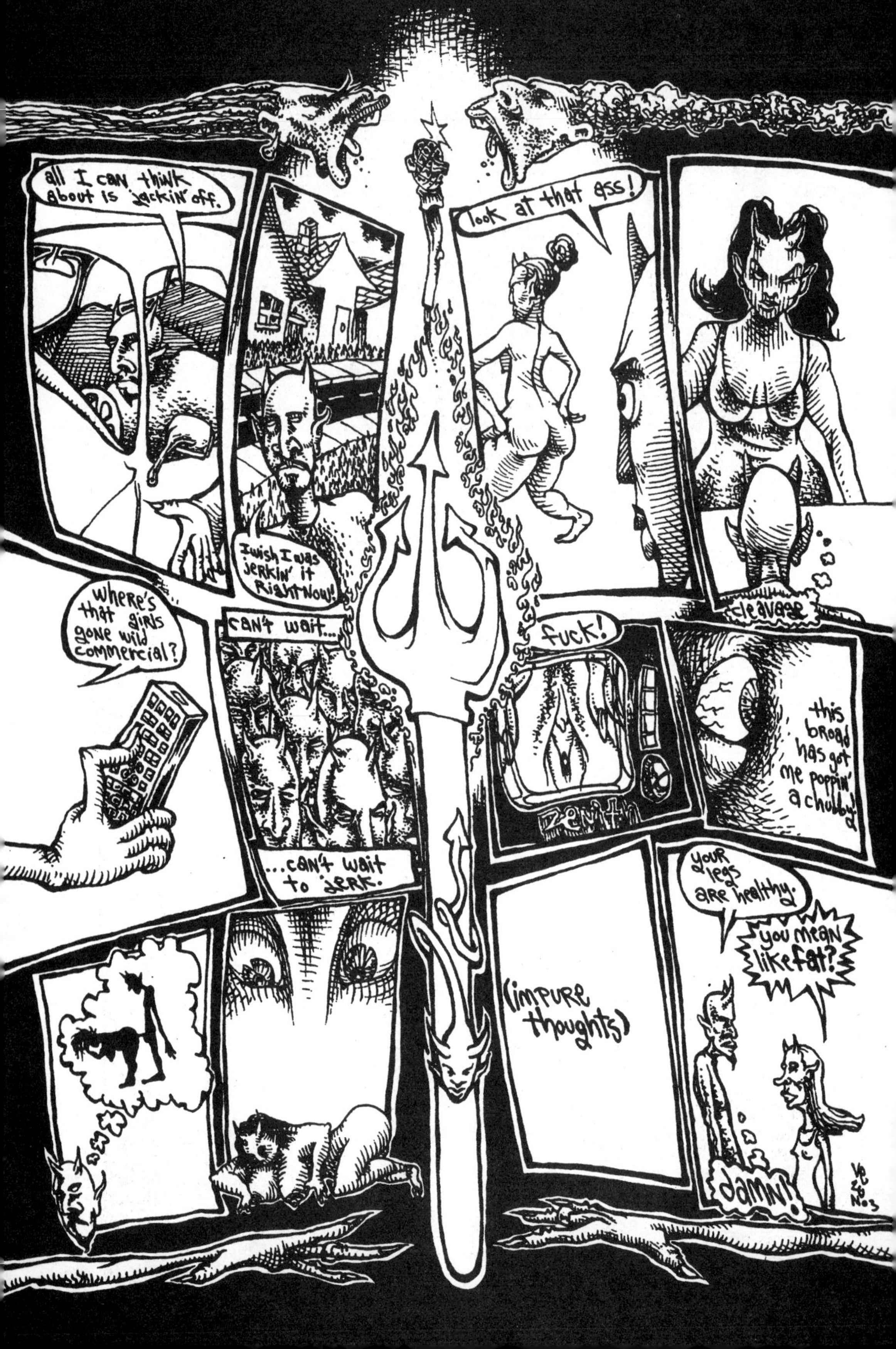
all I can think about is jerkin' off.
I wish I was jerkin' it Right Now!
look at that ass!
cleavage
where's that girls gone wild commercial?
can't wait...
...can't wait to jerk.
fuck!
Zenith
this broad has got me poppin' a chubby!
your legs are healthy.
you mean like fat?
(impure thoughts)
damn!

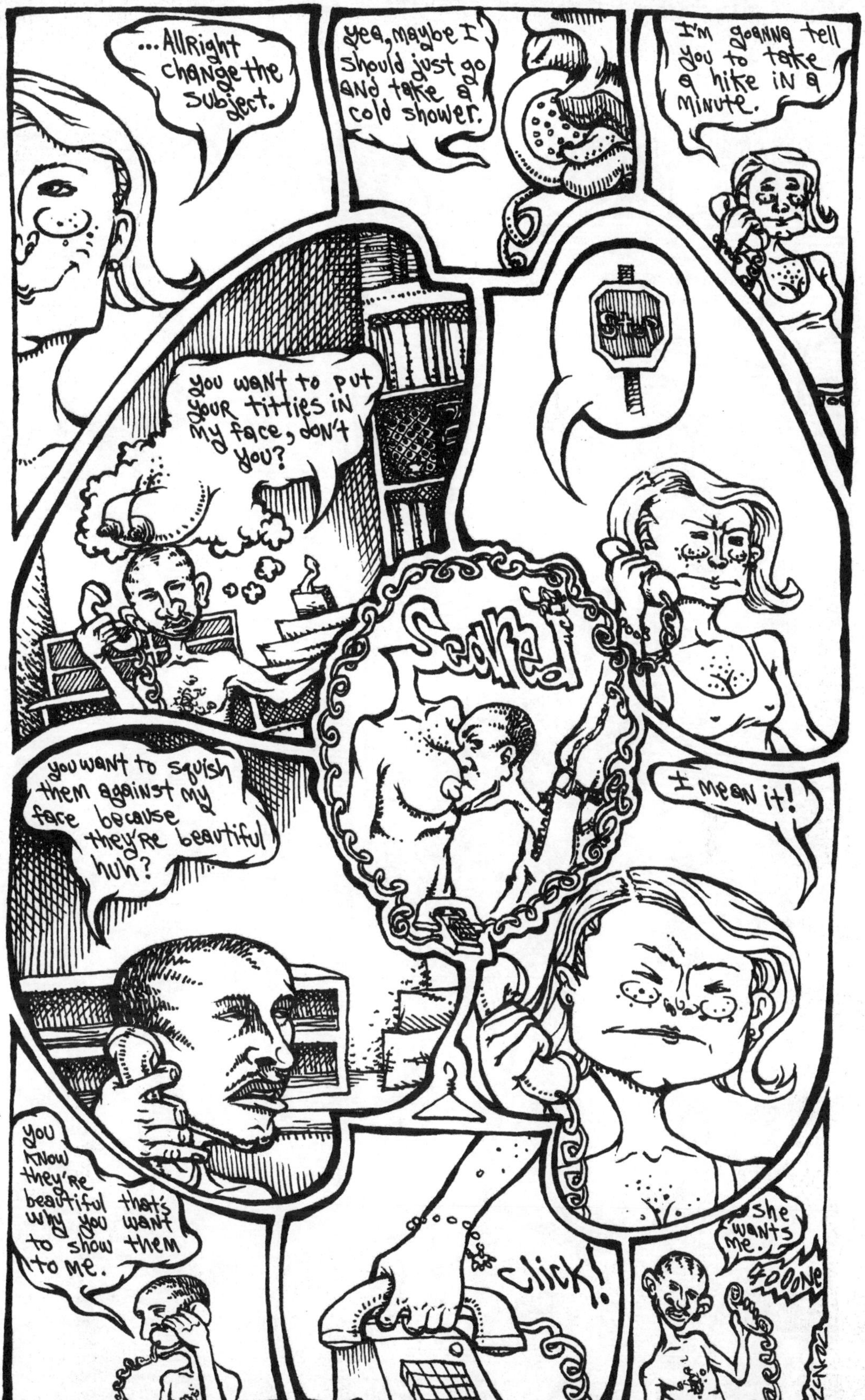
...Allright change the subject.
yea, maybe I should just go and take a cold shower.
I'm goanna tell you to take a hike in a minute.
Stop
you want to put your titties in my face, don't you?
Scored
you want to squish them against my face because they're beautiful huh?
I mean it!
you know they're beautiful that's why you want to show them to me.
click!
she wants me.

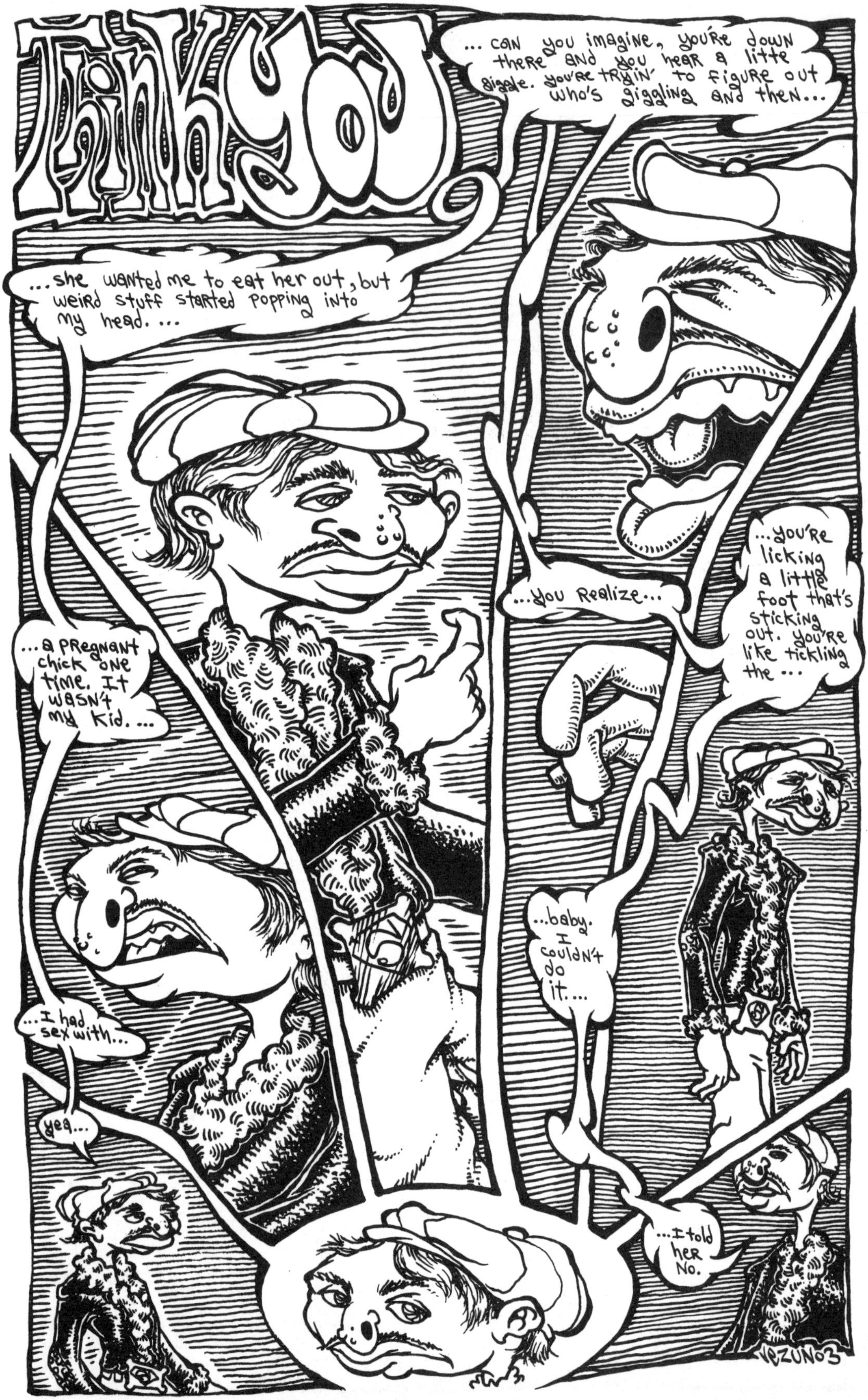
Thank You.
yea...
...I had sex with...
...a pregnant chick one time. It wasn't my kid. ...
...she wanted me to eat her out, but weird stuff started popping into my head. ...
... can you imagine, you're down there and you hear a litte giggle. you're tryin' to figure out who's giggling and then...
...you realize...
...you're licking a little foot that's sticking out. you're like tickling the ...
...baby. I couldn't do it....
...I told her No.
VEZUNO3

Esao Andrews

This bitter old man still lives in the same place in Brooklyn and wishes that everyone hadn't left NY. See his work at www.esao.net and hopefully some other random places too.

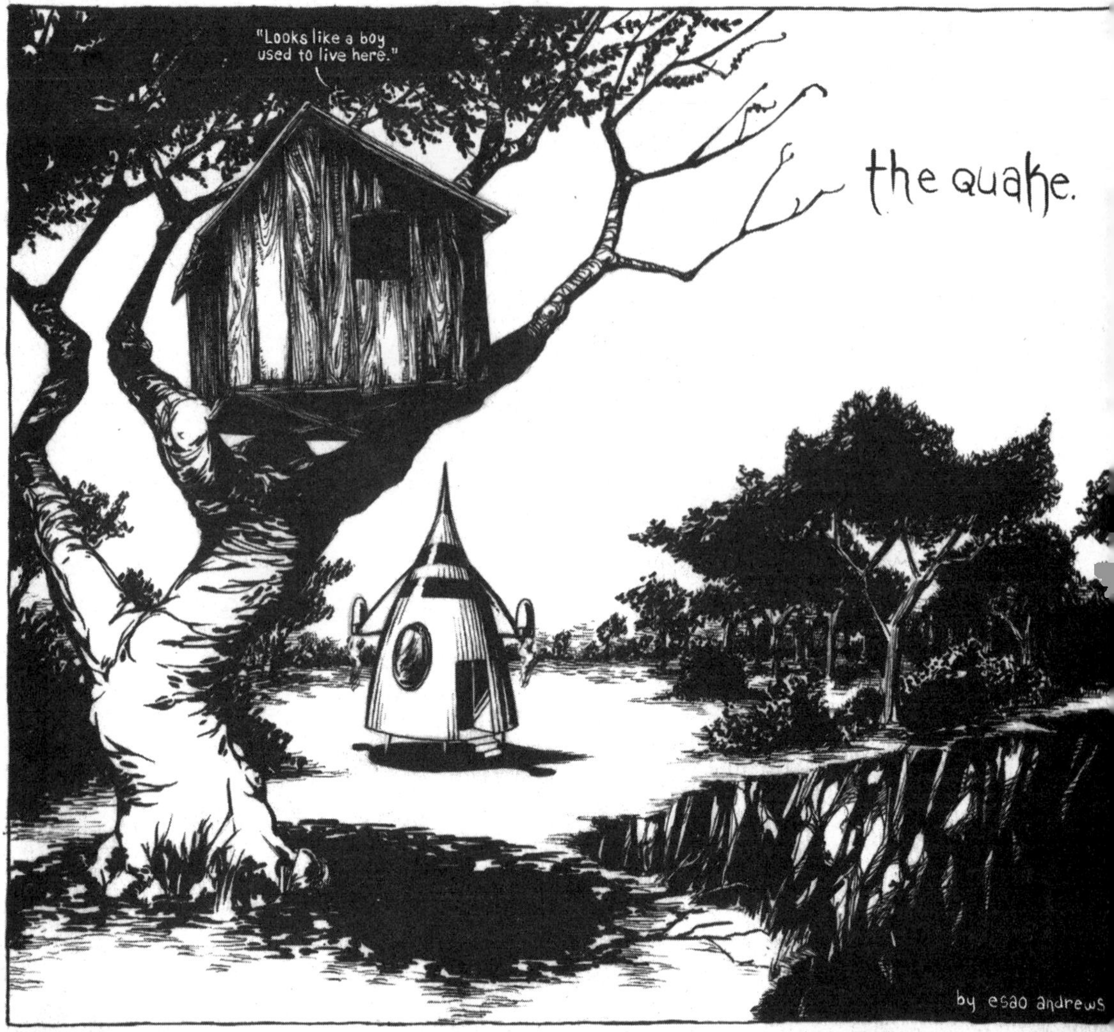
"Looks like a boy
used to live here."
the quake.
by esao andrews

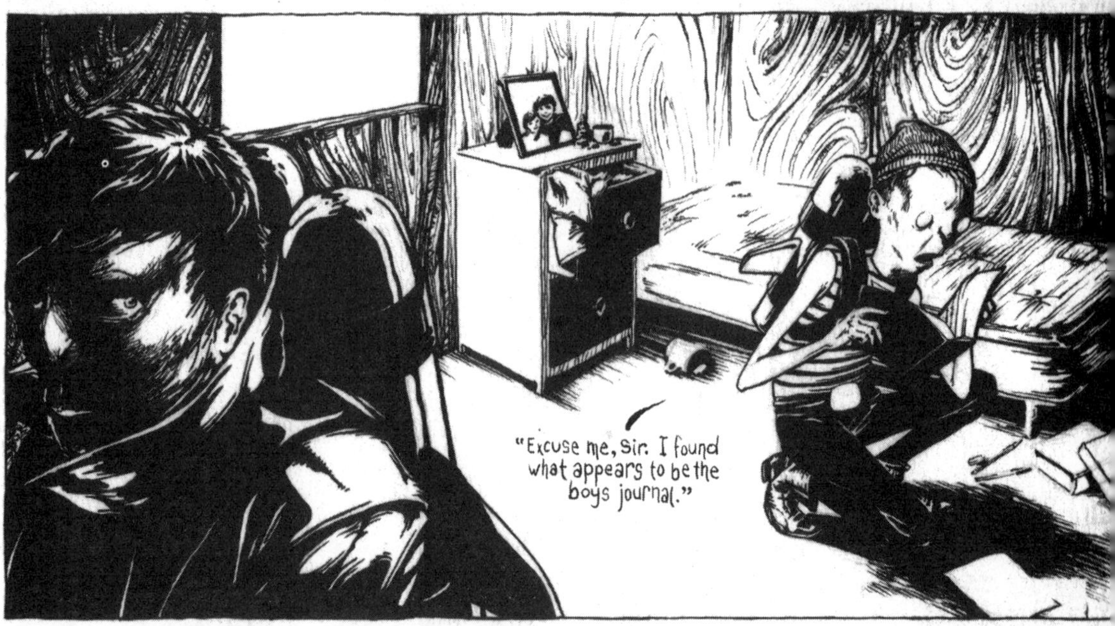
"Excuse me, sir. I found
what appears to be the
boys journal."

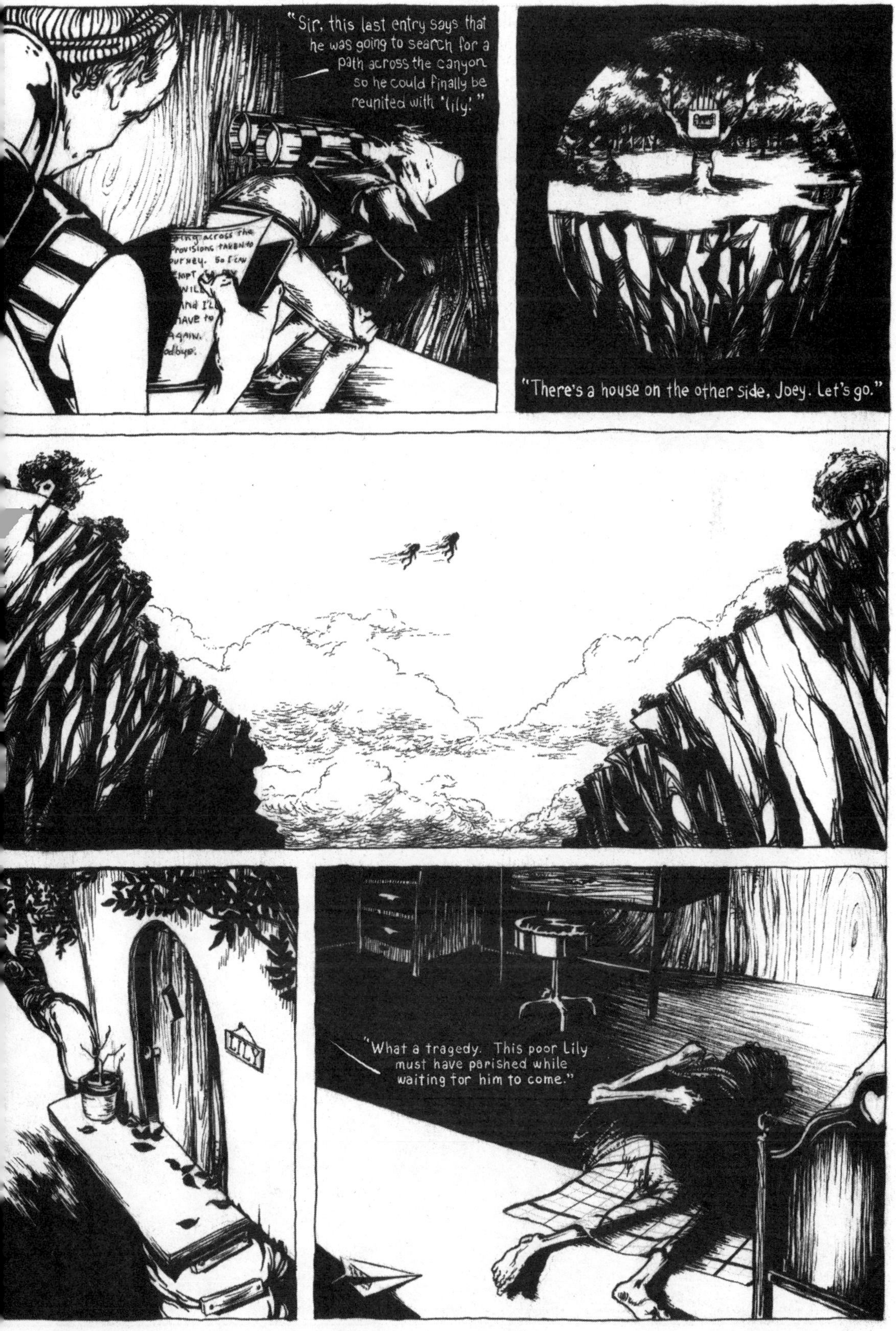
"Sir, this last entry says that he was going to search for a path across the canyon so he could finally be reunited with 'Lily.'"
"There's a house on the other side, Joey. Let's go."
LILY
"What a tragedy. This poor Lily must have parished while waiting for him to come."

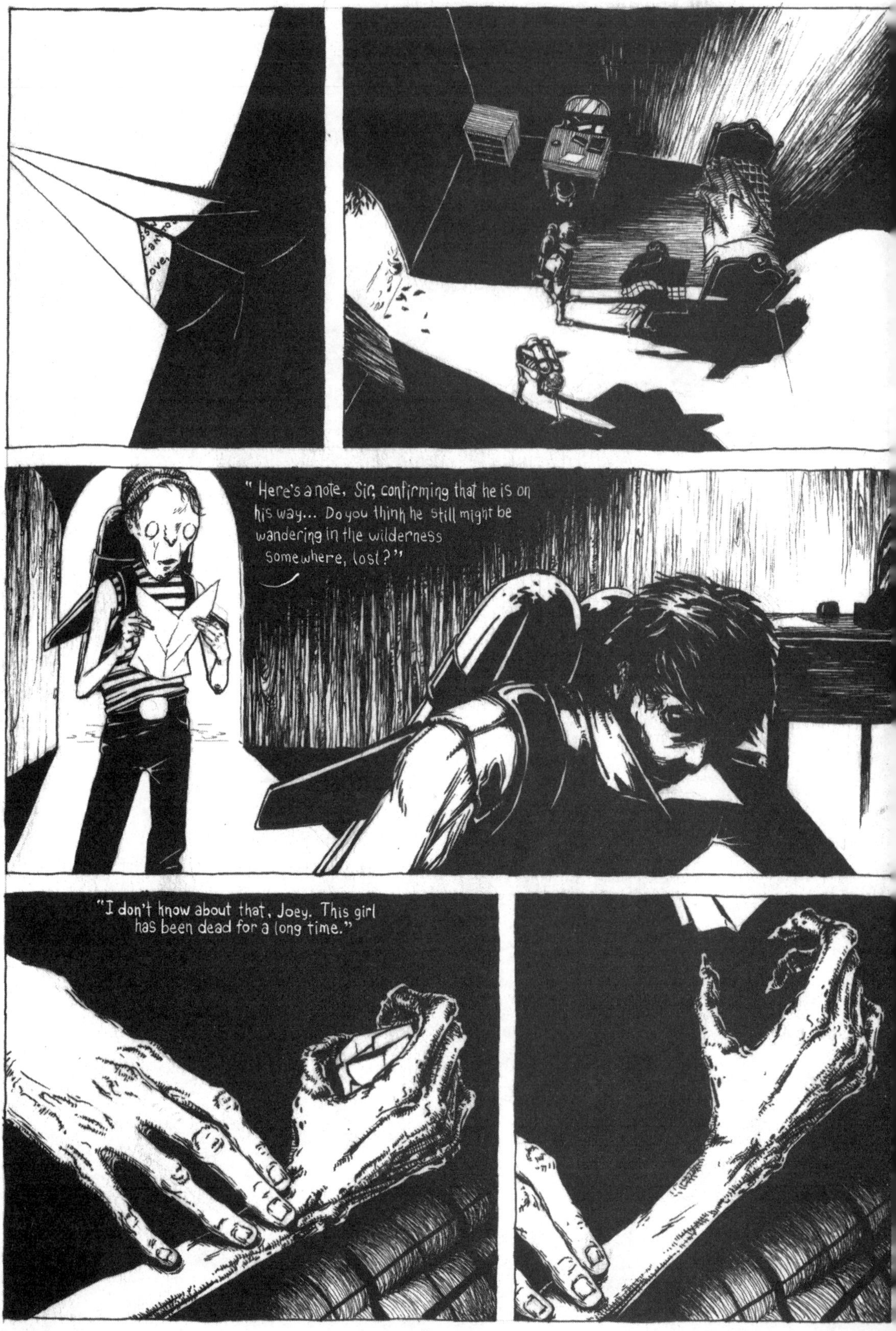
" Here's a note, Sir, confirming that he is on his way... Do you think he still might be wandering in the wilderness somewhere, lost?"
"I don't know about that, Joey. This girl has been dead for a long time."

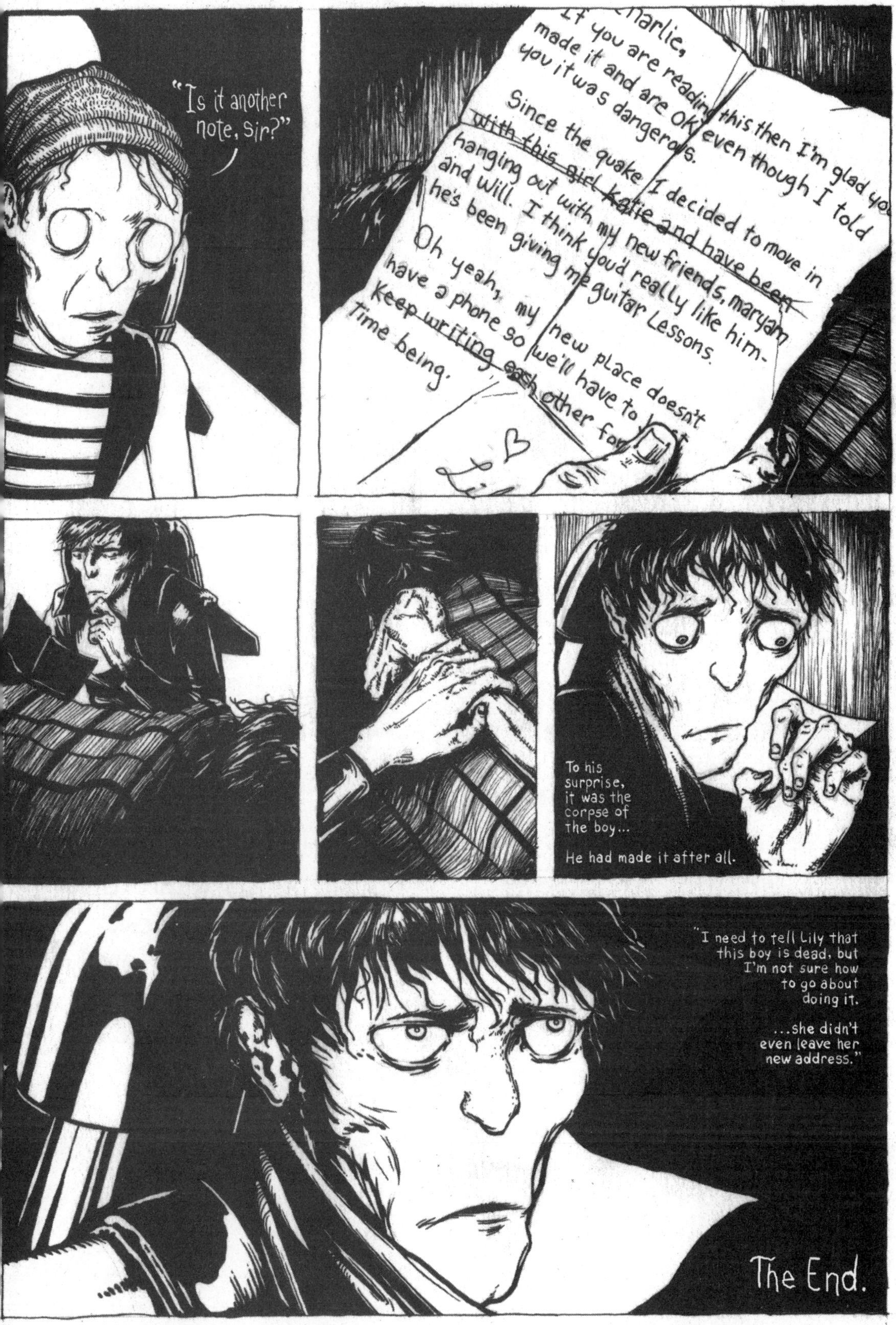
"Is it another note, sir?"
harlie,
If you are reading this then I'm glad you
made it and are OK even though I told
you it was dangerous.
Since the quake I decided to move in
with this girl Katie and have been
hanging out with my new friends, maryam
and Will. I think you'd really like him-
he's been giving me guitar Lessons.
Oh yeah, my new place doesn't
have a phone so we'll have to
Keep writing each other fo
Time being.
To his surprise, it was the corpse of the boy...
He had made it after all.
"I need to tell Lily that this boy is dead, but I'm not sure how to go about doing it.
...she didn't even leave her new address."
The End.

Jonique Williams

What's it like to be me, or someone like me?
This was something I thought would make a great
comic. As a city girl who was raised by a country
born momma. I thought I'd create a story based
on her childhood in Mississippi. Most of what was
laid out are bits and pieces of her life as a girl
who felt different in her own family. I always
related to these pieces as my own life in the
world made me feel out of place too. The world
sees people as only one thing, but what happens
when all of our different backgrounds want to be
in the foreground. I have a mixture of black,
white, and Native American cultures in my family.
Where do I fit in? Where do we all fit in?
Hmmmm....
www.jonique.com and prettymeangirl.com

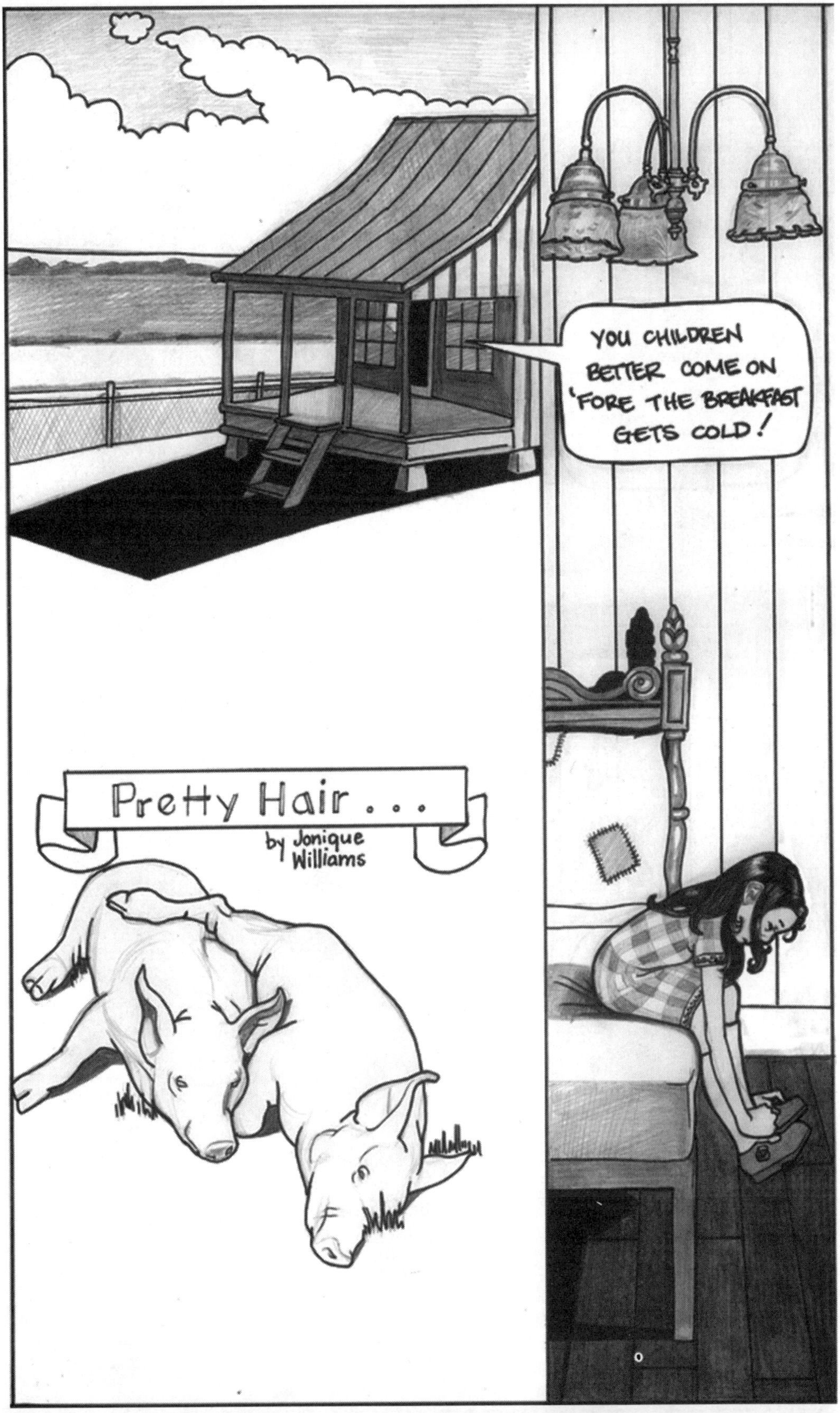
YOU CHILDREN BETTER COME ON 'FORE THE BREAKFAST GETS COLD!
Pretty Hair . . .
by Jonique Williams

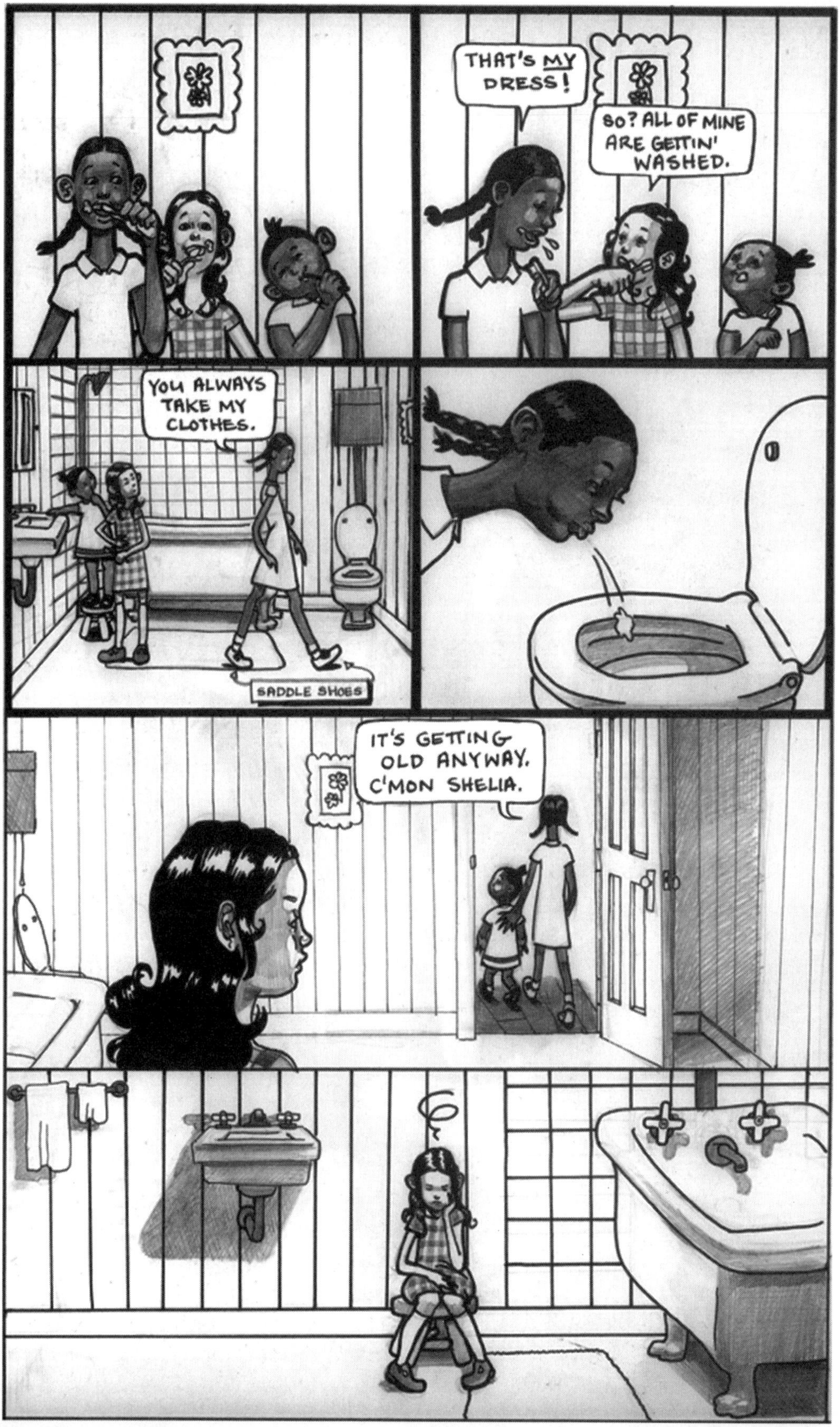
THAT'S MY DRESS!
SO? ALL OF MINE ARE GETTIN' WASHED.
YOU ALWAYS TAKE MY CLOTHES.
SADDLE SHOES
IT'S GETTING OLD ANYWAY. C'MON SHELIA.

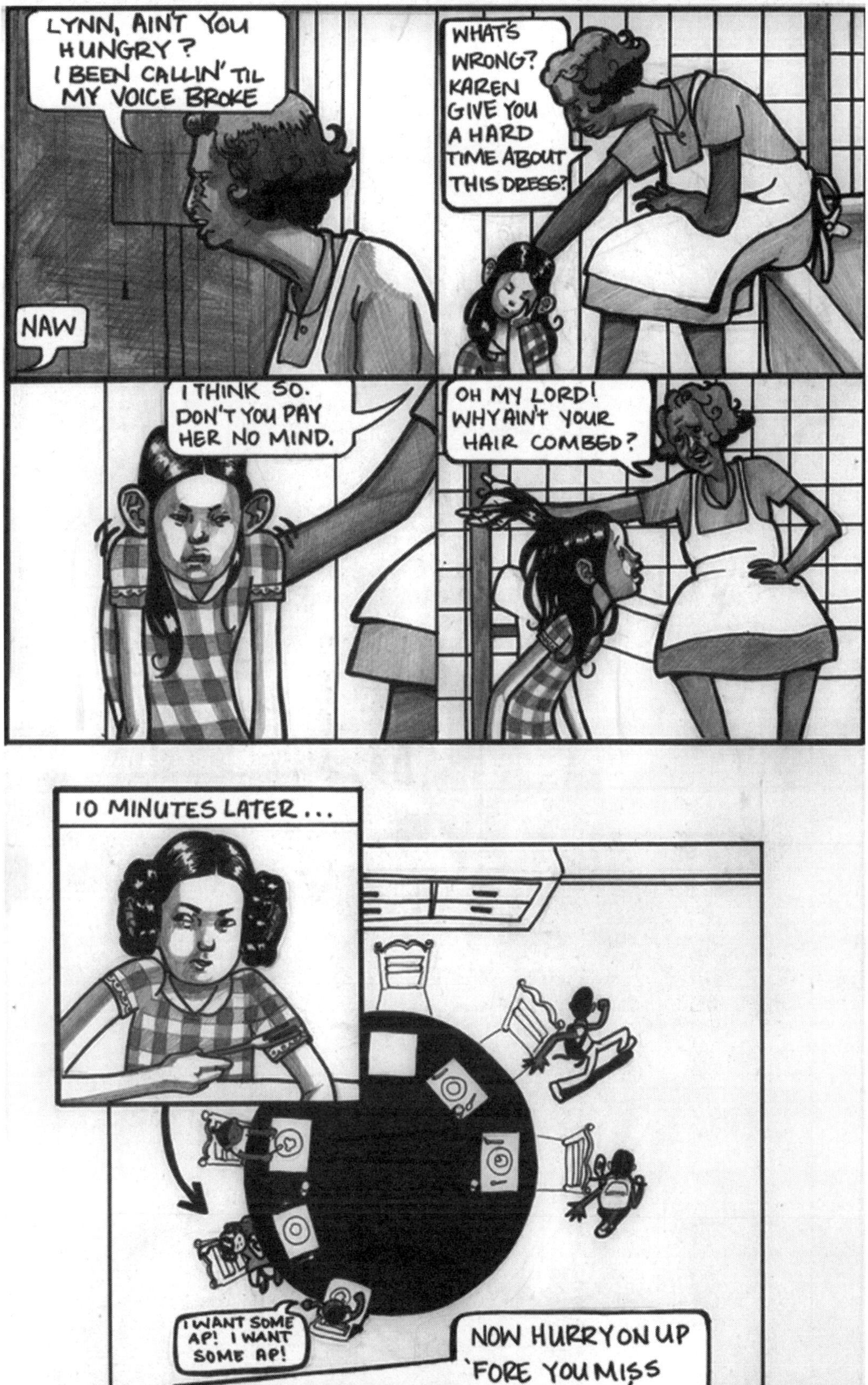
LYNN, AIN'T YOU HUNGRY? I BEEN CALLIN' TIL MY VOICE BROKE
NAW
WHAT'S WRONG? KAREN GIVE YOU A HARD TIME ABOUT THIS DRESS?
I THINK SO. DON'T YOU PAY HER NO MIND.
OH MY LORD! WHY AIN'T YOUR HAIR COMBED?
10 MINUTES LATER...
I WANT SOME AP! I WANT SOME AP!
NOW HURRY ON UP 'FORE YOU MISS SCHOOL!

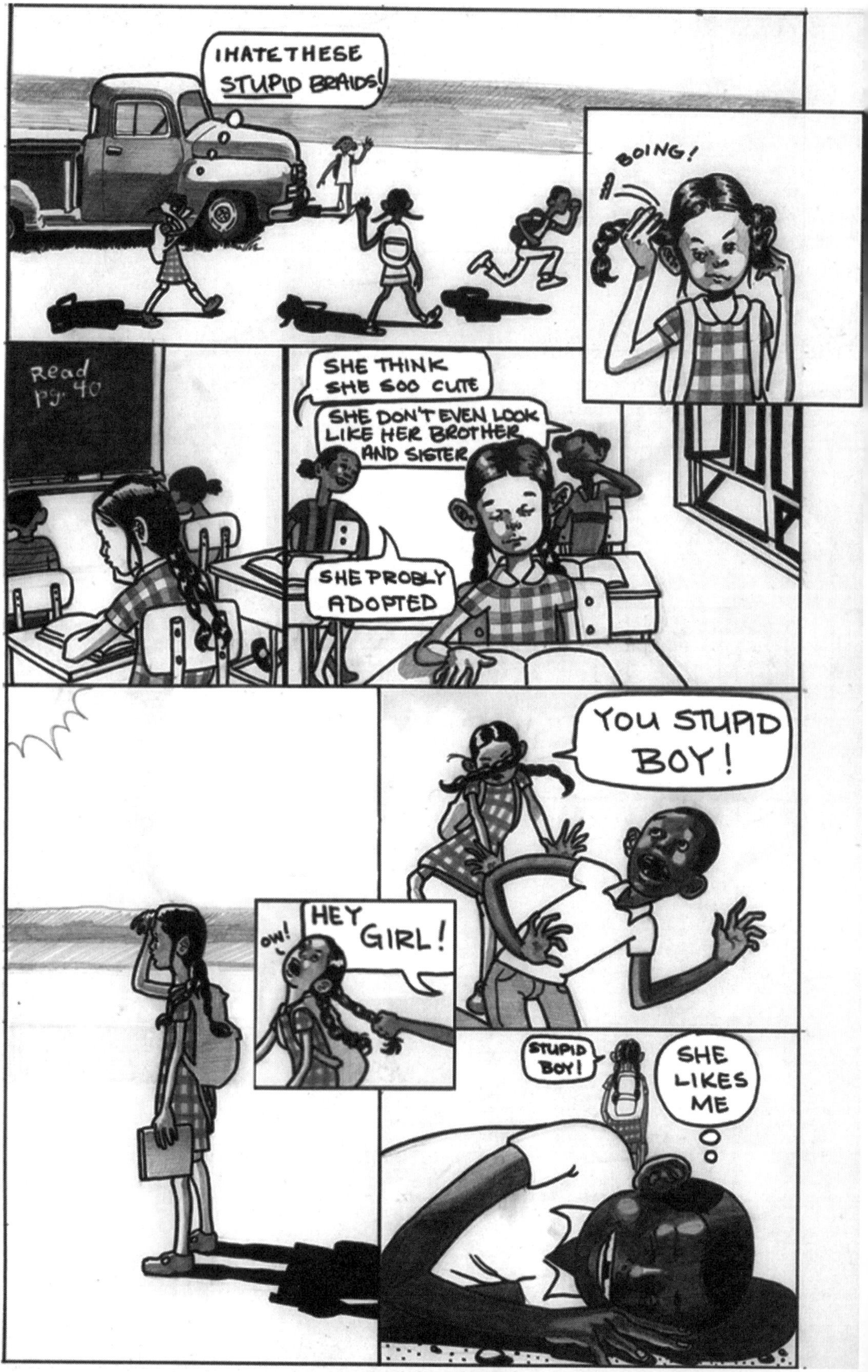

IHATE THESE STUPID BRAIDS!
BOING!
Read pg. 40
SHE THINK SHE SOO CUTE
SHE DON'T EVEN LOOK LIKE HER BROTHER AND SISTER
SHE PROBLY ADOPTED
YOU STUPID BOY!
HEY GIRL!
OW!
STUPID BOY!
SHE LIKES ME

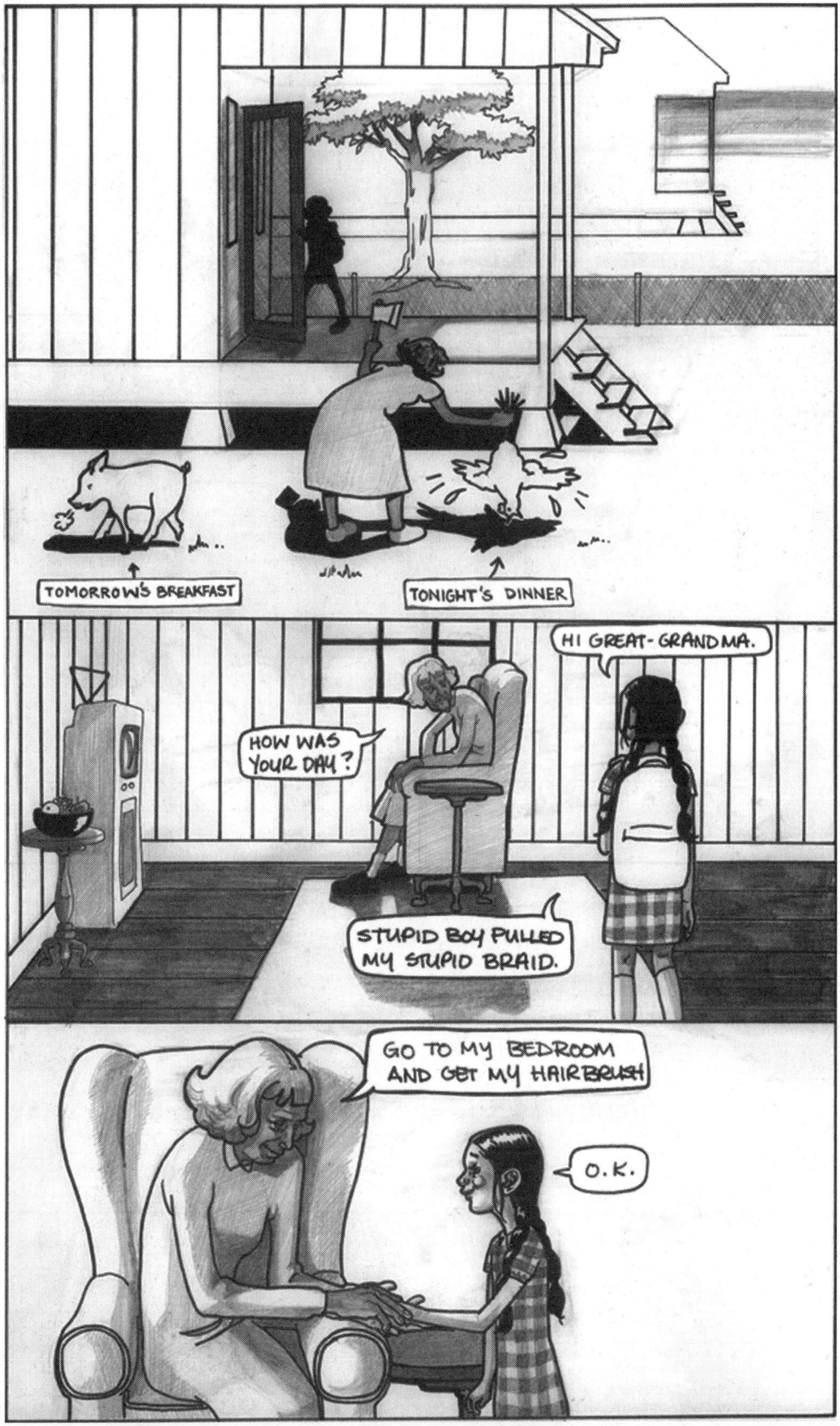
TOMORROW'S BREAKFAST
TONIGHT'S DINNER
HI GREAT-GRANDMA.
HOW WAS YOUR DAY?
STUPID BOY PULLED MY STUPID BRAID.
GO TO MY BEDROOM AND GET MY HAIRBRUSH
O.K.

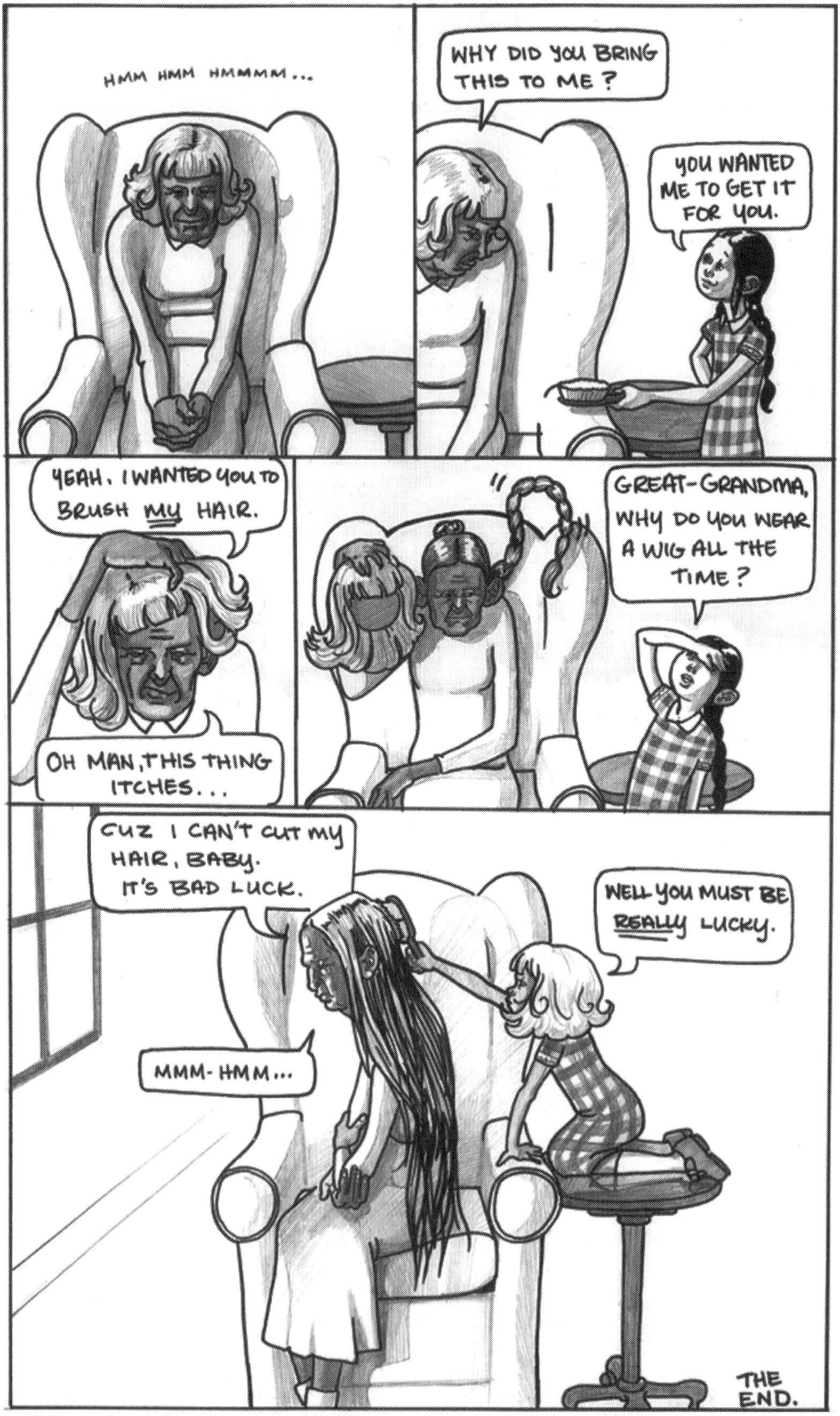
HMM HMM HMMMM...
WHY DID YOU BRING THIS TO ME?
YOU WANTED ME TO GET IT FOR YOU.
YEAH. I WANTED YOU TO BRUSH MY HAIR.
OH MAN, THIS THING ITCHES...
GREAT-GRANDMA, WHY DO YOU WEAR A WIG ALL THE TIME?
CUZ I CAN'T CUT MY HAIR, BABY. IT'S BAD LUCK.
WELL YOU MUST BE REALLY LUCKY.
MMM-HMM...
THE END.

Jasen Lex

Jasen Lex was born and raised in Pittsburgh,
Pennsylvania. His first comic was the Gypsy
Lounge.
His new comic book series is called the Science
Fair, from Antarctic Press.
His email address is jasenlex@hotmail.com.

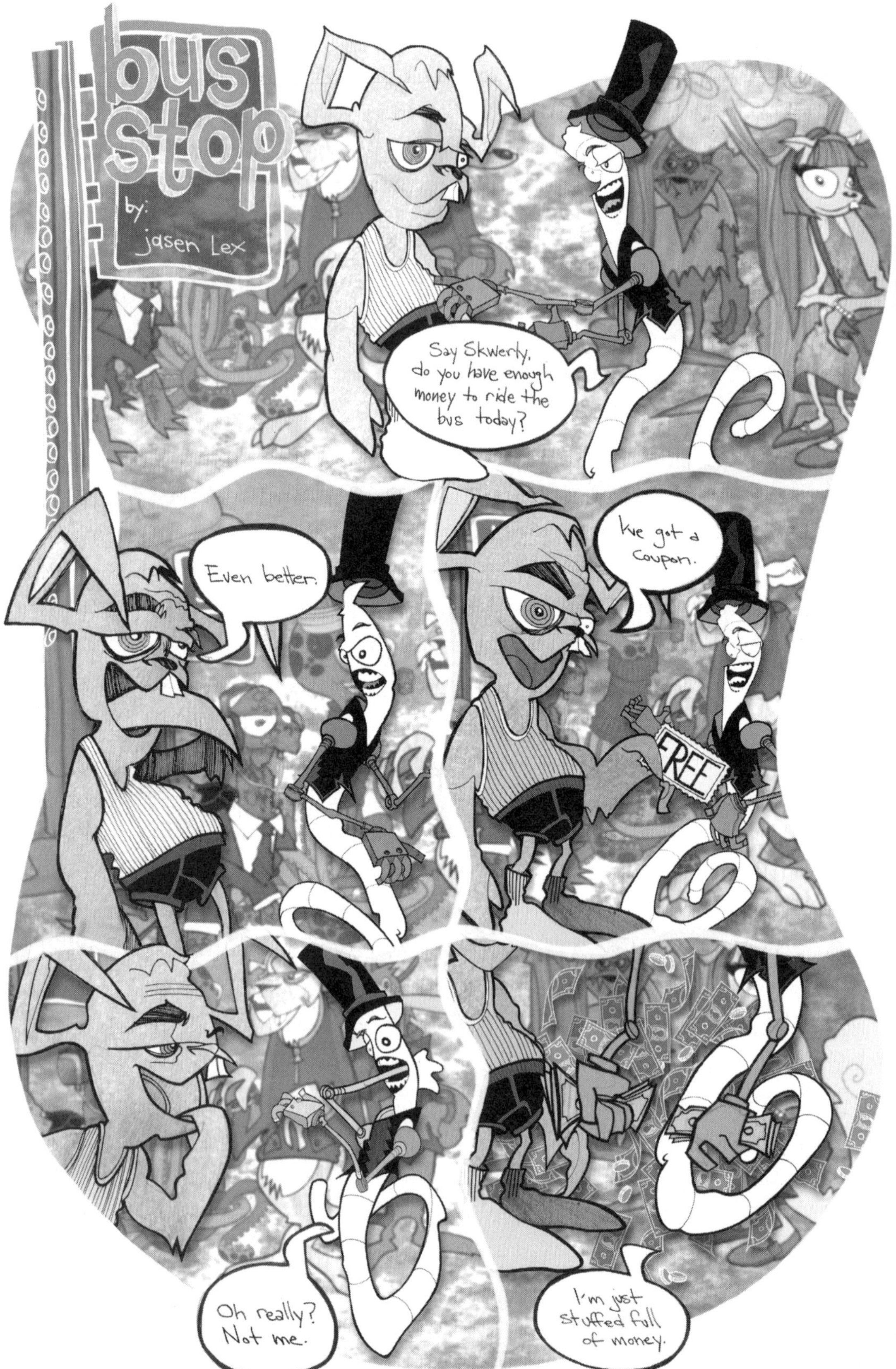
bus stop
by: jasen Lex
Say Skwerly, do you have enough money to ride the bus today?
Even better.
I've got a coupon.
FREE
Oh really? Not me.
I'm just stuffed full of money.

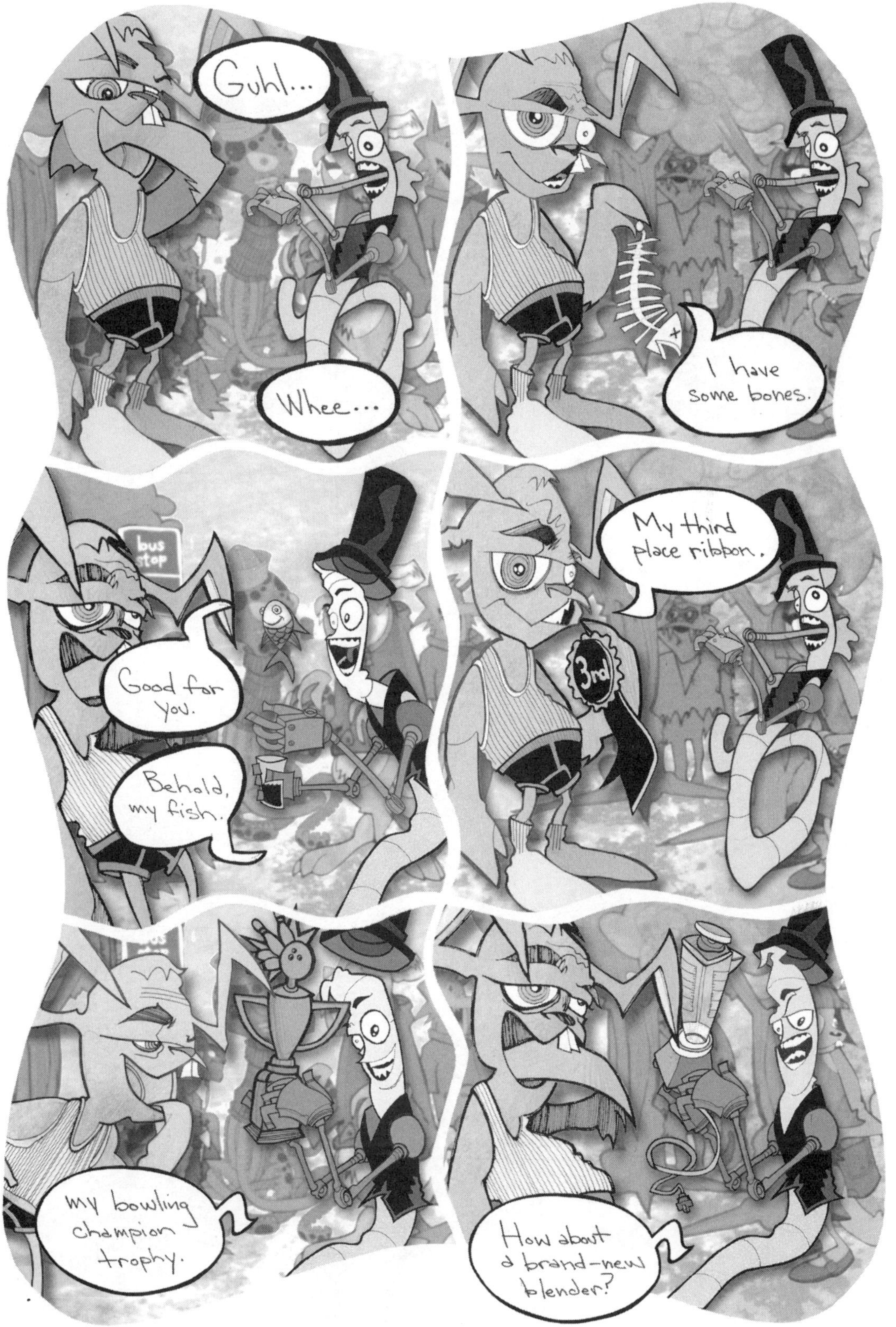
Guhl...
Whee...
I have some bones.
bus stop
Good for you.
Behold, my fish.
My third place ribbon.
3rd
my bowling champion trophy.
How about a brand-new blender?

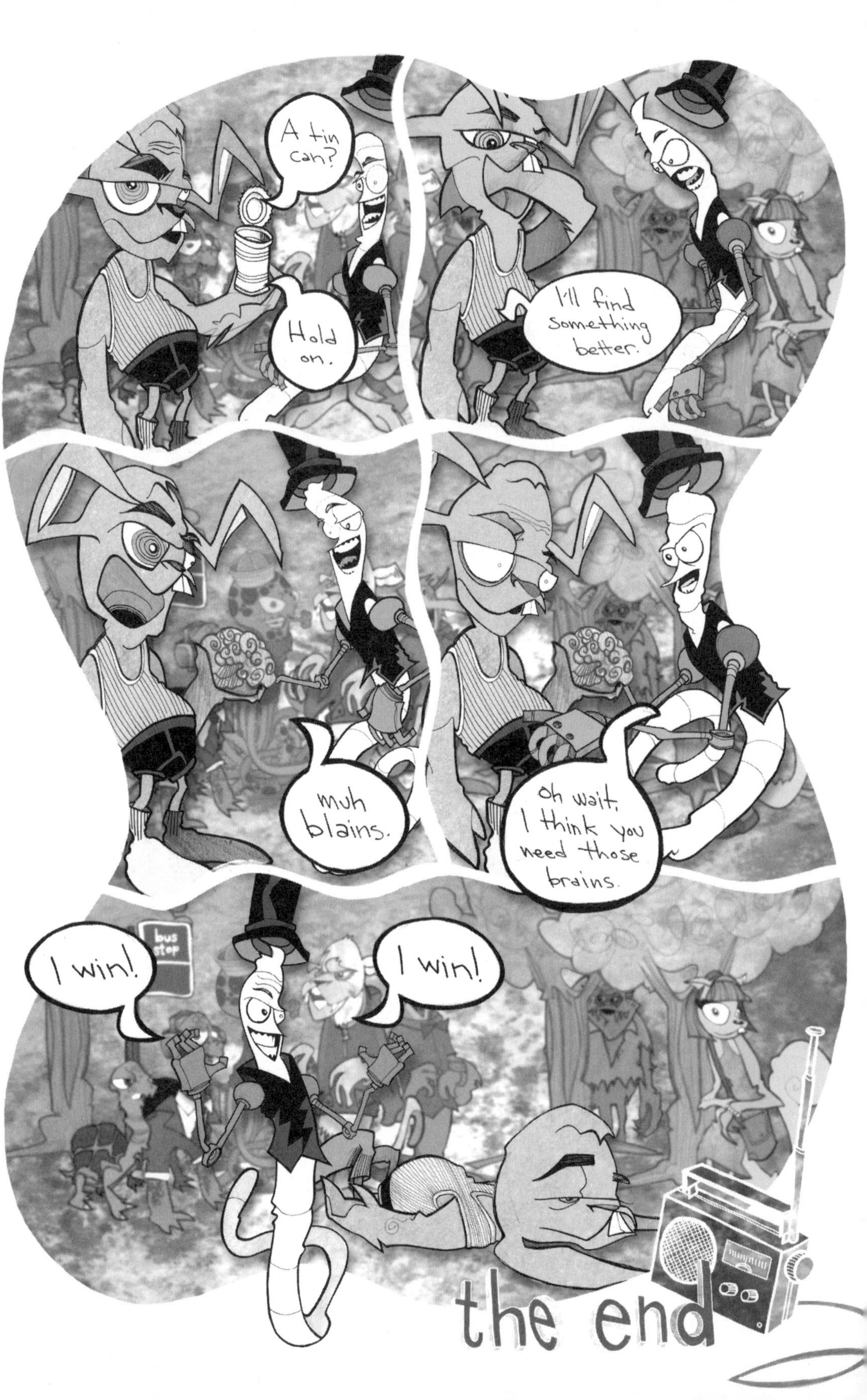
A tin can?
Hold on.
I'll find something better.
muh blains.
oh wait, I think you need those brains.
bus stop
I win!
I win!
the end

Stephen Gilpin

stephen's favorite food is pizza. -- no. candy.
sgilpin.com
sparkgilpin@cox.net

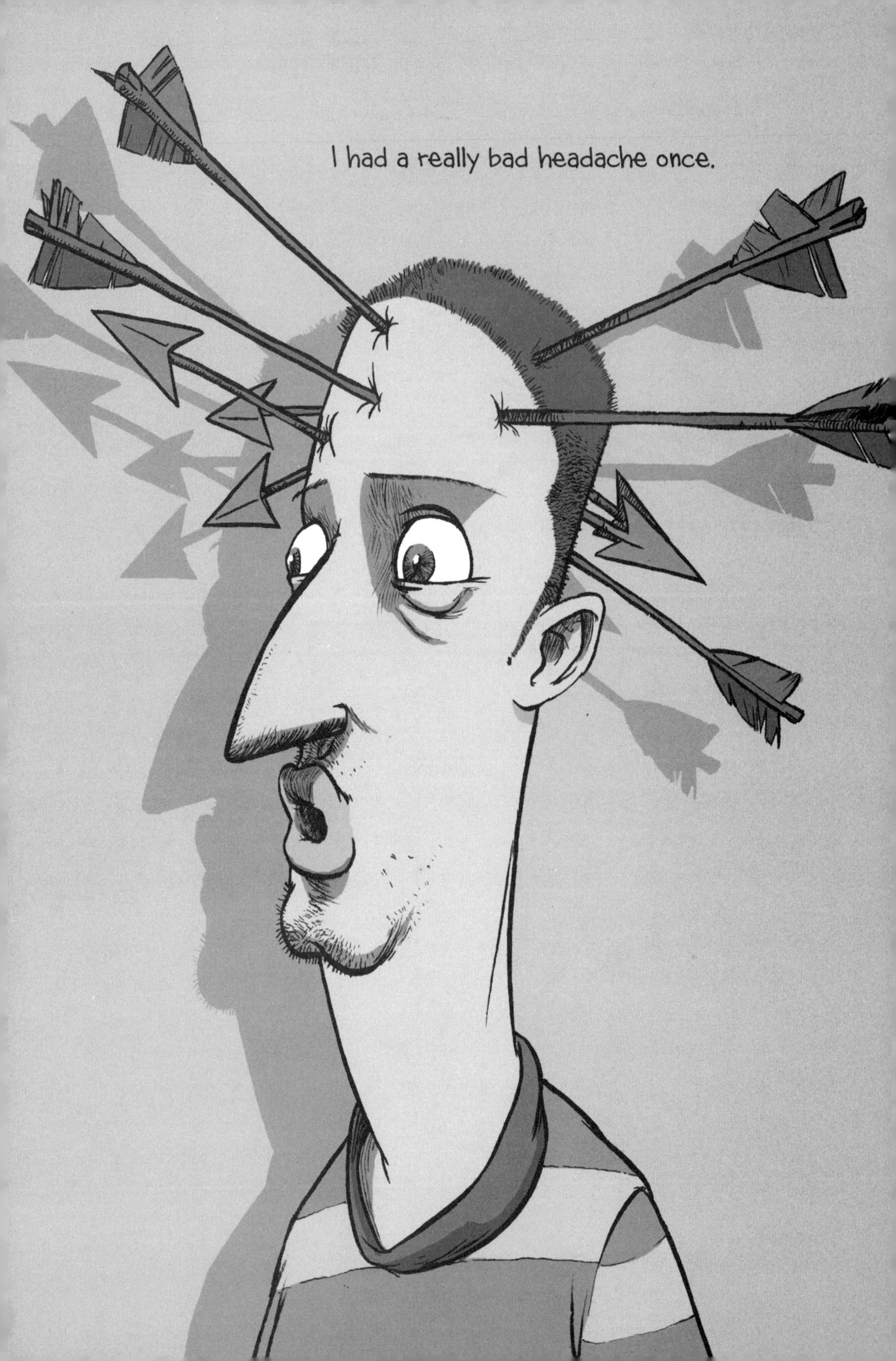
I had a really bad headache once.

My mom used to tell me all kinds of things that needed to be done, directions on how to do them and suggestions on what to do after I was finished. I didn't ever remember what she said.

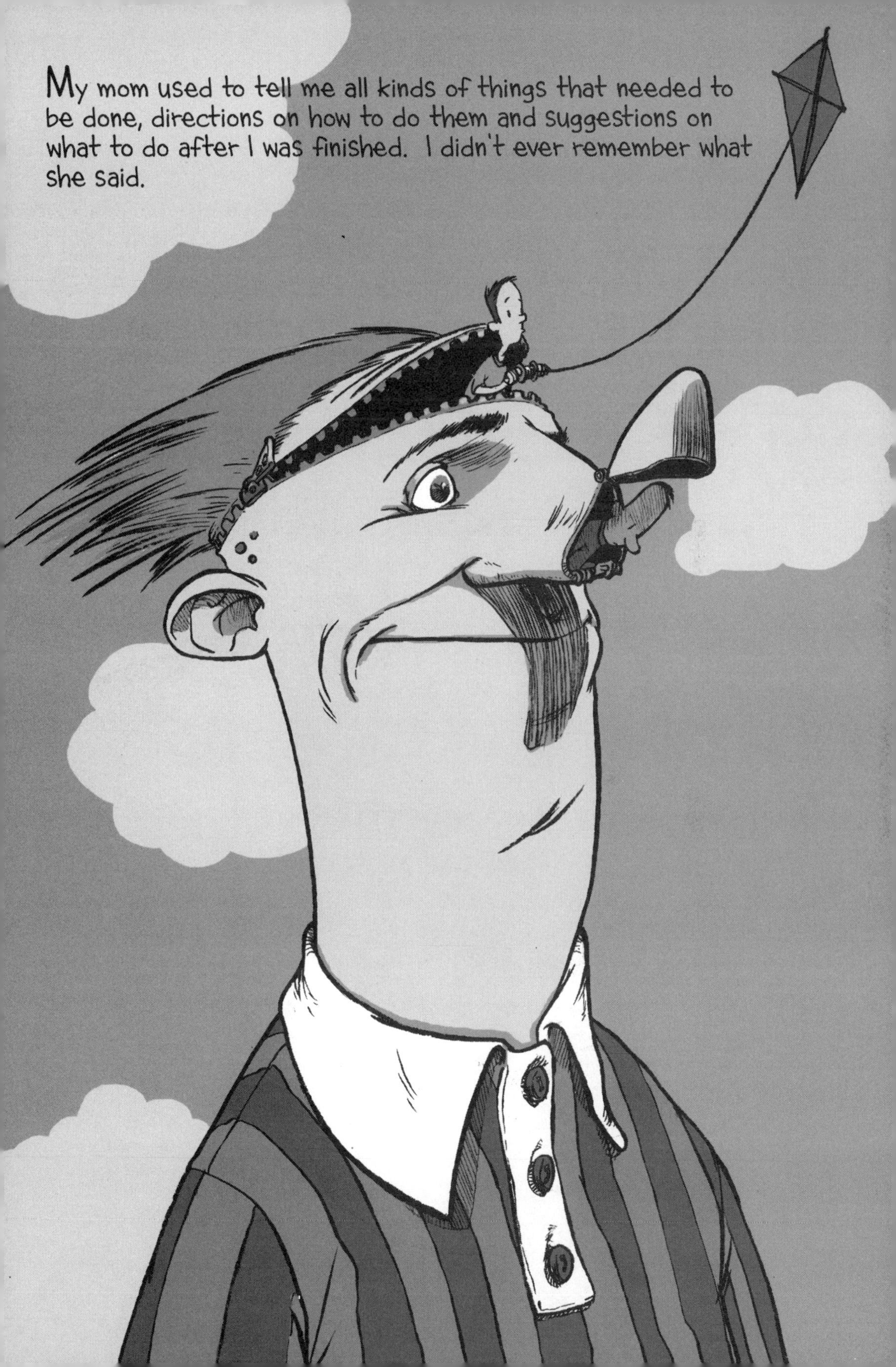

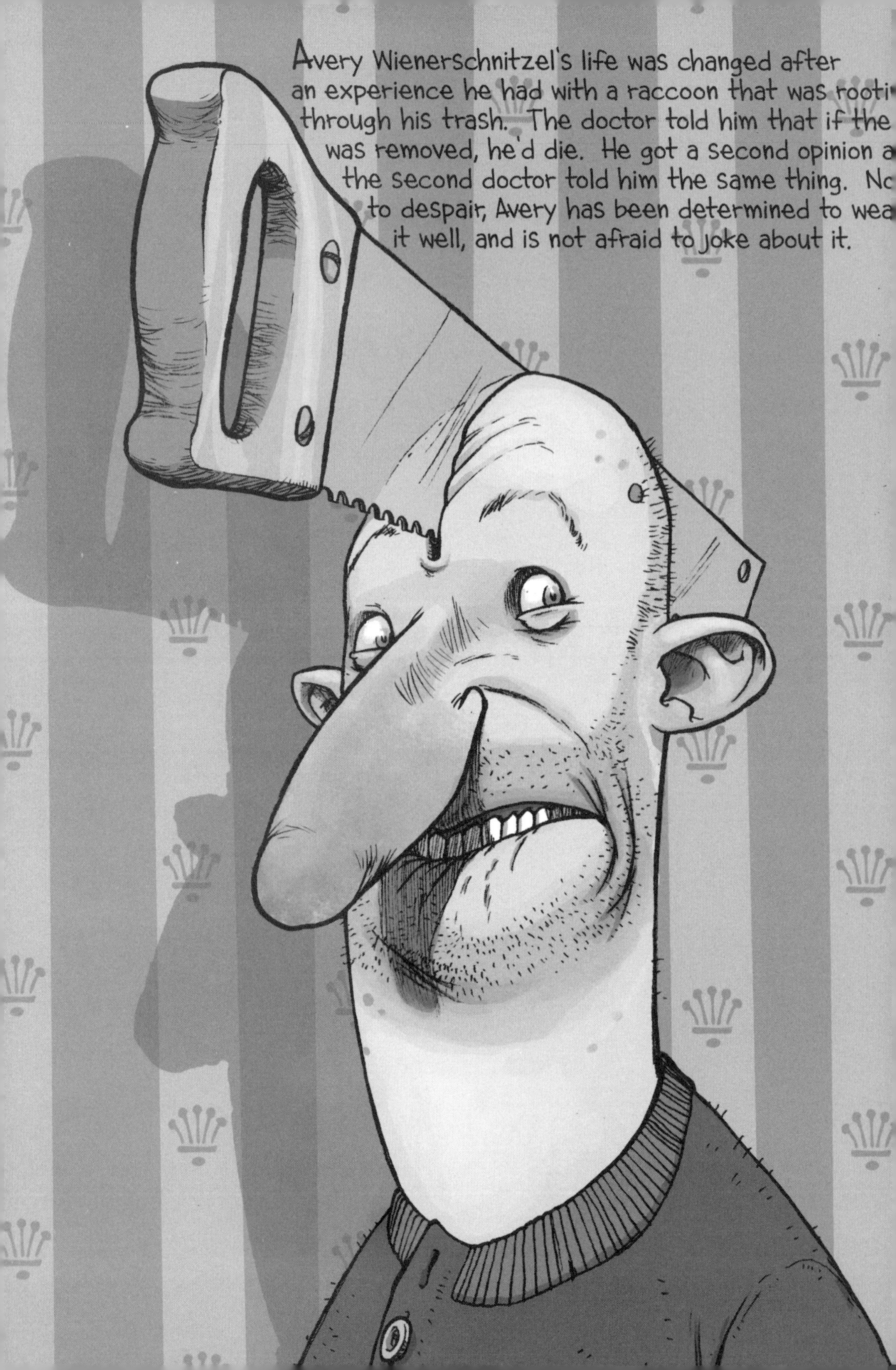
Avery Wienerschnitzel's life was changed after
an experience he had with a raccoon that was rooti
through his trash. The doctor told him that if the
was removed, he'd die. He got a second opinion a
the second doctor told him the same thing. No
to despair, Avery has been determined to wea
it well, and is not afraid to joke about it.

The Whistle Inhibitor

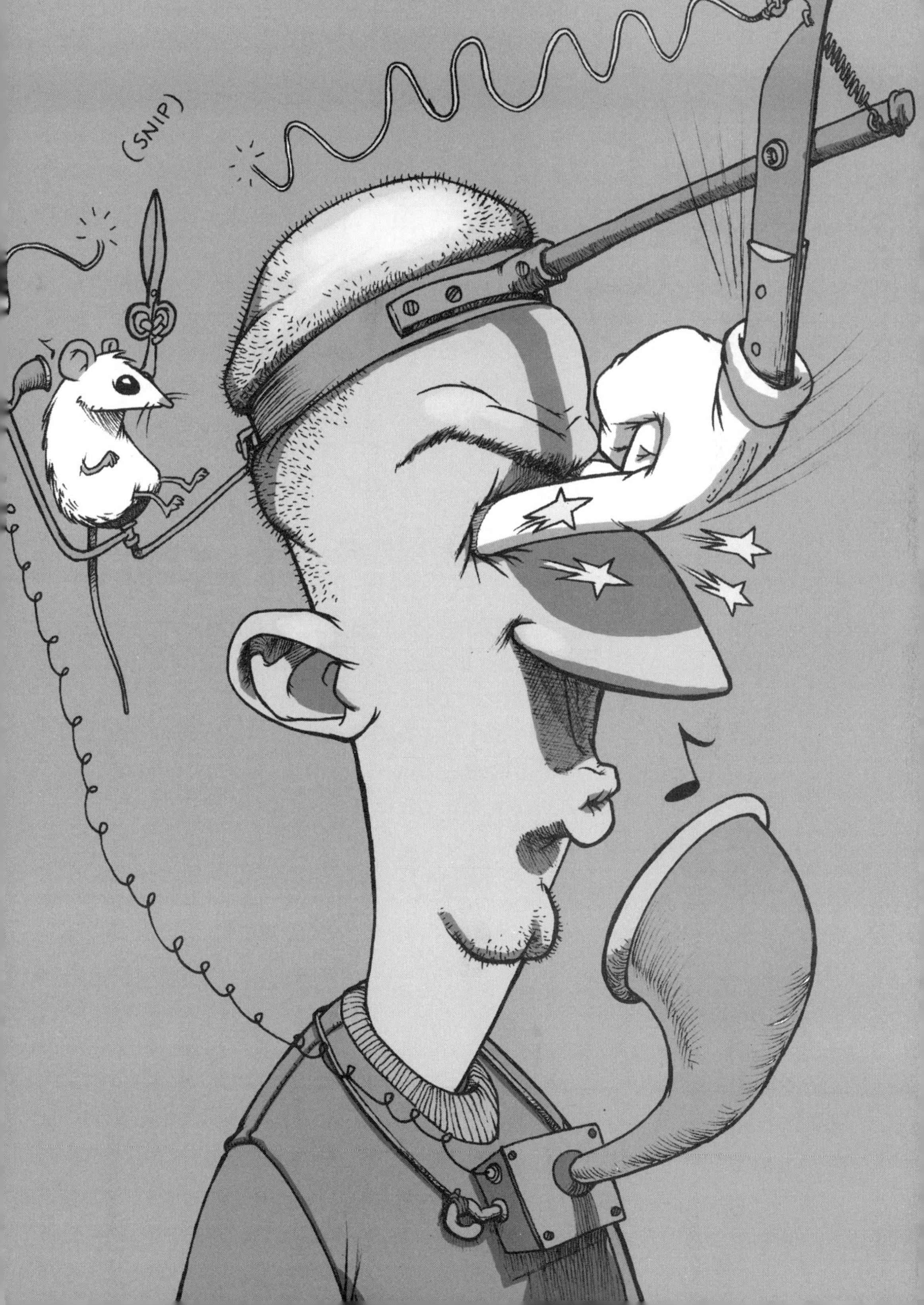
(SNIP)

Nate Powell

Nate Powell is a fidgety, spritely 27-year old fellow from Little Rock, Arkansas. He currently lives in Bloomington, Indiana, where he skittishly draws comics, plans adventures with his band Soophie Nun Squad, runs Harlan Records, works full time doing support for adults with developmental disabilities, plays with animals, eats rice cakes, and romances the stone. His comics include "Please Release", "It Disappears", "Tiny Giants", "Walkie Talkie", and "Conditions". He's currently working on a new book entitled "Wormwood".

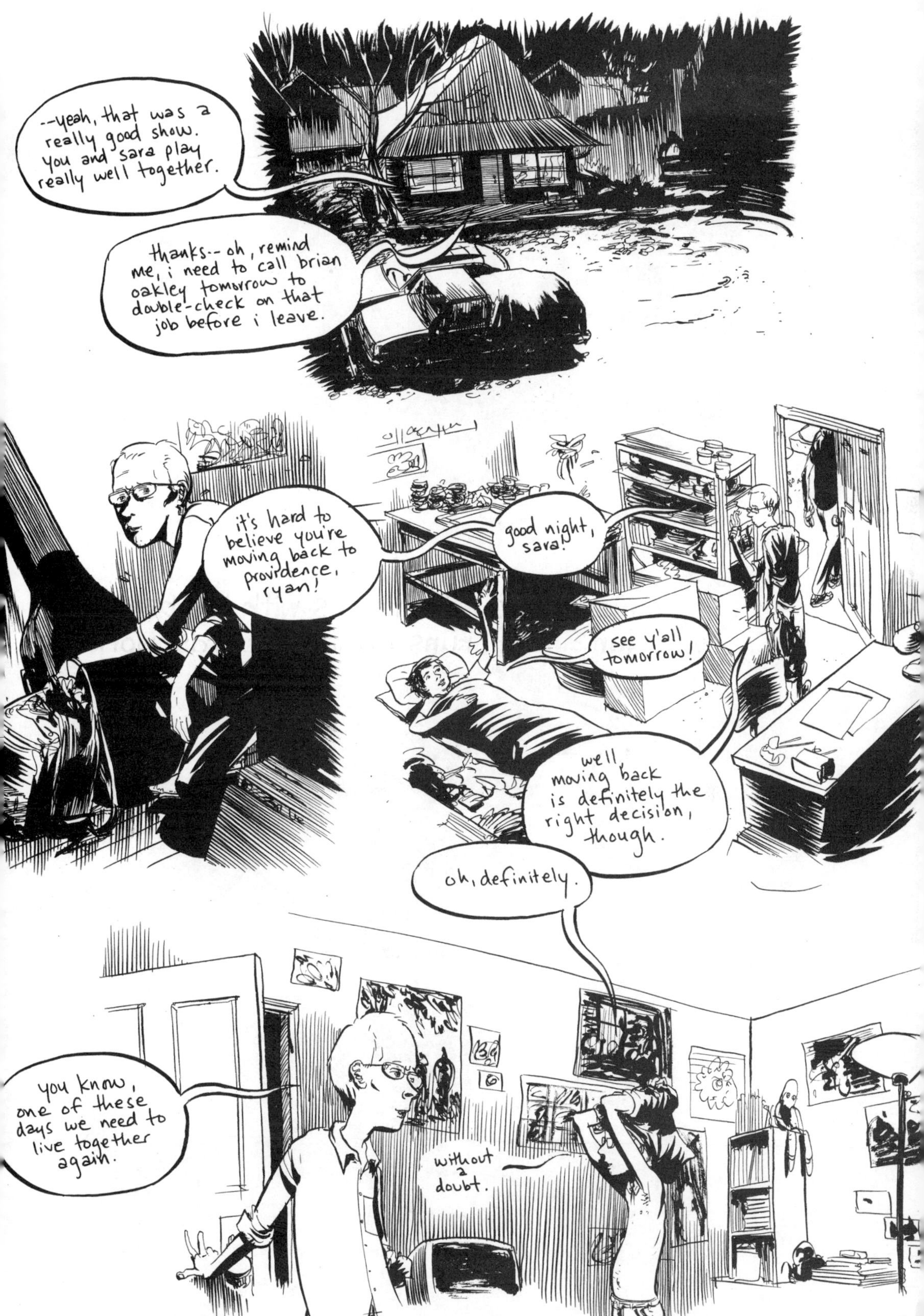
--yeah, that was a really good show. you and sara play really well together.
thanks.- oh, remind me, i need to call brian oakley tomorrow to double-check on that job before i leave.
it's hard to believe you're moving back to providence, ryan!
good night, sara!
see y'all tomorrow!
well moving back is definitely the right decision, though.
oh, definitely.
you know, one of these days we need to live together again.
without a doubt.

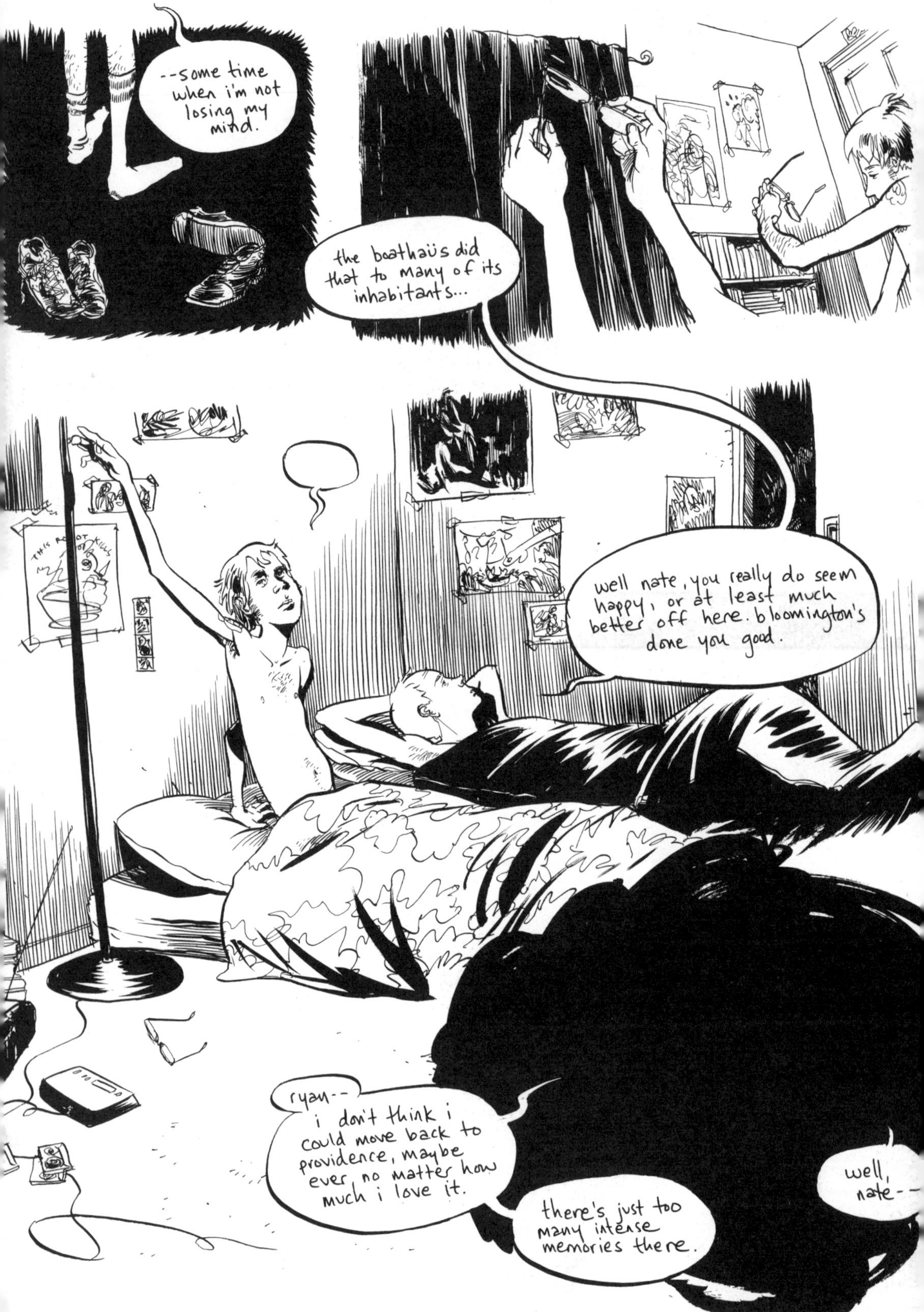
--some time when i'm not losing my mind.
the boathaüs did that to many of its inhabitants...
well nate, you really do seem happy, or at least much better off here. bloomington's done you good.
ryan-- i don't think i could move back to providence, maybe ever, no matter how much i love it.
there's just too many intense memories there.
well, nate--

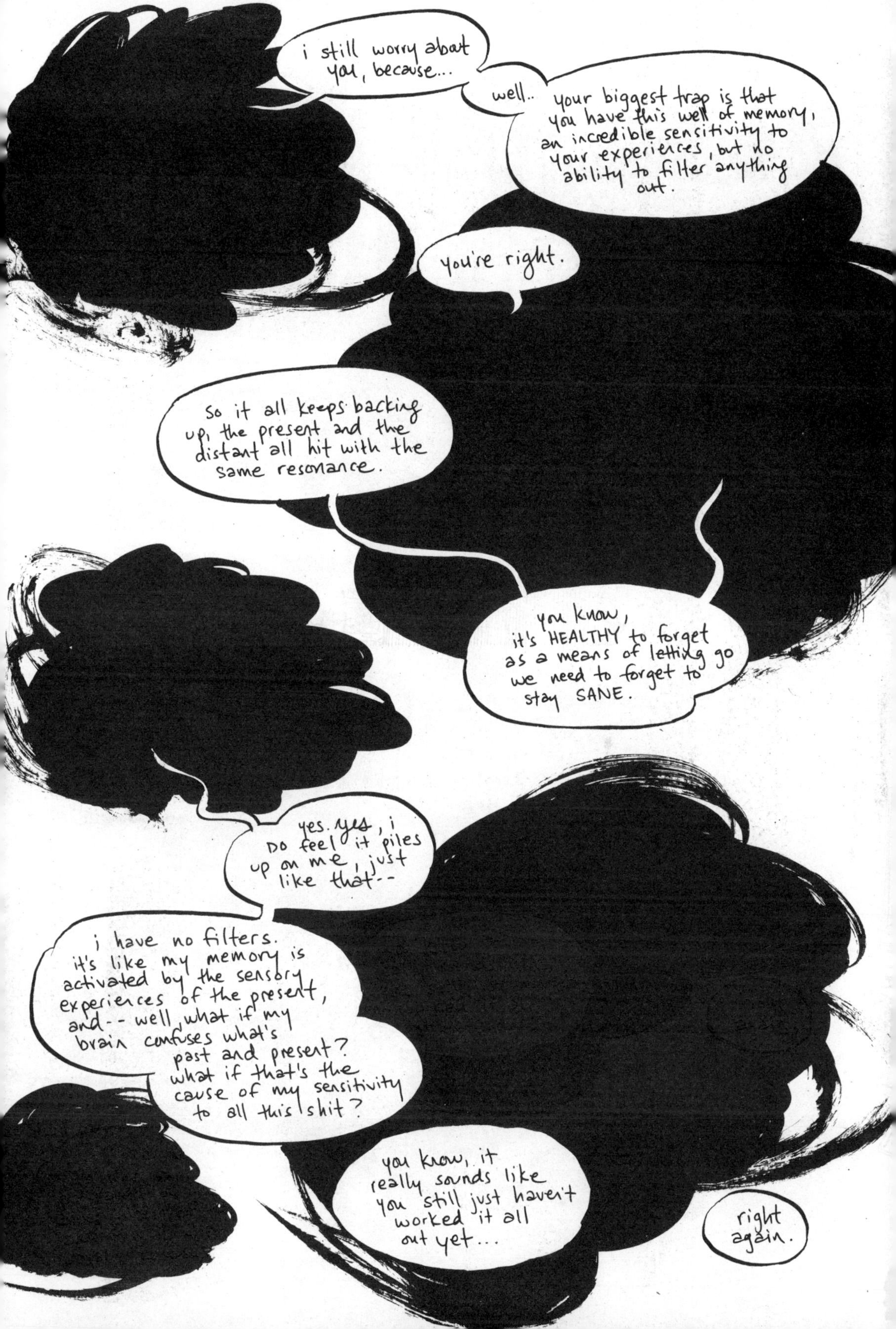
i still worry about you, because...
well.. your biggest trap is that you have this well of memory, an incredible sensitivity to your experiences, but no ability to filter anything out.
you're right.
so it all keeps backing up, the present and the distant all hit with the same resonance.
you know, it's HEALTHY to forget as a means of letting go we need to forget to stay SANE.
yes. yes, i do feel it piles up on me, just like that--
i have no filters. it's like my memory is activated by the sensory experiences of the present, and-- well, what if my brain confuses what's past and present? what if that's the cause of my sensitivity to all this shit?
you know, it really sounds like you still just haven't worked it all out yet...
right again.

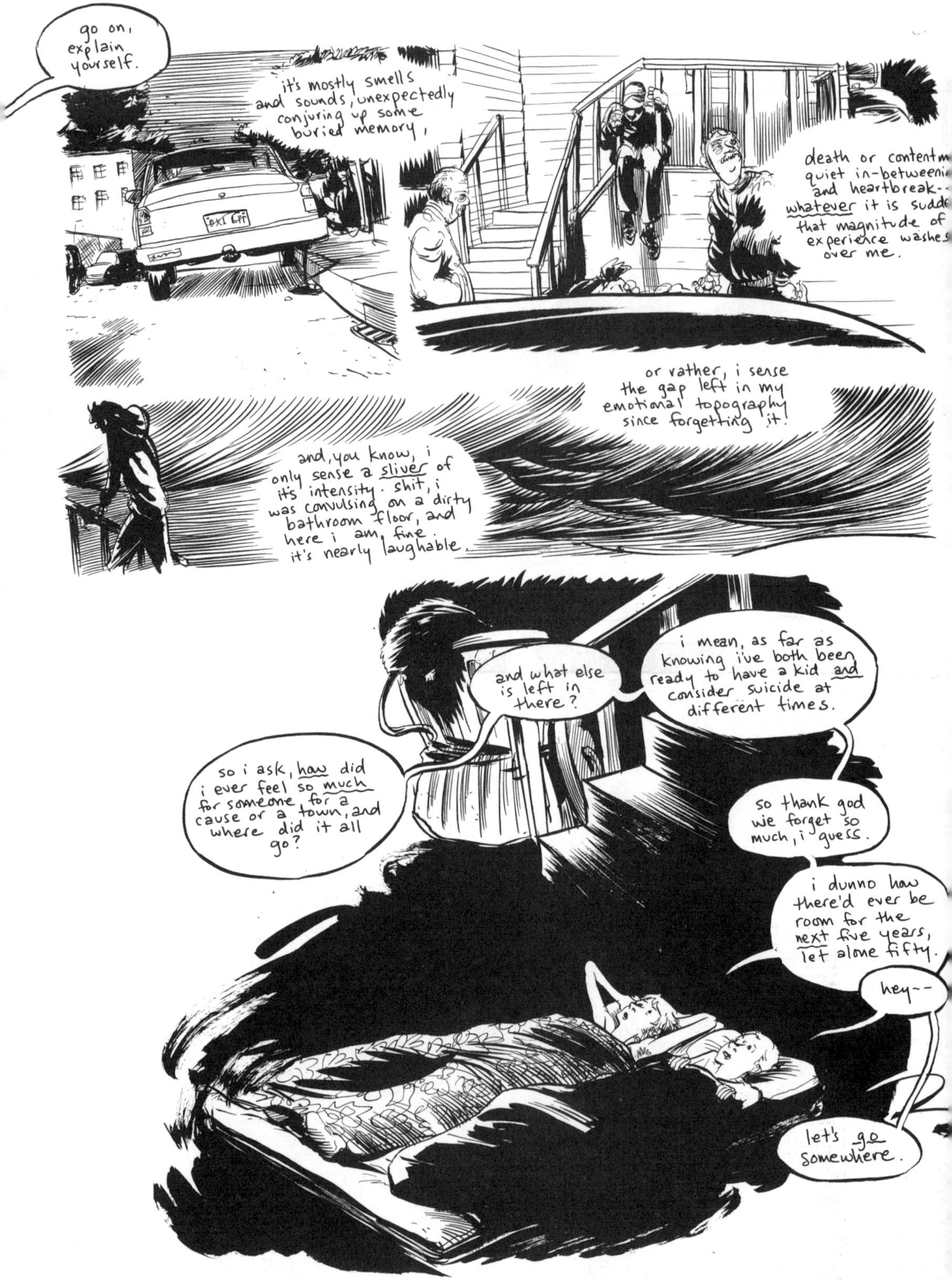

go on, explain yourself.
it's mostly smells and sounds, unexpectedly conjuring up some buried memory,
death or contentm quiet in-betweeni and heartbreak-- whatever it is sudde that magnitude of experience washes over me.
or rather, i sense the gap left in my emotional topography since forgetting it!
and, you know, i only sense a sliver of it's intensity. shit, i was convulsing on a dirty bathroom floor, and here i am, fine. it's nearly laughable.
and what else is left in there?
i mean, as far as knowing i've both been ready to have a kid and consider suicide at different times.
so i ask, how did i ever feel so much for someone, for a cause or a town, and where did it all go?
so thank god we forget so much, i guess.
i dunno how there'd ever be room for the next five years, let alone fifty.
hey--
let's go somewhere.

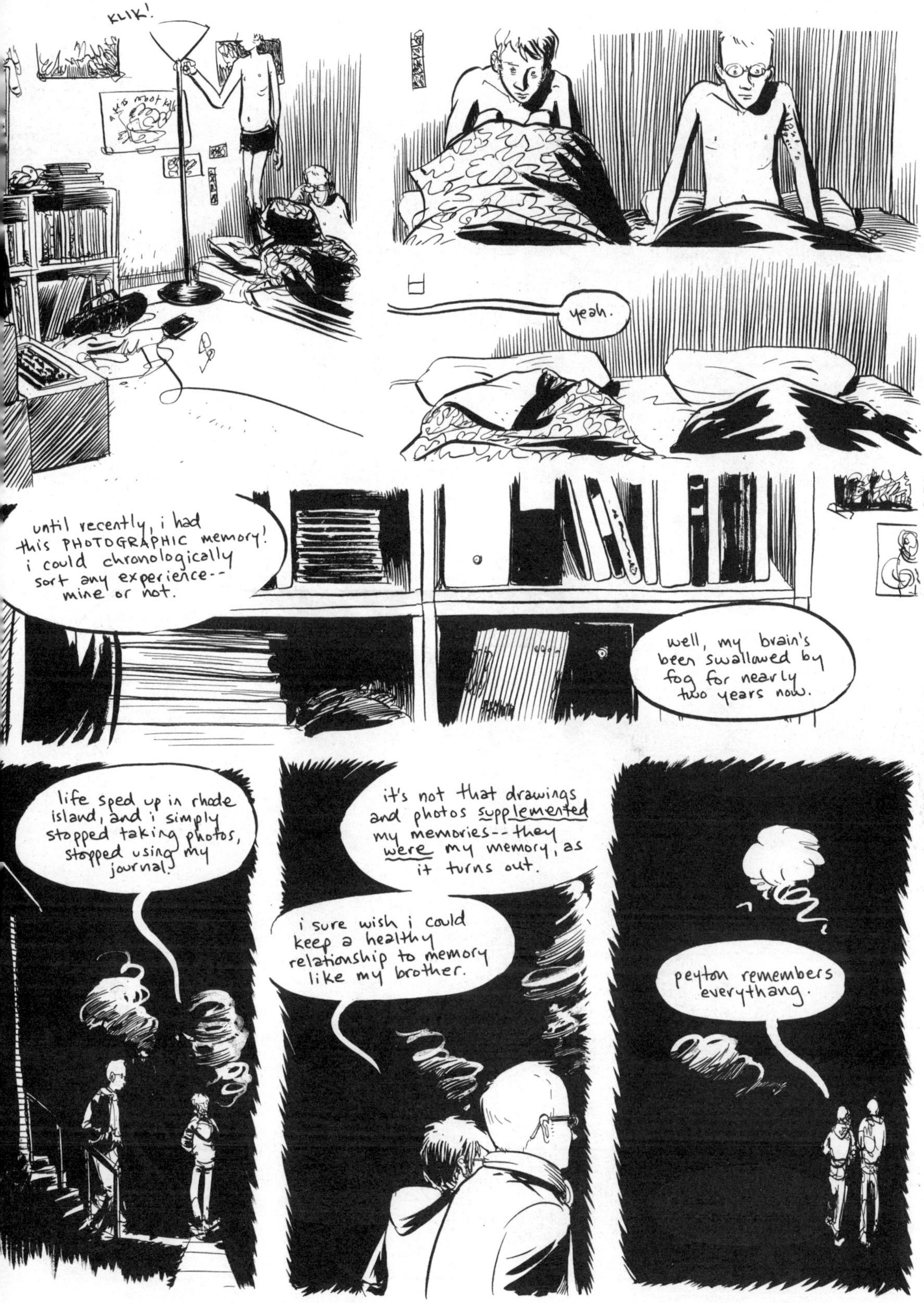
KLIK!
yeah.
until recently, i had this PHOTOGRAPHIC memory! i could chronologically sort any experience-- mine or not.
well, my brain's been swallowed by fog for nearly two years now.
life sped up in rhode island, and i simply stopped taking photos, stopped using my journal.
it's not that drawings and photos supplemented my memories-- they were my memory, as it turns out.
i sure wish i could keep a healthy relationship to memory like my brother.
peyton remembers everythang.

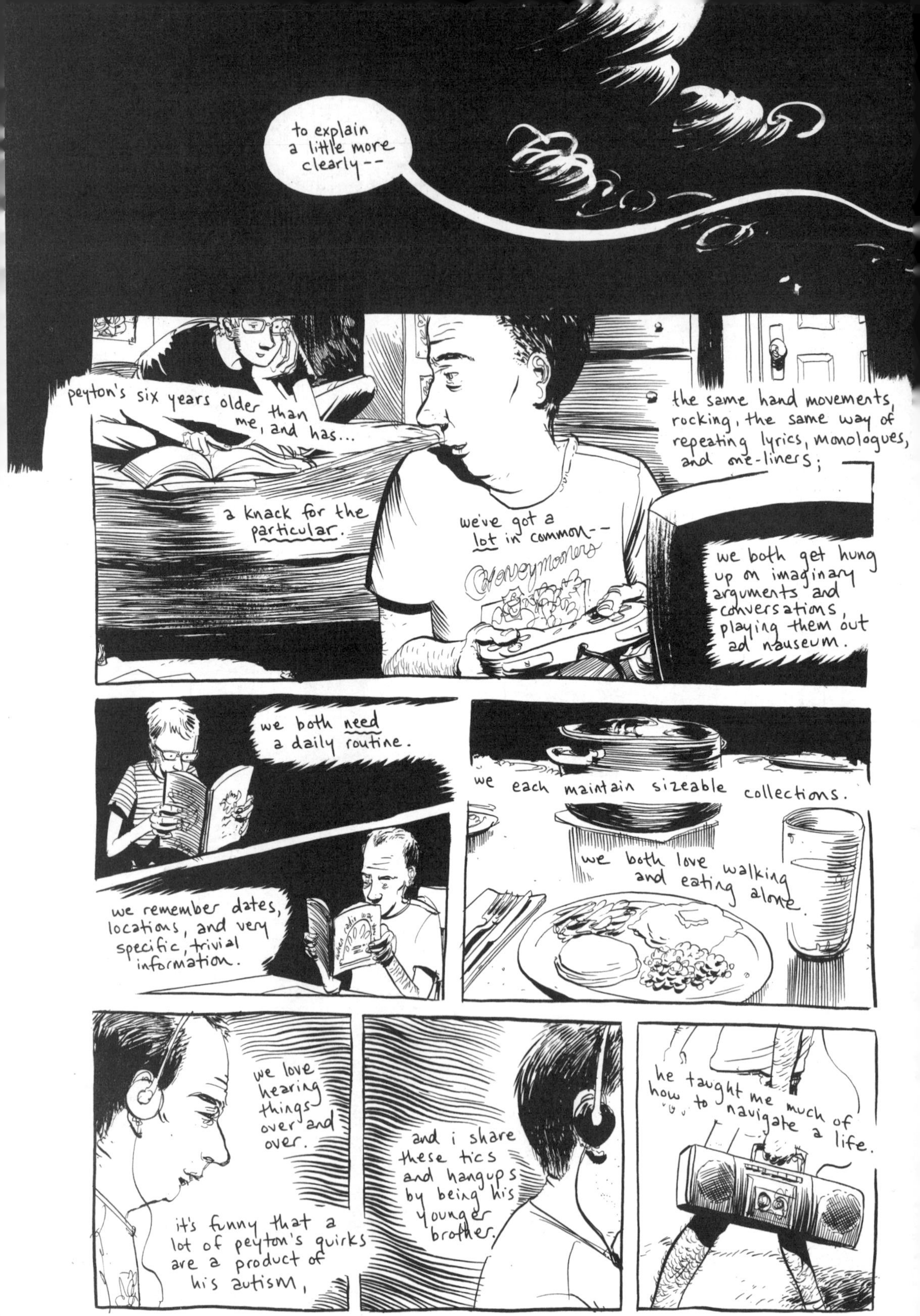
to explain a little more clearly--
peyton's six years older than me, and has...
a knack for the particular.
we've got a lot in common--
the same hand movements, rocking, the same way of repeating lyrics, monologues, and one-liners;
we both get hung up on imaginary arguments and conversations, playing them out ad nauseum.
we both need a daily routine.
we remember dates, locations, and very specific, trivial information.
we each maintain sizeable collections.
we both love walking and eating alone.
we love hearing things over and over.
it's funny that a lot of peyton's quirks are a product of his autism,
and i share these tics and hangups by being his younger brother.
he taught me much of how to navigate a life.

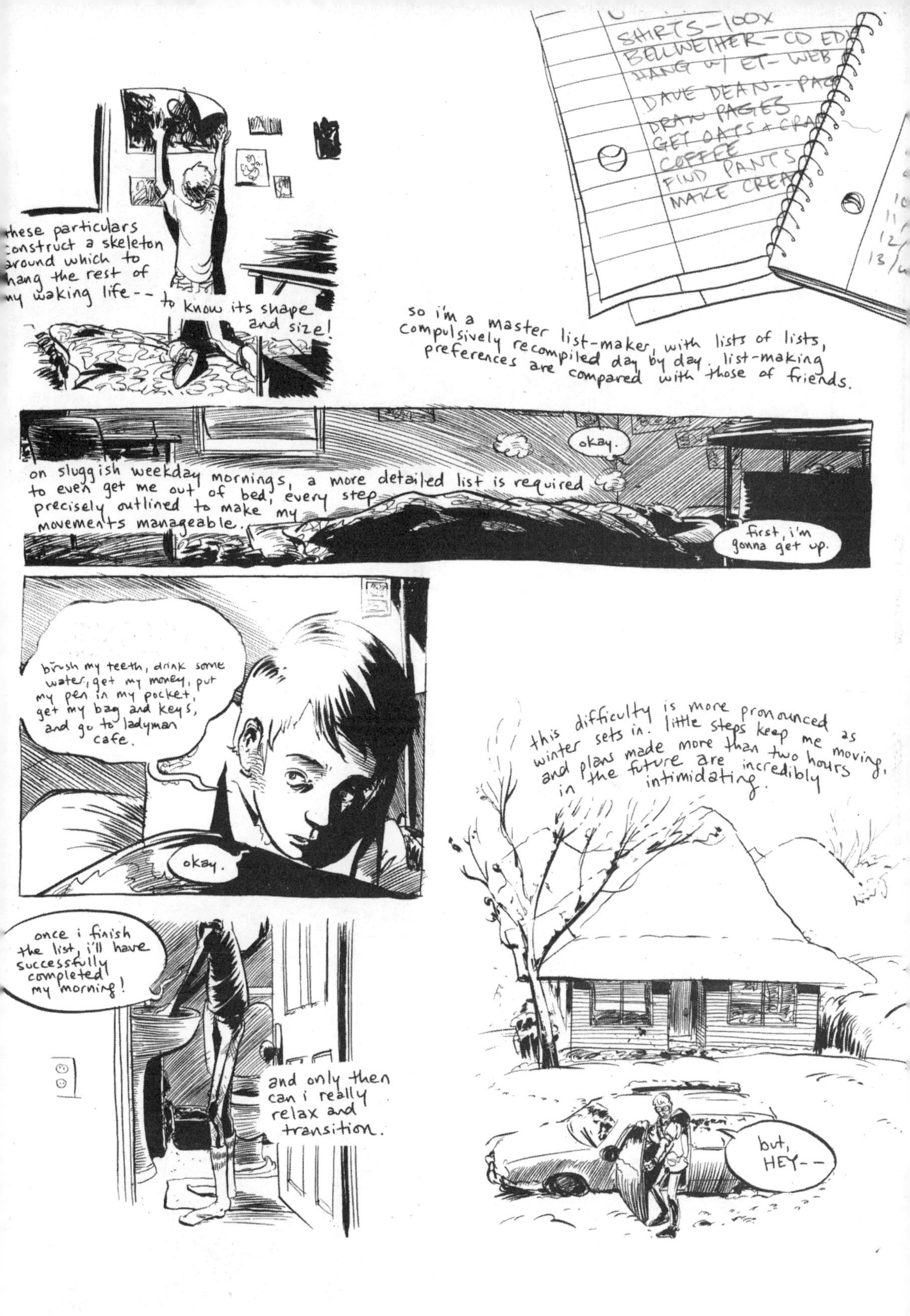
these particulars construct a skeleton around which to hang the rest of my waking life--
to know its shape and size!
SHIRTS—100X
BELLWETHER—CD ED
HANG w/ ET—WEB
DAVE DEAN--PAG
DRAW PAGES
GET OATS + CRA
COFFEE
FIND PANTS
MAKE CREA
so i'm a master list-maker, with lists of lists, compulsively recompiled day by day. list-making preferences are compared with those of friends.
on sluggish weekday mornings, a more detailed list is required to even get me out of bed, every step precisely outlined to make my movements manageable.
okay.
first, i'm gonna get up.
brush my teeth, drink some water, get my money, put my pen in my pocket, get my bag and keys, and go to ladyman cafe.
okay.
once i finish the list, i'll have successfully completed my morning!
and only then can i really relax and transition.
this difficulty is more pronounced as winter sets in. little steps keep me moving, and plans made more than two hours in the future are incredibly intimidating.
but, HEY--

i don't feel so off! not somebody a little agoraphobic and anxious, at least.

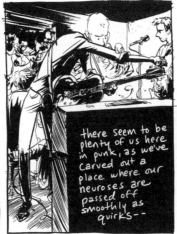

there seem to be plenty of us here in punk, as we've carved out a place where our neuroses are passed off smoothly as quirks--

--brought to the forefront of our personalities, even, shamefully removing more afflicting disorders from our discourse, but at least showcasing parts of our hidden spectrums.

I'LL BE LATE.

i forget.

ah YES, I REMEMBER IT WELL.

YOU KNOW, YOU'RE MY FAVORITE FRIEND WHO'S... PARTICULAR ABOUT CERTAIN THINGS.

SAME TO YOU!

Nº 12/05

Chris McDonnell

Chris McDonnell is always one third of the rock-machine, Ancient Justice.
www.chrismcd.com

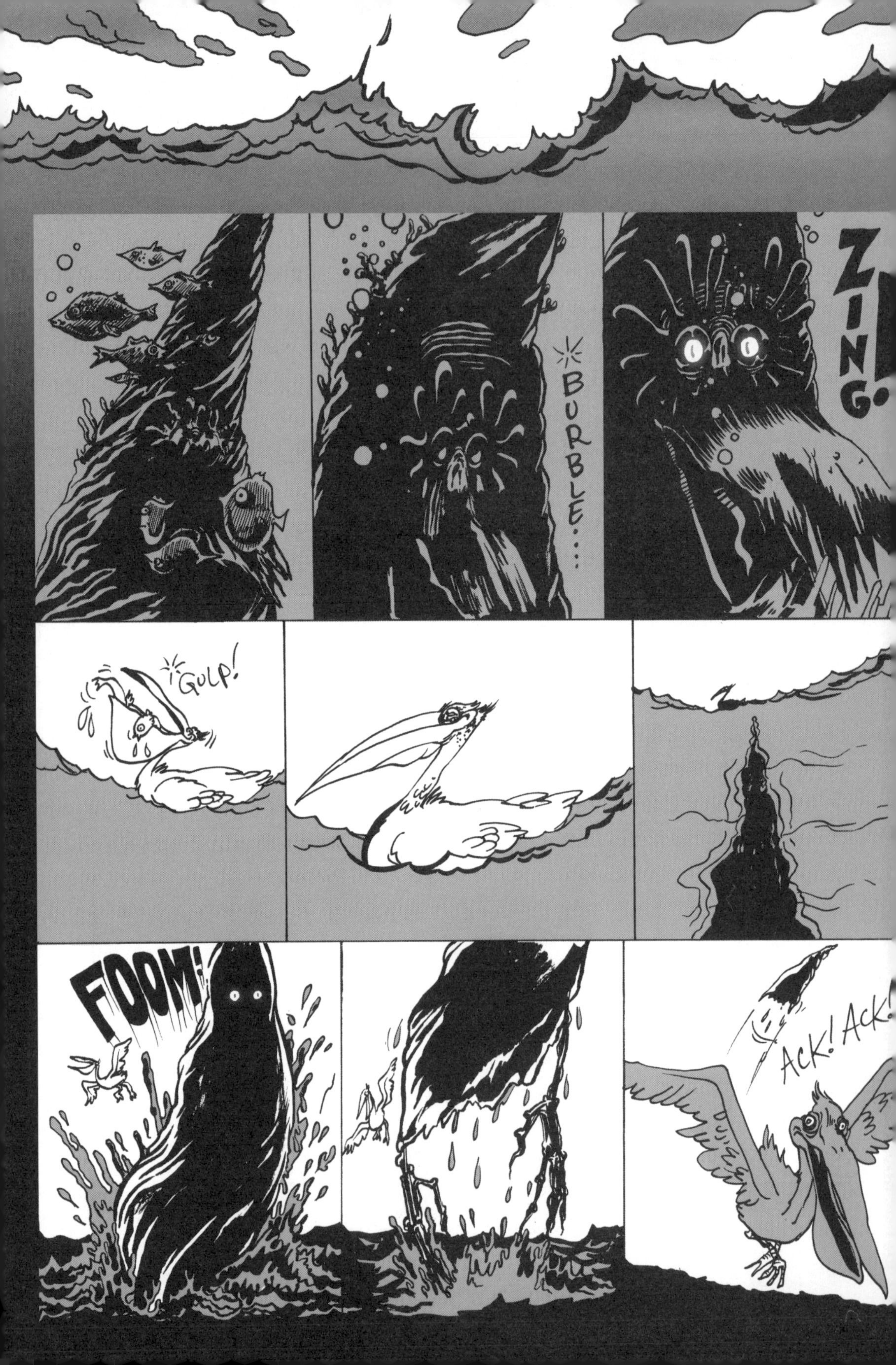
BURBLE...
ZING!
GULP!
FOOM!
ACK! ACK!

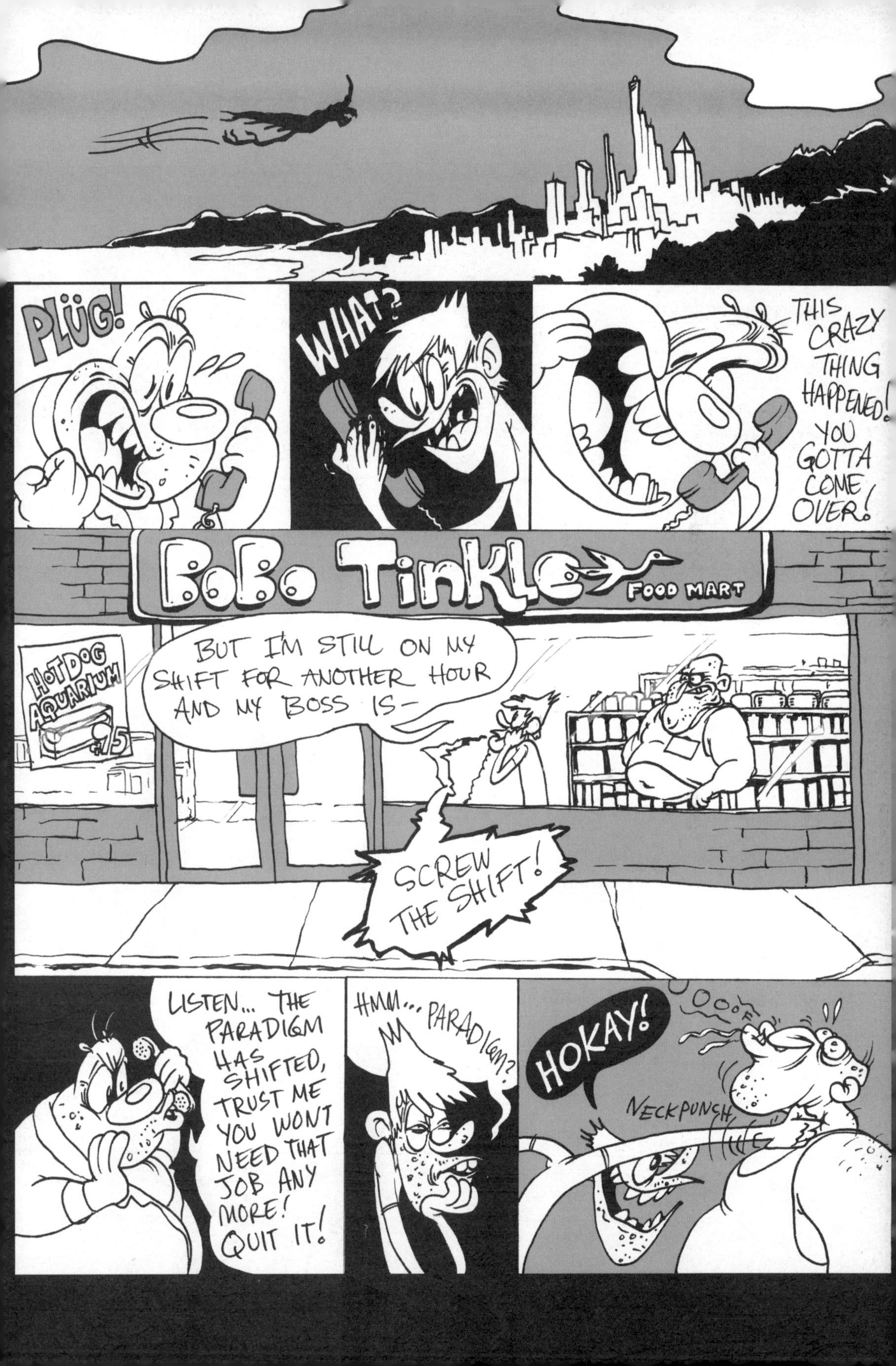
PLÜG!
WHAT?
THIS CRAZY THING HAPPENED! YOU GOTTA COME OVER!
BoBo Tinkle FOOD MART
HOT DOG AQUARIUM
BUT I'M STILL ON MY SHIFT FOR ANOTHER HOUR AND MY BOSS IS-
SCREW THE SHIFT!
LISTEN... THE PARADIGM HAS SHIFTED, TRUST ME YOU WONT NEED THAT JOB ANY MORE! QUIT IT!
HMM... PARADIGM?
HOKAY!
OOOF
NECKPUNCH

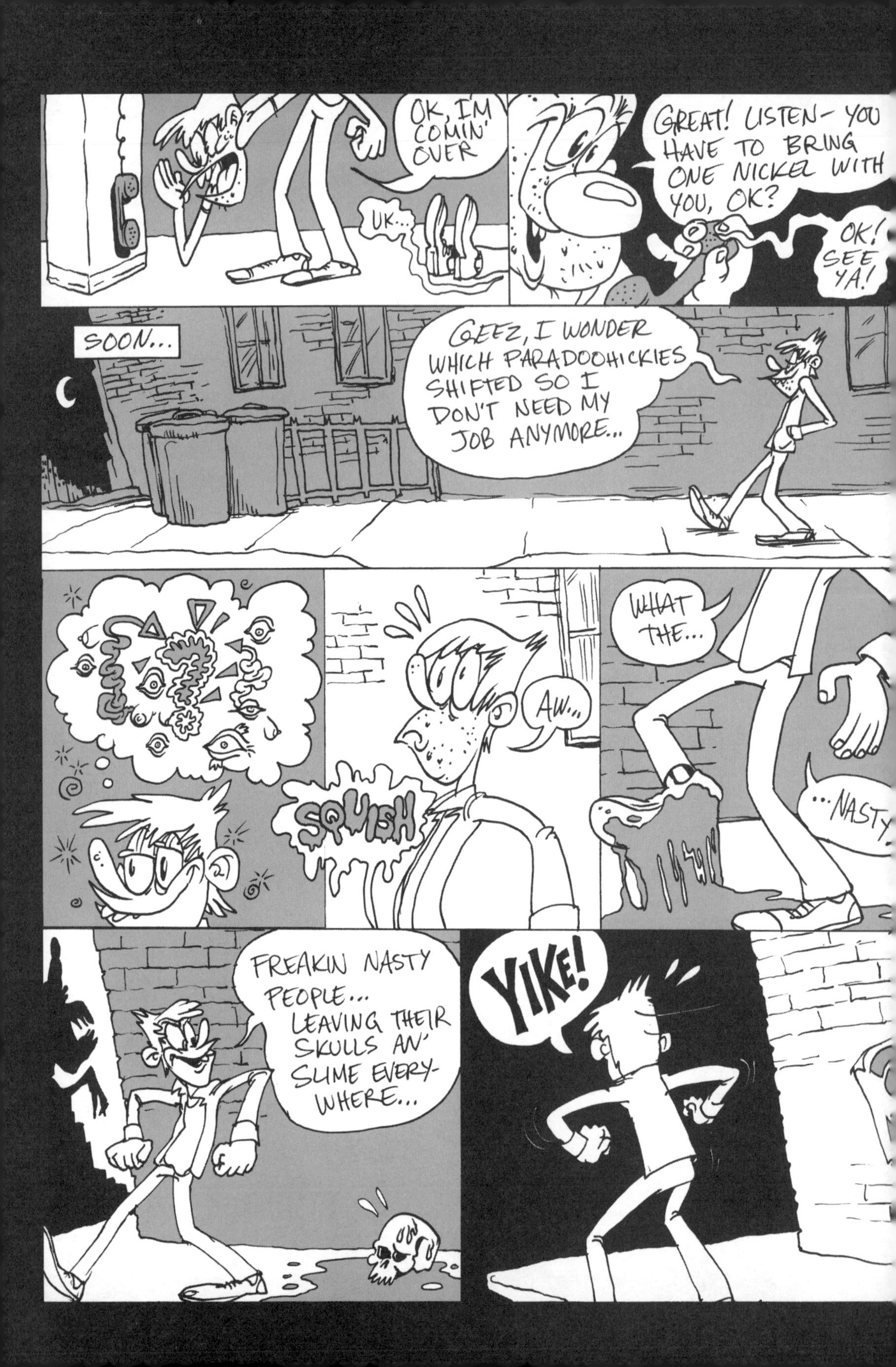
OK, I'M COMIN' OVER
UK...
GREAT! LISTEN- YOU HAVE TO BRING ONE NICKEL WITH YOU, OK?
OK! SEE YA!
SOON...
GEEZ, I WONDER WHICH PARADOOHICKIES SHIFTED SO I DON'T NEED MY JOB ANYMORE...
SQUISH
AW...
WHAT THE...
...NASTY
FREAKIN NASTY PEOPLE... LEAVING THEIR SKULLS AN' SLIME EVERY-WHERE...
YIKE!

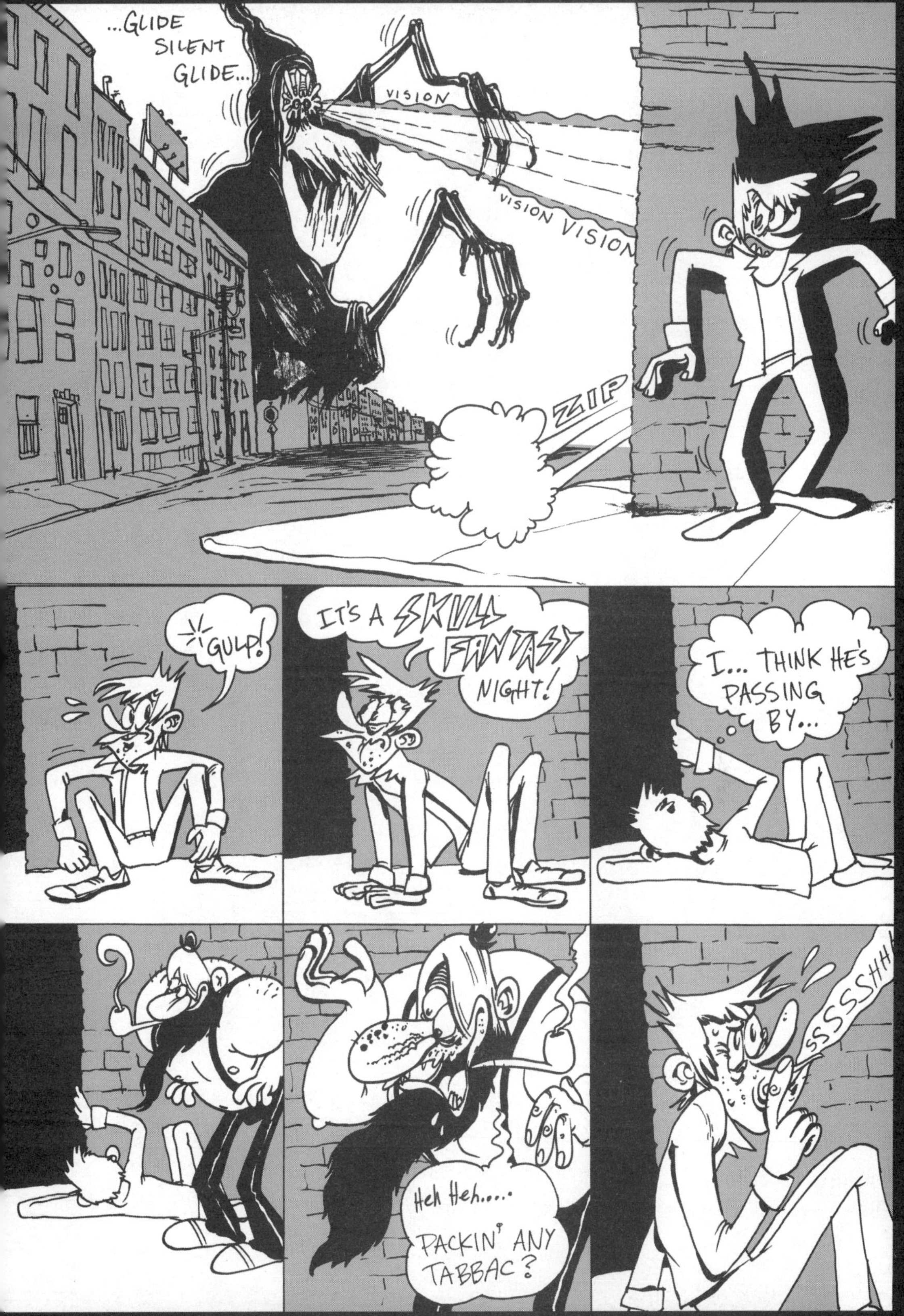
...GLIDE SILENT GLIDE...
VISION
VISION VISION
ZIP
GULP!
IT'S A SKULL FANTASY NIGHT!
I... THINK HE'S PASSING BY...
Heh Heh....
PACKIN' ANY TABBAC?
SSSSSHH

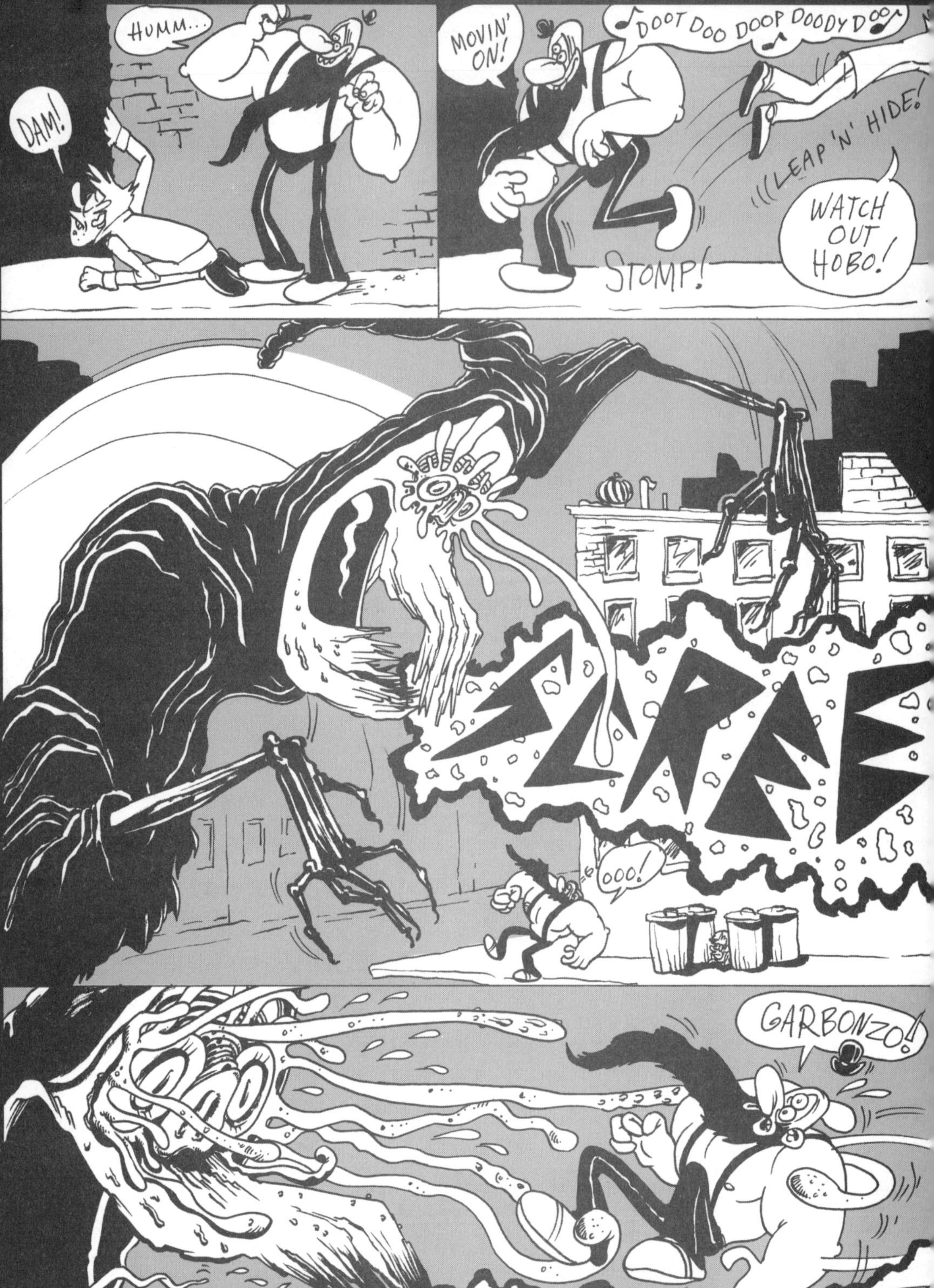
HUMM...
DAM!
MOVIN' ON!
DOOT DOO DOOP DOODY DOO
LEAP 'N' HIDE!
WATCH OUT HOBO!
STOMP!
OOO!
GARBONZO!

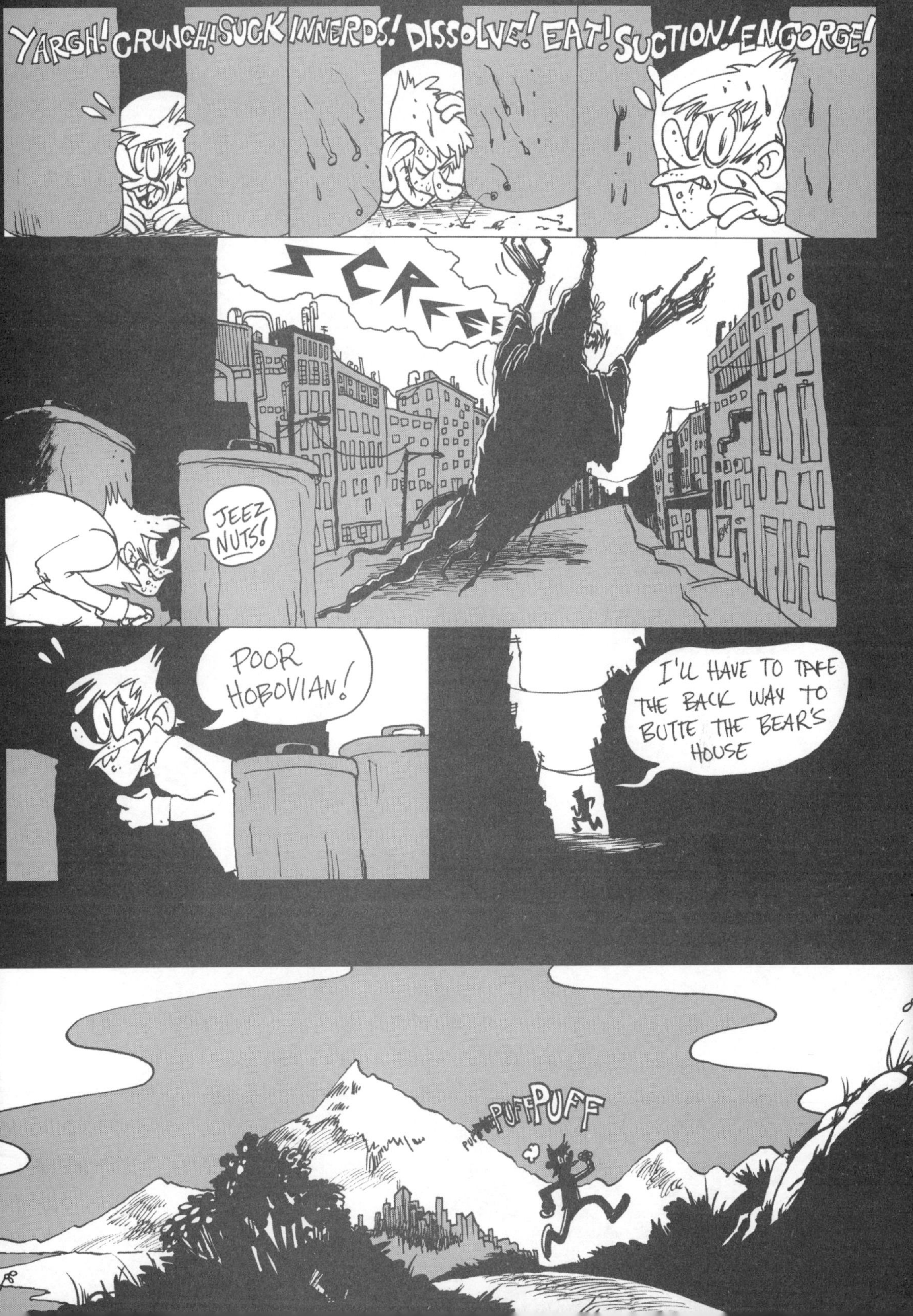

YARGH! CRUNCH! SUCK INNERDS! DISSOLVE! EAT! SUCTION! ENGORGE!
SCRFEE
JEEZ NUTS!
POOR HOBOVIAN!
I'LL HAVE TO TAKE THE BACK WAY TO BUTTE THE BEAR'S HOUSE
PUFF PUFF

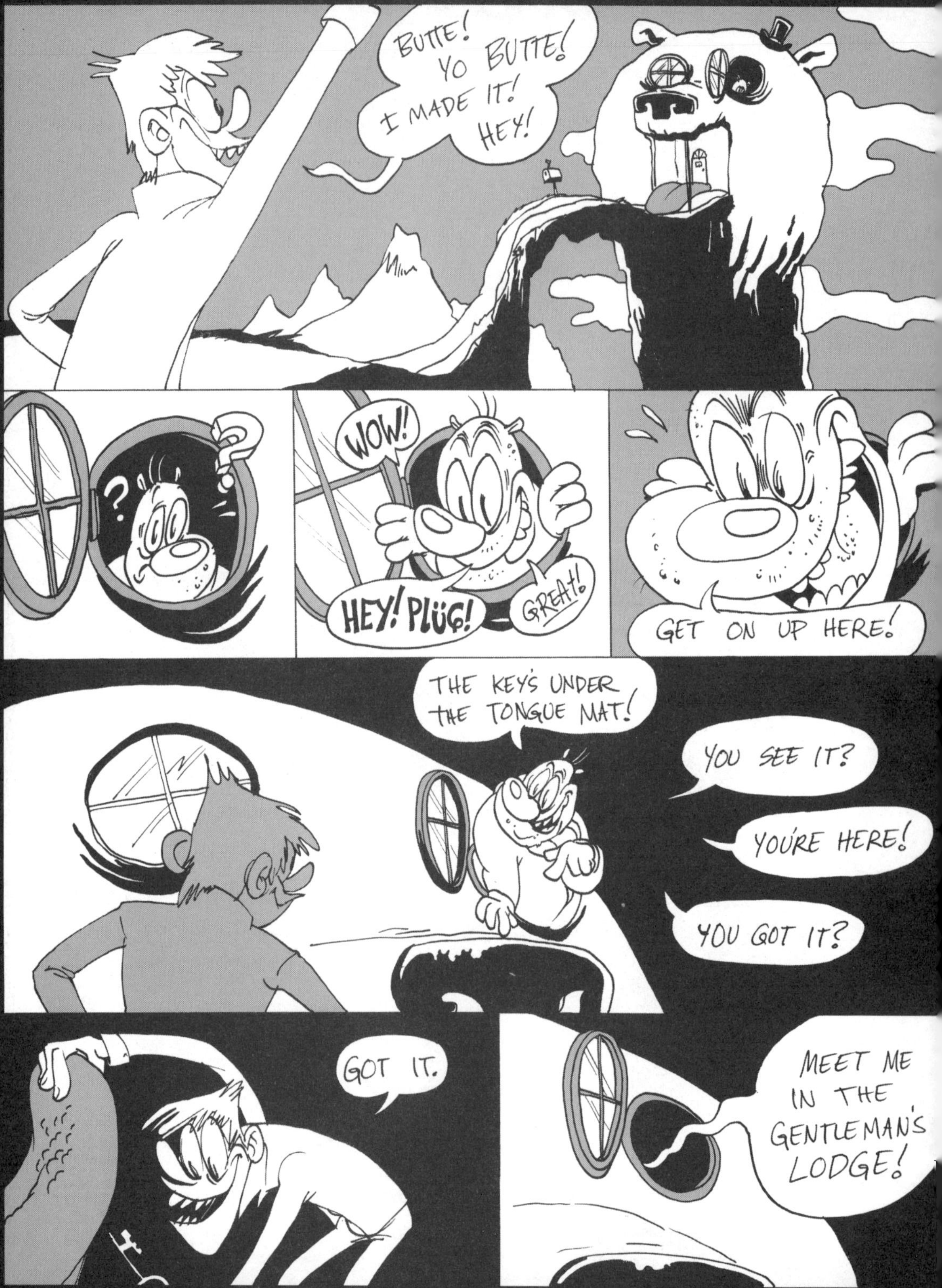
BUTTE! YO BUTTE! I MADE IT! HEY!
?
?
WOW!
HEY! PLÜG!
GREAT!
GET ON UP HERE!
THE KEY'S UNDER THE TONGUE MAT!
YOU SEE IT?
YOU'RE HERE!
YOU GOT IT?
GOT IT.
MEET ME IN THE GENTLEMAN'S LODGE!

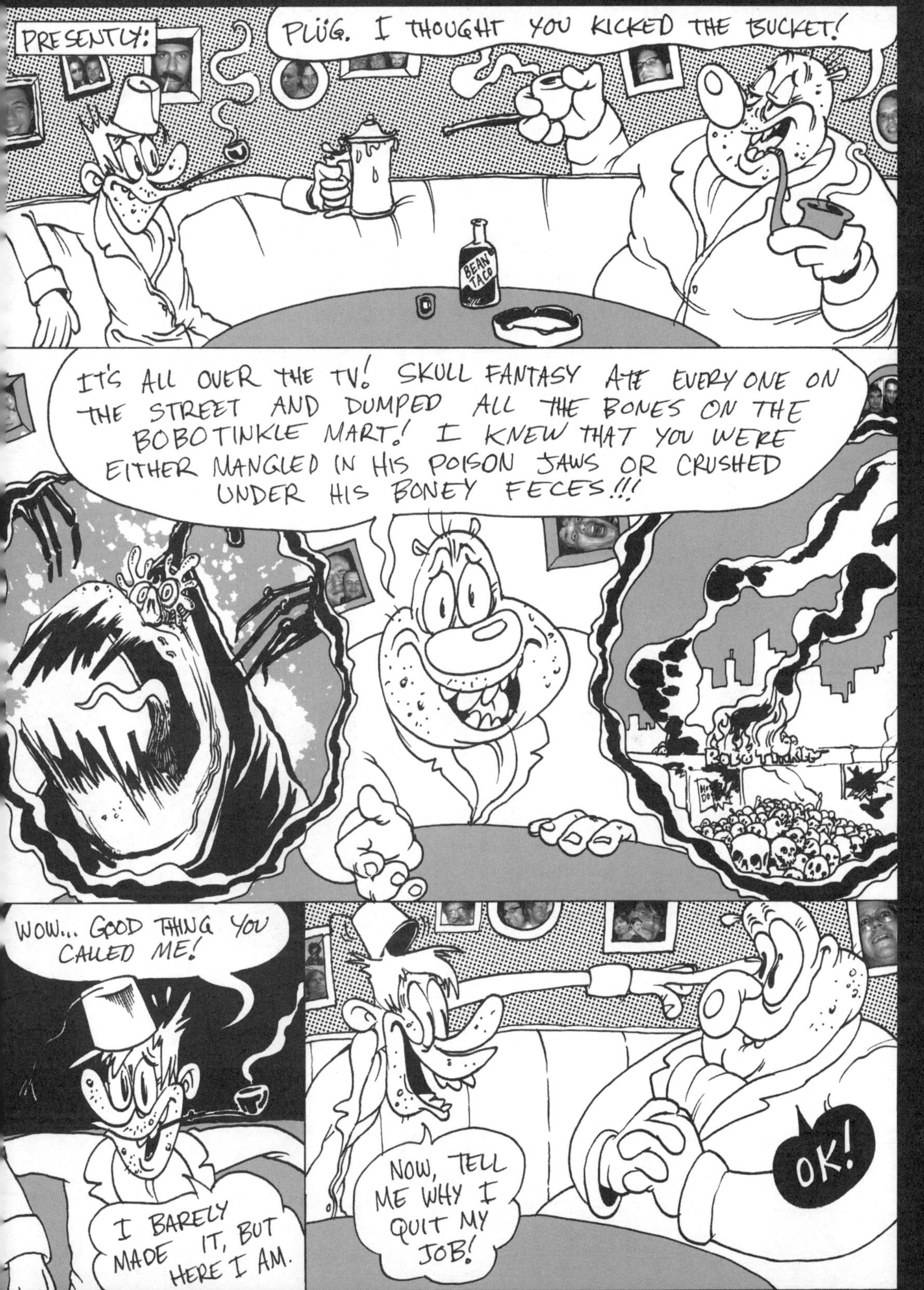
PRESENTLY:
PLÜG. I THOUGHT YOU KICKED THE BUCKET!
BEAN TACO
IT'S ALL OVER THE TV! SKULL FANTASY ATE EVERYONE ON THE STREET AND DUMPED ALL THE BONES ON THE BOBOTINKLE MART! I KNEW THAT YOU WERE EITHER MANGLED IN HIS POISON JAWS OR CRUSHED UNDER HIS BONEY FECES!!!
WOW... GOOD THING YOU CALLED ME!
I BARELY MADE IT, BUT HERE I AM.
NOW, TELL ME WHY I QUIT MY JOB!
OK!

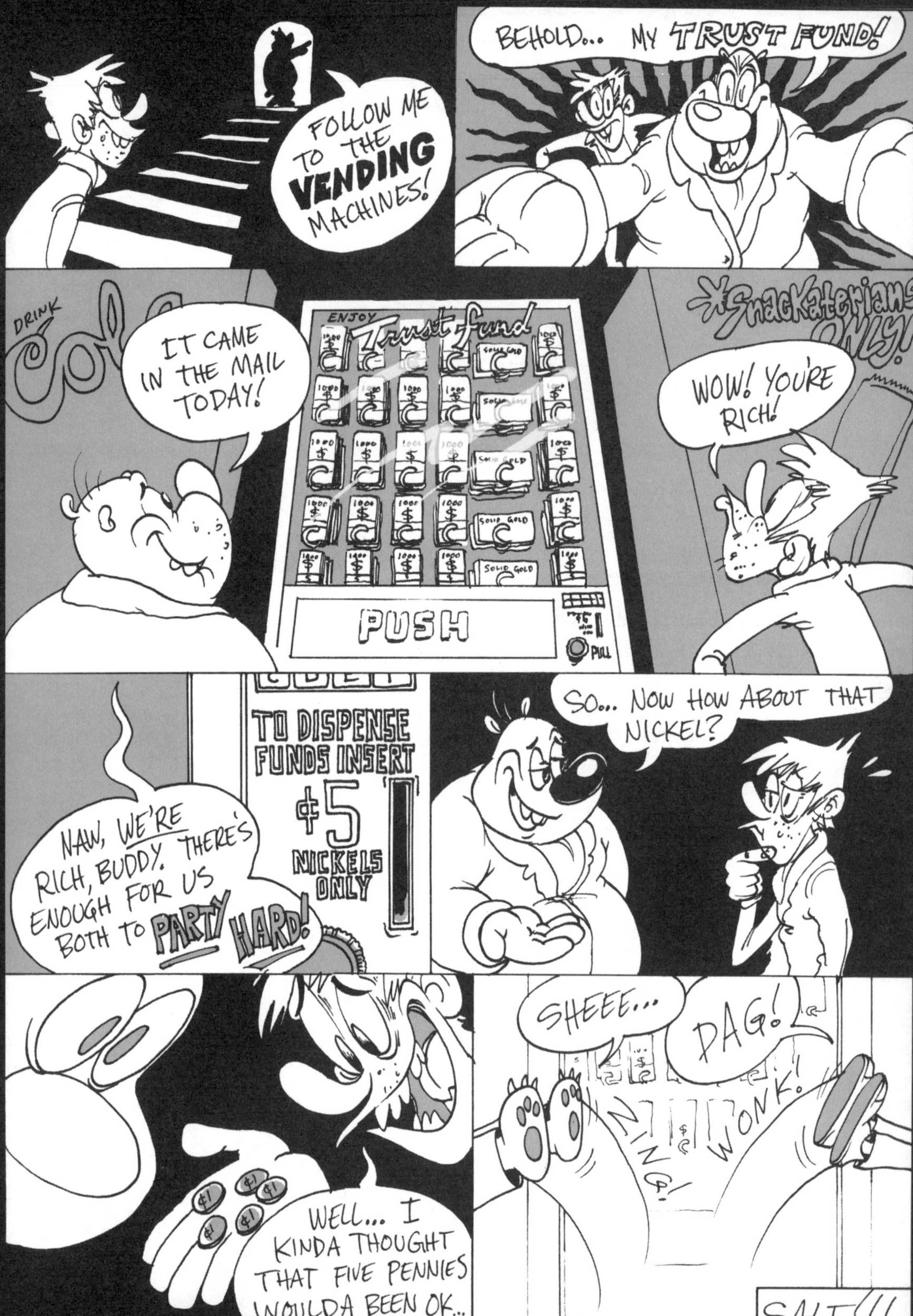
FOLLOW ME TO THE VENDING MACHINES!
BEHOLD... MY TRUST FUND!
DRINK
IT CAME IN THE MAIL TODAY!
ENJOY
Trust fund
SOLID GOLD
PUSH
PULL
Snackaterians ONLY!
WOW! YOU'RE RICH!
TO DISPENSE FUNDS INSERT ¢5 NICKELS ONLY
NAW, WE'RE RICH, BUDDY. THERE'S ENOUGH FOR US BOTH TO PARTY HARD!
SO... NOW HOW ABOUT THAT NICKEL?
WELL... I KINDA THOUGHT THAT FIVE PENNIES WOULDA BEEN OK...
SHEEE...
DAG!
ZING!
WONK!
SALT!!!

Joseph Belden

Joseph Belden lives in Norman, Oklahoma. He
spends his time painting, drawing and working on
his comic POMEGRANATE.
email: josephbelden@yahoo.com
website: www.josephbelden.com

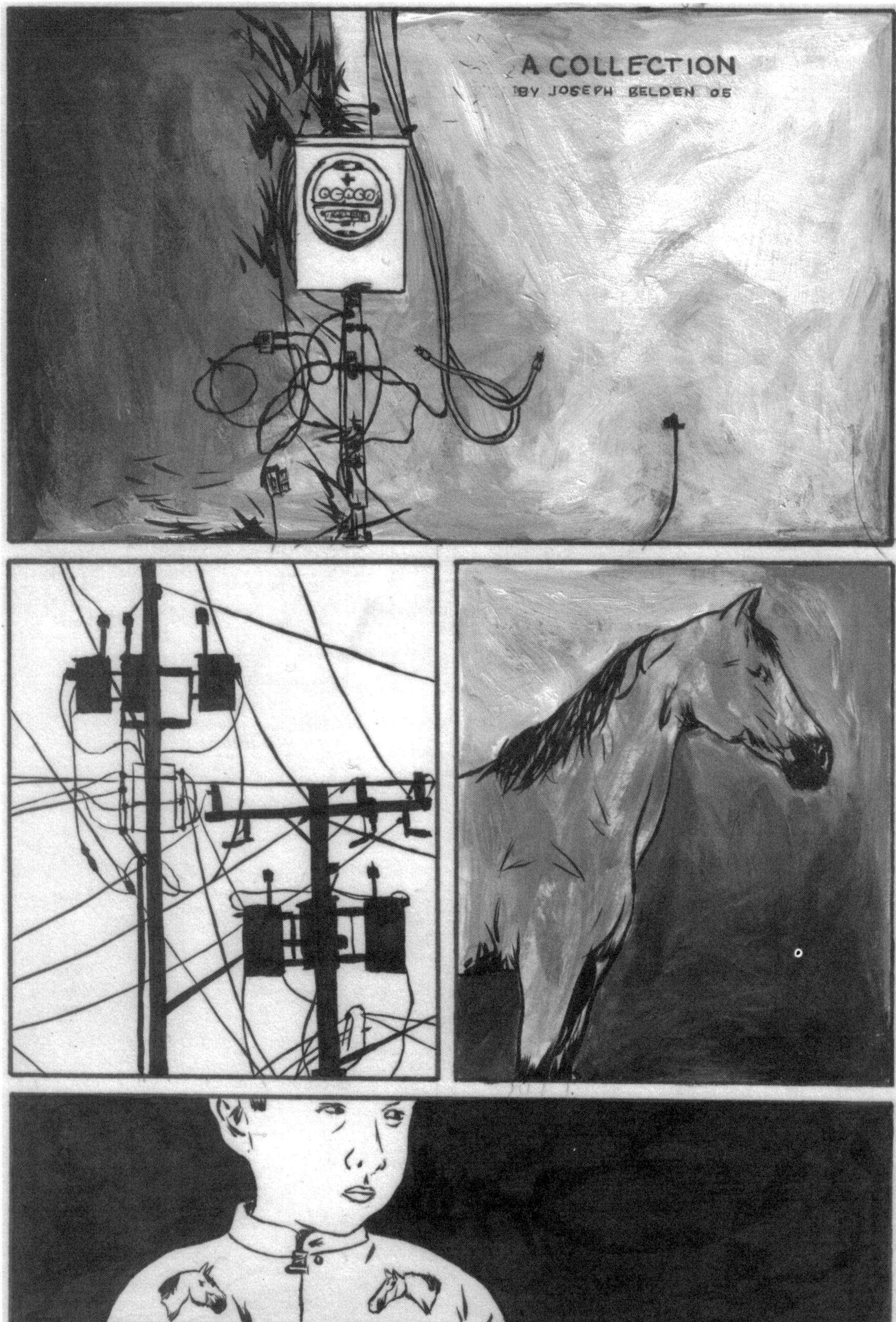
A COLLECTION
BY JOSEPH BELDEN 05

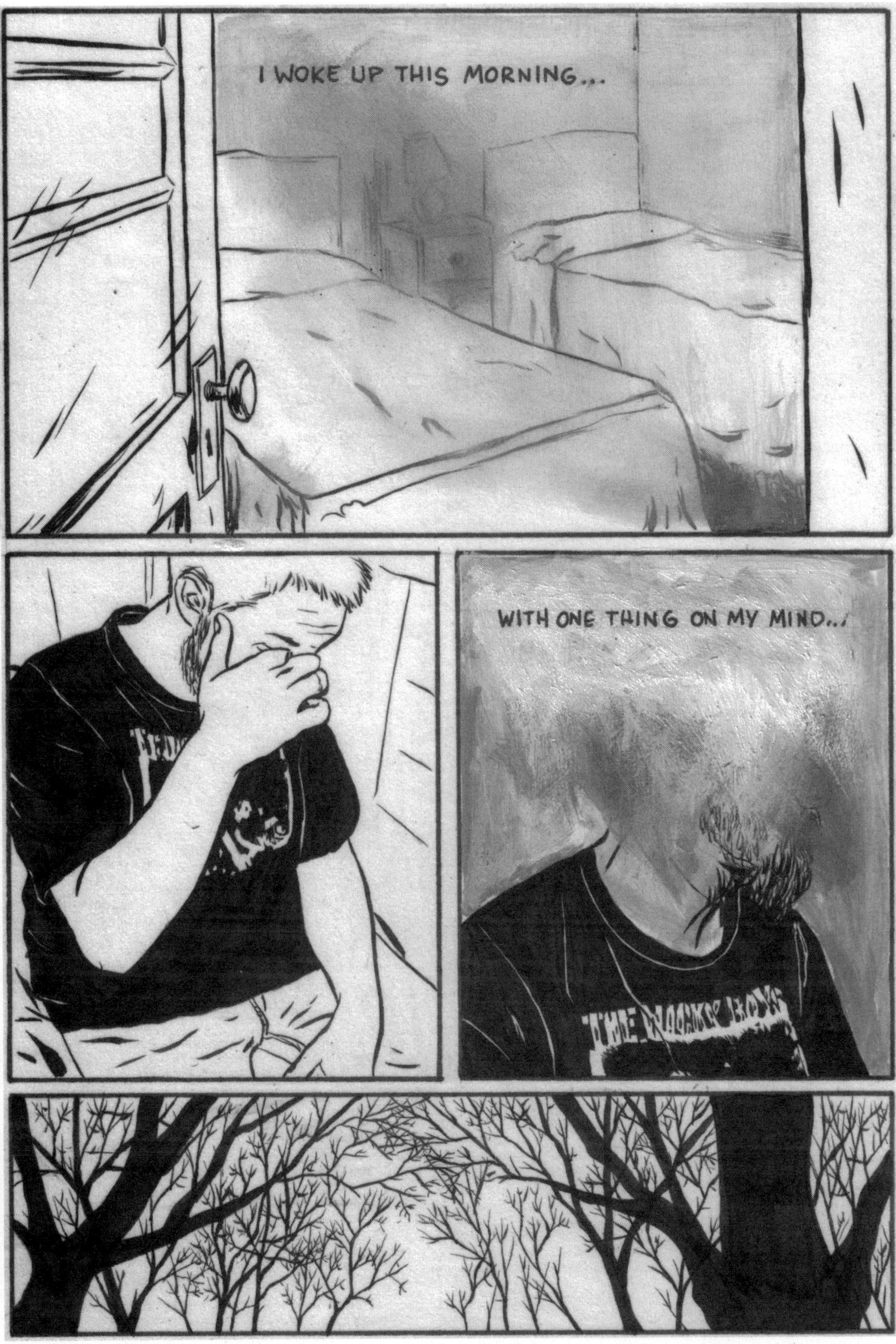
I WOKE UP THIS MORNING...
WITH ONE THING ON MY MIND...

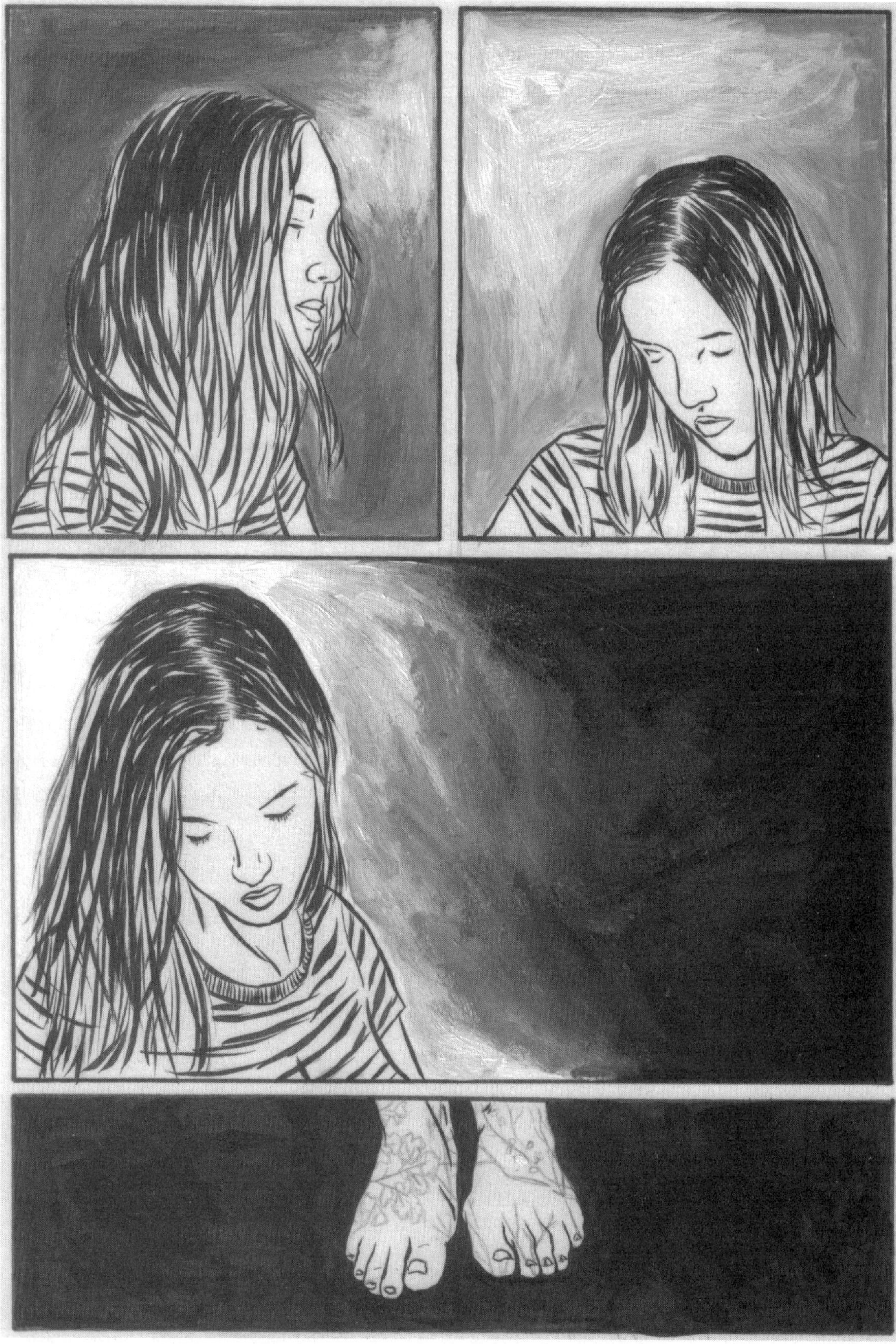

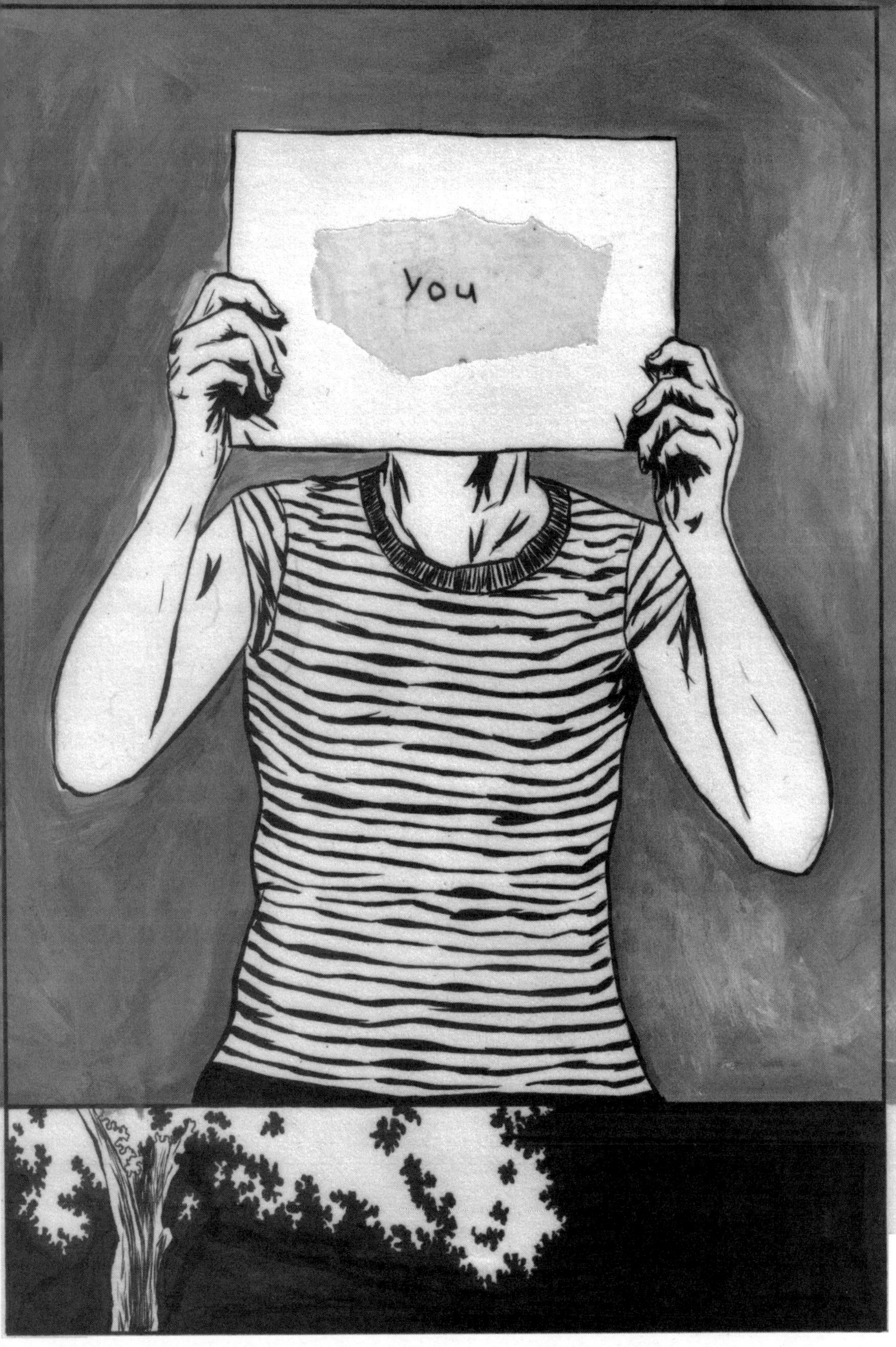
You

Farel Dalrymple

Currently residing in Tulsa, Oklahoma, Farel is working on a new Pop Gun War graphic novel, and is drawing the series, Omega the Unknown with writer Jonathan Lethem for Marvel comics. www.popgunwar.com.

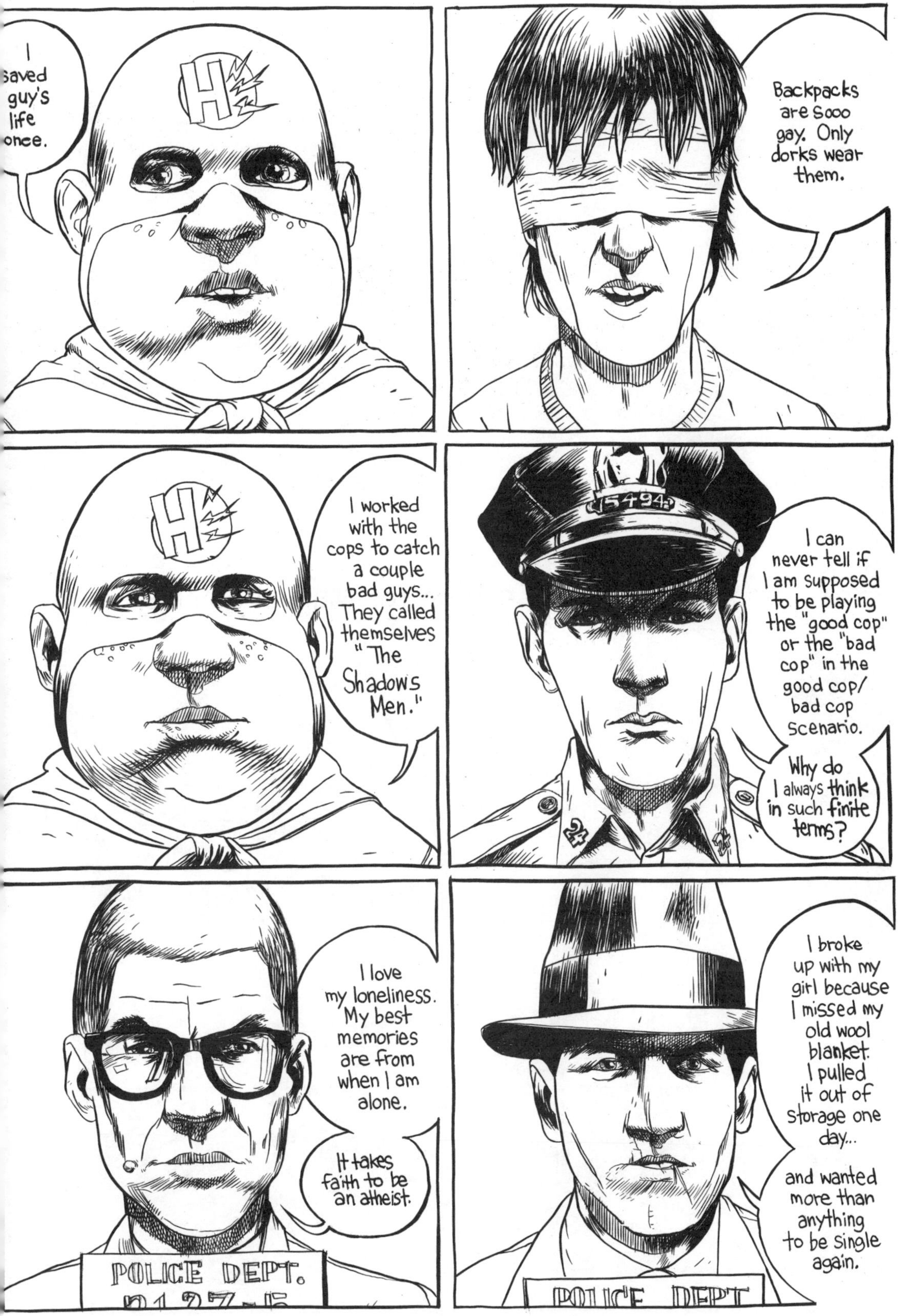

I saved guy's life once.
Backpacks are sooo gay. Only dorks wear them.
I worked with the cops to catch a couple bad guys... They called themselves "The Shadows Men."
5494
I can never tell if I am supposed to be playing the "good cop" or the "bad cop" in the good cop/ bad cop scenario.
Why do I always think in such finite terms?
I love my loneliness. My best memories are from when I am alone.
It takes faith to be an atheist.
POLICE DEPT.
I broke up with my girl because I missed my old wool blanket. I pulled it out of storage one day...
and wanted more than anything to be single again.
POLICE DEPT

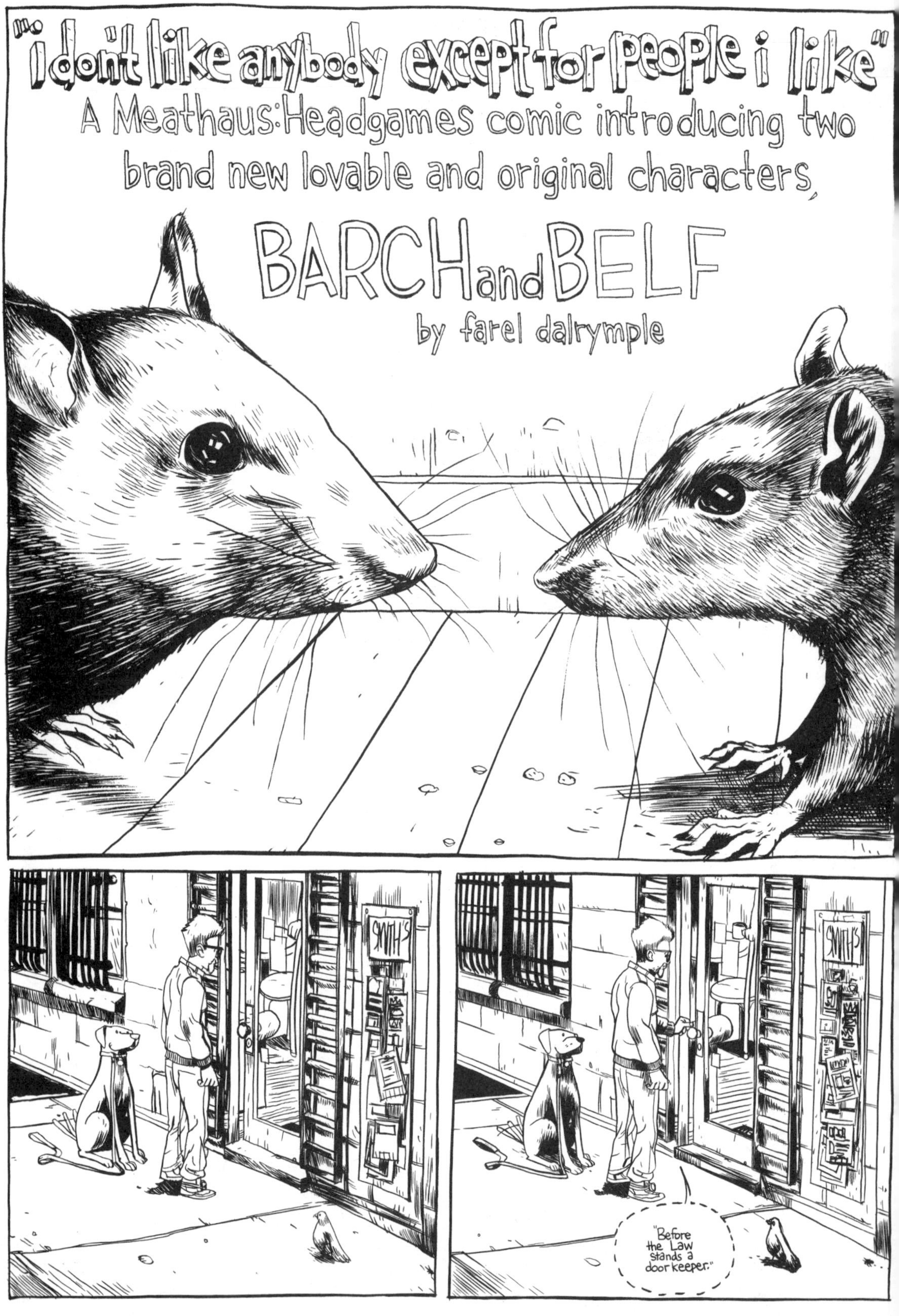
"i don't like anybody except for people i like"
A Meathaus: Headgames comic introducing two brand new lovable and original characters,
BARCH and BELF
by farel dalrymple
SMITH'S
"Before the Law stands a doorkeeper."

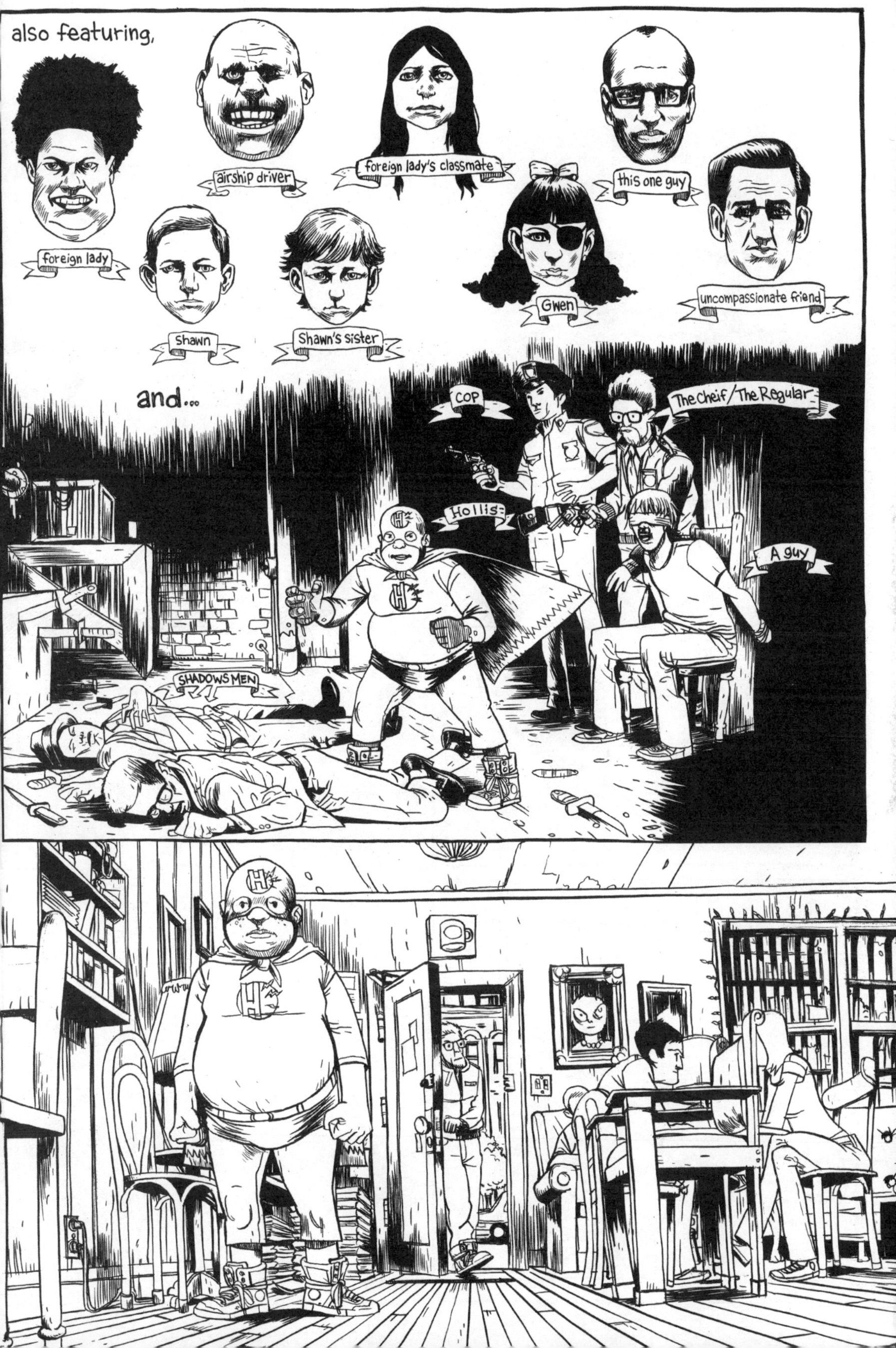
also featuring,
foreign lady
airship driver
foreign lady's classmate
this one guy
Gwen
uncompassionate friend
Shawn
Shawn's sister
and...
COP
The Cheif / The Regular
Hollis
A guy
SHADOWS MEN

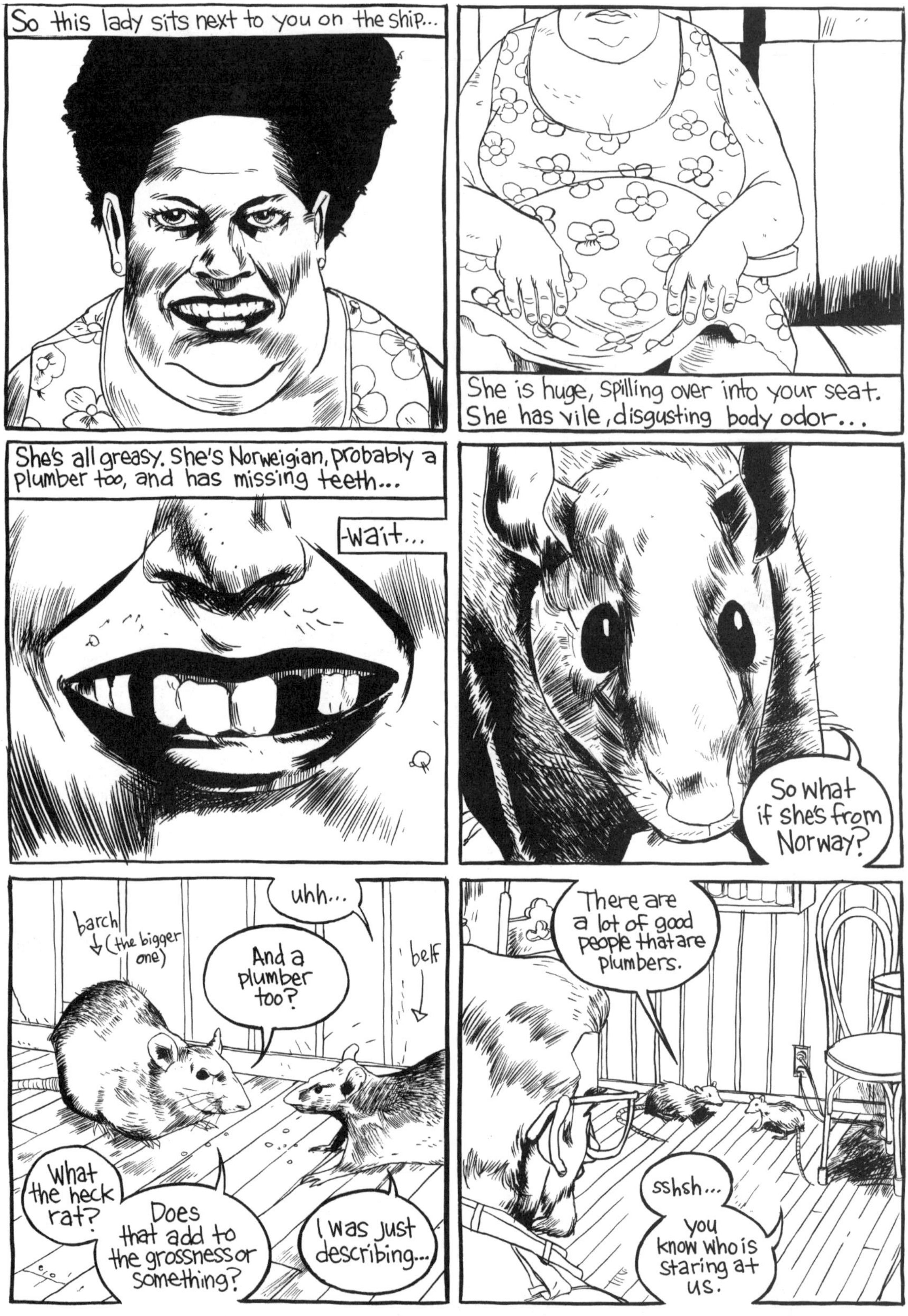
So this lady sits next to you on the ship...
She is huge, spilling over into your seat. She has vile, disgusting body odor...
She's all greasy. She's Norweigian, probably a plumber too, and has missing teeth...
-wait...
So what if she's from Norway?
barch ↓ (the bigger one)
uhh...
And a plumber too?
belf
What the heck rat?
Does that add to the grossness or something?
I was just describing...
There are a lot of good people that are plumbers.
sshsh...
you know who is staring at us.

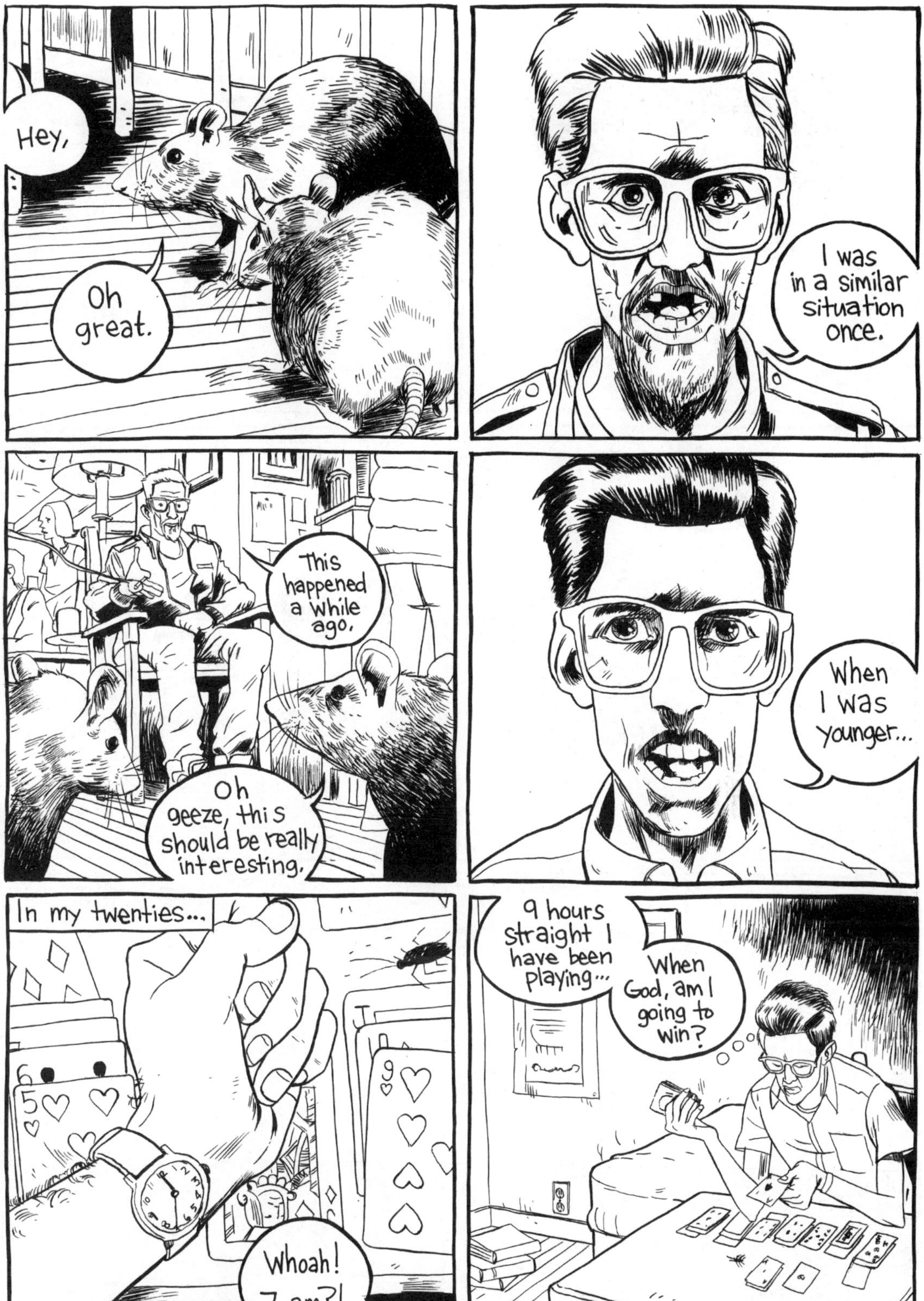
Hey,
Oh great.
I was in a similar situation once.
This happened a while ago,
Oh geeze, this should be really interesting.
When I was younger...
In my twenties...
Whoah! 7 am?!
9 hours straight I have been playing...
When God, am I going to win?

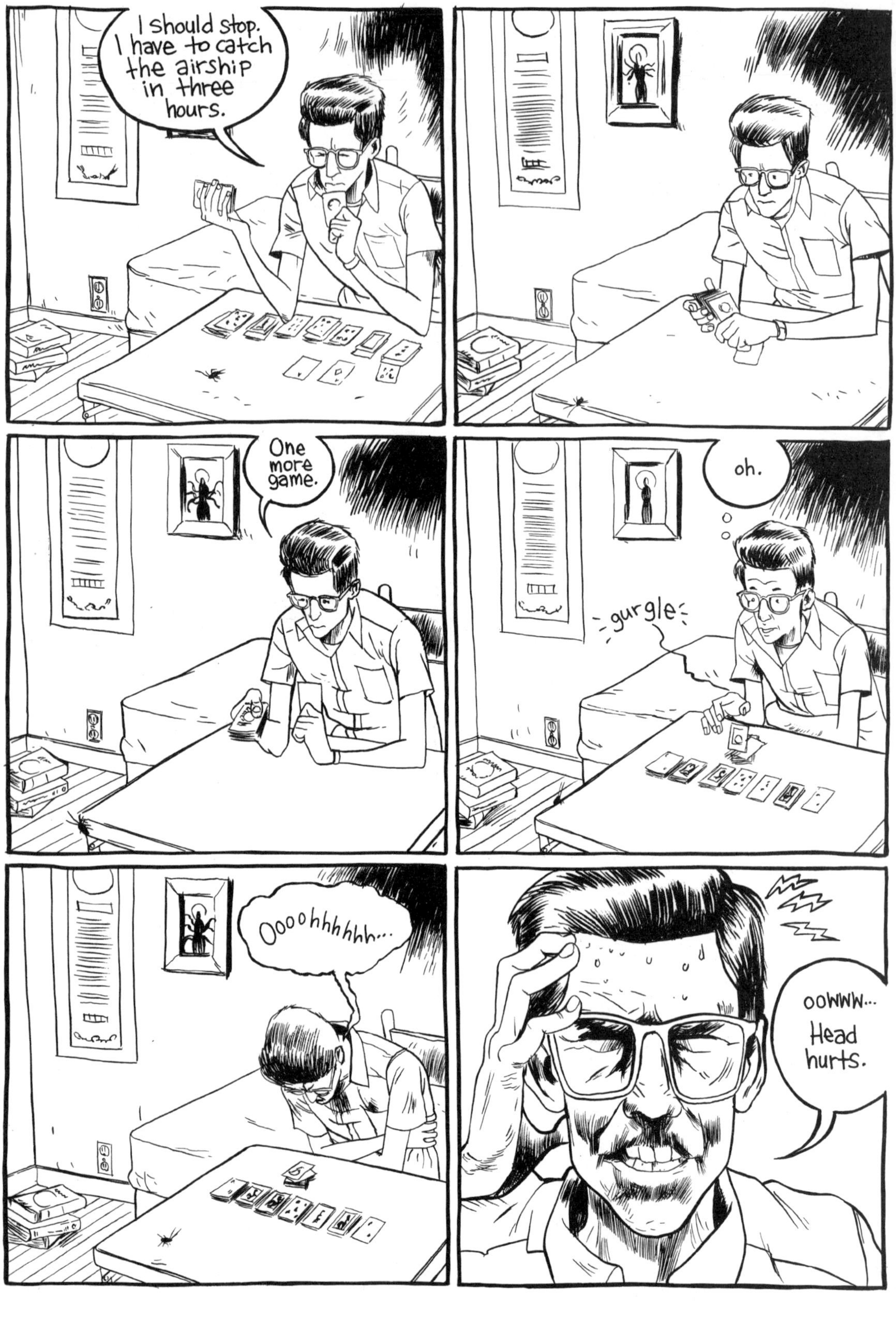
I should stop. I have to catch the airship in three hours.
One more game.
oh.
gurgle
Ooooohhhhhh...
OOWWW... Head hurts.

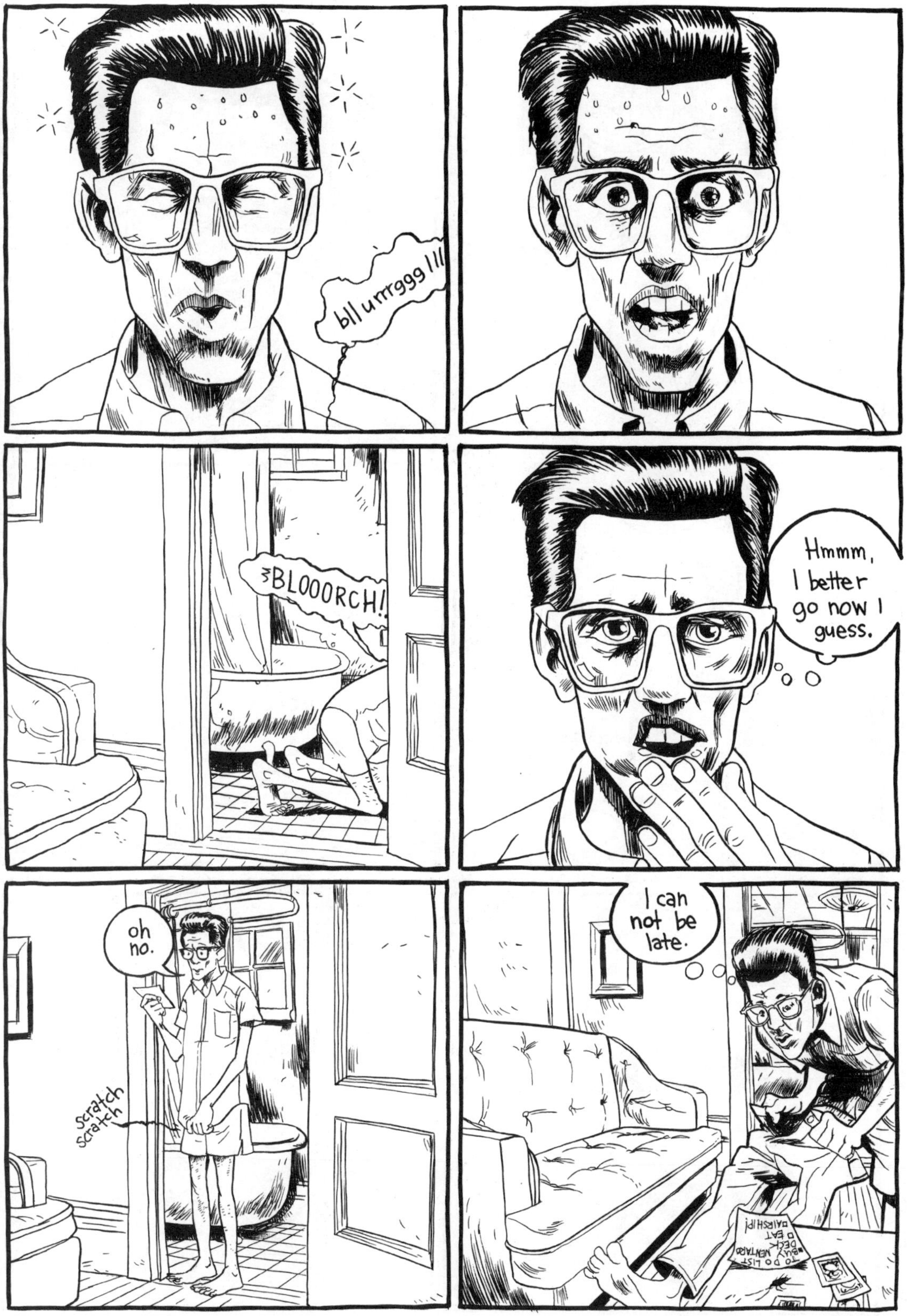
bl|urrrggg|||
BLOOORCH!
Hmmm, I better go now I guess.
oh no.
scratch scratch
I can not be late.

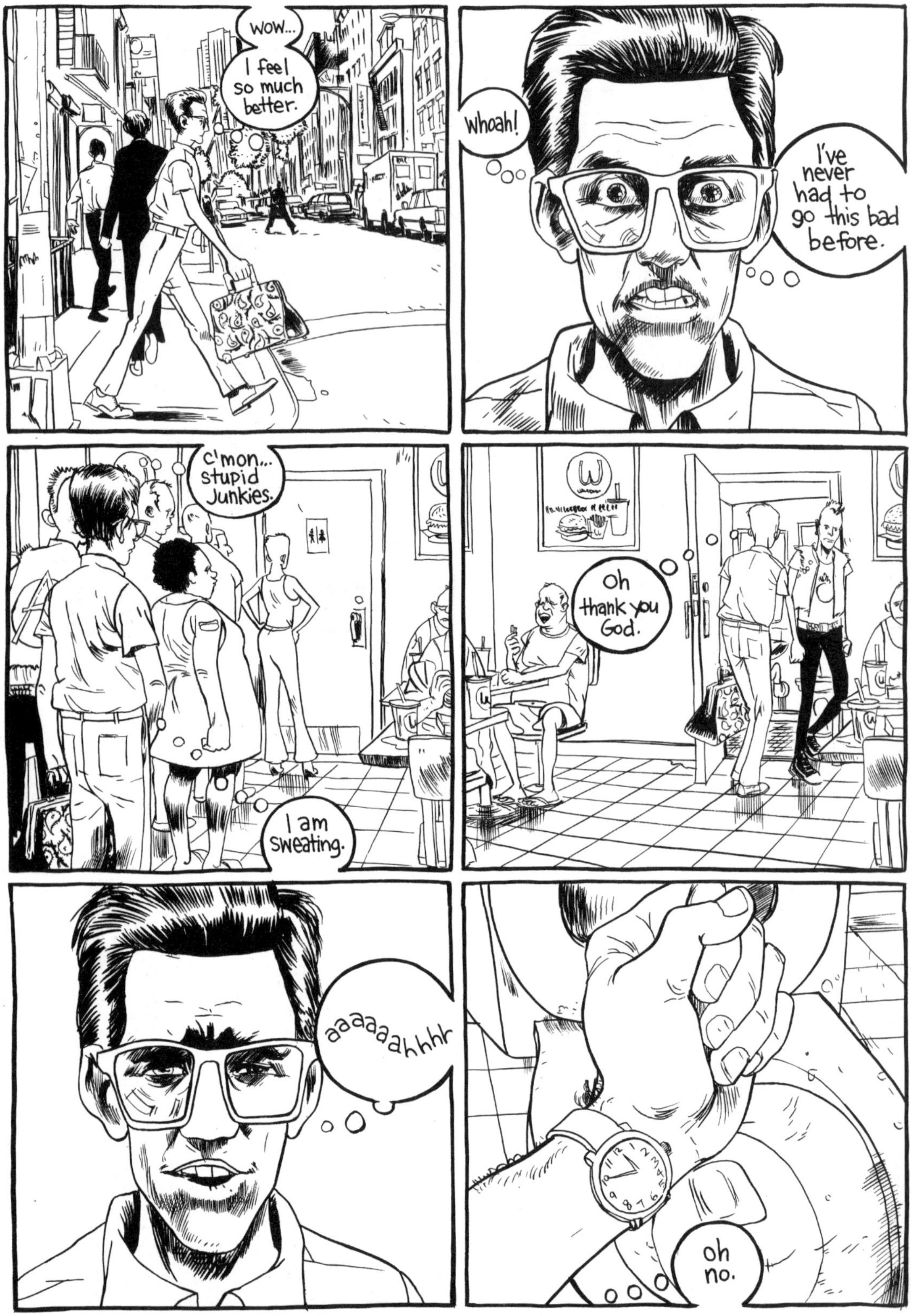
wow...
I feel so much better.
Whoah!
I've never had to go this bad before.
c'mon... stupid Junkies.
I am sweating.
Oh thank you God.
aaaaaahhhr
oh no.

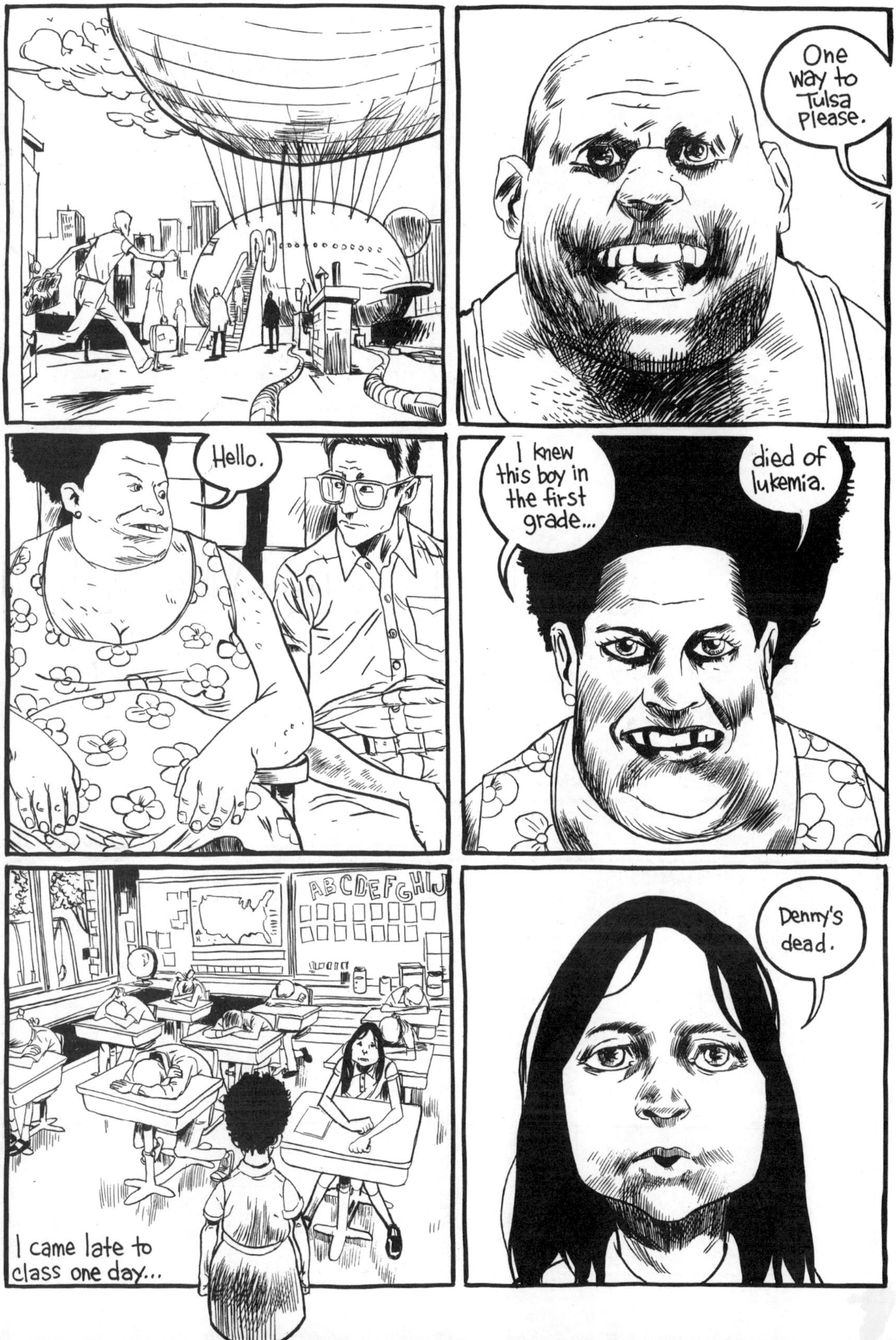
One way to Tulsa please.
Hello.
I knew this boy in the first grade...
died of lukemia.
I came late to class one day...
Denny's dead.

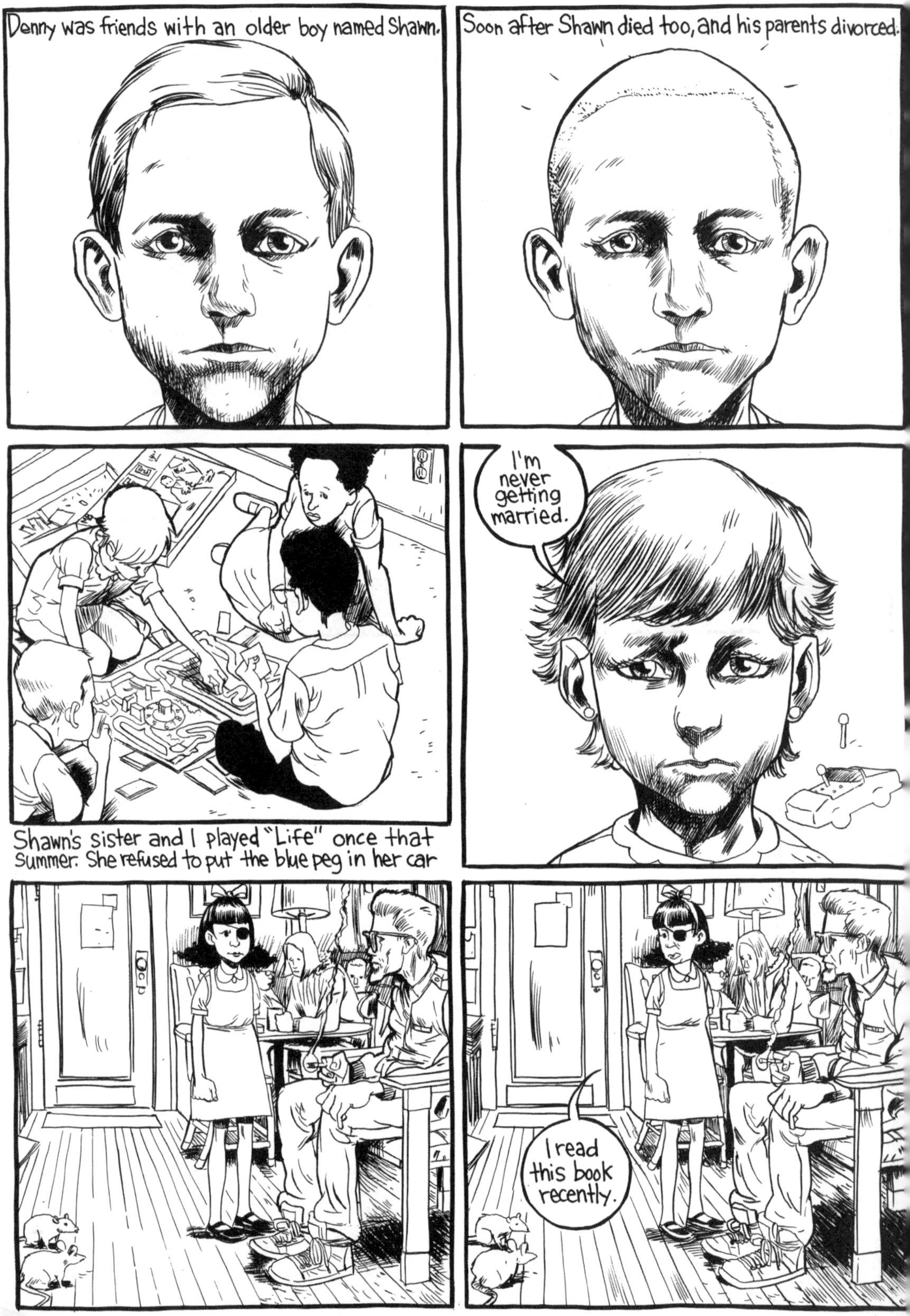
Denny was friends with an older boy named Shawn.
Soon after Shawn died too, and his parents divorced.
Shawn's sister and I played "Life" once that summer. She refused to put the blue peg in her car
I'm never getting married.
I read this book recently.

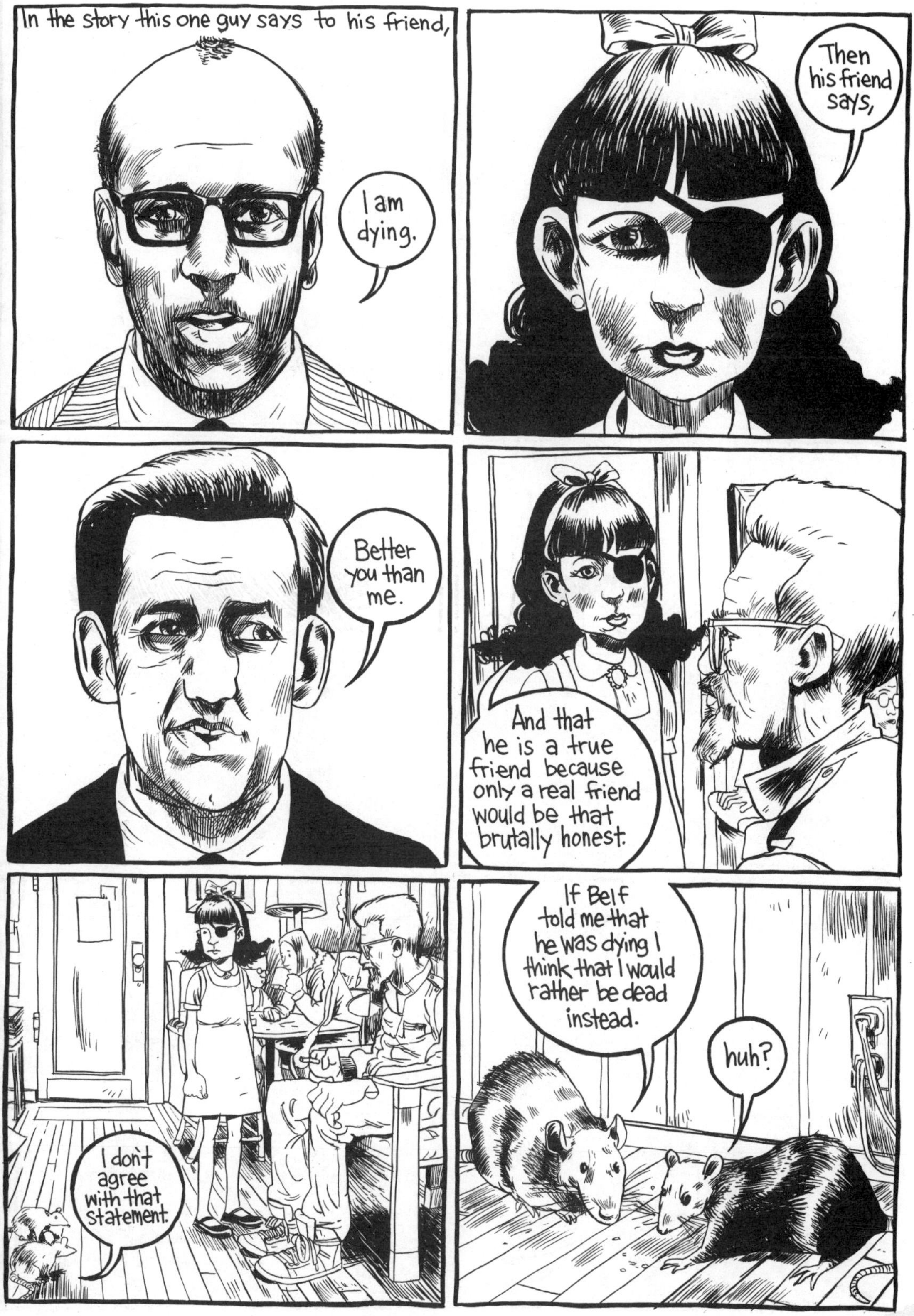
In the story this one guy says to his friend,
I am dying.
Then his friend says,
Better you than me.
And that he is a true friend because only a real friend would be that brutally honest.
I don't agree with that statement.
If Belf told me that he was dying I think that I would rather be dead instead.
huh?

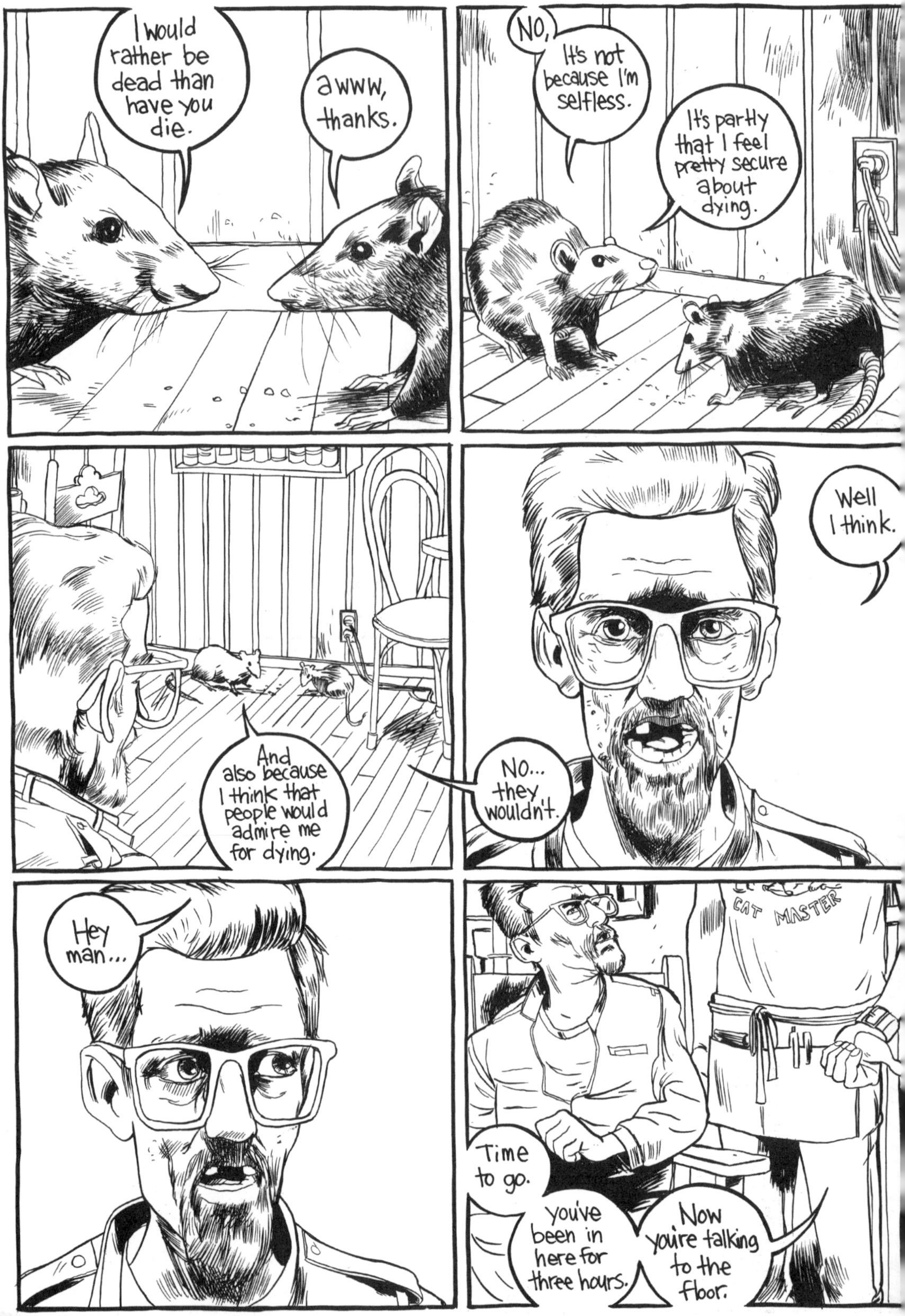
I would rather be dead than have you die.
awww, thanks.
No,
It's not because I'm selfless.
It's partly that I feel pretty secure about dying.
And also because I think that people would admire me for dying.
No... they wouldn't.
Well I think.
Hey man...
CAT MASTER
Time to go.
you've been in here for three hours.
Now you're talking to the floor.

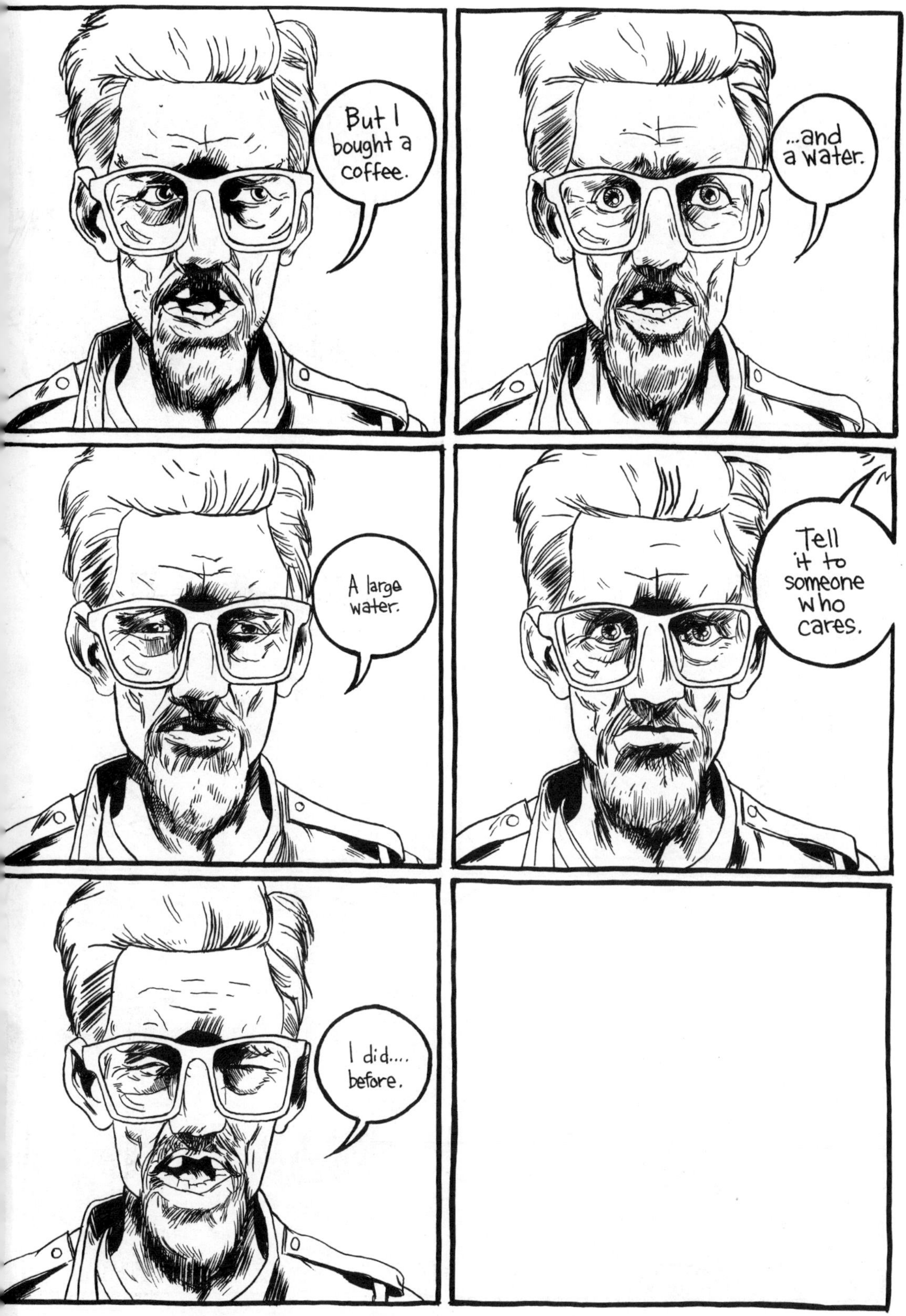
But I bought a coffee.
...and a water.
A large water.
Tell it to someone who cares.
I did.... before.

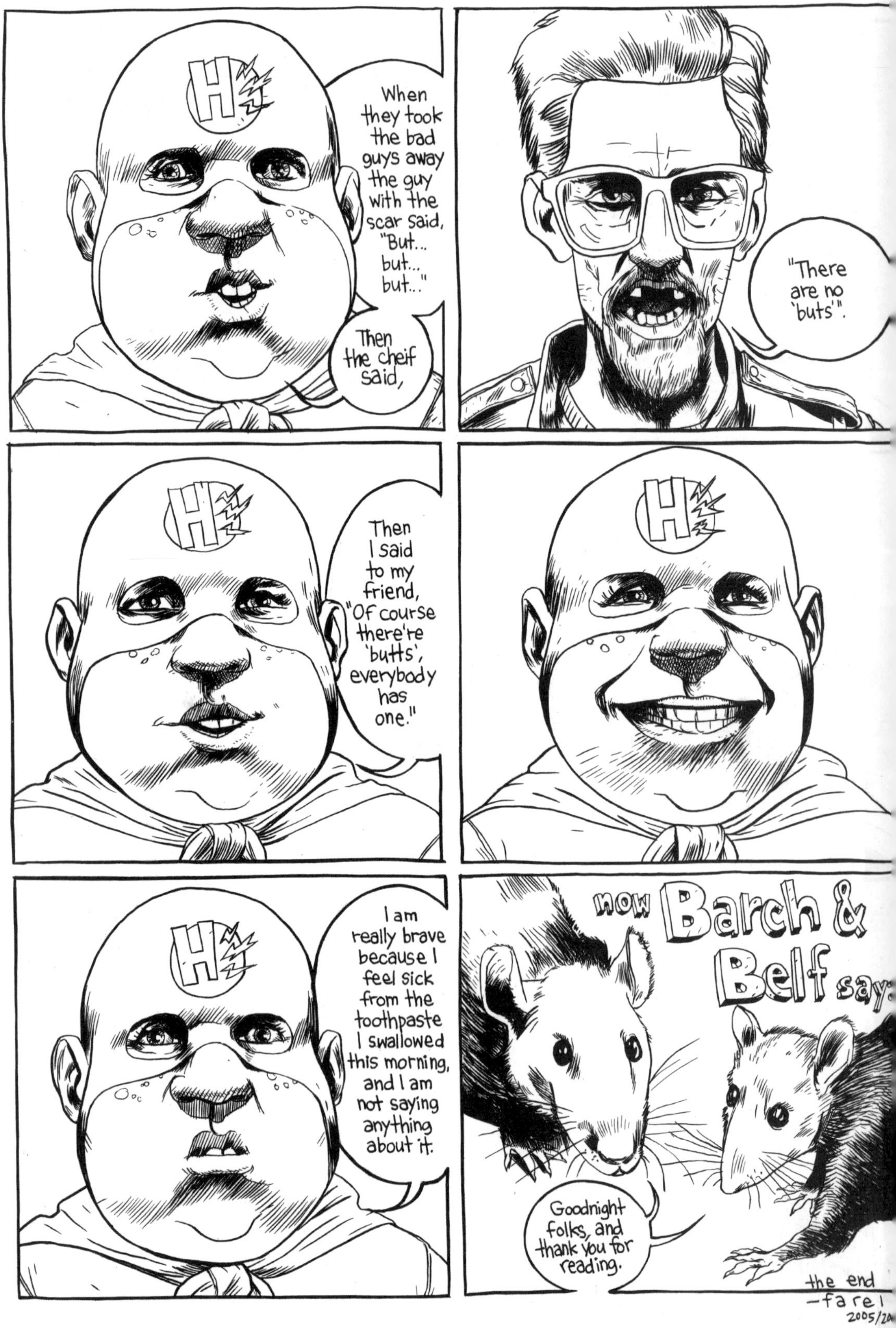
When they took the bad guys away the guy with the scar said, "But... but... but..."
Then the cheif said,
"There are no 'buts'".
Then I said to my friend, "Of course there're 'butts', everybody has one."
I am really brave because I feel sick from the toothpaste I swallowed this morning, and I am not saying anything about it.
now Barch & Belf say:
Goodnight folks, and thank you for reading.
the end
-farel
2005/20